CONTENT WARNINGS

This book contains themes and content that may be upsetting to some readers including: verbal abuse from romantic partners and family members, and drug and alcohol addiction (side characters).

This book also contains graphic sexual content including detailed two-, and three-person sex scenes; double penetration; degradation/praise; public sex; edging; orgasm denial; spanking; and light dom/sub elements. Reader discretion is advised.

PUCKING AMAZING

PUCKING AMAZING

TEAM PLAYERS
BOOK 2

ALEXIS BARLOWE

CHAPTER 1
SYDNEY

How do you survive a first day at a nerve-wracking new job?

Start it with sugar and caffeine. A crapload of it.

The tantalizing aroma of caramel and espresso swirls around my twin sister Selena and me as we settle into a cozy corner booth at Dark Matter, our favorite coffee shop from college. Two frappuccinos topped with whipped cream and drizzled chocolate tower between us.

"To your first day," Selena declares, raising her plastic cup in a toast. Her cat-eye liner is on point, even at this ungodly early hour. It's still surreal, being back near my sister after so many years apart.

I clink my cup against hers. "To new beginnings," I say, meaning the words in more ways than one.

I take a long sip, savoring the icy sweetness. It's already working its magic, taking my mind off of my first day jitters.

Today, I start as the new addiction counselor for the Chicago Blizzards. It's an enormous responsibility. There is a *wild* amount of media scrutiny on the team right now.

I need to prove to the world that I can handle it.

And prove to myself that I'm not the insecure, broken shell of a person Paul left behind.

Selena reaches across the table to squeeze my hand, maybe reading some of that in my eyes.

"You'll be great," she says. "Remember when we'd come here to cram for exams? You always had those ridiculous color-coded notes." She takes a long drag of her sugary drink.

"Hey, those notes were a work of art," I protest.

"Exactly my point. You turn chaos into order. You're going to do the same for those Blizzards boys," Selena says with a smile.

"From your lips to God's ears," I murmur as I raise my cup, the icy coffee concoction soothing more than just my dry throat. It's as if with each sip, the edges of my old self, the one not dulled by Paul's shadow, come back into focus.

"You're brilliant and compassionate and just what those hockey hunks need right now. And can I just say, I'm mad jealous you get to ogle all that eye candy at work." Selena waggles her eyebrows.

I snort. "Yes, I'm sure ogling will be my number one priority in between crisis management and therapy sessions."

But I'd be lying if I said I hadn't thought about it.

The Chicago Blizzards aren't just talented athletes—they're *ridiculously attractive* talented athletes. The kind with chiseled jaws and abs you could grate cheese on. The kind that grace magazine covers and star in commercials for overpriced cologne.

Not that it matters.

I'll be there to do a job, not get distracted by a bunch of muscled jocks, no matter how tempting the fantasy.

Besides, the last thing I need is another man in my life. I'm still figuring out how to be Sydney 2.0 after wasting years as one half of Sydney-and-Paul.

Selena must sense the direction of my thoughts because she leans forward with a wicked grin.

"All I'm saying is, if one of those hotties makes a pass at you, you better climb him like a tree. When's the last time you had some good D?"

"Selena!" I glance around to make sure no one overheard. But I'm laughing.

It's nice, this effortless teasing. Like no time has passed since we used to gossip over frappuccinos between college classes.

Before Paul isolated me from everyone and everything I loved.

Well, I'm taking it all back now. My life, my career, my relationship with my sister.

I hold up my cup. "To ogling hot hockey players. I can't do more than that—" I glare at my sister in mock severity. "—not while I'm working as a counselor for members of the team. But hey, appreciating the view can't hurt, right?"

"Hear, hear!"

Selena clinks my cup again as we dissolve into giggles,

caramel and possibility sweet on my tongue. Maybe I can get the old Sydney back, with my sister's help.

Maybe I can start over in Chicago.

Taking a deep breath to steady my nerves, I push open the glass doors embossed with the Chicago Blizzards logo and step into the expansive lobby of the practice arena.

Whoa.

This place is swanky as hell. Sleek white and black accents are everywhere, with massive action shots of the players frozen in triumphant poses covering the soaring walls.

The clack from my heels on the polished concrete floors echoes up to the vaulted ceiling. I feel tiny as I approach the reception desk, but I paste on a bright smile for the immaculately coiffed woman sitting behind it.

"Hi there! I'm Sydney Nelson, the new—"

"Sydney, welcome!" a booming voice interrupts. I turn to see a distinguished older man striding toward me, arm extended. "Vincent Dale, GM. We spoke on the phone."

"Of course, hi!" I shake his hand, hoping my grip projects confidence. "Pleasure to meet you in person, Mr. Dale."

"Likewise. We're thrilled to have you here. And please, call me Vincent." Vincent claps me on the shoulder, steering me down a hallway lined with framed jerseys. "I'll give you the grand tour later, but let's head straight to the heart of the action, eh? Boys are already on the ice."

My stomach flutters at the thought of meeting the team. "Sounds great. I'm excited to dive in."

"I'll be straight with you," Vincent says, his expression sobering. "We need you. Bad. The incident in Canada...it's a mess. Media's having a field day painting us as a bunch of loose cannons."

I nod, my therapist brain already shifting into gear.

People are used to hockey players getting in a lot of fights —but *usually*, the players are fighting the other teams. The Blizzards got into a massive brawl amongst themselves. Violent, bloody, and nearly career-ending for their starting goalie.

Three players were at the center of the storm, and I'm here to get to the bottom of it and help the team move on.

"I read the reports," I say. "Seems like there's a lot of untapped anger there."

"You could say that." Vincent shakes his head. "But from what Emma's told me, if anyone can get these hotheads to simmer down, it's you. She raved about your work with young addicts. Said you have a gift."

I duck my head, cheeks warming. My friend Emma, who works as the assistant video coach to the team, referred me to Vincent when the team realized they needed to hire a counselor.

Part of me is still not sure if she did it because she thought I was the best person for the job...or if she could see me drowning in Boston and wanted to throw me a lifeline.

Either way, I'm grateful for it.

"I don't know about a gift," I tell him, "but I'll certainly do my best."

"I have no doubt." Vincent pauses outside a set of double doors, his face serious again. "One more thing—the boys don't know the full extent of your role here. As far as they're concerned, you're just providing general counseling and support, not addiction treatment per se. Let's keep it that way for now, yeah? No need to spook them."

"Of course," I agree, though something niggles in the back of my mind.

Secrets are a dangerous foundation for a therapeutic relationship.

But Vincent's the boss. I'll follow his lead.

For now.

He pushes open the doors and I'm hit with a blast of frigid air, the sounds of skates carving ice and sticks slapping pucks.

And then I see them. The Chicago Blizzards in the flesh.

My mouth goes dry at the sheer physical presence of these elite athletes as they fly across the ice, their powerful bodies honed for speed and aggression. The air is heady with the scent of sweat and adrenaline and...testosterone.

Lord almighty. It's a sensory overload.

But the energy seems off, even to my untrained eye. There's a palpable tension, a simmering hostility.

As Vincent and I watch, two players—a stocky D-man and a lanky forward, terms I've learned with Emma's help—slam into the boards, shouting in each other's faces.

"Told you," Vincent mutters. "Powder keg."

As the coaches pull the guys apart, I spot a familiar brunette on the bench.

Emma.

Her eyes crinkle with a warm smile when she sees me. I beam back, fighting the urge to run over and hug her. It's been too long.

Emma and I are way overdue for a catch-up, but I just got into town a few days ago and have been busy unpacking and settling into Selena's apartment. It used to be Emma's apartment, too, until she moved in with her boyfriends—*plural*—earlier in the year.

"All right, let's get you introduced." Vincent strides over to the coaches, waving them over. "Blizzards! Bring it in for a sec."

The men coast to a stop in a loose semicircle, removing their helmets.

And oh... oh boy.

I was not prepared.

Chiseled jaws, smoldering eyes, crooked grins. It's a buffet of raw male beauty.

Down, girl.

But damn, one guy in particular—a tall drink of goalie with dark hair and piercing blue eyes—makes my knees a little weak when his gaze lands on me.

And is *that* guy...? Yep, the tatted-up forward is shamelessly checking me out, a flirtatious smirk playing about his full lips.

I snap my eyes away, heat crawling up my neck.

Pull it together, Syd! You're here to help these guys, not drool over them. I take a deep breath, trying to calm the butterflies wreaking havoc in my stomach.

Vincent points out Coach Daniels, and I do a double take—even the head coach is attractive. Not my type, but silver foxy in that George Clooney kind of way.

Coach Daniels shoots me an encouraging nod, and I immediately sense an ally.

"Gentleman," Vincent booms as I step forward. "I'd like you all to give a warm Blizzards welcome to Sydney Nelson..."

Vincent's voice fades into the background as I step forward, my heels moving awkwardly on the rubber flooring. I paste on my most confident smile, even as my palms grow clammy.

"Hi everyone," I begin, hoping my voice doesn't betray my nerves. "As Vincent said, I'm Sydney Nelson, the new..."

I remember Vincent's warning and trail off for a moment, swallowing the words 'addiction specialist.' I clear my throat.

"Um, the new team counselor. My door is always open to anyone who needs to talk, and anything that we discuss will stay between us. I'm not just here for the three of you," I nod toward Jason, Mikey, and Tomas, who I recognize from all the unfortunate media coverage, "but for any of you who needs support."

I meet the eyes of the three players I'll be working with most, trying to convey warmth and kindness.

They shift uncomfortably, clearly not thrilled to be singled out.

"Again, I want to assure you all that anything discussed in

our sessions is confidential. I'm here to support you, not judge you."

Scanning the group, I'm met with a mixture of guarded expressions and curious gazes. The goalie's electric blue eyes bore into me with an intensity that makes my stomach flip. I quickly glance away, my cheeks warming.

Seriously, Syd? Keep it in your pants.

I swallow, trying to pull my thoughts together. "You all, as professional athletes, face a unique set of challenges and pressures that are difficult to navigate. The important thing is that we work together to create a healthy environment for the entire team."

"We appreciate you being here, Sydney," Coach Daniels chimes in, flashing a megawatt smile. "Alright boys, show's over. Back to drills!"

The players disperse, skating off in various directions. Except for Tattoo Guy, who shoots me a wink before gliding away.

That wink reaches places it definitely shouldn't while I'm on the job.

"Syd!" a familiar voice calls out.

I spin around to see Emma jogging toward me, her dark curls bouncing. A huge grin splits my face.

"Em!" We collide in a fierce hug, giggling like the college girls we once were. "God, I've missed you!"

Emma pulls back, hazel eyes sparkling. "Dude, I can't believe you're actually here! When Vincent said they needed an addiction specialist, I was like, 'I've got the perfect person!' Though I may have oversold your qualifications a bit..." She scrunches her nose impishly.

I gasp in mock outrage, shoving her shoulder. "Wow, thanks for that vote of confidence!"

"I'm kidding. You're gonna be amazing." She links her arm with mine as we meander away from the ice. "So, how's life? How's Selena? Give me all the goss!"

As Emma rattles off questions, I sneak one last glance over my shoulder at the team. Goalie Hottie is barking orders at another player. Tattoo Guy is leaning on his stick, chatting with a group.

My eyes linger on their well-muscled bodies.

The very definition of temptation on ice. Lord help me.

I've sworn off men while I put the pieces of my life back together. I'm here to do a job, not land a date.

Still, a little eye candy never hurt anyone...right?

CHAPTER 2
TYLER

I'm trying my best to focus as the new counselor Sydney introduces herself to the team, but my mind keeps drifting back to that night in Toronto.

What a shit show.

We got our asses handed to us on the ice, then went out and made even bigger asses of ourselves at the bar after. Too many shots, a smartass comment taken the wrong way, and suddenly fists were flying.

Our starting goalie, Adam, ended up with a major knee injury, and several players narrowly avoided getting arrested when the cops showed up. As if the media needed more ammo to make us appear like a bunch of out-of-control frat boys.

And now the pressure is on me to step up as the goalie.

Sydney's voice pulls me back to the present moment.

"The important thing is that we work together to create a healthy environment for the entire team."

Her warm brown eyes meet mine and I relax a bit. She seems like she actually gives a damn, like she's more than just another suit here to babysit us and protect the team's image.

My gaze flicks over to DJ, and I nearly choke on my tongue. He's not even pretending to listen to Sydney, too busy eye-fucking her from across the room with that crooked grin of his.

The same grin that does strange, confusing things to my insides whenever it's aimed my way.

Which has been happening a lot lately.

I tear my eyes away, my face heating.

But I can't help sneaking another glance at DJ. He lounges back in his chair, all toned muscle and shameless confidence. The poster boy for pansexual pride.

I wish I knew what that confidence was like.

To just...feel what I feel, without constantly second-guessing myself. Without worrying what it "means."

I've only ever dated women. I'm straight. Or at least, I thought I was.

And then we were in a club a month ago, a couple weeks before that stupid-ass bar fight. DJ pulled a hot stranger onto his lap and was making out with him in front of everyone.

I've seen guys kiss before, of course. Lukas and Ryan aren't shy in front of the team. But I'd never seen DJ in action like that before. The way his powerful arms wrapped around the other man, the things he was doing with his hands, the absolutely sinful look in his eyes when he eventually pulled back...

All I could think was, *what would that feel like? If it was* me *he was kissing, instead...*

Fuck. I can't even let myself complete that thought.

This team is my shot to prove myself, to make my brother Steven proud after he had to retire early. The last thing I need is my personal life getting even more complicated.

And my thoughts toward DJ since that night have been a monumental distraction.

I just need to focus on hockey. But when DJ catches me looking and throws me a wink, my focus slips away by the second.

Coach Daniels claps his hands, jolting me out of my musings. "Alright boys, show's over. Back to drills!"

I perk up, grateful for the work. It's always settled my nerves, being on the ice. This is what I know, what I'm good at.

Out on the rink, I can just be Tyler the goalie, my mind blank and my mission clear.

We start with basic drills, stick handling and skating suicides. I throw myself into it, relishing the burn in my muscles, the cold air in my lungs. But even as I try to lose myself in the physical exertion, my traitorous eyes keep drifting to DJ.

He's a big guy—hulking, almost—but you'd never know it, watching him on the ice. He's poetry in motion, all grace and finesse as he weaves through the cones. It's hypnotic.

I could watch him for hours—

"Head up, Simmonds!" Coach's bark snaps me back to reality just as a puck whizzes past my left ear.

Shit. I shake my head, trying to clear the cobwebs. I can't afford to be unfocused. Not with Adam out and the starting goalie position squarely on my shoulders.

We shift into a scrimmage and I take my place in the net, determined to redeem myself. For a while, I stay locked in, deflecting shot after shot. But then DJ snags the puck and comes charging towards me, a wicked gleam in his eye.

He dekes left, then right, leaving my defensemen in the dust.

I square up, ready for his shot. But at the last second, he pulls off some kind of action-hero spineroo move and the puck sails over my shoulder into the net.

"Wooooo!" DJ pumps his fist, circling around the back of the goal. As he passes by, he reaches out and taps me on the ass with his stick. "Almost had me there, Ty! Keep those legs closed next time, eh?"

He punctuates it with a wink and a cackle, skating away while I try to remember how to breathe.

It's the same kind of exchange we've had a million times, but somehow it feels different. Loaded with a new tension. The ghost of his stick burns through my padding.

Jesus, get a grip. It's just DJ being DJ. Doesn't mean anything.

But even as I try to dismiss it, there's a tightening low in my stomach, an ache that has nothing to do with hockey.

I towel off in a daze, my mind still reeling from practice. The locker room seems to stretch on forever, rows of empty stalls mocking me as I try to gather my scattered thoughts.

The creak of the door snaps my attention up. DJ strolls in wearing nothing but sinfully tight compression shorts slung low on his hips.

My mouth goes bone dry.

I can't tear my gaze away from the mesmerizing sight of his lean, cut muscles rippling under tanned skin as he moves. Intricate tattoos snake up his sculpted arms and wind across his ribs, practically begging to be traced by fingertips...or a tongue.

DJ's eyes lock with mine and a devilish grin spreads across his face. "See something you like, Simmonds?"

His voice is a low, flirtatious purr that shoots straight to my groin.

Heat floods my cheeks and...other areas. I frantically grab for my towel, almost dropping it.

"What? No, I just—I mean—"

Real smooth, Tyler.

I'm unable to form a sentence like an idiot, but my brain has short-circuited at the nearly naked vision before me.

"Relax, I'm just giving you shit," DJ chuckles, taking pity on me. "Gonna hit the showers. Catch you later, Ty."

He saunters off, treating me to a view of his spectacular ass.

I exhale shakily, my pulse thundering in my ears. This magnetic pull whenever DJ is near—it's getting impossible to ignore, a constant electric hum just under my skin.

What the hell am I supposed to do with these feelings? They don't fit with the image I've always had of myself, of who I'm supposed to be.

In a panic, I throw on clothes haphazardly, desperate to flee the intoxicating air of the locker room and DJ's irresistible effect on me, before I do something crazy like shove him against the tiles and map those tattoos with my mouth...

Nope. Not going there.

I snatch my duffel and practically run for the door, needing to put some serious distance between me and my wild thoughts.

This identity crisis will have to wait—preferably forever.

Shifting in the uncomfortable restaurant chair, I force a smile as my date, Sarah, finishes her story about her latest adventure in hot yoga. She's been enthusiastically chattering on for the past fifteen minutes, but I haven't been able to focus on a single word.

"That sounds... intense," I manage, taking a sip of my water to buy myself a moment. "So, uh, what do you do for a living?"

Sarah blinks, thrown by the sudden change in topic. "I'm a marketing director at a tech startup downtown. I thought your sister mentioned that?"

"Oh right, sorry," I wince. "So...what kind of metrics do you use to evaluate employee performance?" I ask, and then instantly cringe inwardly at how stiff and formal I sound.

Sarah pauses, taken aback. "Um, well, the usual KPIs, I guess...productivity, efficiency, that sort of thing." She tilts her head, looking at me quizzically. "Why do you ask?"

"Oh, no reason," I backpedal, my cheeks heating. "Just, um,

curious about your management style, I suppose." *Seriously, Tyler? This is a date, not a job interview.*

I take a big gulp of wine, hoping the alcohol will loosen me up, help me relax. But all it does is make me vaguely nauseous. I set down my glass and force another smile.

"So, where do you see yourself in five years?" The question slips out before I can stop it. *What the hell is wrong with me?*

Sarah frowns slightly. "Well, hopefully I'll have gotten a promotion by then, be managing my own team. I'd like to—"

I nod along, making appropriate noises of agreement, but my mind is drifting, pulled inexorably back to the locker room this afternoon. To DJ, standing there in those sinfully tight shorts, all lean muscle and bold ink.

The way he looked at me, his eyes hot and knowing...

"Tyler? Did you hear me?"

I snap back to the present to find Sarah watching me expectantly. *Shit.* "Sorry, what was that?"

"I was asking about your plans for the future," she repeats patiently. "What are your long-term career goals?"

"Oh. Um." I fumble for an answer, my mind blank. "Just...to keep playing, I guess. For as long as I can."

It sounds pathetic, even to my own ears.

Sarah nods slowly. "Right. Well, that's... admirable." The conversation limps along from there, every exchange more strained than the last.

By the time the waiter brings the check, I'm exhausted, wrung out from the effort of pretending to be someone I'm not. Someone fully engaged during first dates with random women.

Someone who isn't weirdly obsessed with his teammate.

We say our goodbyes on the sidewalk outside the restaurant. Sarah goes in for a hug and I reciprocate stiffly, patting her back.

"This was fun," I lie. "I'll, uh, call you sometime."

She smiles, but it doesn't reach her eyes. "Sure. Sounds good."

We both know I won't call.

I watch her walk away, her blonde hair swaying, and feel...nothing. No regret, no disappointment. Just a hollow sort of relief that the date is finally over.

But as I climb into my car, the full weight of my situation crashes down on me. I rest my forehead against the steering wheel, gripping it hard enough to turn my knuckles white.

What the hell is wrong with me?

CHAPTER 3
SYDNEY

IT'S STILL EARLY AS I STRIDE INTO THE PRACTICE FACILITY, THE thud of my sneakers echoing in the quiet hallway. The place is mostly empty, but I want to get a head start on my first day of sessions as the team's new counselor.

In my hand I grip my notepad, already covered in scribbles with thoughts and plans. Three names on it jump out at me: Jason Kirkland, Mikey Torres, Tomas Novak.

The players at the center of the bar brawl incident.

My plan today is to meet with each of them individually, to start building the trust and rapport that will be so crucial to helping them move forward.

I find my new office and drop my bag on the chair. It's small but bright, with a window overlooking the practice rink.

I smile, allowing myself a moment to take it in, to appreciate how far I've come since...

No, I don't want to follow that thought right now.

I pull out the slim files I've been given on each player and start leafing through them, my mind snapping into therapist mode.

Jason Kirkland, right winger, known for his aggressive playing style and rebellious streak off the ice. Rumored alcohol abuse. Otherwise, a pretty clean record.

Mikey Torres, the rookie center with a world of talent and a chip on his shoulder. Suspected drug use. Reading between the lines on what I could find online, a seemingly volatile family situation.

And Tomas Novak, the veteran forward, steady and solid on the ice but clearly struggling with something in his personal life. But what exactly that is—anyone's guess. Gambling addiction? Marital problems? Untreated mental health issues?

Hmmm.

Happily, the hockey lingo is starting to make some more sense after my extensive Google and Wikipedia deep dive last night. So at least that part is less of a mystery.

Three men, each battling their own demons. My job is to guide them, to give them the tools and support to find their own way out of the darkness.

Something I know a lot about myself.

A few hours later, I settle into the chair across from Jason, taking in his guarded posture—arms crossed defensively over his broad chest, jaw clenched tight. But there's a vulnerability in his eyes that belies the tough exterior.

"Thanks for meeting with me today, Jason," I begin, keeping my tone warm and non-judgmental. "I know this process can be a little daunting at first, but I'm here to support you however I can. Why don't you start by telling me a bit about what's been going on with you lately?"

Jason shifts uncomfortably, his gaze flicking away before meeting mine again.

"I don't know, doc. It's just been...a lot, you know? The pressure to perform, to be a guy everyone can count on, both here and at home. I've been trying to make my wife and kid proud of me. I guess I've been leaning on the bottle a bit too much to take the edge off."

I mentally wince when he calls me doc. Technically, yes, I am a doctor—I completed my MD. But that fuckwad Paul convinced me to drop out of my psychiatry residency before I could complete it.

He told me that the pressure was too much for me, and I believed him. He convinced me that I would never make a good psychiatrist, that it had been a waste of my time to pursue a MD at all.

So I'm a doctor who isn't licensed to practice medicine... hence, becoming a counselor.

I brush the thoughts awake and refocus on Jason, nodding empathetically. "That's a common coping mechanism, especially in high-stress environments like professional sports. Can you tell me more about what those pressures are like for you day-to-day?"

Jason sighs, rubbing a hand over his close-cropped hair.

"It's like, I'm one of the vets now, you know? The young guys look up to me. I gotta set the tone, be the rock. And with everything that went down in Canada..." He trails off, shaking his head.

"The bar fight, you mean?" I prompt gently.

"Yeah. Not my finest moment." Jason's mouth twists ruefully. "I just saw red, you know? Mike was running his mouth, and I just lost it. I'm so ashamed that my two-year-old will be able to google me and find news stories about that some day. I'm supposed to be better than that. I *am* better than that."

His tone is fierce, almost like he's trying to convince himself.

"Recognizing that is an important first step," I affirm. "It sounds like you have high expectations for yourself, both on and off the ice."

"I guess so." Jason's posture loosens infinitesimally, his arms uncrossing. "I just want to be someone my team can depend on. DJ, Slade, Lukas, Tyler, all the guys—they're like brothers to me."

I perk up at the mention of DJ and Tyler, the two players who caught my eye yesterday. I'd be lying if I said I hadn't eagerly scoured the team roster to find their faces, reading up on their bios last night alongside those of my three patients.

But I keep my expression neutral as I probe further.

"Tell me more about the team dynamics. Who are you closest to?"

A fond smile tugs at Jason's mouth. "DJ for sure. The guy's amazing—so skilled on the ice, but so laid back and fun off it. He's been a real friend, you know?"

I make a mental note of the warmth in Jason's voice. "And Tyler? I noticed you mentioned him as well."

"Tyler's a good kid. Works his ass off out there, real dedicated. I feel bad that my actions contributed to him having to take on Adam's role. To be honest, I don't know him quite as well, but he seems like he's got a good head on his shoulders." He pauses, a slight smirk forming on his face. "And I think he likes DJ even better than I do."

I tilt my head in confusion at his tone. "What do you mean by that?"

Jason waves it aside, laughing. "Oh nothing, nothing."

I steer our conversation back to Jason's personal journey, but I can't help turning over those nuggets about DJ and Tyler in my mind.

There's a part of me that's eager to learn more about whatever is going on between these two gorgeous men—a curiosity that is both professional and, if I'm being honest with myself, personal.

I push aside those distracting thoughts for now, refocusing on the vulnerable man in front of me, who's taken the brave first step of starting to open up. Time slips away as I find myself back in a familiar groove, jotting down notes as Jason patiently answers my questions.

Jason is surprisingly easy to talk to. The session wraps up and he heads out, and the satisfaction rushing through me is a pleasant reminder as to why I got into this work in the first place.

Next, Mikey slouches into my office, all tense shoulders and guarded eyes. He flops onto the couch across from me with an air of insolence.

I have a sneaking suspicion that this appointment isn't going to be quite so productive.

"So you're the shrink they brought in to fix us, huh?" he says with a sneer. "Good luck with that."

I paste on a patient smile. "I'm not here to fix anyone, Mikey. I'm here to listen and provide some tools that could help the team communicate and work together better."

He scoffs. "Right. Because a few heart-to-hearts are going to magically make everything better. News flash, lady—you don't know shit about us or what we deal with."

My smile starts to strain, but I keep my voice even. "You're right. I'm still learning about the team dynamics. Could you give me your perspective? I noticed some tension between you and a few other players yesterday, on the ice..."

Mikey's eyes narrow. "Don't fucking bother. You think you're going to waltz in here and get us spilling our deepest, darkest secrets? Fat chance."

He leans forward, his voice dripping with disdain.

"Let me make this crystal clear—I don't need your touchy-feely therapy bullshit. You shrinks are all just working out your own problems on our dime, anyway. So, how about you just enjoy your cushy office and leave the real work to us?"

With that, he pushes himself up and storms out, slamming the door so hard it rattles on its hinges.

I slump back in my chair and let out a shaky breath. *Holy hell.* That stung more than I want to admit.

Mikey's words hit too close to home, echoing my own fears

that I'm just an imposter, that I have no business trying to help these guys, that my own issues are coloring my work.

For a second, I'm back in that terrible place, broken and defeated after what Paul did to me...

No. I give myself a mental shake. I refuse to let myself go there.

Mikey is hurting and lashing out. I could see the barely concealed vulnerability under all that hostility. The desperate desire to prove himself.

He needs my compassion and deserves my best effort, not my misgivings.

I square my shoulders. Mikey just threw down one hell of a gauntlet. But I've never been one to back down.

I have some time until my next appointment, so I finish dealing with some computer setup tasks I didn't finish yesterday. Eventually, my rumbling stomach becomes too loud to ignore, so I leave my office in search of the kitchen where I stashed my sandwich this morning.

Trying to remember which turn to take, I swing around to glance down the hall and nearly stumble back as I collide into DJ's solid chest.

I catch my balance and look up into his playful eyes, an amused smirk tugging at the corner of his perfectly sculpted lips.

"Well hello there, Doctor," he purrs, his velvety voice sending a shiver down my spine. "Here for a surprise examination? If I'd known I'd be running into you, I would've worn my good underwear."

Heat flushes my cheeks and neck as his shameless flirting catches me off guard once again.

I swallow and will myself to maintain composure, despite the way his chiseled physique and alluring tattoos make my heart race.

"Your underwear, huh?" I raise an eyebrow, attempting to match his playful energy even as butterflies swarm in my stomach. "And what qualifies as 'good' underwear for the great DJ Johnston?"

His eyes sparkle with mischief as they travel slowly down my body and back up again, his tongue darting out to wet his lower lip. My skin prickles with awareness under his appreciative gaze.

"Mmm, maybe you'll find out someday," he says suggestively. "If you play your cards right."

I scoff and roll my eyes, but can't help the smile playing on my lips. The man is incorrigible.

And damn if his cocky confidence isn't a major turn-on.

"In your dreams, pretty boy," I retort, folding my arms. "Some of us are trying to work around here, you know."

DJ shrugs, but there's a softness in his eyes that catches me off guard. "Listen, I was thinking...I'd really like to grab a coffee with you sometime. I could fill you in on some of the team dynamics that might be helpful for your work."

My heart skips a beat at the invitation. *Is he asking me on a date? Or just a work meeting?* I search his face for clues, but his expression is inscrutable.

"Oh, um, sure...that could be useful," I hedge, trying to keep my tone neutral.

"Great," he says with a grin, and I can't help but notice how his eyes crinkle at the corners when he smiles. "I'll email you to set something up."

His hand brushes against my arm as he steps around me to continue down the hall.

"Sounds good," I manage, hoping my voice doesn't betray that I'm flustered. As I watch him walk away, I'm hyper-aware of every flex of his muscles beneath his clothes, the confident set of his broad shoulders.

Sparks of attraction fizz and pop under my skin, and I let out a shaky breath.

What did I just agree to?

Back in my office after lunch, I glance at my watch and sigh. Fifteen minutes past our scheduled appointment and still no sign of Tomas. Drumming my fingers on the desk, I debate how long to wait before officially calling it a no-show.

My phone pings with a new email alert. I pull up my inbox, immediately spotting Tomas's name.

"Hey Doc, sorry but something urgent came up. Gotta bail on today's session. -T."

I frown at the screen.

"Something urgent" could mean anything from a personal emergency like a dead grandparent to partying too hard last night. But given Tomas's history...well, let's just say I have my doubts.

Rather than stew over it, I decide to tackle the mountain of administrative work that comes with starting a new job. Forms to fill out, virtual training sessions to complete, setting up my new email signature...oh, the joys of corporate life.

As I click through the mandatory sexual harassment course, my mind keeps drifting to the three players I'm supposed to help.

Jason, who seems eager to do the work, already facing his problems head-on. Mikey, who barely lasted 5 minutes in session with me before storming out. And Tomas... the mystery.

I want so badly to guide them to a better place, to show them they have the strength to overcome their demons. But first, I need Tomas to actually show up.

Baby steps.

At the end of the day, I have a regularly scheduled status meeting with Coach Daniels and Chloe Bennett, the team's prim and poised PR manager. We're going to be checking in on a weekly basis to discuss the situation at hand, at least until some of the media attention blows over.

The plush leather chairs and mahogany desk in Coach Daniels' office scream "I'm the boss." I settle into a slightly less imposing guest chair, flanked by Chloe.

"So Sydney, what's the game plan?" Coach leans forward, elbows on his knees, his steely blue eyes locked on mine.

I take a deep breath. "Well, first and foremost, we need to create a recovery-positive environment, *without* singling out the three players in counseling. That means rethinking how the team celebrates wins, hosts events, everything. Mikey, Jason, and Tomas need to be comfortable and safe at any team events."

Chloe nods, already tapping notes into her tablet. "We can make that work without calling anyone out. No need to draw extra attention to the fact that some of our events will be dry—we can focus the narrative elsewhere."

"Exactly. Take alcohol out of the equation. Removing temptation will make it easier for Jason, Mikey, and Tomas to maintain sobriety."

The words taste awkward in my mouth—I'm not used to discussing patients so openly. But for this to work, we all need to be on the same page.

Coach runs a hand over his salt-and-pepper hair. "Whatever it takes. Those boys...they're more than just players to me. They're family." His gruff voice cracks with emotion.

"I'll draw up some specific recommendations," I say gently. "Obviously this will be a process. But with the right support, I truly believe they can come out the other side, and the team can too."

Rising from his chair, Coach extends a beefy hand to shake mine. "We're behind you one hundred percent. With you in their corner, I know our boys will beat this."

His confidence buoys my spirits. It's nice to know I'm not in this alone.

After we wrap, I head out for the day, squinting as the bright late-afternoon sun hits my eyes.

What a day. My feet ache, my head is spinning, and I'm exhausted—but also exhilarated to have a challenge ahead of me.

I trudge across the parking lot toward my sensible Honda Civic. Before I reach it, a sleek black Lexus pulls into the spot right next to mine. The tinted window rolls down, revealing a pair of mischievous brown eyes and a roguish grin I'm already getting far too familiar with.

DJ.

Of course. This guy is everywhere today—what, is the universe trying to test my willpower by dangling this tattooed Adonis in front of me 24/7? I'm only human.

"Fancy seeing you here, Doc," DJ drawls, leaning an arm out the window. "If I believed in fate, I'd say this is a sign we should grab that coffee sooner rather than later."

I can't help but laugh as I wrack my brain for a witty comeback. DJ beats me to the punch, shooting me a wink and blowing me a kiss before peeling out of the parking lot, leaving me standing there gaping after him for the second time in one day.

Flustered, I hop into my car and pull out onto the street, heading for home. But my mind is racing the whole drive, thoughts whirling with possibilities I know I shouldn't entertain.

I'm here to do a job, and do it well. That's all. It's important to maintain professional boundaries.

It's just been so long since I've had this kind of spark, this visceral pull of attraction. After what happened with Paul...well, let's just say my self-esteem and sex drive have been lower than the Blizzards' penalty kill percentage.

I laugh at myself—proud that I pulled that hockey term out of thin air but 100% sure I could not define it if my life depended on it.

The glint in DJ's eyes flashes across my mind again and my cheeks flush. Somehow I can't help but think like I'll be learning a lot in this new job...in more ways than one.

CHAPTER 4
DJ

LATER IN THE WEEK, I TAKE JASON OUT FOR BURGERS, TRYING TO get him back in better spirits. The man has been down ever since the fight two weeks ago, and it pains me to see him this way.

I flash the waitress my trademark smirk as she sets down our waters.

"Thanks. And could we get some extra napkins? Things might get messy later, if you know what I mean." I wink and she giggles, flushing pink.

She walks off with an exaggerated sway in her hips and, tearing my gaze away from her cute ass, I turn back to Jason. His shoulders are slumped, and he's spinning his water glass around and around, staring down at the tablecloth like it holds the secrets to the universe.

I frown at his disgruntled expression. *This won't do.*

"So I banged these smoking hot Brazilian twins last night.

Both had bodies like you wouldn't believe..." I launch into a raunchy rendition of my latest sexcapade, trying to get a smile out of him.

Jason just gives a half-hearted chuckle, his mind clearly elsewhere.

Leaning forward, I tap his hand. "Alright man, out with it. You've been like this all week. What's going on?"

He sighs deeply, scrubbing a hand over his face. "Fuck, DJ...I just can't stop thinking about that fight." His eyes meet mine, swimming with guilt. "I was way out of line. Throwing punches, smashing bottles. I'm supposed to be better than that."

I wince, memories of fists and blood and splintered wood flashing through my mind.

"Hey, you're not the only one who lost control." It was ugly, and Jason definitely wasn't the worst of it. In fact, as far as I remember, Jason only really threw a punch or two before he ended up dazed and on the floor.

"I know, but...I can't help feeling responsible, you know? Like I egged them on, made it worse by being so drunk and letting Mikey get to me." Jason's voice rises, the words tumbling out faster. "I keep replaying it, thinking if I had just shut my mouth or walked away..."

"Jase. Look at me." I clasp his shoulder, forcing him to meet my steady gaze. "You fucked up. We all did. But beating yourself up won't change what happened."

"I know," he mumbles. "I just...how do I make this right?"

"Well, you've already apologized to Coach and the team— now show them you're owning your shit. Put in the work to be better." I squeeze his shoulder. "You're a good dude. Learn from this and keep moving forward."

Jason nods slowly, some of the tension easing from his posture. "Thanks, man. I needed to hear that."

"Anytime brother. I've always got your back." I raise my water. "Now, let's enjoy ourselves. Doctor's orders!"

He snorts a laugh, clinking his water glass to mine. I'm relieved to see that the shadows have lifted from his eyes. As for me, I shake off the heavy moment and let my signature smirk slide back into place.

I lean back in my chair, grinning at Jason across the table. "So, speaking of doctors...what do you think of the new counselor they brought in? Sydney?"

I picture the way she blushed when I asked her to coffee and my grin deepens. There's something about her...

Jason catches my expression and shoots me a warning look. "Careful, DJ. You don't want to get yourself in trouble by mixing work and sex. Besides, what about the Brazilians?"

"Hey, a man's got needs," I say with a shrug, just as our burgers arrive. I take a huge bite, savoring the juicy meat. "Mmm. Damn, they make a good burger here. Almost as tasty as Sydney looked in that little sundress today. Did you see the way—"

"Dude, seriously," Jason cuts me off. "She's my counselor, I can't think of her that way. Drop it. Let's talk about something else. Like how Coach is trying to kill us with these extra practices." He rubs his shoulder with a wince.

I nod in commiseration as I chew. "I know, right? I'm so

sore, I can barely lift my arms. Oh, speaking of..." I lean forward excitedly. "I think I finally perfected my post-game recovery smoothie. The secret is a dash of cayenne."

As I expected, Jason perks up at this—the man loves a recipe —but as he discusses the pros and cons of various protein powders I find my mind wandering.

Sydney's warm smile, her quick wit, the way her dress hugged her lush curves...

Fuck, I can't help but imagine ripping it off her, kissing every inch of her soft skin. What do her moans sound like? Is she an aggressive lover, or does she like other people to take the lead?

I shake my head, trying to clear the mental images. I know Jason's right, I shouldn't go there.

Or should I?

The city lights blur past my windshield as I guide my Lexus through the late-night streets, antsy. Dinner with Jason was great as always, but I'm still amped up, craving more excitement before calling it a night. At a red light, I punch out a few texts to my favorite club buddies, seeing who's down to get a little wild.

My phone buzzes with replies almost immediately—looks like Marcos and Shay are out at The Gilded Lily. *Perfect.*

I hang a sharp left, tires screeching, and gun it towards the West Loop, adrenaline already surging in my veins.

After parking I stride past the velvet rope line snaking

around the block and flash a grin at the bouncer. He unhooks the rope without hesitation, ushering me inside. The pulsing beats and flashing lights envelop me as I swagger over to the bar.

Shay spots me first, their neon skintight dress leaving little to the imagination as they grind up against me.

"Hey sexy, about time you showed up," they purr in my ear, their lips grazing my neck. I slip my hands around their tiny waist and pull them close.

"You know I couldn't stay away," I whisper, relishing the heat of their body.

"DJ!" Mateo, the bartender, calls out with a grin. "The usual?"

I flash him a smile and lean across the bar to accept the shot of whiskey he slides my way. "You know it." I give Shay a final squeeze before downing the drink and turning to chest-bump another of our friends, Eli. "Sup man, how's life?"

"Can't complain," Eli shrugs with a smirk. "Especially now that you're here to spice things up."

I laugh, signaling Mateo for another round of shots. "Let's get this party started then, shall we?"

Suddenly, fingertips trail suggestively down my spine and I catch a whiff of perfume. I'd know that intoxicating scent anywhere. Lila.

I spin to face her, drinking in the sight of her dangerous curves poured into a slinky silver dress.

"Hey there, hot stuff," Lila murmurs, a mischievous look in her eyes. "Fancy a dance?" She presses her body against mine.

Pounding back my shot, I allow her to drag me into the pulsing crowd, my blood already on fire.

The bass reverberates through my body as Lila and I move together on the crowded dance floor, our bodies slick with sweat.

My head is pleasantly fuzzy from the two shots I did back-to-back, but as Lila grinds against me, I gaze out across the gyrating mass of bodies and suddenly get an odd flicker of dissatisfaction.

The song ends and I lean in, my lips grazing Lila's ear. "Another round?"

She grins wickedly. "Thought you'd never ask."

We weave through the gyrating bodies to the bar, where I flag Mateo down. "Two more, my good man." I turn to Lila, admiring how her dress barely covers her. She looks good tonight. Hell, she always looks good.

But as we wait for our drinks, another wave of melancholy washes over me.

Must be the alcohol making me all introspective and shit.

I lean in close to Lila again, having to shout over the thumping music. "You ever feel like something's missing? Like you're just going through the motions?"

She cocks an eyebrow at me. "Since when did you get so deep, DJ?"

I shrug, staring out at the crowd again. "I don't know...maybe I need to slow my roll."

Lila throws her head back and laughs, the sound barely audible over the din.

She leans in, her lips curling into a smirk. "Careful there, stud. You're starting to sound like you wanna be tied down. Whatever would your adoring fans think?"

I can't help but laugh along with her. *Me? Tied down?* She always knows just what to say to snap me out of my funks.

Our drinks arrive and we clink glasses. "To living in the moment," Lila toasts with a wink.

"I'll drink to that." The liquor burns pleasantly down my throat.

Lila sets down her empty glass and grabs my hand. "Now, enough of this heart-to-heart bullshit. We've got some dancing to do." She pulls me back to the floor as a new song starts up, the beat already melting away my strange mood.

The music throbs through my body as I spin Lila around, her curves brushing against me suggestively. But then I catch a glimpse of familiar dark hair and smoky eyes in the crowd, long limbs moving sensually to the rhythm of the music.

My heart jumps into my throat. *Sydney.*

Without even thinking, I extricate myself from Lila's embrace, plastering on my most charming grin as I beeline towards her.

The alcohol has me bold and reckless.

"Well, fancy meeting you here," I drawl, my words only slightly slurred. "Care to dance with me?"

But as I get closer, I squint my eyes and a vague realization swims through the booze: this woman isn't Sydney at all.

It's her twin—Selena. Coach Emma's friend. *Whoops.*

"DJ Johnston." Selena arches one perfectly sculpted brow, red lips quirking. "I've heard a lot about you."

"All good things, I hope," I quip back, attempting to cover my initial blunder.

I eye Sydney's twin with curiosity, wondering how I realized my mistake so quickly. They really are identical—the resemblance is uncanny—but for some reason I can't picture Sydney wearing something this...fussy. Selena looks like she just stepped off a runway, all curves and glamor.

"Sounds like Sydney's been talking about me, huh?" I continue. "I'm intrigued."

Selena flicks her perfectly manicured hand, feigning nonchalance. The diamond studs on her nails glint in the club lights. "A lady never tells," she shoots back playfully.

"Pity." I click my tongue in mock disapproval. "And here I was hoping to get the scoop. Guess I'll just have to use my imagination about what Sydney's been saying..."

I'm hoping Selena will relent—god, I would kill to know what Sydney's been saying about me—but she just crosses her arms and gives me a long, unreadable look.

"You do that." Selena smirks, leaning in close enough that I catch a hint of her perfume. "But I'd guess your imagination is already running wild enough as it is."

Before I can retort, she turns on her stiletto heel and saunters away, hips swaying. I watch her go, wishing it were the other twin that I was watching.

I frown. Why? What is it about Sydney that has me so intrigued? Is it just because she's off-limits?

My frown deepens. I'm never one to conform to society's rule, but even I know when to draw the line. Getting involved with Sydney could jeopardize not only my career but the whole team.

We *need* her to get us through this mess.

The thought sobers me. The team always comes first.

Pulling myself together, I head back to where Lila is still swaying on the dance floor, watching me with a lifted eyebrow.

"Friend of yours?" she asks, half-laughing.

But I just absentmindedly wrap my arms around her, letting the music wash over me again.

Hoping the music and the dancing will melt away the thoughts of Sydney that still dance through my head.

If only it was that simple…

CHAPTER 5
SYDNEY

I LEAN BACK IN MY CHAIR, THE SOFT CREAK OF LEATHER NOW A comforting backdrop to the countless hours I've already put in. The first two weeks have been a whirlwind of emotions and responsibilities, with therapy sessions bleeding into team meetings and brief interludes of quiet that I snatch greedily whenever I can.

I'm rifling through my notes from Jason's latest session, pleased that we've been making progress, but my focus fractures as my thoughts are drawn yet again to the issue of Tomas's missed appointments.

If Tomas dodges one more meeting, I'll have no choice but to get Coach involved. I hate the idea—it's important that Tomas *wants* to get help rather than be forced—but I can't just stand by.

I can't help the man if he refuses to show up.

A cacophony from the hallway, sudden raised voices sharpened by frustration, breaks my concentration. Concerned by the disruption, I rise and inch toward the door, my skin prickling with tension.

Cracking the door open, my eyes widen as I'm met with a scene charged with anger.

DJ and Tyler are squared off, their faces red with the heat of their argument. DJ's tattoos seem to dance on his arms as he gesticulates, while Tyler stands like a bull ready to charge. In the eye of the storm is Jason, hands raised in a futile attempt at peace.

"Your head isn't even in the game anymore, Jason!" Tyler's accusation slices through the air. "It's obvious! You assholes had to go act out, and now we can't win a game to save our lives!"

DJ frowns, stepping in front of Jason defensively. "Back off, Simmonds. We're a team, remember?" DJ's tone is acid laced with honey, sharp but impossible to dismiss.

The three move farther down the hallway and I ease my office door closed, my heart sinking. The headache that's been lurking behind my eyes blooms fully now, a thorny ring tightening around my temples.

The accusation in Tyler's eyes, the distrust in the team's ability to pull together and break their losing streak...this is more than a spat; it's a crack in the foundation of the team.

And it's my job to be the glue.

Ten minutes later, the door swings open and a sheepish Jason steps into my office. His shoulders slump in a way that screams defeat, his usual easygoing charm nowhere to be seen.

"Could you hear us?" he asks, rubbing the back of his neck with a nervous chuckle that doesn't quite reach his eyes.

"Hard to miss," I admit, folding my arms across my chest and leaning my elbows on the desk. "Wanna talk about it?"

He exhales, a heavy gust that seems to carry the weight of the entire team. "It's like we're split down the middle, and I have no idea how to stitch us back together. No one trusts each other anymore."

"Maybe it would help to sit down and talk to everyone one-on-one," I suggest. "Address what happened and how you're committed to doing better in the future. Face the music, clear the air."

Jason nods, the gears visibly turning in his head as we toss ideas back and forth like a puck in overtime. By the time he leaves, his stride has regained its confidence.

I sink back into my chair and allow myself a smile. It's a small victory, but it's a step toward mending the fractured spirit of the Blizzards.

If only my own tangled mess of a life could be sorted with a good pep talk.

Later that afternoon DJ swings by my office, a crooked grin lighting up his handsome face. His presence immediately fills the small room, sending a little thrill through me despite my best efforts at maintaining professional distance.

Over the past week, my office has turned into a revolving

door of stressed-out hockey players seeking a moment of peace amidst the team's chaos. Tensions are simmering and occasionally boiling over—fights keep erupting on and off the ice.

It's no wonder that the players want a safe space to vent about the mounting pressure.

To my surprise (and secret pleasure), both DJ and Tyler have become regular visitors, often dropping in unannounced. Sometimes they want to dish about team drama, other times they simply seem to crave friendly conversation that has nothing to do with hockey.

Technically, they aren't my official patients—I'm only formally treating the three players struggling with addiction. But I never have the heart to turn DJ and Tyler away when they appear at my door.

There's just something magnetic about them, as different as they are.

DJ with his easy charm and flirtatious energy.

Tyler with his quiet intensity, the simmering emotions hidden just beneath the surface.

I constantly have to check myself, to remember my role as their team's counselor and not...whatever forbidden fantasies threaten to carry me away.

Let's just say it's getting harder to banish inappropriate thoughts of them from my mind, especially late at night alone in bed.

"Hey, Doc," DJ greets me now, plopping down on the chair across from my desk.

God, even the way he sits is sexy. *What is wrong with me?!*

"Got a minute for your favorite player?" His voice is pure seduction, sending tingles to all the right places.

Wrong places! Wrong places, Sydney!

I shoot him a look, trying to seem stern even as I fight back a grin. "You know I don't play favorites, DJ. But of course, I always have time for you. What's on your mind today?"

His smile falters slightly as he leans forward, resting his elbows on his knees. "Honestly? I'm worried the team is fracturing...that we won't recover from that shit-show. The guys are at each other's throats constantly. I'm trying to stay positive, but..."

I nod, feeling DJ's concern as if it's my own—and in some ways it is. I've had basically the exact same thought nearly every day this week.

"Has something new happened that makes you think that?" I ask.

We've just started digging into things when a knock sounds at the door. I glance over to see Tyler hovering in the doorway, his brawny frame practically filling it. His gaze darts between me and DJ, uncertainty flickering across his classically handsome face.

The tension in the room instantly ratchets up a notch.

Tyler frowns slightly, his chiseled jaw clenched tight. "Sorry, I didn't realize you were with someone," he mutters, already turning to leave.

But DJ jumps up, waving him inside with a grin that skates the line between friendly and wicked. "Don't be silly, man. I was just heading out, anyway. Besides, Doc could use a visit from her second favorite player, right?"

There's an edge to his tone that I don't have time to interpret before DJ winks at me and motions to leave, but Tyler doesn't budge from the doorway. After a charged standoff, DJ strides over to Tyler, grabs his muscular arm, and practically hauls him into the room.

I watch, transfixed, as DJ's tattooed hand lingers on Tyler's bicep a moment longer than necessary, his fingers trailing across the bulging muscle.

Tyler stiffens at the touch, his blue eyes avoiding DJ's face.

The sexual energy between them is so electric, I swear it crackles across my skin.

Finally it breaks as DJ grabs his jacket and swaggers out, shooting one last look over his shoulder that I sense deep in my gut. I realize that I've been holding my breath, and inwardly roll my eyes at myself as I take a gulp of air.

Tyler clears his throat, looking everywhere but directly at me. "Second favorite, eh? Guess I drew the short straw, eh? Always the backup..."

The ghost of the heat from their exchange still hanging in the air, I force myself to focus on Tyler, noticing how his gaze lingers on the door.

Just what exactly is going on between Tyler and DJ?

An image of the two men together in bed, their muscular bodies slick with sweat, flashes through my mind.

A flicker of something hot unfurls low in my belly—jealousy? Curiosity?

I firmly push this line of thinking aside. Tyler is here because he needs my help to sort through his issues, not because he wants me perving on him and his teammates.

"What's on your mind, Tyler?" I ask in my most professional voice, folding my hands on the desk and giving him my full attention. Time to do my job.

That night, I sit down across a small table from Selena, gazing with longing at a sashimi platter in the hands of a passing waitress. Selena arches a perfectly sculpted eyebrow at me, a teasing grin playing on her bold red lips.

"Food can wait. Spill," she demands. "I want to hear all about these hot hockey hunks you're spending your days with."

I roll my eyes but can't help the grin tugging at the corners of my mouth.

"Oh, they're nothing special. Just giant, muscular men with chiseled jaws and eyes you could drown in, gracefully gliding across the ice and smashing each other into the boards."

"Mmm, sounds rough," Selena purrs, propping her chin on her hand. "Any frontrunners emerging from the pack to sweep you off your feet?"

I snort. "Please. Even if it weren't wildly unprofessional, I'm not ready for that. No matter how tempting their...stick handling skills may be."

But even as the words leave my lips, my mind flashes to DJ

and Tyler—their intense gazes, the crackling tension when they're in close quarters...

Selena watches me knowingly as I squirm in my seat. *Damn twin intuition.*

Desperate to change the subject, I ask about her latest Tinder exploits, and soon we're giggling over cringe-worthy pickup lines and debating the merits of bad boys versus geeks.

As our sushi arrives, Selena's eyes light up. "Ooh, we should plan a spa day soon! Massages, mani-pedis, the works. God knows we could both use some pampering and girl time."

"Mmph, yessh," I mumble around a mouthful of rice and fish. Swallowing, I nod enthusiastically. "I'm so in. My treat, for putting up with my moping lately."

Selena waves a dismissive hand. "Please, what are sisters for? Besides, maybe a little TLC is just what you need to get your groove back. Among other things..."

She wiggles her eyebrows suggestively.

I groan, fighting a blush. As much as I adore my incorrigible twin, her well-meaning meddling is so not what I need right now.

Selena's phone pings and she dives for it, eyes scanning the screen.

"Potential suitor?" I tease. She winks at me saucily as her thumbs fly over the keyboard.

I prop my chin on my hand, letting the cheerful chatter of the restaurant wash over me as I gaze at my sister. This moment might be mundane, but after everything I've been through, something as simple as dinner with Selena makes me feel like the luckiest woman in the world.

Putting down her phone, Selena takes a sip of her lychee martini and leans in across the table. "So, Syd, seriously, when are you going to get back out there and find yourself a man?"

I nearly choke on my tuna roll at her blunt question.

"Wow, way to ease into that topic," I mutter, wiping my mouth with my napkin.

"I'm just saying," she shrugs unapologetically. "It's been months since you and Paul. You can't let that douchebag ruin dating for you forever. There are plenty of great guys out there."

"Can we not talk about Paul right now? Or my love life in general?" I snap, my fingers tightening around my chopsticks.

Selena holds up her hands in surrender. "Okay, touchy subject, got it. But I worry about you, sis. I don't want you to close yourself off because of how badly things ended with him."

I take a deep breath, trying to shake off the surge of irritation.

Selena means well, but she has no idea how deeply I was wounded when Paul shattered my heart and my self-esteem.

Okay, maybe she doesn't know because I haven't really told her much. But still.

"I appreciate the concern," I say tightly. "But I'm doing just fine on my own. My career is taking off. I have great friends. I don't need a man to complete me."

Selena studies me over the rim of her glass, one brow arched. "If you say so. But if a hockey hottie does come along, don't shut him down just because of Paul. You deserve to be happy in a relationship again."

I stab my chopsticks into my dragon roll, my appetite fading.

Is Selena right? Am I still letting that toxic relationship taint my future, without even realizing it?

The thought unsettles me more than I care to admit.

The next day, Tomas finally shows up.

The dark circles under his bloodshot eyes match the invisible weight dragging his broad shoulders into a slump as he settles into the chair across from me. I study him, my relief at finally seeing him after the missed sessions tinged with unease.

Tomas runs a hand through his rumpled hair.

"Sydney, hey. Sorry about flaking on you before. Things have been..." He shakes his head, not meeting my eyes. "Complicated."

I lean forward, offering what I hope is an encouraging smile. "It's okay, Tomas. I'm just glad you're here now. Do you want to tell me what's been going on?"

He's quiet for a long moment. When he speaks, his voice is ragged at the edges.

"It's Gina. My girlfriend. Ex-girlfriend, I guess. I don't know anymore."

A chill prickles my skin. I know that lost, hurting look in his eyes all too well. "What happened?"

"She's always had a temper. But lately it's gotten bad. The things she says..." He swallows hard. "That I'm pathetic. Stupid. Lucky she puts up with me. I try not to let it get to me, but..."

My chest tightens, Tomas's words hitting too close to home. Memories of Paul's cruel taunts echo in my mind—how he'd tear me down one moment then beg for forgiveness the next until I didn't know which way was up. I take a steadying breath, focusing on Tomas. I can see the desperation in his eyes and I choose my words carefully.

"Tomas, I want you to listen to me. What Gina is doing—the yelling, the insults—that's verbal abuse. It's not okay, and it's not your fault."

He meets my gaze, his dark eyes glassy. "I know. Deep down, I know that. It's just hard..." Tomas takes a deep breath. "I need to break away from her. I can't keep letting her control me like this."

I nod, my heart aching for him. Escaping an abusive relationship is never easy. He has a long road ahead of him.

"Have you ever reached out for help before now?" I ask. "A support group, or therapy?"

Tomas runs a hand through his hair again, his expression conflicted. "I mean, I know I should have but...I don't know. I guess I've been too ashamed to admit that I'm in this situation."

I place a reassuring hand on his arm. "Tomas, there's no shame in seeking help. It takes courage to acknowledge that you need it."

A small smile tugs at the corners of his mouth as he meets my eyes. "Thanks, Sydney."

We spend the rest of the session discussing different resources he could explore in addition to his sessions with me.

By the time Tomas leaves, he looks exhausted but determined. We have a lot of work still to do—aside from going over coping strategies that don't involve alcohol, we barely touched on Tomas's substance abuse. But we made a good amount of progress in just one session.

While I pack up my things for the day, my mind wanders back to Paul and our tumultuous past together. He had been my first serious boyfriend in college—charming and charismatic at first, but slowly revealing his true colors as our relationship progressed.

It wasn't until years into the relationship that I realized how bad everything had gotten.

How he'd convinced me that I was worthless and unlovable.

My heart breaks for Tomas because I know exactly how hard it is to break free of a toxic relationship. How easy it is to convince yourself that *you're* the problem.

As I lock up my office and head out into the chilly evening air, I remind myself that I've done it. *I've* broken free from my own personal demons. I got away from Paul and have started rebuilding my life. But Selena's words echo in my mind.

"You deserve to be happy in a relationship again."

Maybe it's time to admit that I'm having trouble believing that.

CHAPTER 6
TYLER

WE'RE HEADING HOME FROM A BRUISING AWAY GAME, AND AS THE plane hurtles down the runway, I grip the armrests like they're the only thing keeping me from plummeting to my death. My stomach churns, a cocktail of post-loss misery and pre-flight jitters.

Those damn pucks slipping past me replay in my head on a sickening loop.

The plane lifts off with a shuddering jolt and I swallow hard. Flying and losing—my two least favorite things. *What a banner day.*

Suddenly, the seat beside me dips and DJ's woodsy cologne invades my nostrils. I glance over to find him grinning at me. My pulse kicks up a notch that has zero to do with the turbulence.

"Tough game, eh?" DJ bumps his knee against mine. The

brief contact sends a shockwave straight to my groin. "Their offense was killer."

"More like I sucked," I mutter, jaw clenched. "Let in way too many."

DJ tsks. "Aw, don't be so hard on yourself, Ty. We win as a team, lose as a team, right? Besides..." He leans in, voice a low rumble. "I happen to know you're amazing at playing hard and fast. On the ice, of course."

A surprised laugh bursts out of me. Trust DJ to pull me out of my self-loathing with some well-timed innuendo. It's one of the things I lo—appreciate about him.

As a friend. A teammate. Because that's all we are.

I clear my throat, willing my body not to react to his proximity. "Of course. Thanks, man."

DJ studies me a beat longer, gaze drifting to my mouth, before he sits back with a smirk. "Anytime, babe. Anytime."

My breath hitches at how easily the endearment rolls off his tongue. I both crave it and curse it.

"We all had a rough game," DJ says, squeezing his eyes shut momentarily.

DJ starts rehashing a play he thinks he screwed up, and my fear of flying is momentarily forgotten. Realizing that his presence is pulling me out of my spiraling negative thoughts, he launches into a funny incident from the locker room and his body seems to angle towards mine unconsciously, our shoulders nearly touching.

I can't help but notice the spark between us, a terrifying, thrilling magnetic pull.

At one point, he throws his head back laughing at something I said and his hand lands on my thigh, squeezing gently. I tense for a millisecond before allowing myself to relax into it. *There's nobody around to see, everyone's zonked out asleep...what's the harm in enjoying this closeness, just for a bit?*

DJ's thumb rubs circles on my leg and I suppress a shiver. This is straying into dangerous territory but I can't bring myself to pull away.

Not when it feels this good, this right.

"Y'know, you're something else, Tyler Simmonds," DJ murmurs, holding my gaze with an intensity that steals my breath. "Funny, humble, talented as hell...the whole package."

"Look who's talking," I shoot back, emboldened by the heated gleam in his eyes. "DJ Johnston, resident puck god. You've got half the women in Chicago ready to drop their panties for you."

"Only the women?" He arches an eyebrow. "Clearly I'm not trying hard enough."

My heart races at the implication of his words. *Is DJ trying to tell me something, or is this just his typical flirtatious bullshit? And if he is trying to tell me something—if he is attracted to me, too—then what?*

I open my mouth to respond, but before I can form any coherent words, the plane hits a patch of turbulence and DJ's hand instinctively tightens its grip on my thigh. My heart catches in my throat as we both brace ourselves for the sudden shaking.

As soon as the turbulence subsides, DJ pulls back slightly,

his hand staying firmly planted on my thigh. But this time, it's different—more possessive, more intentional.

Our eyes lock for a moment and I see something raw in DJ's expression. It's as if we're both silently acknowledging the unspoken tension between us.

The sudden rattle of a flight attendant's cart passing down the aisle startles me and I flinch. DJ clocks my unease and smiles, leaning back into his seat and eyeing me with those deep brown eyes that always seem to see right through me.

"So yeah, about the game tonight," he starts, his tone casual. "I was thinking we need to adjust our strategy for next time."

My jaw clenches involuntarily. The loss is still raw, like an exposed nerve, and I can't help but wonder if what DJ means is that *I* need to adjust my strategy.

"Oh yeah? What did you have in mind?" I try to keep my tone light but there's an edge to it.

"Well, a couple things. Like, their forwards were getting past our D pretty easily." *Read: they were scoring on you nonstop.* "Maybe we need to tighten up the gaps, put more pressure on them in the neutral zone."

He says it lightly, but I can't help hearing it as pointed, a reminder of how incapable I am of defending the net if they let anyone near me.

"You saying it's my fault? That I let in too many goals?" My face gets hot, my hands curling into fists at my sides.

DJ's eyes widen. "What? No, man, that's not what I meant at all. The whole team needs to—"

"Because it sure as hell sounded like it," I cut him off,

straightening up abruptly in my seat. "Sorry I'm not fucking perfect like you, DJ. Sorry I can't just shrug off another goddamn loss and act like everything's fine."

"Ty, c'mon, I never said that. I'm not blaming you." DJ tentatively raises his hand, reaching out like he wants to touch me, but I jerk away.

"Right. Because nothing's ever your fault, is it? Must be nice, being so goddamn flawless."

I'm in his face now, blood pounding in my ears. I know I'm overreacting, I know he doesn't deserve this, but it's like a dam has burst inside me, all the fear and inadequacy and self-doubt pouring out.

DJ's jaw tightens, a muscle ticking in his cheek. "You know what, screw you. I'm just trying to help the team. Sorry for giving a shit."

"I don't need your fucking help!" The words tear out of me, louder than I mean them to be. Raw, exposed, like an open wound. "I can handle it myself. I don't need you—or anyone else—telling me how to do my job."

We're both breathing hard, chests heaving, glaring at each other. My heart hammers against my ribs. I'm stripped bare under DJ's gaze, all my flaws and weaknesses laid out for him to see.

How did we get here? Minutes ago we were laughing together, the warmth of his body pressed against mine a sweet torture. Now it's like a chasm has split open between us, jagged and deep.

And I put it there.

I drag a hand over my face, suddenly exhausted. "You know what, just…forget it. I can't do this right now."

I turn away, needing to put some distance between us before I say something else I regret.

Before I let him see how much he affects me.

"Fine. Be a dick then. See if I care." DJ's voice is rough, strained. Hurt. I flinch at the sound of it but I don't turn back, can't bear to see the look on his face. To see how much damage I've done.

I sink down in my seat, grabbing my headphones from my backpack and pulling them down over my ears, a clear signal that this conversation is over.

Fuck. How did I let my stupid insecurities ruin everything?

Because that's what this is really about, if I'm being honest with myself. It's not about the game, not really. It's about me and my fragile ego, so easily threatened by someone like DJ. Someone confident and secure in who he is, on and off the ice. Everything I wish I could be but I'm not.

Everything I…

No. I can't go there. Can't even let myself think it. With all the pressures of the team on my shoulders right now, I do not have the bandwidth for an identity crisis.

So I do what I always do—I bury it down deep, lock it away.

Pretend it's not there, eating away at me, hollowing me out bit by bit.

❄

In the airport, I spot Sydney walking ahead of the players with Coach Emma, her long brown hair swaying as she walks. I jog to catch up with her. After we really got into it about my stress this season last week, Sydney told me she was always available to talk if I needed it.

And after everything that just went down, my mind is a tangled mess.

I need a distraction, something to get my head on straight. Maybe I've been reading into things too much, but I've felt a flicker of attraction from Sydney over the past few weeks. Right now, nothing sounds better than some alone time with a beautiful woman who just happens to be an incredibly easy person to talk to.

"Tyler, hi!" Sydney says as I pull up beside her, shooting me a warm and sweet smile.

"Hey, I was wondering if you might want to hang tonight?" Sydney's eyes grow large and I plow ahead. "I know it's a bit unorthodox since you're working with the guys, but technically I'm not your patient so...maybe it's okay to grab a drink?"

There's a pause and for a second I think she'll turn me down. But then—

"You know what, I'd love to! It's been a hell of a week and I could use a chance to unwind. I need some time to head home and change my clothes though; meet you at Finnegan's at 9?"

"Perfect, it's a date. Well, not a *date* date but—" *God I'm an idiot.* I hope I'm not blushing.

"I know what you mean," she laughs. "See you then!"

I wave and then peel off to get a cab home.

Sydney has this way of making me so at ease, like she really gets me. It's refreshing. When I stop and think about it, I can't remember the last time I felt that way—like a woman saw me as *me* and not as NHL Player Tyler Simmonds.

And if I'm being totally honest, focusing on her helps keep my mind off a certain brown-eyed enforcer who shall remain nameless.

So tonight, it's all about forgetting that drama and enjoying the company of a gorgeous, intelligent woman who sees me for me.

The cozy booth is warm and intimate as I slide in across from Sydney. She gives me a small smile, tucking a lock of dark hair behind her ear. There's an awkward beat of silence. We've only ever talked in her office before, with the barrier of counselor and client between us.

Now, in the low light of the bar, it's just the two of us.

I clear my throat. "So, uh, thanks for coming out with me tonight."

"Of course." Sydney leans forward, resting her elbows on the table. "I'm glad we could do this. Get to know each other in a more...casual setting."

Her voice is playful, flirtatious even. A flicker of interest crackles through me as we lock eyes. She really is gorgeous. And kind, and smart. Exactly the type of woman I would want to be with.

The type of woman who could help me forget about my inconvenient—

I clear my throat, pushing thoughts of DJ out of my mind.

"Yeah, it's nice," I say. "To hang out. Outside of your office."

Jesus, I sound like a moron. I take a big gulp of my beer, hoping the alcohol will loosen my tongue. Sydney just smiles at me, patient and understanding, and my chest relaxes.

"So tell me about yourself, Tyler," she prompts gently. "I know the surface level stuff from our sessions. But I'd like to know more about what makes you tick."

I hesitate, not used to talking about myself. But something about Sydney's warm look compels me to let my guard down.

"Well, a lot of it is hockey," I admit. "Trying to live up to expectations. Especially my brother's."

"Your brother Steven, right? The one who used to play in the NHL?"

I nod. "Yeah. He was—is—amazing. Growing up, all I wanted was to be like him. To make him proud."

"That's a lot of pressure to put on yourself."

"I guess." I shrug. "But Steven...he demands a lot. He always has."

"In what way?" Sydney asks.

"Oh, you know...pushing me to train harder, skate faster. Yelling at me when I let in a goal." I try to keep my tone light, but some bitterness creeps in. "He didn't like it when I made mistakes. Still doesn't."

Sydney's brow furrows in concern. "That doesn't sound like he was a very supportive brother."

"Naw, it's fine," I say quickly, not wanting her to get the wrong impression. "Steven's great. He just wants me to be the best. And I want that too. It's just...a lot sometimes. Trying to fill his skates."

"I can understand that," Sydney says quietly. "Feeling like you're not enough. Like you'll never measure up, no matter how hard you try."

There's a knowing look in her eyes, and somehow I get the impression that she has her own demons. Her own past hurts and insecurities.

"Yeah. Exactly." I take another sip of beer, emboldened by her understanding. "And with playoffs less than a sure thing this season...I don't know, Syd. I'm worried I'm going to choke. Let the team down. I'm the goalie—everything rests on me. If I don't play a fucking perfect game, it's over."

"That's an awful lot to carry on your shoulders alone," she murmurs. Her hand slides across the table, coming to rest lightly on my forearm. "I know we just met, Tyler...but I can already see how much heart you have. How much you care. The Blizzards are lucky to have you."

Her touch sends a tingle up my arm. I stare at her slender fingers against my skin, swallowing hard.

"I don't always feel so lucky," I mutter. "Especially lately, with everything that's been going on..."

I stop myself, realizing I'm veering into dangerous territory. I can't tell Sydney about DJ. If I say the words out loud, it makes them real.

And I'm not ready for that.

Sydney is watching me carefully, her expression soft and open. "It sounds like you're going through a lot right now. I know how hard it can be, to think you're fighting a battle alone. My ex, Paul...our relationship really did a number on my self-esteem. He always made me feel like I needed to be someone else to make him happy."

My heart clenches at the vulnerability in her voice. I turn my arm over, grasping her hand in mine.

"You are good enough, Syd," I tell her firmly. "You're more than enough. Fuck Paul for making you think otherwise."

A ghost of a smile crosses her lips. "Thanks. I'm working on believing that."

She squeezes my fingers gently.

"The point is," she continues, "I understand how suffocating other people's expectations can be. Even well-meaning ones. At the end of the day, you have to be true to yourself, Tyler. Figure out what you want. What makes you happy."

"What if I don't know what that is?" The words slip out before I can stop them, laced with a raw desperation.

Sydney's thumb rubs soothingly over the back of my hand. "That's okay. You don't have to have all the answers right now. Just...be gentle with yourself. Let yourself feel whatever it is you're feeling. The rest will come in time."

I nod slowly, lost in thought.

My brain keeps circling back to DJ. The jolt of electricity I have when our eyes meet across the locker room. The way he calmed me down on the plane today—well, at least until I blew up in his face like an asshole....

I'm on the verge of blurting out my confused, inappropriate feelings when a wave of panic slams into me.

What the hell am I doing? I can't say any of this out loud. I'm on a goddamn date with a beautiful woman, for fuck's sake.

Bracing my elbows on the table, I shift closer to Sydney, fixing her with my most charming smile. "You've given me a lot to think about. But enough about me. I want to hear more about you, Syd. And not just the counselor side. The real you. Hopes, dreams, dirty little secrets...I'm all ears."

I layer my voice with innuendo, letting the implication hang in the air between us. Sydney arches an eyebrow, a slow grin spreading across her face.

"Oh, I see how it is. You want to get to know the real me?"

"Absolutely," I murmur.

I'm finding that Sydney makes it easy to focus on her—the look she gives me sends heat racing straight to my groin.

"Also I should have said—you look stunning tonight, Sydney. That dress is...wow." My eyes flick down to the V of her neckline before meeting her gaze again.

"Thank you," Sydney smiles shyly, a pink blush creeping into her cheeks. "You look very handsome yourself."

I grin, and the excitement of the moment makes my head light. For the first time in a long time, I'm really connecting with someone. Flirting is natural, easy.

Not like my tortured angst about DJ.

As the evening progresses I find myself inventing excuses to touch Sydney—tucking an errant lock of hair behind her ear, offering my jacket when she shivers slightly in the air conditioning, letting my hands linger on her bare shoulders as I help her slip it on.

"Thank you," Sydney says quietly, her eyes meeting mine as she leans slightly towards me.

My thumb strokes over the soft skin at the nape of her neck and my breath catches. My body is reacting strongly to her nearness—my tight jeans, already constricting, become far *too* tight around my hardening length.

Inhaling the subtle floral scent of her perfume, I have the sudden urge to trail my lips along the graceful column of her throat.

To skim my hands lower, over her curves...

Stop it, I chastise myself. *This is Sydney. The Blizzards' counselor.* I need to keep things in check, take it slow—if there's any chance of something happening between us, we'd have to be careful about it. *But damn if she doesn't look incredible in that clingy dress, her full breasts straining against the fabric...*

I clear my throat, leaning back in my seat. "Another drink?" I signal the waitress.

"I'd love one." Sydney smiles up at me through her lashes. She looks flushed, and there's an inviting gleam in her eyes.

Fuck. I fidget in my seat, trying to will down my growing erection. Suddenly all I can think about is getting my hands on her luscious body, tasting her.

Making her cry out my name in ecstasy.

My fingers tremble with the overwhelming desire to touch her. To pull her into my lap and lose himself in her intoxicating presence. As the waitress sets down our next round of drinks, I wonder...

Will I be strong enough to stop myself?

CHAPTER 7
SYDNEY

SAYING YES TO DRINKS WITH TYLER IS SEEMING MORE AND MORE LIKE it was a bad idea.

It must have been my travel-addled brain that convinced me we could just keep things friendly. Because this date has been anything but.

I've been thinking nonstop about Selena's implication the other week that I wasn't opening myself up to love. I *don't* want to let things with Paul impact my future happiness, she's right. So when Tyler asked me out, I ignored the voice inside that shouted, "unprofessional!"

If a man this hot and nice asks you out, you say agree. But god, I was not expecting this instantaneous and easy chemistry.

I tune back into the conversation as Tyler leans in close, those chiseled features softened by his smile. He rests his warm hand on my knee, his piercing eyes sparkling with boyish charm.

"I've never met anyone like you, Sydney. You just...get me, y'know?"

My breath catches. The weight of his touch, the timbre of his voice, sends tingles racing up my thigh. I fight the urge to squirm.

"I feel the same way," I say honestly, pulse quickening as I meet his open gaze. "Like I can tell you anything." *Anything except how badly I want to climb into your lap right now and grind against those rock-hard hockey thighs...*

I mentally slap myself. I can't let my hormones hijack my brain, not when Tyler is being so real with me. Especially when it seems like he needs a friend more than a hookup.

But lord, the way he's looking at me, gaze dipping to my lips—is he feeling this too? This magnetic tug, this need simmering just under the surface?

I lick my lips, trying to corral my wild imagination. "So, um, you were saying? About the pre-game rituals?"

"Right, yeah." He blinks, shaking his head slightly as if emerging from a trance. "It's just, with all the pressure lately, I dunno...I'm in my head too much. Psyching myself out."

"That's understandable." I squeeze his hand, enjoying the solid warmth, the slight calluses. "You've got a lot on your plate. New starting position, your brother, figuring out...things..."

I trail off delicately, not wanting to put him on the spot about his sexuality or what's going on with DJ. He's never come out and said anything about it to me, but it's pretty obvious. Tyler seems to catch my meaning, swallowing hard.

"I just...I've never..." He huffs out a breath, shoulders sagging.

"I don't know how to make sense of it all. What I'm feeling, what I want..."

His thumb strokes absently over my knuckles and I suppress a shiver, my skin tingling at the gentle touch. I know we're not talking about us—*or are we?* I'm losing track of everything, consumed with the heat pooling low in my belly.

But I can't pounce on him when he's lost. Can't take advantage or risk scaring him off with my own selfish desires.

So I simply lean into him, resting my head on his broad shoulder, savoring the spicy scent of his cologne.

"You'll figure it out, Ty. I know you will. And I'll be right here while you do."

He lets out a shaky exhale and drops a kiss on my hair, his scruff grazing my temple. "Thanks, Syd. You're a good...friend."

Friend. I try not to wince at the word, reminding myself that maintaining boundaries is for the best.

"You have no idea how nice it is to just talk like this," he says, his hand grazing mine and sending traitorous electric tingles up my arm. "I can really open up to you, Syd."

My heart flutters at the huskiness in his voice, the emotion shining in those mesmerizing eyes. It would be so easy to throw professionalism to the wind and kiss him. But Tyler's struggling and I can't do that to him, not when it seems like he and DJ are on the verge of figuring out...something.

"So, tell me more about DJ," I say, trying to steer the conversation away from the two of us. "You guys seem really...close."

Tyler fidgets with his drink, suddenly tense. "Oh, uh,

yeah...DJ's my bro, you know?" He looks away and forces a laugh. "God, I could tell you some insane stories about him."

Curiosity officially piqued. I raise an eyebrow. "Oh yeah?"

"I mean, the man is a fucking legend—literally. I'm talking like, hooked up with an entire cheerleading team. In the penalty box." He clears his throat, "Got caught by the janitor, all of them just..."

He trails off, a slight flush rising on his cheeks, and suddenly I wonder if we're imagining the same scene: a naked, muscular DJ surrounded by writhing bodies, sweat dripping on the ice...

My eyes lock with Tyler's and I see a flash of heated jealousy that takes me straight back to the confrontation in my office, to the palpable tension between the two men.

And just like that the scene in my mind shifts.

Now it's DJ and Tyler together, all hard muscles and hungry mouths as they give in to the explosive attraction that crackles between them. DJ pinning Tyler against the locker room wall, kissing him hard, big hands roaming possessively over all those sculpted contours...

I gulp my drink to cool my overheated brain.

Jesus, Syd! These are practically your patients. You cannot be fantasizing about them ripping each other's clothes off, no matter how insanely sexy that mental image is. Focus on being a supportive friend.

I take a steadying breath and meet Tyler's smoldering gaze. *Damn, it should be illegal for a man to have eyes that knee-weakeningly blue.*

"Well, it definitely sounds like you and DJ have an interesting relationship," I say, attempting a light chuckle.

"You could say that," he replies slowly. His fingers brush my knee under the table and I nearly combust on the spot. *This charming, sensitive man is going to be the death of me. But oh, what a way to go...*

We wrap up the evening and the cool night air hits my flushed skin as Tyler and I step out of the bar.

My body is still buzzing from his closeness all night, every accidental brush of his arm sending sparks through me. I can hardly breathe as he turns to face me, his deep blue eyes intense on mine.

He leans in, achingly slow. "I had a great time tonight, Syd."

His husky voice is barely above a whisper. My heart pounds wildly as his face draws nearer, those full, sensuous lips just inches from mine...

I can almost taste him already...

A jolt of panic suddenly clears the fog of lust. I jerk back, stumbling slightly in my heeled boots. "Tyler, wait. We can't..."

Hurt and confusion flash across his strong features. God, he's gorgeous, a marble statue come to life. But there are so many reasons why we can't do this. I'm his team's counselor, first and foremost. And I know that he needs to deal with whatever's going on between him and DJ.

Talk about unethical.

Never mind that he makes me weak in the knees.

"I...I'm sorry," I stammer, cheeks blazing. "I shouldn't have let things get this far. You're not technically my patient but still..."

I take another step back, needing distance before I change my mind and let my heart—and other areas—make my choices for me.

"No, I get it. My bad." He runs a hand through his tousled hair, flashing a self-deprecating smirk that doesn't reach his eyes. "You're just so damn beautiful, I got carried away."

"I should go," I blurt out. "Goodnight, Tyler." I spin on my heel and hurry around the corner to my car without looking back, pulse thundering in my ears.

Safe in the driver's seat, I sink back against the leather and squeeze my eyes shut, trying to steady my racing heart. But behind my eyelids, tantalizing images of Tyler and DJ dance through my mind.

Tyler's broad, muscular chest pressed against DJ's lean, tattooed torso. Their strong hands roaming demandingly over each other's bodies.

I imagine myself sandwiched between them, their calloused fingers gliding over my heated skin, tracing the curves of my breasts, my hips, my thighs. Soft lips and hot breath trailing kisses down my neck as they take turns tasting me.

A shiver races down my spine, and I suddenly have an almost unbearable urge to touch myself.

Glancing up at the rearview mirror, I confirm that Tyler's car is gone. I'm parked on a side street behind the bar, dark and residential. There's no one else around and all the buildings in the immediate vicinity are dark.

Perfect.

I'm not comfortable touching myself at home, not with Selena's room a thin wall away. I know *just* how thin, thanks to several late-night sleepovers she's had lately with Tinder guys.

What am I thinking?

I really shouldn't indulge these fantasies, not when I'm parked on a public street, where someone could see.

But the ache between my legs is insistent, demanding attention, and I know I won't find satisfaction at home. I glance around my dark surroundings, a dizzying sense of danger and excitement coursing through me.

Biting my lip, I slip a hand between my thighs, brushing over the damp lace of my panties. I stifle a gasp as my fingers find my sensitive clit.

Closing my eyes again, I lose myself in the delicious daydream of Tyler and DJ.

Tyler's deep, rumbling groans vibrating against my throat as he suckles my pulse point. DJ's wicked tongue flicking over my nipples before drawing one into his hot mouth.

Both of them whispering dirty promises of all the filthy things they want to do to me.

I rub desperate circles over my clit, hips rocking against my hand, chasing release.

In my mind, it's their fingers stroking me, Tyler's blunt and thick, DJ's long and clever, taking turns plunging into my wet heat. Their hard cocks prodding against my thighs, aching to be buried inside me... each wanting to claim me as their own.

I imagine them fighting over who is allowed to take me first, taking turns pushing inside of me, pounding me.

My breath catches in my throat as the fantasy spirals, my mind spinning with the vivid images of their bodies intertwined with mine, all three of us pushed against each other in a hot tangle of limbs.

I bite down on my lower lip, stifling the moans that threaten to escape. Sensation builds and crests. Waves of ecstasy crash over me, leaving me trembling and breathless in the aftermath.

Clarity seeps back in as my body quiets. Shame wars with satisfaction.

What the hell am I doing, getting myself off in public to completely inappropriate fantasies, like some sex-crazed degenerate?

But even as I straighten my clothes with shaky hands, I can't deny how right it felt to surrender to those sinful fantasies, if only for a stolen moment. With a sigh, I turn the key in the ignition.

Time to head home, where a cold shower should set me right.

Hopefully I'll be able to meet Tyler and DJ's eyes at work tomorrow…

I step into the apartment, hoping against hope that Selena is already asleep so I can avoid rehashing every detail of my date. But as luck would have it, there she is on the couch with Emma, munching popcorn and sipping white wine like the night is still young.

"Well look what the cat dragged in!" Selena calls out with a grin. "How was your hot date, sis? We want all the juicy details!"

I groan, kicking off my boots. "Can't a girl get some rest around here? I'm beat."

But they're having none of it. Emma pats the cushion between them. "Oh no you don't! Park that booty and spill, girl. How was Tyler? What was he like off the rink?"

With a sigh, I flop down on the couch and snag a handful of popcorn. The buttery scent makes my stomach rumble. "It was...nice," I say carefully. "He took me to that bar that all the guys like, Finnegan's."

"And?" Selena probes, eyes gleaming. "Did you two hit it off? Any sparks flying?"

I shrug, trying to play it cool even as memories of Tyler's strong hands and smoldering eyes flash through my mind, making my cheeks heat.

"I mean, the conversation flowed well. He's easy to talk to. But it's too soon to tell if there's anything...more there yet." I shake my head in frustration. "There shouldn't be anything anyway—even if he isn't technically one of my three patients, he's still, you know, a client of sorts."

"Uh huh, sure," Emma says knowingly. "You just keep playing coy then. But I think you'd be crazy not to go for it, that man is *fine!*"

"Enough about my love life," I say, eager to change the

subject before they weasel anything else out of me. "What's new with you, Em? How are things with your boys?"

That does the trick. Emma happily launches into a story about Slade and Alex and some hilarious miscommunication between the three of them recently.

I try to listen, but my mind keeps circling back to her unique relationship dynamic. Emma always seems so content, so fulfilled, balancing four incredible men who support each other just as much as they adore her.

I can't help but wonder—could something like that ever work for me? The thought of being with both DJ and Tyler, of all of us together, like the illicit fantasy I indulged in before heading home...

It sends a naughty thrill through me.

Shit, I think I have a crush. On Tyler...*and* on DJ.

CHAPTER 8
DJ

MY BLADES SEND OFF A SPRAY OF SNOW SHAVINGS AS I SLICE TO A stop beside Ethan. The kid's been struggling with his puck control at higher speeds, and since our trusty team captain has his hands full with all the tensions on the team right now, I've made it my mission to help him level up before practice, take a bit of that pressure off Slade.

Gotta pay it forward, right?

"Alright, let's run it again," I say, snagging a puck. "Remember, soft hands on the stick. Guide it, don't grip it."

Ethan nods, brow furrowed in concentration beneath his helmet as we take off down the ice. I keep my speed in check, watching his technique, and feel a surge of pride. *He's getting there.*

We weave through a series of cones, passing back and forth. As we hit the far blue line, I call out, "Now faster on the crossovers!"

Ethan digs in, powerful strides eating up the ice. The puck wobbles on his blade but he maintains control. *Beautiful.*

"Hell yeah!" I whoop as we reach the end. "You're getting it, man. Those hands are pure silk right now."

"Thanks, Deej," Ethan says, flashing a grin. "It's way better after those tweaks you showed me."

"Anytime, kid. I'm always here if you need advice, on or off the ice. Us Blizzards gotta look out for each other, yeah?" I reach out for a fist bump.

Ethan returns it with enthusiasm. "For sure. Means a lot."

I can't help but smile as we set up for the next drill. Folks like to run their mouths about my rep as a player, on and off the ice. And yeah, maybe I play a little fast and loose when it comes to sex and my personal life. OK, a lot.

But the tabloids don't see moments like these.

I vividly remember being the rookie, wide-eyed and eager to prove myself. If it wasn't for leaders taking me under their wing back then, I wouldn't be the player I am today.

Nah, this right here—building up the next generation, making sure they know they've got support—this is the legacy I wanna leave.

As Ethan and I finish up our last drill, a sudden stab of pain shoots through my knee. *Aw shit, not again.* I wince and stumble, catching myself before I face-plant on the ice.

"You good, DJ?" Ethan calls out, skating over with a look of concern.

"Yeah, yeah, I'm fine," I say through gritted teeth, trying to stretch out the ache that's radiating from my kneecap. "Just the old war wound acting up again."

But even as I brush it off, memories of that fateful game all those years ago come rushing back...

It was conference finals my sophomore year of college. We were neck and neck with our biggest rivals, fighting for a chance at the national title.

I intercepted a sloppy pass and rocketed down the ice, the roar of the crowd spurring me on as I deked around their d-man. I was about to snipe top shelf when out of nowhere, their goon of a defenseman slammed into me from behind.

My skate caught an edge and my knee twisted at a sickening angle as I smashed into the boards. White-hot agony exploded through my leg and I collapsed on the ice, screaming. Next thing I knew, I was being stretchered off to the hospital.

Sitting out that whole next season, watching my team struggle without me, was pure torture. Hockey was my life, my identity. Who was I if I couldn't play?

I fell into a dark spiral of self-pity and doubt, only pulling myself out of it by focusing on rehab after my surgery, the promise of being able to play again senior year my only light at the end of the tunnel.

I shake my head, trying to dispel the painful memories. I can't let myself go down that road again. I'm at the top of my game, one of the best players on the Blizzards.

But at thirty-three, I'm not exactly a spring chicken anymore. The NHL is a young man's league. *If I get sidelined again...*

Anxiety knots in my stomach at the thought. The team could easily cut me loose. Then how would I keep supporting my mom? She depends on me to help cover her mortgage ever since she got screwed over by a shady investment scheme.

I can't let her down. I *won't* let her down.

I take a deep breath and gingerly test my weight on my aching knee. I'll just have to grin and bear it for now. Tape it up, pop some Advil, do whatever it takes to push through. *No one can know I'm hurting.* I paste on a cocky smile and wink at Ethan.

"Race you to the locker room, slowpoke. Loser has to buy lunch!"

I take off across the ice, ignoring the twinge of protest from my knee. Mind over matter. I've beat this once before and I'll beat it again. Nothing's gonna keep DJ Johnston down for long.

As Ethan and I glide off the ice, I spot Tyler perched on the bench, his sandy hair tousled and damp with sweat. There's a hesitancy in his chiseled features, like he's not sure how to approach me after our little spat on the plane.

Well, can't let my favorite goalie stew in awkwardness, now can I?

I skate over with my most dazzling grin and clap a hand on Tyler's broad shoulder. "Hey man, we good?"

Relief washes over his face at my friendly expression. "Yeah, totally. Sorry about before, I was just stressed about starting and—"

"No worries, water under the bridge." I pull him into a quick bro-hug, his solid muscles pressing against me for a brief, tantalizing moment before we separate.

And that's when I notice it—the pink rising in his cheeks, the way his blue eyes drop to my mouth and linger just a beat too long.

Well, hello there...

A thrill zings through me.

I've been into Ty for a while now—how could I not be, with that chiseled jaw and the way he fills out that uniform? And I've definitely caught a vibe from him before, a spark in his gaze when he looks at me.

I mean, what was that on the plane?

But he's never been this obvious about it.

My mind races with the possibilities. I know he's always considered himself straight, but maybe he's finally ready to explore this thing between us. My pulse kicks up at the thought.

I've never been one to deny myself pleasure, in any of its delightful forms.

And Tyler? I have a feeling he'd be very pleasurable indeed...

Instead of stepping away after our hug, I trail my fingers down the firm muscles of Tyler's forearm, marveling at the heat rising off his skin.

His breath hitches and those stunning blue eyes darken with desire.

God, he's gorgeous. And so close to giving in to what we both want.

"You know Ty, we could slip away right now," I murmur,

leaning in until my lips brush the shell of his ear. "No one would even notice we're gone. There's still at least an hour until practice starts officially."

Tyler shivers and for one glorious moment, I think I've got him. His tongue darts out to wet his lips and my eyes track the movement hungrily.

But then he's pulling back, shaking his head.

"DJ, I... I can't. Not yet." His voice is strained, apology and frustration warring in his expression.

Damn. I want him so bad it hurts. But I get it. Coming to terms with a new side of yourself is a big deal.

As much as I'm dying to take this further, I respect Tyler too much to push.

"Hey, no worries man. I didn't mean to pressure you." I take a step back, giving him some breathing room. "You take all the time you need to figure things out."

Relief floods his face and he nods gratefully. With one last heated look, he turns and walks away. I watch his perfectly muscular ass until he disappears around the corner.

Well, well. Not a yes...but definitely not a never either.

I grin to myself. *Tyler Simmonds, I am going to rock your world so hard when you're ready for it. Just you wait.*

The icy breeze stings my skin in the most delicious way as I stand shirtless on the practice facility's rooftop terrace, my heart rate finally slowing.

I close my eyes for a moment, savoring the chill rippling across my torso. The perfect way to cool down after that encounter with Tyler, get my head on straight for practice.

The metal door clangs open and I spin around. Sydney freezes mid-step, coffee mug in hand, bundled adorably in her thick winter coat. Looks like great minds thought alike about getting some fresh air this morning.

Sydney's surprised eyes lock on my bare chest before darting away and the corner of my mouth curls into a grin.

I can't resist the opportunity to tease her a little. Keeping my movements slow and deliberate, I grab my shirt and tug it over my head, pulling the fabric tight across my abs.

Sydney's gaze traces down my body and a pretty blush stains her cheeks.

Gotcha.

"Morning, Sydney," I drawl, flashing her a wink. "Enjoying the view?"

"Oh! Um, I was just—I didn't expect anyone else to be out here," she stammers, fidgeting with her mug.

I take a few steps closer, drawn to the way the wind ruffles strands of her dark hair. "Guess it's your lucky day then."

Sydney raises an eyebrow. "Is that so?" Her eyes sparkle with amusement and...something else. Something heated that sends a jolt straight through me.

Interesting. This is new. My pulse kicks back up a notch.

I'm not trying to be a total sex pest, but I have a laser-sharp ability to sense when people are into me. The way Sydney is looking at me right now is different from normal.

Darkened, and slightly guilty, like she's been thinking about me naked.

Has she?

After my cock-tease interaction with Tyler, I can't resist playing this out.

I lean my hip against the railing, acting casual while my body buzzes with awareness. "C'mon, admit it. Seeing me is totally the highlight of your morning."

"You're awfully sure of yourself," she observes, but a smile plays at her mouth.

"Nah, just calling it like I see it, sunshine. I mean, look at you, you're practically swooning."

Sydney bursts out laughing and the sound wraps around me like a caress. "In your dreams, hot shot."

"Every night, baby." I let my smile drop until my expression is dead serious and give her a smoldering look. "Every night."

She laughs at first, rolling her eyes, and I join her. But when she meets my eyes again, there's another jolt of attraction between us and I know she senses it too. Her breath hitches and I swear the air between us sparks.

I want to reach for her, to see if her skin is as soft as it looks...

I step closer to Sydney, my hand coming up to trace the line of her neck above her coat. Heady desire courses through my veins.

Another wave shoots through me as Sydney melts into my touch, tilting her head to the side to give me better access. The winter air might be cold, but everything about this moment is burning hot.

"DJ," she whispers, her voice a mixture of warning and invitation. Her fingers graze my wrist gently, not pulling away but holding on.

It's all the encouragement I need to lean closer, my thumb brushing softly against her jaw, our breaths mingling in the icy air.

"You okay with this?" I ask, because I want her all in.

A shy nod and a small smile escape her before she meets my gaze fully, vulnerability and desire shining back at me.

"Yes, I'm okay with this," Sydney confirms, her voice firmer now, seemingly emboldened by our obvious shared lust.

I close the distance between us entirely, my lips capturing hers in a kiss that feels like the first spring day after a relentless winter—warm, promising, revitalizing. She tastes like coffee and peppermint, a combo I'm already addicted to.

Her arms wind around my neck, pulling me closer as if she's afraid I'll vanish if she lets go.

The world narrows down to just the two of us on this rooftop, surrounded by the sounds of the city below and blanketed by the crisp morning.

Before I can think better of it, I'm pulling off her coat, then reaching under her skirt, my hand skimming up her thigh as I deepen the kiss, reveling in the softness of her skin.

Sydney gasps against my lips, her body pressing closer to mine, her hands wandering over my back, tracing the outlines of my muscles. The cold air nips at us, but the heat between us could melt the ice in the rink below.

She winds her fingers in my hair. I break the kiss to catch my breath, both of us panting slightly, cheeks flushed with more than just the chill, and then I watch her face as my hand edges up higher…

"DJ…" Sydney murmurs, her voice catching as my fingers dance dangerously close to crossing a line.

Her eyes lock onto mine, wide and exhilarated, a silent question passing between us.

I pause, letting the moment stretch out deliciously.

"Too much?" I ask, my voice low and husky, my breath visible in the cold air.

She shakes her head slowly, her eyes never leaving mine. "No," she whispers back, her breath hitching. "Just enough."

Encouraged by her response, my hand moves higher, eliciting a soft moan from deep within her as I explore further, pushing back the fabric of her thin panties, my fingers teasing the sensitive skin beneath, caressing her wet folds before starting to tease her opening, one finger slipping in, then two.

Sydney's breath turns ragged, her grip on me tightening as if she's clinging to sanity by a thread.

Her legs tremble slightly and she leans more fully into me for support. The city's distant noises fade away, drowned out by the sound of her quickening breaths and the soft moans that escape her lips every time my fingers move against her clit, her pussy getting wetter and wetter.

Her back arches, pressing her closer to me, and heat rises between us, scorching against the cold morning air.

"DJ," she gasps again, this time her voice laced with urgency, her hands pulling at my hair.

I chuckle softly as I kiss her, the sound rumbling from my chest and vibrating against her lips.

"You like that?" I murmur, increasing the pressure just a bit, circling her clit faster and then slowing, teasing her, delighting in the way her body responds so beautifully to my touch.

"Yes," she breathes out, almost desperately. "Don't stop. I want—"

But before she can finish, a sudden noise has us both freezing. The moment fractures, and we break apart, both glancing toward the doorway, but nobody is there. Sydney pulls back further, grabs for her coat.

She wraps it around herself quickly, the flush of our activities still painting her cheeks red.

The sudden return to reality makes my heart hammer against my ribs, not entirely from the exertion.

There's a flicker of something like regret in Sydney's eyes, maybe for the interruption or perhaps for the line we had just crossed. But I'm glad to see that underneath that, there's an unmistakable glint of exhilaration.

"I—we should probably cool down," she stammers, her voice husky from our escapade. "This was... I mean, I don't want you thinking—"

And then she flees, leaving me standing alone, my heart still racing as the vivid recollection of our heated encounter makes it impossible to think straight.

I take a few deep breaths, letting the cold air fill my lungs and chill my heated skin. My fingers still tingle from the warmth of her touch, and I wipe them against my sweatpants absently.

Running a frustrated hand through my hair, I take a deep breath and try to compose myself. Hockey practice is going to be pure torture after that. Time to take a cold shower and think about grandmas before I head to the rink.

It's going to be a long fucking day.

CHAPTER 9
SYDNEY

A COUPLE OF WEEKS AFTER MY MOMENTARY LAPSE IN JUDGMENT with DJ, I take a deep breath and step into a glittering ballroom, my stomach doing somersaults.

A sleek emerald dress hugs my body as I totter in unsteady stilettos, silently cursing my sister for convincing me these would make my legs look amazing. Crystal chandeliers drip from the ornate ceiling, illuminating the elegant place settings on white linen tablecloths.

It's all so...fancy, worlds away from my usual grungy sports bars and pizza joints.

The team really went all out sponsoring this swanky charity gala, no doubt trying to repair their image. Here's hoping a massive donation and some schmoozing will get the media vultures off their backs.

I'm beyond flattered they included me, the team's lowly new

girl, but my excitement wars with jangling nerves at the thought of seeing DJ and Tyler.

Things have gotten...complicated with those two, to say the least.

Heat rises in my cheeks as I remember my tryst DJ on the rooftop. I can't believe that I let something like that happen between us, especially after turning down Tyler in part because I knew he had feelings for DJ.

But after that night out with Tyler and my conversation with Emma, my thoughts were a constant revolving spiral around Tyler and DJ. And when I walked out onto that roof and it was apparent that DJ was immediately more than game to hook up...I found that all of my mental resistance had disappeared.

God, the way his hands felt skimming my body, his lips on my skin...

I pinch my arm, pulling myself out of my horny memories. Can't let anything like that happen here amid the city's elite and a gaggle of nosy reporters.

I find my place card and nearly choke. *Of freaking course.* I'm seated at the same table as both Tyler and DJ.

Fate has a twisted sense of humor.

Grabbing the lone empty chair next to Tyler, I will my racing heart to calm the hell down, but he's not making it easy. That tailored suit does sinful things to his broad shoulders. His sandy hair looks extra tousled, like he's been running anxious hands through it.

Tyler meets my gaze and quirks a tiny uncertain smile that has my insides flipping.

"Hey Syd. You look stunning," he murmurs, eyes roving over me appreciatively before he seems to catch himself and glances away. The tips of his ears turn adorably pink.

"Thanks, Ty. You clean up pretty well yourself," I tease gently, trying to dissipate the awkward energy crackling between us. We've been dancing around each other for weeks, this unspoken attraction pulling us together even as Tyler's feelings for DJ push us apart.

DJ chooses that moment to drop smoothly into the seat on my other side, his woodsy cologne swirling around me.

Trust him to convince my other seatmate to switch spots in 30 seconds flat.

Memories of his lips, his hands, the delicious hardness of his athletic body flash through my mind. I swallow hard.

"Well, doesn't this cozy seating arrangement just make you want to send fate a fruit basket?" he drawls, signature smirk firmly in place as his brown eyes smolder.

His gaze drags over me slowly, raising goosebumps in its wake.

"Damn, Sydney," he continues. "Forget the fruit, fate deserves a case of good bourbon for putting you in that dress."

I roll my eyes even as a blush heats my cheeks. "Keep it in your pants, Casanova. In case you haven't noticed, we're in public. At a charity event. For sick kids."

"Hey, I've got nothing but pure thoughts over here," he says, all wide-eyed faux innocence. "For instance, I'm thinking about how much I'd like to make a *sizable* donation. To the kids, of course."

Tyler nearly chokes on his water. I glare at DJ, trying and failing to stop the corners of my mouth from twitching. *Damn him.*

This night is going to be...interesting.

My head spins as introductions are made around the table, a whirlwind of unfamiliar names and handsome faces, members of the business teams I haven't met yet, and a few players that haven't taken advantage of my counseling sessions.

The guys waste no time drawing me into the conversation, their good-natured ribbing and easy camaraderie quickly putting me at ease.

"So Sydney, what's the craziest thing you've seen as a team doc so far?" one of the players asks. "Any wild rookie initiation rituals?"

I hesitate, not wanting to admit that the Blizzards are the first team I've ever worked with, then grin.

"Well, once during med school, I watched a teacher stitch up a med student who tried to impress a girl by doing a keg stand...totally naked. Not a pretty sight, let me tell you!"

The table erupts in guffaws. Warmth spreads through me as DJ and Tyler lean in, their solid frames bracketing me on either side. It feels good to let loose.

"Where are you originally from, Sydney?" Another innocent question, but it makes me tense up.

"Oh, I just moved here from Boston," I say lightly, determined not to let my smile falter. Eager to change the subject, I turn to DJ. "So, hot stuff, regale us with a tale from your rookie days. I'm sure you have some gems."

DJ grins and launches into a raunchy story involving a bottle of tequila, a stripper named Cinnamon, and a live chicken, much to everyone's delight. And as the guys swap increasingly wild tales, I find myself forgetting all about Boston for the moment, too caught up in the laughter and the intoxicating pull of the two men beside me.

I'm digging into my short rib when the voice of Nikolai, a player I don't know as well, booms from the other side of my table.

"Lightweights couldn't handle a real party!" he guffaws, and I suddenly tense.

I know he's referring to Jason, Mikey, and Tomas, who couldn't join the event tonight because booze is flowing freely.

My jaw clenches. Irritation prickles under my skin at the crude jab about my patients. Pushing away from the table, I make an excuse about saying hi to Vincent, the general manager, seated three tables over with some of the biggest donors.

Weaving between the tables, snippets of gossip reach my ears. I slow my pace as two well-coiffed women, dripping in diamonds, huddle together in scandalous conversation, their eyes darting back to my table.

"I heard the...what did you call them, Gretchen? Oh, puck bunnies!" Giggles erupt. "Well, I heard the *puck bunnies* throw themselves at that DJ Johnston especially. He has quite the...reputation, if you know what I mean."

The women exchange a knowing look.

"Oh, I know what you mean! That body and those tattoos...mmm. I wouldn't kick him out of bed!"

"Right? No wonder everyone's absolutely feral for him."

Laughter trills again and heat flares in my chest, my pulse picking up speed. Irritation, yes. But a thorny tangle of something else too...something green-eyed and possessive.

I shake my head and quicken my steps, trying to outpace the unexpected sting of jealousy.

Smile plastered on my face, I greet Vincent, Coach Daniels, and Chloe, determined not to let idle gossip get under my skin, and I relax as they assure me that the event is going well. But as we're talking a flash of movement catches my eye.

It's DJ, leaning against the bar with a devilish grin, two champagne flutes dangling from his fingertips. He tilts his head, beckoning me over with a come-hither look that sends shivers down my spine.

After excusing myself I approach the bar cautiously, pulse quickening as DJ hands me a glass.

His fingers graze mine, lingering just a moment too long. Memories of our rooftop rendezvous flood my mind—his strong hands caressing my thighs, slipping higher and higher...

Choking on my champagne, I sputter inelegantly as DJ chuckles.

"Careful there, Doc. Wouldn't want you to hurt yourself." His eyes sparkle with mirth and...something darker. Desire.

We make innocuous small talk, but the air crackles between

us, sparks threatening to ignite at any second. *I need to shut this down before I spontaneously combust.*

"Well, guess we should rejoin our table..." I hedge, looking for an escape.

But DJ leans in close, his warm breath tickling my ear. My toes curl in my crazy stilettos as I hear his murmur.

"Or we could find somewhere a little more private to continue our conversation." His voice is low, seductive, and despite my better judgment, it tugs at every nerve ending in my body.

Flushing scarlet, I stumble back a step, mind reeling even as my body responds to his brazen words.

"I, um, I should really finish my dinner before they clear the plates..." I stammer.

His eyes practically burn into my back as I turn and rush back to my table.

Collapsing into my seat beside Tyler, I watch as Tyler quirks an eyebrow but says nothing. Doesn't need to. The heat staining my cheeks is all the confirmation required: he saw everything.

I catch the jealousy that flashes across his face and feel terrible and then even more terrible for wondering whether he's jealous of DJ or of me.

The uncomfortable moment stretched between us until Tyler clears his throat, turning towards me with a softness in his eyes that contradicts the stoic mask of his face.

"You alright?" he murmurs, voice barely audible above the laughter and clinking of glasses around us.

I nod, trying to muster a less shaky smile. "Yeah, just... a lot of people here tonight." It's a feeble excuse, and we both know it.

Luckily, the sound of the live band starting up saves me from my misery—staffers clear our table and waiters start circulating the room with delicate desserts and pots of coffee.

Tyler stands and glances my way. For a moment I wonder if he's going to ask me to dance but instead, he excuses himself to use the restroom.

I sigh, not knowing if I'm more disappointed or relieved. *At least I can give my aching feet a rest.*

I'm sipping an after-dinner cappuccino, relaxing on a plush velvet couch at the edge of the ballroom and deep in conversation with Chloe about the hockey team's recent troubles, when there's a tap on my shoulder.

Turning, I find DJ grinning down at me, his hand outstretched in invitation. The colorful tattoos snaking up his muscular forearm seem to dance in the pulsing lights.

The formal dinner and keynote speeches have given way to dancing, the ballroom floor filling with swaying couples, groups of friends, and tipsy laughter. Many of the older attendees started to head home, and the party became livelier for the younger crowd.

"May I have this dance, gorgeous?" DJ's deep brown eyes sparkle mischievously.

I hesitate for a moment, knowing I'm just asking for trouble if I take his hand.

DJ is charming and persistent, and there's no denying our sexual connection. But I'm still the team counselor, and this is a *work event*.

He looks unfairly handsome in his crisp tuxedo, a few strands of dark hair artfully escaping to frame his chiseled face. The champagne bubbles pleasantly in my veins, making my reasons for ignoring him seem silly.

What's the harm in one dance, when half the team is out there on the dance floor with donors and staff?

Throwing caution to the wind, I accept DJ's hand and let him lead me onto the dance floor. Shimmering strands of lights crisscross the high ceiling, casting an intimate glow. The bass thumps as he pulls me close, one strong arm circling my waist.

We start to move in sync to the sensual beat.

"Well this is a nice surprise," DJ murmurs near my ear. "I was hoping you'd say yes."

"Don't let it go to your head," I tease, trying to play it cool despite the way my heart races at his proximity. "I'm just here for the dancing."

"Mmm, is that so?" His lips curve. "We'll see about that."

DJ spins me out dramatically, the skirt of my dress flaring, before tugging me back flush against his firm chest.

I can't help but laugh. "Not bad, hotshot. You've got some moves."

"You haven't seen anything yet, babe." He waggles his eyebrows comically.

We continue to banter playfully as we twirl and sway to the music, my initial nervousness fading.

"I have to say, Syd, you're equally beautiful in evening wear and office attire...although I prefer you in a slightly shorter skirt..." he says, voice low and intimate as his fingers skim my lower back.

A pleasant shiver runs through me at his insinuation, and it's like I can feel his fingers inside me again. I struggle to catch my breath and push the memory away.

"Does this routine usually work for you?" I ask tartly.

"Who says it's a routine? Maybe I'm just enraptured by your devastating wit and beauty." His tone is light and flirty, but there's an underlying sincerity in his eyes that makes my breath catch.

We move together effortlessly as the song builds, DJ's strong arms guiding me. My body relaxes into his, letting the rest of the room fall away.

The song ends and DJ draws me in, his face just inches from mine. For a breathless moment, I'm sure he's going to kiss me, right here in front of all our coworkers.

I'm unable to move, my heart thundering with anticipation.

Suddenly Tyler is here, and DJ and I both turn to him. It looks like he wants to cut in, a flicker of uncertainty on his handsome face.

Then a reckless look crosses his features and before I know it, I'm sandwiched between Tyler and DJ, their hard bodies moving in perfect sync as the pulsing beat surrounds us.

Holy hell, is this really happening?

My head swims, the heat of the crowded dance floor nothing compared to the fire igniting between the three of us, hands and hips brushing in a tantalizing promise of what could be. I lose myself in the music, letting go of my inhibitions as I grind back against Tyler.

His strong hands grip my waist possessively, pulling me flush against him.

In front of me, DJ is all sinful hips and wicked grins, his dark eyes blazing with raw desire as he gazes at me. I can sense his hardness through our clothes, and he's not making any effort to conceal it.

He moves closer, pressing his body against mine, and my breath hitches at the contact. The intensity of the situation makes my head spin—a delicious dizziness fueled by the combination of DJ's allure and Tyler's strong presence behind me.

DJ leans in, his lips brushing against my ear as he whispers, "We're not playing fair, are we?" His voice is a tantalizing mix of temptation and tease.

I manage to stammer out a reply, my voice barely above the music. "Who said anything about fair?"

Tyler's hands tighten slightly on my hips, his breath warm against the back of my neck. The air between us is electric, the heady thrill of being desired by these two gorgeous men too powerful to resist.

I'm drunk on their touch, dizzy with arousal.

Part of me can't believe I'm doing this, dancing with not just one but two professional hockey players on the team I work for, right in front of everyone I work with. But that part of me is drowned out by the rumble of DJ's voice as he leans in, his lips grazing the shell of my ear.

"Mmm, you like being in the middle of a Tyler-DJ sandwich, don't you babe?" he purrs, his deep voice sending shivers down my spine.

I bite my lip to stifle a moan, my core clenching at the dark promise in his words. Behind me, Tyler growls, his fingers digging into my hips. I can feel exactly what our dancing is doing to him.

Knowing I'm driving them both wild is a heady rush unlike anything I've ever experienced.

It's only when the band switches over to a slower song and the floor empties except for swaying couples that I'm finally hit with the reality of what we're doing, realizing how visible we've become now that we aren't surrounded by bodies.

Shocked at my own behavior, I mumble an excuse about needing the restroom as I practically sprint off the dance floor.

I burst into the blessedly empty bathroom, my chest heaving as I lean back against the cool tile wall. Closing my eyes, I try to calm my racing heart, to quell the ache of arousal pulsing between my thighs.

I stagger to the sinks and splash some cold water on my flushed cheeks, but it does little to extinguish the fire DJ and Tyler ignited inside me. The door suddenly swings open and I whirl around, only to meet the knowing eyes of Emma.

I flush crimson as Emma takes in my disheveled appearance, her eyebrows raising.

"Wow, Sydney, you look like you got hit by a hurricane," Emma quips, shaking her head. "A tall, dark and handsome hurricane. Or two."

Her eyes dance with mirth and maybe a hint of sympathy at my guilty, deer-in-headlights expression. She saunters over to use the mirror next to me, pulling out her lip gloss.

"What? No, I was just, um..." I stammer lamely, my mind scrambling for an excuse and coming up blank. "Fixing my hair! You know how hot it gets on the dance floor at events like this..."

"Mm-hmm, I'm sure there was a lot of steam out there, alright," Emma jokes, her voice dripping with innuendo. "Careful, or you might fog up the mirrors."

She winks suggestively.

My cheeks burn even hotter. Emma's no fool—she clearly saw right through my terrible attempt at a cover story. Her eyes are all-knowing as she gives me a final pointed look.

"Well, I'll leave you to, ah, finish primping. Catch you later, Syd."

With that, Emma slips out of the bathroom, the door clicking shut behind her. I slump back against the vanity, my legs like jelly. *Holy shit.*

I stare at my reflection, taking in my just-fucked appearance. There's no denying the truth anymore, at least not to myself.

I want DJ and Tyler. Both of them. Desperately. Every inch of my body is still tingling from their touch, aching for more.

But my work with the team...it wouldn't be right to get involved with either of them. Would it?

And what about the electricity simmering between DJ and Tyler? The heated looks they kept exchanging, the electric spark when they touched...

There's definitely something brewing there, something intense and urgent.

What if the real attraction is only between them? I think that would break my still-fragile heart.

I need to just...ignore this. Forever.

Shouldn't be too difficult, considering that I see them every day at work.

CHAPTER 10
TYLER

I YANK OPEN MY LOCKER, THE METAL DOOR CLANGING AGAINST the others. The dank smell of old hockey pads assaults my nose.

My head's not in this today. All those late-night workouts, the extra time on the ice—I'm putting in the hours to get my game back. But if I'm being honest with myself, it's also been a damn good distraction from a certain someone.

No, scratch that. Two someones.

Sydney's dark eyes, beckoning me closer on the dance floor. DJ's penetrating gaze, undressing me with his eyes as I pressed against the soft curves of Sydney's body…

The images are all burned into my mind and I can't shake them loose. I've been ducking the two of them for days now, unsure what the hell I even want.

"Yo, Ty!" Slade's booming voice pulls me out of my daze. "You bringing your A-game today or what, bud?" He chucks a roll of stick tape at me.

I catch it against my chest. "Aye aye, Cap'n." A weak attempt at a joke.

"Better get your ass in gear," pipes up Ethan, the rookie. "Or Slade might make you bag skate again!" The guys chuckle.

"In your dreams, rookie." I force a grin and busy myself taping my stick. Their good-natured ribbing washes over me but I'm still lost in my own world.

The locker room fades away and I'm back under the lights of the dance floor, my body moving against Sydney as DJ stares at me, eyes never leaving mine.

Heat coils in my gut, and I shake my head to clear it.

This is a locker room, for God's sake, not some porn site fantasy. I need focus—we've been winning more games lately, but our playing has still been erratic, like my thoughts bouncing from one memory to another. I tighten the grip on my stick, willing myself to keep my head in the net.

The team is counting on me.

I head to the ice for practice, my body thrumming with energy. All the extra hours I've been putting in, working on my technique and mental game—today, it all seems to click into place. As I take my position in the net, a sense of calm washes over me, a quiet confidence I haven't felt in weeks.

The pucks come flying at me, but I move with fluid grace, my glove hand snagging even the trickiest shots. Sweat drips down my brow but I'm laser-focused, anticipating each shot before it happens.

"Way to go, Ty!" Ethan hollers from defense. "You're on fire, man!"

My teammates whoop and holler their assent, their sticks tapping against the ice in a rousing chorus of support. The sound sends chills down my spine. This is what I live for, these moments when it all comes together.

I glance over at Coach Daniels. He gives me a rare nod of approval, his usual stony expression softening with pride. Validation courses through me.

All the long hours, the sore muscles, the self-doubt—it's all worth it for this feeling.

"Keep it up, Simmonds," Coach barks. "Don't let it go to your head. We've got a long way to go."

"You got it, Coach." I flash him a grin, invigorated by his praise but humbled by his reminder. He's right: I've got to keep my head in the game.

As drills continue, I'm in the zone, unstoppable. Puck after puck meets my glove, my pads, deflecting away. I could do this forever, just lose myself in the rhythm and the thrill.

It's damn good to turn my brain off, after how much I've been torturing myself with memories of the event last weekend.

Too bad practice has to end.

Afterwards, I'm on a bench packing up my bag, taking my time getting ready for the showers, wanting some space to myself once everyone else clears out. Most of the team has either left or is still showering off, and I'm taking in the quiet, letting that confidence from today sink in, willing it to stick around.

Then the locker room door swings open from the showers

and DJ saunters in, his hair damp and tousled, a cocky grin on his face.

My breath catches in my throat as he makes his way over to me, eyes locked on mine, just like they were on the dance floor at the gala.

"Damn, Ty, I know basically the whole team has already said it, but you really were on fire out there today," he says, his voice low and smooth. "Watching you in the net...it was something else."

My cheeks flush at the compliment, my body thrumming with nervous energy. "Thanks man, I was really in the zone. Felt good."

DJ steps closer, crowding into my space. The scent of his body wash envelops me. "I bet it did. You were incredible. Superhuman, even."

A laugh bubbles out of me as I look up at him. "Nah, c'mon, I'm not that good."

He arches an eyebrow. "Don't sell yourself short. That glove save during our scrimmage? Unreal. Had me all worked up."

There's a glint in his eye that makes my pulse race.

"Well, I aim to please," I joke, trying to play it cool.

DJ chuckles, his gaze dragging over my body in a way that is almost physical. "Mmm, I bet you do..."

Fuck. I shift on the bench, arousal coiling in my gut.

I'm still not sure I'm ready to acknowledge what I'm feeling —no matter how many times I've replayed images from the dance floor the other night, relived having DJ's eyes searing into mine.

And god, the way he's looking at me now...

He notices my squirming and smirks, flopping down next to me, his towel falling slightly open. "You doing okay there, Ty? You seem a little...tense."

I avert my gaze from the lean muscles of his legs. "No, no, I'm good," I stammer. "Just uh, tired from practice, y'know?"

"Right. Practice." His hand lands on my thigh and I nearly jolt out of my skin. "Gotta make sure you take care of this body. It's your greatest asset, after all."

His fingers start tracing teasing circles against my pants.

I swallow hard, trying to remember how to breathe.

"You could help me with that," I blurt out before I can stop myself. "Taking care of my body, I mean." *What am I talking about? Where did that come from?*

DJ's grin turns positively wolfish. "Oh I'd be more than happy to...take care of you, Ty. Anything you need."

His double meaning rings out clear as a bell. I know I should put a stop to this, laugh it off, but... I don't want to. DJ's thumb keeps stroking, higher now, and it's sending sparks of want zinging through me.

I lean into his touch, craving more.

"Yeah?" I ask, my voice rough to my own ears. "I might have to take you up on that..."

DJ hums, looking extremely pleased with himself. "Standing offer. Trust me, I've got mad skills...on and off the ice."

I'm sure he does. The thought alone has me half hard already.

This flirty back-and-forth promises so much more, and I'm quickly getting addicted to the rush. I've never wanted anyone so badly in my life. And from the hungry look in his dark eyes, it's mutual.

Fuck it.

Before I can even process what I'm doing, I stand up from the locker room bench and lean in to kiss DJ, finding his lips soft and insistent against my own.

My mind goes blissfully blank, my body taking over as I kiss him with a hunger that surprises us both.

DJ responds instantly, his hands gripping my waist, pulling me closer until there's no space left between us. Heat radiates from his body, the firm muscles under his skin pressing against mine. His kiss deepens and I let out a low moan, my hands moving to tangle in his damp hair.

We stumble back and I press him against the lockers, our bodies aligning perfectly.

Breaking the kiss for air, DJ rests his forehead against mine, his breath coming out in ragged pants.

"Tyler," he murmurs, his voice thick with desire. And then his lips are back on mine.

The kiss deepens, and I can taste the mint on his breath as our tongues slide together. It's intoxicating, dizzying. We lose ourselves in the sensation, hands roaming and tongues tangling.

Until the sound of approaching footsteps jolts us back to reality and we spring apart.

Several of our teammates burst in from the showers, joking and laughing loudly, and in the chaos I grab a towel and practically sprint out of the room, leaving a stunned DJ in my wake. I don't stop running until I'm safely locked in a shower stall.

I turn on the water and lean my forehead against the cool tile, trying to calm my racing thoughts.

Holy shit. Did that really just happen? Did I seriously just make out with DJ?

The hot water cascades over my body as I replay that electrifying kiss with DJ in my mind. *Fuck, his lips felt so good on mine.* My hand unconsciously drifts lower, wrapping around my aching cock as I imagine DJ's strong, capable fingers in place of my own.

I bite back a moan, hips rocking into my fist.

I squeeze my eyes shut against the pleasure, imagining that I'm back in the locker room, where DJ slams me up against the lockers, hands sliding beneath the waistband of my pants to grip my ass. He sinks to his knees, tugging my pants down and taking my throbbing length deep into his skillful mouth.

The fantasy of DJ's lips wrapped around me is almost too much to bear. I pump faster, the slick sound of my hand slapping against my skin echoing in the steam-filled shower.

My breath catches as pleasure builds, and I imagine DJ redoubling his efforts, my cock hitting the back of his throat, him moaning around my rock-hard length. I picture Sydney suddenly walking in on us, eyes dark with unmistakable desire as she watches DJ work me over.

The erotic image pushes me over the edge. My body shudders as I spill over my fist with a muffled cry of pleasure. As the intense high fades, confusion clouds my post-orgasmic bliss.

Where the hell does Sydney come into all of this?

CHAPTER 11
DJ

A FEW DAYS AFTER MY ELECTRIC LOCKER ROOM KISS WITH TYLER, I stretch out on a lounge chair by the hotel pool, soaking up the Florida sun. My shades are on but my eyes keep drifting to my phone sitting on the little table next to me.

I keep hoping it'll buzz with a text from Sydney. Or Tyler. But it stays annoyingly silent.

Tyler seemed so eager the other day. I was thrilled that he was finally admitting that there was something between us, that he finally seemed ready to explore it. But then...nothing.

He's obviously still working through it. I know sexuality isn't a simple thing, particularly if you're learning something new about yourself as an adult, when you already have a set idea of who you are.

But man...I hope he figures it out soon. I'd *really* like to pick up where we left off.

I sigh and let my head fall back, my mind drifting to last

night's game instead. We kicked ass out there on the ice, and I can't help grinning as I replay the sick goal I made in the second period. Their defense was all over me but I deked left, then right, leaving them grasping at air as I flicked the puck top shelf, bar down. The red goal light flashing was sweet vindication.

At least something's going right. I rub my knee absentmindedly.

The steady regimen of Advil, icing, and babying it between practices seems to be keeping the ache to a dull roar. *Gotta stay on top of that if I want to keep bringing my A game...*

My phone trills suddenly, making me jump. I snatch it up, hoping—but it's just my mom calling.

Ah well, I need to talk to her too, make sure she doesn't need more help. I stifle my disappointment and answer.

"Hey Ma, what's up?"

"Hi honey, how's Tampa treating you?" Her voice is warm but sounds tired.

"Can't complain. Wish you could see this resort, you'd love it. How are things back home?"

She sighs. "Oh you know, same old same old..."

I frown, hearing the exhaustion in her voice. "Everything okay? You know I can transfer more money if…" *If she'd just tell me exactly how much she owes on her cards after that ruinous investment.* But she won't share the details, insisting that she doesn't want to worry me.

"No, no, I couldn't ask you to do that again..."

"Hey, I'm happy to help. You're my number one girl, you know that."

She laughs softly. "What am I gonna do with you and that silver tongue?"

"Let me transfer some cash to get you through the next couple months? No arguments?" I say, rolling over to one side to keep my conversation shielded from some of my teammates who are hanging out a few chairs down.

"Alright, alright. You win," Mom concedes with a sigh. "I don't know what I'd do without you, kiddo. I'm so proud of the man you've become..."

"Aw geez, you're gonna make me blush," I joke. "Love you, Ma."

"I love you too, DJ," she replies, and I can hear the emotion in her voice. "So much. Thanks for looking out for your old mom."

"Anytime," I assure her. "Talk soon, okay? Try to relax a little."

She agrees and we say our goodbyes. I toss my phone down and rub a hand over my face.

I'm grateful I can help her out, but I wish she wasn't too proud to just share all the details so I could pay off her debts once and for all. Right now I could afford it, I'm sure—we all got a sweet holiday bonus since the team has been winning games again.

I'm planning to transfer it all to her, she needs it more than I do.

I take a deep breath and push the stress aside. Today's about rewarding myself for playing well and giving my body some much needed R&R. My eyes drift shut as I let the warm sun melt the tension away, but my thoughts keep drifting back to bronze skin, soft curves and hard muscle...

Dammit, why doesn't Tyler just text me back?

The team's big win last night has me on top of the world...and horny as hell. What can I say, crushing it on the ice always gets me amped up and ready to celebrate in my favorite way—by making somebody scream my name in ecstasy.

My mind keeps flashing back to the charity event—the press of Sydney's lush curves against me as we danced, those come-fuck-me bedroom eyes. And Tyler behind her, his heated gaze locked on mine.

I can still feel the solid heat of his body pinning me against the lockers, taste the desperation on his tongue right before he bolted like the hounds of gay panic hell were nipping at his tight little ass.

Fuck, I'm getting hard again just thinking about it. I palm my dick through my board shorts, then throw a towel over my lap in consideration for my teammates just across the pool. *Not the time.*

Snagging my phone, I pull up my texts with Tyler, scanning the series of increasingly thirsty messages I've sent him. The dude is an Olympic-level ghosting champ—my texts get read almost instantly but no reply.

Maybe turn receipts off, my guy.

I toss the phone aside with a sigh, sinking lower in the recliner and adjusting myself lewdly. *When did I turn into a lovesick teenager, moping over unrequited crushes?*

This is some bullshit. DJ Johnston waits for no man. Or

woman. There are plenty of hotties in my contacts who'd come running to bounce on my dick. I should call one of them...

But I don't want them.

I want Sydney. Or Tyler. *And* Tyler.

Fuck.

The day drags on without a single text from Tyler. I'm getting restless, pacing around the pool, when a burst of laughter draws my attention.

It's Sydney, looking like a goddamn snack in her modest one-piece and cover-up. I grin, soaking up the sight. I bet she thinks the suit is a professional choice but the joke's on her—it's sexier than all the barely there bikinis around put together, the way it teases and conceals her considerable attributes.

I'm captivated.

Screw it, I'm making my move. If Tyler isn't ready to pick things up where we left off, that's his business. And my business...well, tonight it'll be Sydney. Throwing on my most panty-dropping grin, I saunter over to where she's chatting with some of the staff.

"Can you believe that turnover in the third period?" Coach Alex is saying animatedly as I join the group. "Absolutely clutch."

"Hell yeah! We're on a roll," I chime in, reveling in the post-win high.

Sydney smiles at me, her eyes sparkling with mirth. "Well,

well, look who decided to grace us with his presence. To what do we owe the honor, Mr. Bigshot?"

"What can I say, I couldn't resist the allure of hearing everyone say nice things about me," I quip back, holding her playful gaze.

Coach Emma chuckles. "C'mon DJ. That assist in overtime was pure luck and you know it."

"Bullshit, it was all me. They don't call these magic hands for nothing!" I joke, wiggling my fingers.

The group dissolves into knowing laughter—my salacious reputation isn't really a secret on the team. Or anywhere, for that matter.

As the conversation turns to post-game analysis, I sidle closer to Sydney. Leaning in, I murmur, "So, I was thinking... How about you and I explore the Tampa nightlife tonight?"

Sydney arches an eyebrow, looking adorably conflicted for a moment.

"I don't know, Johnston. You keep getting me into trouble."

Her words say no but her eyes are issuing a challenge. And damn if I don't love a challenge.

"Hey, I'll be on my best behavior. Scout's honor," I vow, throwing up three fingers in salute.

She laughs, shaking her head. "Fine, you've got yourself a date. But no funny business, you hear?"

I grin as images of just what kind of funny business we could get up to cross my mind. *It's a good thing I'm not actually a scout.* "Mmm."

❄

After some killer fish tacos and a bit of restaurant hopping in search of the perfect key lime pie, Sydney and I find ourselves in the back of a tiny local joint I heard about from a friend who went to school down here.

The twangy notes of an old man strumming a beat-up guitar on a cramped platform blend with the clinks of glasses and chatter filling the dive bar. I lean in close to Sydney so she can hear me over the noise.

"Is it just me or do these lyrics make absolutely no sense?" I ask with a smirk.

Sydney giggles. "It's like he picked random words out of a country music dictionary and strung them together." She puts on an exaggerated Southern drawl. "My truck got towed, my dog done died, drinkin' whiskey by the riverside."

I laugh and throw an arm around her shoulders, pulling her against me in the booth. "Don't quit your day job to become a country star now."

She fits perfectly tucked into my side, her curves pressing deliciously against me. I know I promised, I know I should behave myself, but damn if I don't want to slide my hand down and grab that fine ass.

Sydney looks up at me through her dark lashes. "You don't think I could make it in Nashville?"

She juts out her bottom lip in an adorable pout. I want to bite it.

"Oh, I think you'd be a star no matter what you did, beautiful." I reach out and gently run my thumb over her lip. "But I like having you all to myself."

Her breath hitches and she parts her lips slightly. I'm so fucking tempted to lean in and capture that pouty mouth with my own. Instead, I force myself to pull back, trailing my fingers down her arm and noticing how her skin prickles with goose-bumps at my touch.

I clear my throat and force myself to look away. "Another beer?" I ask, my voice coming out rougher than I intended.

Sydney nods. I signal the bartender for two more of the potent domestic drafts. *Is it getting hotter in here?* I shift on my stool, trying to adjust myself discreetly. *This woman turns me on without even trying.*

I want to peel that sundress off her and lay her out on my bed, kissing a path down her throat, between her perfect tits, over her soft belly. Burying my face between her thighs and tasting her sweet honey until she's writhing and begging for more...

The beers appear in front of us and I take a long swig of the cold liquid. It does little to cool the desire raging inside me.

Sydney watches me over the rim of her glass, her cheeks flushed and her eyes dark. She senses this electric pull between us too, I can tell. But neither of us makes a move, the exquisite tension simmering in the scant space separating our bodies.

Sydney told me to behave, so behave is what I'll do.

For now...

❄

The hotel is totally deserted when we get back.

The silence of the lobby amplifies every step we take, the clicking of Sydney's heeled sandals on the marble floor echoing like a metronome ticking down to something inevitable. I glance at her, catching the slight tremor in her fingers as she brushes a loose strand of hair behind her ear.

We've kept things friendly tonight, but the night isn't over yet. I call the elevator, gesturing for Sydney to step in first. She hesitates for a fraction of a second before sliding past me, the subtle scent of her perfume filling the small space—something floral and wickedly intoxicating.

The doors close with a soft ding, and we laugh as we both reach for the same button, realizing we're staying on the same floor. And suddenly it's just us, surrounded by mirrored walls that only seem to multiply the tension.

I lean against the wall, trying to look casual, and not like I'd like to rip her clothes off and fuck her right up against that mirrored wall. *Not at all.*

"So," I start, breaking the quiet. My voice sounds unnaturally deep in the confined space. "Did you have fun tonight?"

Sydney leans back against the opposite wall, mirroring my posture.

"I did," she admits. "Thank you—I needed this."

The elevator pings and the doors slide open to reveal the dimly lit hallway. Sydney and I step out in unison, our footsteps muffled by the plush carpet. We don't speak but an electric current builds between us as we walk side by side down the deserted corridor.

My room is coming up on the left. I pause with my keycard in hand, my heart suddenly pounding. *It's now or never.*

I turn to Sydney, my eyes searching her face.

"Listen, I know you think this is a terrible idea, but if I don't at least ask if I can kiss you right now, I'm not going to be able to sleep tonight." I swallow hard. "But no pressure, the decision is totally yours."

Sydney stares back at me, her eyes glinting in the low light. The moment stretches between us, taut with unspoken desire.

Then she lunges forward, crashing her lips against mine.

Suddenly we're a tangle of roaming hands and gasping breaths as we stumble backwards into my room. I kick the door shut and press Sydney up against the wall, my body molding to hers.

Holy shit, is this finally happening?

CHAPTER 12
DJ

MY HEAD SWIMMING AND MY COCK THROBBING, I KISS SYDNEY again but release her when she suddenly hesitates, pulling back slightly. Her eyes search my face, uncertainty dancing across her delicate features.

I cup her face gently. "Hey, if you're not comfortable with this, I'm happy to back off. No questions asked."

Even as I say the words, they ring hollow.

Who am I kidding? Walking away from Sydney right now would be the hardest thing I've ever done.

We both know we're teetering on the precipice here, the point of no return. The air is thick with the scent of her perfume and pheromones. Every cell in my body is screaming at me to tear her clothes off and take her right here against the door.

But I force myself to wait, letting Sydney call the shots.

She stares at me, eyes glimmering in the low light, seeming

to weigh something in her mind. After an agonizing pause, she nods slowly.

"Let's do this," she whispers, her voice husky. "But just for tonight. To get it out of our systems. And then we go back to normal tomorrow, agreed?"

"Agreed," I breathe, already leaning in to capture her lips again. *No time to waste.* If we're only going to have one night together, I have a hell of a lot of things to get out of my system.

Starting with getting those clothes off her.

I pull her toward the middle of the plush hotel room, into the light. "Undress for me," I growl.

Sydney undresses tantalizingly slowly, sliding her dress off one shoulder at a time, revealing her smooth, golden skin inch by agonizing inch. Her dark hair tumbles down her back as the dress slips to the floor. She shoots me a coy smile, knowing exactly what she's doing to me.

Be careful, babe, two can play at this game.

"Get on the bed," I order, my voice low and rough with desire. "Show me how you touch yourself when you're all alone."

Her eyes widen, darkening with lust. "Like this?" she purrs, crawling onto the bed and running her hands over her generous curves. "Talk to me, DJ. Tell me exactly what you want to see."

Fuck, that's hot. Quickly, I tear my own clothes off, not bothering with a strip tease. I can't take my eyes off the sight before me.

I've been fantasizing about what might get Sydney off.

Turns out she's a girl that likes a little direction, huh? My cock twitches at the thought.

"Start at your collarbone," I direct as I advance on her. "Trail your fingertips down...slowly. When you reach your pussy, take it real slow."

She obeys with a breathy moan, propping herself up on the hotel pillows so she can watch my face as I watch her pleasure herself. Her fingers trace down, stopping to circle one hard nipple, then continuing across her soft belly.

When her fingers reach her slick folds, she moans again as she slides a finger inside herself.

God damn. The way she responds to my commands is intoxicating. I want to just throw her down and fuck her senseless, but I'm enjoying this power trip too much.

Needing to touch her silky skin, I grab her hips, yanking her to the edge of the bed and spreading her thighs wide. It takes every ounce of my restraint not to plunge my rock-hard cock into her right then and there. Breathing heavily, I step back, stroking myself slowly and watching her as she rubs her clit, faster now.

"DJ," she begs shamelessly, reaching for me. "I need you inside me. Fill me up."

"Not yet," I growl and sink to my knees before her, spreading her legs even wider so I can see every movement of her slender fingers against her dripping-wet center.

I gently bite my way up the inside of one thigh, letting my breath ghost against her clit before biting my way back down the other side.

"Please, I want your mouth on me," she pleads, but I'm not done watching her pleasure herself.

"Stretch yourself out for me," I order.

She meets my eyes boldly before complying, fitting two fingers inside that hot little hole, then three. The sight of her fingers pumping in and out of her dripping opening drives me wild.

Her gaze is locked on mine, her breath ragged and needy. I watch her touch herself, fascinated by the way she moves, the little sounds she makes driving me insane, cataloging every flick of her fingers, every little trick she uses on herself, filing it away for later.

Only tonight be damned.

"Good girl," I murmur. "Get yourself close, but don't come yet. Take your time."

Sydney's eyes glint with a mix of defiance and arousal, her breathing harsh against the silent hum of the hotel's AC. Her fingers move more deliberately now, dipping and curling inside herself while her other hand works her clit in frantic circles.

She's close—I can tell by the way her body starts to shake and the pitch of her moans elevates.

"Let me come, DJ..." she gasps, her voice laced with desperation.

"Let me come, *please*," I order.

My cock gets even harder than I thought was possible when she obeys, moaning, "Please, let me come DJ, please!"

"Good girl. But it's not time yet."

Standing, I wrap my hands around her hips as she lets out a

breathy moan of frustration, and flip her over roughly. "Get on your hands and knees."

Sydney does as I say, her body shaking with anticipation and need. Positioning herself on the bed, she raises her ass invitingly, a perfect, irresistible sight.

I get on the bed behind her, running my hands over the curves of her hips, her ass. Then finally feel her wet warmth, teasing her clit gently for just a second, and thrust two fingers inside her.

Her moan is nearly a scream as she pushes back against my hand, wiggling her perfect ass to drive my fingers farther inside of her.

I lean down to whisper against her ear, my voice dark with lust. "I want you to feel every second of this. I'm going to make you come so hard, you'll forget your own name."

Without another word, I roll on a condom then align myself at her entrance, teasing her with just the tip, enjoying the way she tries to push back against me.

"Easy," I chide her. "I'm giving the instructions here, remember? Stay still, that's a good girl."

I push in slowly, groaning at her heat around me. She's so tight, so perfect around my cock.

Sydney moans loudly, the sound echoing off the walls of the room. Her fingers clutch at the sheets as she adjusts to my size, and I stay deep in her as I reach my hand around to rub her clit again.

I start an even, agonizing pace as I continue to stroke her, pulling nearly all the way out before pushing back in deep.

Every thrust is measured, deliberate, meant to build us both up to the brink and then pull back just enough to keep us hanging there. My fingers slow on her clit, then speed up, never letting her reach her climax.

Sydney's moans fill the room, each one a mix of frustration and ecstasy.

"Faster, DJ, more," she pleads, her voice breaking with need.

"Not yet," I tell her, my voice strained as I fight against the urge to let go. "You're gonna wait for me, baby."

Underneath me, Sydney moves with a desperate energy, trying to speed up the pace, but I grip her hips tighter, controlling the rhythm as I pound into her. My other hand continues its relentless massage of her clit, pushing her closer to the edge with every touch.

"DJ... please...please!" she gasps, her body shaking under mine.

"Just a little longer," I whisper into her ear, then lean over her back and gently sink my teeth into her soft shoulder.

The mix of pain and pleasure seems to send a shockwave through her and Sydney cries out, a raw, primal sound that nearly undoes me.

"Yes, right there!"

I grit my teeth, determined to hold off just a bit longer, to draw this out into the perfect crescendo for both of us. My strokes become even more deliberate.

"You're doing so well," I praise her, my voice hoarse with effort. "Hold on for me, Sydney."

Her response is a nod and another moan as she buries her

face into the pillow. Her body begins to tremble under the strain of prolonged arousal, her movements growing more frantic. She clenches around my cock, right on the verge, again and again.

"DJ... I can't..." she whimpers, her voice muffled by the pillow.

I lower my voice, a soft command laced with promise. "You can, Sydney. We're not done."

With a deep, controlling breath, I adjust my angle slightly, hitting that sweet spot inside her that makes her jerk beneath me. Her back arches off the bed, her moan turning into a shriek of pleasure. My fingers move faster now on her clit, a relentless rhythm that matches the steady thrusting of my hips.

"Are you ready?" I ask, my voice rough with my own desire.

"Yes!" She barely manages to get the word out between moans.

Her breathy voice undoes me. I grab her chin, forcing her to look me in the eye over her shoulder. "Then come for me, Sydney."

Her climax crashes over her like a wave, uncontrollable and all-consuming. Sydney's body convulses beneath me, each wave of pleasure making her clench over my cock. I continue to drive into her, prolonging the bliss as long as I can until I can't hold back any longer.

With a deep groan that comes from somewhere primal within me, I feel myself coming, and my mind goes white. We collapse together, a tangle of limbs and heavy breath, the world outside our bubble seeming inconsequential and far away.

I trace her cheek with my finger, breathing hard, and she smiles slowly at me. "That was good."

I nod, then roll onto my back to stare at the ceiling.

Damn, understatement of the century. That was the hottest sex I've had in a long time. And I have a lot of hot sex.

I know we said this was just for one night.

But now that we've had a taste, how are we possibly going to resist this?

CHAPTER 13
SYDNEY

I JOLT AWAKE, MY BODY BUZZING WITH ELECTRIC AROUSAL FROM the vivid dream still playing in my mind.

DJ's strong hands roaming my curves, his soft lips blazing a trail of desire across my flushed skin. His long fingers plunging deep into my aching cunt as I writhe and moan beneath him. The thick length of his cock pounding into me, taking me to dizzying heights of ecstasy.

Five days. It's been five excruciatingly long days since our night of reckless passion in Tampa, but I can't stop reliving every sinful second.

The forbidden thrill, the insatiable need, the explosive release.

Giving into temptation with DJ was more incredible than I ever could have imagined.

Biting my lip, I slide a hand beneath the covers, teasing myself as the erotic memories wash over me. *The way his eyes darkened with lust as he growled filthy commands. How he edged me for what felt like hours until I was desperate and begging.*

Finding my clit, I start to circle it slowly, prolonging the delicious sensation. I close my eyes, letting the fantasy take over once more.

DJ's voice echoes in my head, low and husky, dripping with desire. *"Come for me, Sydney."*

"Yes," I whisper back to the empty room, my breath hitching as my fingers quicken their pace.

The buildup of pleasure crescendos, my orgasm sweeping through me like a tidal wave, my body convulsing in silent, shuddering waves. As the aftershocks ripple through me, I lie still, panting softly, the echo of DJ's voice and the way his cock felt inside me slowly fading away.

I roll over, checking the clock. It's early, barely dawn, but sleep is now a distant possibility, chased away by lingering arousal and restlessness.

Groaning in frustration, I throw off the blankets and swing my legs over the side of the bed. The cool air nips at my skin, causing goosebumps to rise.

"I need a shower," I mutter to myself, standing and padding toward the bathroom. The hot spray of the shower is soothing, washing away the remnants of my dream—or at least attempting to.

As water pours over me, the image of DJ's intense gaze and the ghost of his body pressed against mine invade my thoughts yet again. I lean my head against the cool tile, closing my eyes and letting out a long, slow exhale.

What have I done? I'm the Blizzards' counselor, and DJ is on the team...

The thought of the team suddenly has my stomach in knots for an entirely different reason: what would Tyler think if he knew what happened?

A flash of guilt pinches at my heart. Would it destroy our friendship? Our working relationship? What would it do to the team dynamics?

Shaking my head, I turn off the water, determined to push those thoughts away for the morning. Wrapping a towel tightly around myself, I catch a glimpse of my reflection in the mirror. My cheeks are flushed, hair damp and tousled—evidence of the turmoil swirling inside me.

I pull on a pair of jeans and a loose sweater, then grab my keys and bag and wrap my biggest winter scarf around my neck, ready to step out into the frigid morning air. As I close the door behind me, I envision myself shutting the door on the memories of DJ in bed.

Putting it behind me, for good.

Jason is first on my agenda for the day, and I'm pleased to see his smiling face in the doorway as he arrives a few minutes early.

"Morning, Syd!" Jason beams, his enthusiasm infectious. I find myself beaming back. "Ready to tackle the world today?"

I nod, shuffling some papers on my desk until I find my notes from our last session. "Absolutely, let's get started."

"I used those breathing techniques you showed me during our last game, when things got heated," Jason shares as he drops into the chair across from me, eyes shining with excitement. "Totally kept my cool. You were right, it works! Felt awesome!"

"That's amazing progress, Jason!" I feel a burst of pride for him.

It's moments like these that remind me why I love my job. It's so rewarding to see someone building back up from a low place, and Jason has done exactly that.

The morning continues with back-to-back meetings, both with my patients and some of the team staff. I'm relieved to find that everything is going smoothly today.

Even prickly Mikey seems slightly less hostile during his appointment. Sure, he still tosses out the occasional barb, but hey, at least he's not storming out anymore. *Baby steps.*

I staunchly avoid any thoughts of DJ, repeating my new mantra: *That night was just a much-needed release, a way to move past the tension. Totally healthy, totally fine. Totally...normal?*

I drop my head into my hands, realizing how crazy I sound in my own head, and that's how Eva Rodriguez finds me when she knocks.

I look up and take in the serious expression of the head athletic trainer, my optimism deflating further at the worry in her eyes.

"Eva, come in, take a seat." I straighten quickly and gesture at the chair across from me. "What's up?"

She closes the door behind her as she enters and I gulp discreetly. *That's never a good sign.* "I wanted to talk to you about Mikey."

Uh oh. What now? I try to keep my face neutral. "Of course. What's going on?"

Eva leans forward, hands clasped on her lap. "I've been noticing some concerning patterns with him lately. I mean... worse than usual."

We both laugh grimly at that—Mikey has a reputation with the Blizzards staff for being difficult.

"Mood swings, erratic behavior," she continues. "He'll be joking around one minute, then irritable and withdrawn the next."

A sinking sensation begins to form in my stomach. "I see. Have you noticed anything specific triggering these changes?"

"Not that I can pinpoint. But it's definitely affecting team dynamics." Eva's brow furrows with worry. "Just yesterday, he snapped at Ryan over a simple miscommunication during practice. It was way out of proportion."

Shit. This isn't the progress report I was hoping for. I chew my bottom lip, mind racing.

"Has he seemed like he's been using anything to you? Any signs of drinking, or other substances?"

Eva shakes her head. "No, nothing specific. But he's been able to hide this from us before, so..." Her gaze is earnest, almost pleading. "Sydney, I know you've been working closely with him. If there's something going on, we need to address it immediately. For his well-being and the team's."

I nod slowly, the weight of the responsibility settling heavily on my shoulders. Eva's words trouble me more than I'm letting on—I thought Mikey and I were making strides, that he was starting to trust me.

But clearly, I've only scratched the surface.

"I understand," I say, injecting more confidence into my voice than I feel. "I'll dig deeper with him, see if I can get to the root of what's going on. I'm not giving up on him, Eva. I promise you that."

She offers me a small smile, some of the tension easing from her posture. "I appreciate that, Sydney. Keep me in the loop, okay?"

As Eva leaves my office, my mind is already spinning, strategizing my next move with Mikey.

I refuse to let this setback derail the progress we've made.

I'm staring down at the remnants of my sad reheated stir fry in the break room, fruitlessly trying to come up with ideas to get through to Mikey, when I hear someone clear their throat. I look up to see Tyler standing in the doorway.

"Hey," he says softly, sauntering over. "Mind if I join you?"

I nod mutely as he settles into the chair next to me, his broad shoulders and chiseled features making the spacious room suddenly seem very small. Despite myself, despite all the hours I've spent thinking about DJ this week, his presence next to me still makes me go all hot and tingly.

"How are you holding up, Syd?" Tyler asks, those piercing blue eyes seeing right through me as usual.

I shrug. "Oh, fine. You know, just living the glamorous life of an underpaid counselor."

A ghost of a smile flickers across his face, but his eyes stay distant. "Well, if it makes you feel any better, hockey stardom isn't all it's cracked up to be either."

"Really? The fame, the fortune, the women throwing themselves at you...sounds terrible," I tease gently.

Tyler chuckles before his expression grows serious again. "Sometimes it's like a huge act. Everyone either wants a piece of me or expects me to be just like my brother. It's like no one actually sees *me*."

My heart stutters in my chest at the confession. I'm honored that he's opened up to me and swallow hard, not wanting to spook him.

"I know the feeling," I murmur. "It's like you're trapped in a box of other people's perceptions."

Tyler nods, reaching out to lay his hand over mine. The familiar electricity zings through me at his touch.

"Exactly. You're the only one I can really discuss this with, Syd." He pauses, studying my face, then shakes his head. "I don't know why you're so damn easy to talk to."

He's leaning closer, those full lips parted slightly, beckoning me.

For a crazy moment, I imagine closing the distance between us, finally giving in to the attraction that's been bubbling beneath the surface between us for so long.

But then Tyler sits back, his brow furrowing. "There's something else... It's DJ. I think—I think I might have feelings for him. Like more-than-teammate feelings."

He laughs awkwardly, his face flushing.

"God, I sound like a kid. But you know what I mean. I don't...I don't know what to do, so I've just been avoiding him, but I can't keep going this way."

His voice is soft and uncertain, his eyes searching when they meet mine again.

And just like that, reality comes crashing back in. My heart clenches.

As much as it pains me, as much as it causes a flood of jealousy on both ends, I know the best thing I can do is encourage Tyler to explore this, now that he's finally owning up to it. Saying this out loud—this is big for Tyler, I know it.

I can't get in the way of this connection.

I squeeze his hand. "Ty, if you like DJ, you owe it to yourself to see where it leads."

"You really think so? Even if..." He trails off, looking at me searchingly.

"Even if," I confirm around the lump in my throat, though I'm not entirely sure how he intended to finish the sentence. "You deserve to be happy."

We continue chatting as we rise and walk out of the break room. The easy rapport is still there, but there's a new undercurrent charged with all the things we're leaving unsaid.

When we reach my office door, an awkward silence falls. I fumble for the knob.

"Well, I guess I'll see you around," I mumble.

But then Tyler is pulling me into his arms, enveloping me in a hug that makes my treacherous body light up despite my heart continuing to sink lower and lower. He smells like pine and fresh ice.

"Thanks, Syd," he rumbles near my ear. "For everything."

And then he's gone and I'm closing the door, sinking down against it, my heart a riot of confusion.

Oh God. What have I done?

CHAPTER 14
TYLER

My feet pound against the frozen sidewalk, breath rising in visible puffs as I push myself through the neighborhood. The frigid morning air bites at my lungs but I welcome the sting, hoping the cold can numb the chaos churning in my mind.

I can't escape the memory of DJ's lips on mine, the heat of his hands gripping my hips, pulling me into him. A lot has happened since we kissed but that moment in the locker room has haunted me continuously. DJ smashed through the careful walls I've built around the truth I've been running from for years.

I'm into him. DJ. A dude. Like, really fucking into him.

A groan escapes me and it has nothing to do with the stitch in my side. I've gotten so good at pushing those desires down, locking them away. Pretending to be the cocky straight bro, fooling everyone—hell, even myself most days.

But that kiss...fuck.

It changed everything.

I think about how Sydney looked at me yesterday when I finally shared my truth with someone out loud.

Her face, always so open and honest, held no judgment. Only warmth and understanding.

"You owe it to yourself to see where it leads."

I reach my building and slump against the brick wall by the door, gasping to catch my breath.

Holy shit. Am I actually going to do this? Risk alienating my family, endure vicious press scrutiny, upend my entire fucking identity...to explore things with DJ?

My mind conjures an image of him. Strong jaw, full lips quirked in that cocky smirk that never fails to piss me off and turn me on. Broad shoulders, muscular arms, and big, rough hands I've secretly imagined on my body for years.

Yeah. Years. The thought strengthens my resolve—*I'm doing this. This has been a long time coming. No more running.*

Feeling ten pounds lighter, I haul myself upright and head inside, mind spinning as I think through my next steps.

First things first—it's game day.

The arena thrums with palpable energy as I skate out to take my place between the pipes. Thousands of eyes bore into me but I block them out, my world narrowing to the puck and the players before me. I'm clearheaded, focused.

Ready.

The whistle blows and the game begins in a flurry of motion. I move on pure instinct, my body an extension of my will as I deflect shot after shot. *Stick, blocker, glove*—each save is met with a deafening roar from the crowd.

"Let's go Simmonds!" they chant, their voices filling me with a heady surge of adrenaline.

I feel untouchable, invincible, like a goddamn superhero in my pads and mask.

The clock ticks down, seconds stretching into eternity. *One more shot, one more save.* The buzzer sounds, and the arena erupts.

3-0, a flawless shutout.

Gloves and sticks rain down around me as my teammates mob the crease, their shouts of elation blending with the crowd's. Strong arms wrap around me from all sides and I'm swallowed up in a sea of sweaty jerseys and fist bumps.

In this moment, I'm on top of the world. The doubts and insecurities that plague me off the ice melt away, replaced by an unshakable confidence. With my team at my back, I can face anything.

Something deep in me clicks into place, and I know I'm finally ready to talk to DJ. Tonight.

The team is packed into our favorite pizza joint, the smell of pepperoni and victory hanging heavy in the air. Laughter and loud voices reverberate off the scuffed wooden tables as the guys relive the game's biggest moments, riding high on our win.

"Simmonds, those saves in the third were fucking clutch!" Matthews grins, lifting his beer towards me.

I flash him a smile and nod in thanks, but my eyes are tracking DJ across the table as he chats animatedly with Cooper. His easy laughter draws me in like a magnet.

I can barely focus on the banter flying around me.

And then our gazes lock and everything else fades to the background entirely. That familiar current of electricity sparks to life between us, unspoken but undeniable.

DJ's lips quirk up at the corner and his eyes glint with a look I've been fantasizing about for months.

The confidence from our win pulses through my veins, mingling with the thrum of anticipation. Sydney's advice echoes in my ears and I take a deep breath.

Fuck it, it's now or never.

I catch DJ's eye again and tilt my head subtly towards a door marked "emergency exit" in the back—or rather, towards the dark hallway that I know is behind it, from past mistaken searches for the bathroom. He looks confused and my heart pounds in my throat. For a harrowing second, I think I've misread everything.

But then a grin slowly spreads across his face, turning almost feral.

"Be right back," I mutter to no one in particular, sliding out of the booth. The guys barely look up from their heated debate over a ref's missed call.

I make my way to the dimly lit back hallway on shaky legs, hyper-aware of DJ's presence a few steps behind me. As soon as the door swings shut behind us, he pins me against the wall, his hands sliding over my hips and his breath hot against my ear.

"Been waiting for you to make a move," he growls, his voice rough with want.

Any coherent response I might have had is swallowed by his mouth on mine, passionate and demanding. I fist my hands in his shirt and pull him closer, kissing him back just as fiercely.

DJ's hands are everywhere, leaving trails of heat even through my clothes. I melt into his touch, craving more, all my pent-up desire pouring out. He starts fumbling with my belt and I freeze for a second, a spike of shocked excitement piercing the haze of lust.

It's finally happening.

"This okay?" DJ breaks the kiss to ask, his eyes searching mine.

I swallow hard and nod firmly. "Yeah. I want this. Want you."

It's all the encouragement he needs. DJ undoes my pants and takes my cock in hand, confident and sure. *Oh, Jesus.*

I let my head fall back against the wall as he starts to stroke me, teasing and exploring. Sparks of pleasure shoot through me as I harden in his grip.

"Fuck, your hands," I groan, my hips jutting forward.

"You have no idea how many times I've imagined this," DJ says, his voice strained. "God, Tyler, I've been thinking about this huge cock nonstop."

His words send a thrill through me, imagining that he's

touched himself thinking about me—the way I have about him, so many times.

I clutch him tighter, bucking into his hand, and he meets my movements with his own, a perfect sync that drives every thought from my mind but him. The walls of the hallway are cold against my heated skin, a stark contrast to the warmth between us.

"Don't stop," I breathe out, and DJ chuckles lowly, his breath tickling my ear.

"Not a chance," he promises, and shifts his position slightly to give himself better leverage. His other hand slides up under my shirt, fingers exploring the plane of my back before digging possessively into flesh.

DJ crushes his lips against mine, trailing down the side of my neck before kissing me deeply again.

"Your cock feels incredible," he murmurs against my mouth. "I need to taste you."

I exhale with desire and anticipation and he grins against me.

"That's right, I'm going to blow you now. As long as that won't freak you out?"

He drops to his knees and glances up at me, his lips parted and eyes dark with lust. My heart nearly pounds out my chest at the sight.

This is real. This is actually happening.

"God, yes," I rasp out. "Please."

DJ doesn't need to be told twice. He takes me into the wet heat of his mouth and I stuff my fist against my lips to muffle my moan. His tongue swirls and teases as he bobs his head, taking me deeper.

The sensations are almost too much, overwhelming in their intensity. DJ is thorough, deliberate in his movements, and I can tell he's just as caught up in this as I am. His mouth is unbelievable, each stroke of his tongue sending shivers down my spine.

DJ's lips come up to circle the head of my cock and he sucks hard.

The way he looks up at me through his eyelashes, eyes alight with mischief and lust—it ignites something inside me and I grab his hair and fuck his mouth hard once, twice, before I realize what I'm doing and begin to back off.

But DJ grabs my thighs to stop me, taking me deeper into his throat and then groaning around me, the vibration adding another layer of pleasure that has my knees buckling.

"Holy shit, DJ..."

He pulls back slightly, lips shiny and swollen as he grins up at me.

"You like that?" he teases, voice husky.

I nod, unable to form words. His hands have come up to play with my dick and I watch as he uses his fingers to smear his spit and my pre-cum up and down my straining cock.

The sight turns me on more, if that's even possible, and I moan and lace my fingers into his hair again, guiding his hot mouth back to my cock until his lips are pressed against the head.

DJ's gaze is locked on mine, intense and unyielding as he

takes me all the way again, until my tip is hitting the back of his throat. The sensation is mind-blowing, his mouth a perfect heaven of pressure and wetness.

The rush is building from deep within, threatening to overwhelm me.

"DJ...I'm gonna—" My voice breaks off into a ragged gasp as he increases his pace, his hands gripping my hips to hold me steady.

He hums around me again, sending vibrations through my entire body, and then I'm gone. The world narrows to the blinding pleasure cresting through me and I throw my head back against the wall, my orgasm ripping through me in waves.

DJ doesn't let up until I'm spent, gently easing me through it with soft licks and sucks, drinking down every ounce of the hot cum I'm shooting into his mouth.

When I finally open my eyes, DJ is standing up, his lips curved in a self-satisfied smirk. "Fuck yeah," he rumbles, standing to press against me once more. "I'll suck you off for dessert anytime."

I laugh, the sound more breathless than I'd intended. "You... God, DJ, that was—"

"Everything you hoped for?" he interjects as he wipes the back of his hand across his mouth with a cocky raise of his eyebrow, his voice still rough.

"More," I admit, pulling him into another fierce kiss. My lips are hungry against his and I can taste my own cum in his mouth —it's intoxicating. His arms wrap around me, strong and secure, and I can't help but press closer, wanting his body against mine without any barriers.

As we break for air, my forehead rests against his.

"I didn't know it could be like this," I confess, my voice scratchy, not even entirely sure what I mean.

DJ's smile gentles, the usual playful spark in his eyes giving way to something softer.

"It can be whatever you want it to be," he whispers back, brushing a stray lock of hair from my face. His fingers linger against my skin, heart-stoppingly tender compared to the animalistic roughness moments ago.

Someone passes by the door, talking loudly, and the hallway suddenly seems too public despite the seclusion. DJ seems to sense my unease. Leaning in for a quick final kiss, he gestures towards the door.

"Come on," he says. "Let's get out of here."

We try to be subtle as we grab our coats, making casual excuses individually to the team before meeting back up outside.

Out in the night air, the usual charged energy between us shifts into something calmer but no less present. The city lights cast shadows over DJ's features, making him look both mysterious and impossibly handsome. We walk in silence for a few blocks, each lost in our thoughts.

I'm frowning slightly when DJ wraps his hand around mine and tugs me to a stop.

"Hey," he says gently. "I hope you're not freaking out." He

quirks an eyebrow at me, our breath steaming between us in the winter air.

His words are casual but I can see a crease of concern on his forehead.

I smile and shake my head, trying to find the right words.

"No, I'm not freaking out," I assure him, squeezing his hand. "Just...overwhelmed, I guess."

DJ laughs softly, looking relieved. "Good overwhelmed or bad overwhelmed?"

"Definitely good," I reply without hesitating.

"Good. Because for me it was fucking amazing." His easy words take the air out of me. "So...my place is just over there, but I'm not asking you back..." For a moment I'm stung, but then he grins and continues. "Because if I do, I can't be held responsible for what I do to you, and I think I've probably given you enough firsts for one evening."

DJ's hands have come up to fist in my hair, and all I can do is stare at him as his words light up my skin, my cock already stirring with arousal again.

"But you think we can do this again sometime?" he asks.

"Yes," I say, my voice only shaking a little. "I'd like that a lot."

DJ's smile widens, and he leans in, his lips brushing against mine in a kiss that's sweet and slow. It's another stark contrast to the intensity we shared minutes ago, yet it sets off a whole new range of tingles through my body.

As he walks away, he turns back to shoot me one last mischievous grin and a small wave. I watch him until he turns the corner, and then I'm left standing alone under the street-lights, every moment of tonight whirring around my mind in vivid detail.

I'm going to be replaying this night for a very long time.

CHAPTER 15
DJ

I GRIN WIDELY AS I ADD MORE WEIGHT TO THE BAR, ELICITING A raised eyebrow from Eva, the Blizzards' head athletic trainer.

"Damn DJ, what's gotten into you today? This energy is off the charts."

I wink at her cheekily. "What can I say, I woke up on the right side of the bed...and the left side...and in the middle. Multiple times, if you catch my drift."

Eva rolls her eyes but can't hide her amused smirk. "Yeah, yeah, we get it, you get laid. No need to rub it in for us mere mortals."

I let out a bark of laughter as I settle under the bar, a satisfying strain in my muscles as I start my reps. The endorphins are flowing and I'm riding a natural high, my body buzzing with adrenaline.

With a playful glance, I grunt between reps, "Hey now, don't shame me for living my best life! Don't be jealous, be inspired!"

This earns me a swat from Eva with a rolled-up towel. "Alright hotshot, focus on your lifts before that ego makes you drop the bar on that pretty face."

I stick my tongue out at her but oblige, channeling my pent-up energy into each rep. My muscles burn as I push myself harder than usual but I barely feel them protest.

I'm so keyed up, I could bench-press a fucking Zamboni right now.

Maybe it's the thrill of anticipation thrumming through my veins, knowing I'll be seeing a certain backup goalie at practice soon. The memory of our hot encounter last night is burned into the back of my eyelids.

I can't wait to get my hands on him again. My mouth.

I want to throw him down and crawl on top of him and—

"Uh, DJ? You still with us, bud?"

Eva's sarcastic voice snaps me out of my horny daydreaming. *Fuck, I'm at full mast in my compression shorts.*

Hoping she doesn't notice my raging hard-on, I hastily re-rack the weight and hop up, flashing him a megawatt smile. "Yep, all done! What's next, boss?"

Shaking her head in bewilderment, Eva sighs. "I think we better call it, man. Any more and you'll pull something. Go grab something to eat and save some of that for practice, yeah?"

"Sir, yes sir!" I give her a cheeky salute and prance off toward the locker room, my heart racing with excitement rather than exertion.

Practice can't come soon enough. *I wonder if I'll have Tyler coming soon too...*

I'm still grinning like an idiot as I glide onto the ice for practice, my adrenaline only having ratcheted up. My body is electric, like I just chugged ten espressos and chased them with a Red Bull.

But it's not just the caffeine high, and it's not just seeing Tyler—the whole team is on fire lately, our passes tape-to-tape, our shots so money they should have their faces printed on bills.

It's clear that Sydney's work with the team is really having an effect.

Sydney.

She's been dodging me since that night in Tampa, true to her word about keeping it a onetime thing. I really thought she'd want a repeat—god knows I did—but I have to respect her for keeping her word.

And anyway, I've had my hands *more* than busy in the meantime...

Mikey rips a one-timer past the d and the boys whoop and holler, tapping his shin pads as he cruises by the bench. I join in, relieved that things finally are back to normal after all that shit went down in Canada.

Well, almost normal.

I catch Tyler's eye from across the ice and—*hot damn.* The way he's looking at me, like he wants to melt the ice and pin me against the boards... Let's just say it's not just the physical exertion making me sweat right now.

I stare back at him, wondering what it is about him that's

got me so tied in knots. I've always been the king of casual. Hit it and quit it, a different body in my bed every weekend.

Feelings are messy, relationships are work, and I don't play with that.

But with Tyler... God, there's just something about him. Those soulful eyes, that shy smile, the bulging muscles that strain against his pads... I want him. Not just his body, but like, all of him. Heart, mind, soul, the whole shebang.

It's thrilling and terrifying and confusing as hell.

"Hey DJ, stop staring at Ty's ass and get in the drill!" Jason chirps, jolting me out of my surprisingly wholesome daydreams.

I flip him the bird. "You're just jealous I'm not staring at yours, Jace!"

"In your dreams, bud!" Jason cackles.

But as we run passing drills, I can't help sneaking more glances at Tyler in the crease. *I need to get my hands on him again, and soon.*

After a brief water break, we resume practice. Tyler skates back onto the ice and of course, my eyes can't help but follow the lines of his muscular body as he takes his place in the goal crease. I find myself drifting closer, looking for any excuse to get near him again.

Finally the team is busy shooting offensive drills and I take advantage of the moment, skating right up beside him.

"Keep your glove hand higher," I murmur, leaning in close. My fingers graze his hip, lingering just a moment too long.

Tyler shivers slightly and I catch the hitch in his breath.

"Like this?" he asks, voice husky.

"Almost. Let me show you." I wrap my hand around his wrist, manually making the adjustment, and he leans into me, trying to get closer.

I smirk. He's so responsive, it's intoxicating. The feeling is heady, as if he's completely under my spell.

Or is it the other way around?

We switch up the drills but I contrive to be near Tyler every chance I get.

"Your five-hole is open, Ty," I say with a wicked grin as I slide another puck between his legs. "Wanna stay after practice for some one-on-one training?"

Tyler flushes so red I can see it through his goalie mask.

"You offering private lessons now, DJ?" His voice is light but there's an undercurrent of heat.

God, the things I want to teach him... I lick my lips, filthy lesson plans flooding my mind.

"For you? I'll make an exception."

I'm high on the shy glances Tyler sneaks my way when he thinks I'm not looking, the pink that lingers across his cheeks.

Coach Daniels skates over to a cluster of defensemen at the other end of the rink, his face displeased.

"Marquez, keep your stick on the ice and shoulders square. King, tighten up that gap. You're giving the forwards too much space to make a play."

I glide up behind Tyler while the rest of the men on the ice focus on Coach's notes. *Now's my chance.* I lean in close, my lips grazing the pink shell of his ear.

"Hey you. Come over tonight," I murmur, my voice low and inviting. "I've got...plans for you."

Tyler starts slightly and whips his head around to look at me, eyes wide with surprise. His tongue darts out to wet his plump lips, and he nods, almost imperceptibly.

Fuck yes.

A thrill of anticipation rips through me and I have to stop myself from checking him against the boards and ravishing him right here on the ice, team and coaches be damned.

My mind races with thoughts of all the delicious, wicked things I'm going to do to him later—strip off that tight Under Armour, get my hands and mouth all over those chiseled muscles, make him moan and tremble under my touch until he's begging for more...

Fuck, I can hardly wait to get him naked and into my bed. Finally.

Distracted by thoughts of the promising evening ahead, I'm skating into formation for our final scrimmage of the day when pain explodes through my knee.

Shit. Not now.

I grit my teeth and try to straighten and skate on, doing my best to ignore the throbbing, demanding ache that's radiating from the old injury. *Power through it, DJ.*

But each stride sends another jolt of agony shooting up my

leg. I stumble and nearly face-plant onto the ice. My heart begins to race, my mind already spiraling.

This is bad. Really bad. I can't risk blowing out my knee again, not when the team needs me.

Not when Mom needs me to keep earning that NHL paycheck.

"Coach!" I call out, masking my grimace with a tight smile and waving my cell phone in the air. "Gotta bail early. Family emergency."

Coach raises an eyebrow but, engrossed in a discussion with Slade, waves me off. I gingerly move off the ice, each stride sending a fresh wave of pain through my knee.

Fuck. Fuck! This can't be happening. Not now, when it looks like we actually have a chance to make it back to the playoffs this year, against all odds.

As I head into the tunnel to the locker room, I catch Ty's eye across the ice. He shoots me a questioning look laced with concern.

I flash him a grin and mouth: "Still on for tonight."

Ty nods, his lips curving into a smile that sends heat rushing through me. *Knee be damned, I'm not about to cancel my plans with him. I've waited too long for this.*

CHAPTER 16
TYLER

My pulse pounds in my ears as I weave through the Chicago traffic, visions of DJ dancing through my head. His smoky eyes, that sexy smirk, the way his body moves on the ice - and how it might move against mine...

I shift in my seat, jeans tightening. I can't believe this is finally happening, that I'm letting myself go there with him.

I imagine DJ answering the door shirtless, tattoos on full display. Running my hands over his chest, his abs. His lips on my neck, hands roaming lower. Tumbling into bed, a tangle of limbs and sheets.

I'm so lost in the fantasy I almost miss the turn onto his block.

Just as I pull up in front of his building, my phone starts buzzing. It's my sister Leah. I hesitate, finger hovering over the screen, then sigh and pick up.

"Hey sis, what's—"

"Tyler?" Her normally perky voice wobbles. "I'm so sorry to bother you, I just...I didn't know who else to call."

My stomach clenches at her tone. "Leah, what's wrong? Are you okay?"

She lets out a shuddery breath. "Not really. Nate and I had a huge fight. He stormed out and I'm just sitting here crying and...ugh, I'm a mess. I know you're probably busy, but is there any way you could come over? I really need my brother right now."

Disappointment and then guilt twists through me as I glance up at DJ's window.

"Of course, Leah. I'm on my way, just sit tight."

I disconnect the call and thunk my head back against the headrest, a frustrated sigh escaping my lips. *I was so close.* But Leah needs me, and she's always been there for me.

No matter how badly I want DJ, my sister comes first.

I fire off a quick text to him before pulling away from the curb.

"Hey, I'm so sorry but something came up with my sister and I have to go be with her. Family emergency. Rain check on tonight? I'll make it up to you, promise."

The reply comes seconds later.

"No worries man, family first. Hope she's alright. Let me know if you need anything."

Disappointment sits heavy in my chest, but I know I'm doing the right thing. I navigate on autopilot to Leah's, my mind no longer filled with thoughts of DJ, but worry for my older sister.

Since I can remember Leah's been my rock in the family, always looking out for me. I used to love hanging with her and her husband and their crazy poodle mix, Bananas. It's still great to see Bananas but lately, spending time with them has felt like navigating a minefield thanks to the constant tension between her and Nate.

Just two weeks ago, we were all out having dinner to celebrate Leah's promotion at work. But instead of congratulating her on her accomplishment, Nate griped about her long hours the whole time.

"I don't know why you even need this job, I make plenty for both of us," blah blah blah.

It ruined the night; Leah didn't even eat anything at her favorite restaurant, just pushed the food around her plate.

Then last weekend, I went to their place to watch the football game. Leah came in from running errands and Nate immediately started in on her.

"I thought you said you'd be home an hour ago to make snacks. Guess hanging with your work friends is more important than your own husband, huh?"

The words were bad enough but his tone, dripping with accusation—it pissed me off. And obviously Leah too, though she just muttered an apology before escaping to the kitchen.

I grip the steering wheel tighter, my stomach twisting at the memories.

This isn't the Leah and Nate I know - the cutesy high school sweethearts who used to be downright nauseating with their PDA. These days, it seems like they can barely stand each other.

Thirty minutes later, I'm pulling into her driveway, noting the absence of Nate's car. I take a deep breath and head for the front door, readying myself to be the supportive big little brother she needs, shoving down my own selfish wants for the night. *Duty calls.*

Leah's silky hair brushes against my neck as her head drops onto my shoulder. She lets out a shuddering sigh, sniffling softly. A wave of fierce protectiveness surges through me. As the baby of the family, I'm used to Leah taking care of me, not the other way around.

It's good to return the favor, finally.

"What happened, sis?" I murmur, rubbing soothing circles on her back. "Talk to me."

Leah takes a shaky breath.

"It was so stupid. Nate made some offhand comment about how I've let myself go since the wedding. Said my ass is getting flabby." She rolls her teary eyes. "I snapped back that maybe he should spend less time staring at other women's asses and more time appreciating his wife. It escalated from there into this whole blowout fight."

I frown defensively. "Dick move."

Nate's usually a decent guy, but he definitely has his moments of assholery.

"I just..." Leah's voice cracks. "What if he's not attracted to me anymore, Ty? What if this is the beginning of the end?

We've only been married three years, and it already feels like we're unraveling."

"What if he's not attracted to you anymore?" I repeat incredulously, my protectiveness turning into frustration. "Come on, Leah. Nate is a shallow idiot sometimes, but he loves you. No matter what. You know that."

Leah shrugs and wipes her eyes with the back of her hand.

"I just...I don't know. Maybe we should never have gotten married."

I shake my head, refusing to let her spiral down this rabbit hole of self-doubt.

"Don't even go there, Leah. You guys have been through so much together. Remember high school? College? All those stupid breakups and makeups? This is just a rough patch. You'll get through it. You just need to talk to Nate, explain how he's making you feel—I'm sure he'll shape up. And if he doesn't, I'll kick his ass."

She nods slowly, sniffling again.

"You're right," she says quietly, leaning into me for comfort.

We sit in silence for a few minutes before I break the peace with a question that's been nagging at me since I arrived. "So where is Nate, anyway?"

Leah pulls away from me and looks down at her hands, fidgeting with her wedding ring.

"He went out with his work friends," she mumbles.

My eyebrows shoot up in surprise and concern. Since when does Nate have work friends? In all the years I've known him, he's always been a total loner when it comes to his job.

"Work friends?" I ask skeptically.

Leah shrugs again noncommittally, focusing on her mug of tea.

"Yeah, they're new coworkers or something."

I narrow my eyes suspiciously but decide not to push it for now.

"Well, let's try to relax and enjoy our night in then," I say with forced enthusiasm, hoping to cheer Leah up.

She manages a small smile and looks at me with watery eyes.

"Thanks for listening, Ty. I didn't realize how badly I needed to get that off my chest."

I squeeze her hand. "Anytime, sis. I'm always here if you need to vent. Or cry on my manly shoulder." I flex jokingly.

Leah snorts out a half-laugh and swats my arm.

"Dork." But I can see the gratitude shining in her eyes. Knowing I could make her feel even a tiny bit better fills me with warmth.

And suddenly, I realize I might be ready to get my own burden off my chest.

My heart pounds in my ears as I nervously clench my fists, steeling myself for a conversation I've been putting off.

I glance over at my sister. Her tears are gone, and she's looking at me with knowing eyes, as if she can sense the words I'm struggling to form.

I take a deep, shaky breath.

"Leah, there's something I need to tell you." My voice trembles.

She sets down her mug, giving me her full attention. "What's up, Ty?"

"I..." My palms are sweaty. I wipe them on my jeans. "I think I'm bi. Bisexual, I mean."

I freeze—*I think that's the first time I've said the word out loud.*

Leah's eyebrows rise but she stays quiet, letting me continue. The warmth in her eyes gives me confidence and suddenly the words are tumbling out in a jumbled rush.

"There's this guy on the team...I mean, I've always felt this attraction to guys too, not just girls. But with DJ...the way he makes me feel, it's intense. Unavoidable. I don't know how to explain it; I've never experienced anything like it before."

I rake a hand through my hair, hot and frazzled, and Sydney's face inexplicably pops into my mind.

"But I'm still into girls too! I'm so confused..."

My leg bounces anxiously under the table. *What in the rambling hell am I talking about?* Leah sees my consternation and reaches over to squeeze my hand. Her touch is gentle and reassuring.

"Tyler, breathe. It's okay," she soothes, smiling. "There's nothing wrong with being bi. I'm so proud of you for telling me."

I blink back the sudden wetness in my eyes.

"You are? I was so scared you'd think I was...I don't know. A freak or something."

"Never," Leah says firmly. "You're my brother and I love you, no matter what. I just want you to be happy. To be yourself."

A lump rises in my throat. "Thanks, sis. You have no idea

how much that means to me. But...don't tell Steven, yet, okay? I'm not sure..."

I trail off, my voice catching with unspoken fears of rejection. Our brother...he's not as understanding as Leah. Leah nods immediately, understanding my hesitation.

"Of course, Ty. Your truth is safe with me until you're ready to share it with anyone else," she promises firmly, squeezing my hand again for emphasis.

Relief washes over me, mingled with a newfound sense of freedom. It's like a weight has been lifted off my shoulders. I hadn't even realized how heavily hiding this part of myself had been holding me down.

Leah's eyes soften as she looks at me, her features etched with loving concern. "So, this thing with DJ...is it serious? I mean, do you think it might go somewhere?"

I shrug, a small smile playing on my lips despite my inner turmoil.

"Maybe? I don't know. We're just...seeing where things go right now." My smile fades a bit as I add, "It's complicated, since we're teammates. And he's...well, he's a lot more experienced than I am, if you know what I mean."

I blush. Why does he make me feel like I'm a teenager again? I've got goddamn butterflies in my stomach just thinking about him.

Leah chuckles softly, her face brightening up with a mix of amusement and understanding.

"Oh, I see! The notorious DJ." She teases gently, nudging my foot under the table. "Just remember, it's all about communication, Ty. It doesn't matter how experienced or inexperienced someone is, if you're not on the same page, things can get messy."

I nod, absorbing her words with slight trepidation. Communication has never been my strong suit in relationships. Maybe that's why they rarely lasted long or ended well.

"You're right," I admit begrudgingly. "And I guess I want to be sure about whatever's going on with DJ before I get too deep into it."

The conversation shifts as we dive into lighter topics— movies we want to watch, vacation plans, and Leah's new recipe experiments. But through it all, I'm only half-present; my thoughts keep drifting back to DJ.

Is this just a fling for him? He's notorious for moving on from one lover to the next, and open with the team about not being monogamous. Should I just assume whatever's going on is purely physical?

I chide myself internally—wasn't I just saying that I wanted to take things slow? It shouldn't matter to me whether DJ sees this as serious or not, not if I don't even know what I want.

So why does it feel like my heart is sinking?

CHAPTER 17
SYDNEY

My last meeting of the day is a status update. I lean forward in my chair, meeting Coach Daniels' keen gaze across his cluttered desk.

"Jason's been making real strides lately," I say. "He's been consistently attending AA meetings with the support of his wife and really opening up during our sessions about his drinking. I think he's starting to understand how it's been a crutch for him to avoid dealing with deeper issues."

Coach nods thoughtfully. "That's great to hear. I've noticed a change in him on the ice too. He seems more focused, more at peace with himself."

"Absolutely," I agree. "And Tomas too. He's been journaling every day, unpacking a lot of the anger and resentment that was fueling his drug use. We've been working on healthier coping mechanisms and he's really embraced the process."

Pride swells in my chest as I recount their progress, hard-won through vulnerability and courage.

But my smile fades as my thoughts turn to Mikey.

"I have to admit though, I'm worried about Mikey," I confess with a sigh. "He still refuses to try group therapy or AA. I haven't been able to get him to open up at all. And Eva mentioned some behavior that has me concerned."

Coach's brow furrows, his expression grave.

"I've noticed he's been withdrawn, irritable," he says. "You think he's still struggling with active addiction?"

"I suspect so," I say grimly. "Addiction is insidious. It thrives in isolation and secrecy. If he won't let anyone in, won't admit he needs help..." I trail off, my heart heavy with concern for him.

"What do you recommend?" Coach asks, his troubled gaze reflecting back my same worry. "I don't want to see the kid throw away his future."

I'm about to reply when my phone buzzes against my hip. Slipping it out of my pocket, I glance down to see DJ's name lighting up the screen.

My pulse quickens. *Why is he calling me?* DJ isn't the type to call out of the blue, so my instinctual reaction is that something is wrong, either with him or with someone on the team.

"I'm so sorry, Coach, would you excuse me for just a moment?" I say. "I really need to take this."

He nods understandingly and I step out into the quiet hall-way, my thumb already swiping to answer. As I lift the phone to my ear, I can't help the tingle of anticipation that runs through me.

"DJ? Is everything okay?"

DJ's smooth voice tickles my ear through the phone.

"Syd," he purrs, and my knees go weak at the sound of my name in his mouth. "My plans tonight fell through. I'm sitting here all alone with enough sushi for an army. You like Izumi's, right? The place near my apartment?"

I scoff, even as my mouth waters involuntarily at the thought of their signature dynamite rolls.

"That's what this is about? God, DJ, I thought something was wrong. But, yes, it's my favorite sushi spot in the city. How did you know?"

"Oh I have my ways," he says mysteriously. I can practically hear the cocky smirk in his voice. "So what do you say, want to come keep me company? I promise to be a perfect gentleman." His voice drops. "Scout's honor."

I bite my lip, goosebumps erupting on my arms at his reference to the last time he promised to be a gentleman. Hanging out alone with DJ, just the two of us, is dangerous. *Exciting.*

"I don't know, I have an early morning tomorrow..." I hedge.

"Come on, live a little! I'll have you home before curfew."

His playful tone is impossible to resist.

My resolve, already weak, crumbles.

"Okay, fine, you've twisted my arm. I'll be there in an hour."

"Can't wait."

What am I doing? My heart hammers as I head back inside to wrap things up with Coach Daniels. I try to convince myself this is totally casual—two friends, some sushi, no big deal.

But deep down, I know I'm only fooling myself.

This growing thing between DJ and I refuses to be ignored, no matter how hard I try to tamp it down. It's magnetic, constantly pulling us into each other's orbit against our better judgment.

What would it mean to stop fighting it and see where this gravitational pull takes me?

Two hours later, I find myself spread out across DJ's bed, totally naked. The sushi he'd ordered sits forgotten on the kitchen counter, abandoned in favor of a much more delectable meal.

When I first arrived, DJ was the perfect gentleman, just like he promised. But we both knew why I was really there. One charged moment, a devilish glint in his eye, and I couldn't resist going in for a searing kiss.

Things rapidly heated up from there, clothes frantically shed and discarded on the way to his bedroom.

I know I should feel guilty, having once again crossed the boundaries I set for myself. But right now, sated and boneless, it's hard to be anything but blissful.

DJ isn't my patient, we're both consenting adults, we're not hurting anyone…

Except for Tyler.

I frown, the thought sobering. Clearly I was delusional for

thinking DJ and I could have a one-off hookup. This energy between us is too explosive to ignore. But what does this mean for my own relationship with Tyler—and the growing connection between him and DJ?

Am I getting in between them?

I flash back to that night at the charity event, when I was literally sandwiched between them on the dance floor.

I'd like to get in between them again, my filthy mind responds.

DJ's skillful hands skim over my sensitive skin, his full lips trailing fiery kisses in their wake, and I can't bring myself to worry anymore.

"Mmm, your body is so gorgeous. I can't wait to fuck you again," DJ murmurs against my neck, his deep voice sending shivers down my spine.

He captures my lips in another hungry kiss before trailing his mouth lower, worshiping my breasts with licks and nibbles that make me whimper and arch into him.

I grin when I feel him already rock hard against my thigh. Emboldened by his eagerness, I push against his sculpted chest until he rolls onto his back, allowing me to straddle him. DJ's hands immediately go to my hips as I bend down to plant open-mouthed kisses across his chest.

"I want to blow you," I whisper against his abs, glancing up at him from beneath my lashes.

DJ's eyes darken even further, his grip on my hips tightening.

"Fuck yeah, baby. Take my cock in that pretty mouth."

I don't need to be told twice. I shimmy down his body until

I'm eye level with his impressive erection. Wrapping my hand around him, I give a few teasing pumps before I swirl my tongue around the tip, lapping up the bead of moisture there.

DJ groans, a hand coming down to tangle in my hair. "I'm going to tell you what to do. If it's ever too much just tap my thigh, okay?"

I swallow and nod, gazing up at him. I can feel myself getting wetter and wetter. *Fuck, it turns me on to hear him order me around.*

"Good. Then take it deep, Syd," he commands. "Fuck my cock with your mouth."

His gravelly voice lights a fire in my core.

Following his instructions, I start bobbing my head, taking him slowly into the soft wetness of my mouth.

I've never blown someone with a cock this big, and the new sensation drives me crazy. Then his other hand grabs the back of my neck and he yanks me down, filling my mouth, pressing his hard cock deep into my throat until I'm choking on him.

DJ's grip is steady but gentle, as if he's fully aware of my limits and holding me right at the brink. My eyes water slightly, the moment thrilling in its intensity.

I manage a slight nod, signaling I'm okay, and DJ's features slacken with pleasure as I start to move up and down his cock, taking him all the way in each time.

As I build my rhythm, DJ watches me intently, his dark eyes glazed with passion. He starts directing me again, his voice husky.

"Just like that...you're doing so good," he encourages as I

work him deeper with each motion, his moans urging me on, taking him into my throat over and over until I'm lightheaded.

"Tell me what to do next, DJ," I manage to gasp out. There's something exhilarating about giving in to this act, letting him order me around. *I've never felt so turned on.*

DJ's smirk turns decidedly wicked, his eyes dancing with mischief and yearning.

"Get up here," he commands, the authority in his voice sending a shudder of anticipation through me. "I want that tight pussy on my cock."

Eager to please and equally eager to have him inside me again, I shift my position and crawl up until I'm straddling him. I align myself above him as he rolls a condom on.

DJ's hands remain firmly on my hips, guiding me down fast and hard, lifting me up and then slamming me back down. His movements are deliberate, a perfect blend of rough and tender, as if he knows exactly how much I can handle.

I groan as his huge cock stretches my pussy out almost to the point of pain, wanting more.

"You feel so fucking good," DJ groans, his voice strained with effort.

I lean forward to capture his lips in a fevered kiss, my hands exploring the defined muscles of his chest. Every thrust sends waves of pleasure coursing through me, blurring the line between pain and ecstasy.

DJ's hands are everywhere, pulling me closer, and the world narrows to the electrifying sensations overwhelming my body

—DJ's powerful strokes, his hot skin against mine, his fingers digging into my thighs.

As the intensity builds, I'm spiraling toward a climax. DJ senses it too and holds me down on his cock, tight, so that I can't move, can't give myself the friction I'm craving.

I half moan, half sob, desperately trying to break his grasp and move on his cock again.

"Naughty girl," DJ chides. "It's not time to come yet."

Tears of frustration prick my eyes, and I beg him for release.

"Please DJ, fuck me. I need your cock, I need to come now!"

His hand loosens slightly, and I take the opportunity to grind against him, my movements frenzied with need.

"Little slut," he laughs approvingly and slaps my ass hard, the pain pulling me back from the edge again, and it feels *so fucking good.*

I grit my teeth and will myself to stop moving, to obey his every command.

DJ notes my reaction and his low laughter resonates through the room, a low, seductive sound that only builds my need. One hand remains firmly on my hip, his control absolute, as the other one caresses the skin he just spanked, making me shiver, and then he slaps the spot again.

"That's right, stay still for me, little slut," he murmurs, his voice thick with desire.

I'm panting now, desperate for release but held captive by his will.

He lets me catch my breath, his gaze locked on mine, smoldering and intense.

"You're so beautiful like this," he whispers as he runs a thumb across my cheek, wiping away a stray tear from my cheek, pulling back my bottom lip with his thumb before anchoring his hand back on my hip, keeping me locked down on his hard cock, so deep inside me.

"This is how I want you, all the time," he continues, his voice husky. "Completely at my mercy."

The words send a shiver through me, a mix of fear and excitement sparking deep in my belly, and I clench over his cock, gasping.

"You aren't going to move until I tell you, are you, my good girl?"

I shake my head mutely, and he frees one hand to start playing with my clit—alternating between feather-light strokes, hard insistent caresses, and small painful tweaks that jolt me back from the edge, over and over again.

The tension builds to a fever pitch and I'm losing my mind with it, a delicious torment orchestrated by DJ's skilled touch. He keeps me teetering on the brink, pushing me closer with each caress, then pulling back just as I'm about to tumble over into oblivion.

The mixture of frustration and anticipation is intoxicating, overwhelming my senses until I'm not sure how much more I can take.

"Look at me," DJ commands.

I lift my gaze to meet his, finding his eyes burning with need, his expression one of intense focus as he watches the alternating pain and pleasure written across my face.

"Let go, Sydney," he murmurs, his voice quiet but commanding, as if he's willing me to break apart under his touch. "It's time. Let go for me."

I can hardly breathe, the ferocity of his gaze pinning me as surely as his hands. His fingers are relentless, skimming over my clit until, in a wave of torturous bliss, he sends me crashing into orgasm.

My body convulses around the rock-hard length of his cock inside me, waves of release sweeping over me in an unending rush.

As I shudder and gasp, DJ slowly eases his grip, allowing me to collapse against his chest. His arms wrap around me in a firm embrace, his heartbeat strong under my ear. He kisses the top of my head gently, looking down at me with affection filling his dark eyes.

"Perfect," he breathes out.

CHAPTER 18
SYDNEY

I ROLL BACK ONTO THE BED, MY BODY STILL QUIVERING. *HOLY shit*. I stare up at the ceiling, my chest heaving as I try to catch my breath.

DJ chuckles, his fingertips trailing lazily over my sweat-slicked skin. "Mm, look at you. Delicious. I guess that was more than okay for you, huh?"

I blush. Despite the intimacy of what we just did together I'm unsure of how to respond.

All of this is so new for me. With Paul, sex was always vanilla, almost perfunctory, more about his needs than mine. I can't remember the last time I came that hard.

Or rather, I can: never.

And I've never had a partner prioritize my orgasm over his own. I'm aware that DJ hasn't come yet.

I always felt so self-conscious with Paul, like he'd make fun of me if I ever voiced what I truly desired. But with DJ...

My blush deepens. With DJ, I'm safe to let go completely and explore the naughtiest fantasies buried deep in the recesses of my mind. There's no judgment, only acceptance and encouragement.

I'm still trembling, the aftershocks still hitting me, when DJ raises one dark eyebrow.

I nod, belatedly remembering his teasing question. "More than okay."

He grins in response, his eyes darkening hungrily. "Ready for more?"

"Please," I breathe. "But can we take the condom off? I'm on birth control and I've been tested recently."

"I have too, and fuck, I would love to really feel you around me."

DJ pulls the condom off, then stands up at the edge of the bed and drags me toward him until I can wrap my legs around him.

Taking himself in his hand, he skims his head over my clit, so sensitive that it sends a jolt throughout my whole body. Then he notches his dripping cock up against my entrance. DJ grins again, that devilish twinkle in his eyes promising more delicious torment.

I moan in anticipation, lifting my hips, suddenly desperate to have his hard length back inside me.

To my surprise he slides into me smoothly, almost gently, a stark contrast to the rough fucking we were doing before. This time his thrusts are slow, deliberate, as if he's memorizing every reaction, every moan that escapes from my lips.

He watches my face closely from his position above me, each stroke deep and thorough, exploring me in a way that is new and yet familiar.

"Tell me what you want next," he commands, moving his hips so that his cock hits even deeper inside my pussy, sending shivers down my spine. "Tell me what to do to you."

I bite my lip, my breath hitching as I try to form coherent thoughts. His gaze is intense, almost daring me to voice my deepest desires.

I've never felt so uninhibited.

"Spank me again," I whisper, the words barely audible over the pounding of my heart. I almost can't believe the words that spill out of me next. "And while you do it I want—I want your cock deep in my ass."

I've never had anal sex before but it's something I always wanted to try. Paul was too prude, too judgmental. I was always afraid that he'd look at me differently if I told him what I craved.

But DJ's eyes flare with a mix of surprise and excitement. He leans down to press a soft kiss against my lips, the tenderness another surprise after the dark desire I just voiced. His voice is low, a husky whisper that sends shivers up and down my spine.

"With pleasure."

He pulls back slightly, giving us both a moment to breathe as he reaches for the bedside drawer, fishing out a bottle of lube. His movements are calm, his slow, deliberate actions only ratcheting up the heady tension in the room.

DJ coats his fingers and then his cock with the slick

substance, his gaze never leaving mine, filled with unspoken promise.

With one hand, he lifts up one of my legs to rest my heel on his shoulder, spreading me wide, exposing my pussy and ass to his eager fingers. It's an obscene position and for a moment I have the urge to cover myself, but when I take in the worshipful expression on his face, I relax and open for him, my heart racing with anticipation.

Slowly, he begins to prepare my ass, one finger slipping inside with ease, gradually adding more until I'm breathing heavily from the stretch and sensation.

I'm breathless, eager for more, so when he suddenly stops and pulls away I whine in frustration. He chuckles, then his expression grows serious again.

"Are you sure about this?"

Our eyes meet and I nod, my throat dry. "I'm sure."

"If anything is too much just tell me," he says, waiting until I nod again.

Then all at once he flips me over and I don't even have time to catch my breath before his hand comes down hard on my ass cheek. The sting is sharp and sudden.

"You like that?" he asks, his voice laced with both amusement and desire.

"Yes," I groan. "Spank me again. Fuck me while you spank me, DJ."

I have no idea where this version of myself is coming from but I don't have time to analyze my newfound boldness. Almost as soon as I get the words out, the head of his cock nudges up against my tight, virgin ass, slowly pushing in.

The sensation is intense, a slow, stretching pressure that has me gripping the sheets beneath me, gasping hard, my face pressed down into the mattress.

DJ pauses, letting me adjust to him for just a moment, confirming I'm ready before swiftly pushing the rest of the way into me and slapping my ass again, harder this time.

His hands grip my hips tightly and he begins to move, each thrust slow and deliberate, driving deeper into me with a controlled ferocity that has my toes curling. The dual sensations of pain and pleasure mingle exquisitely, sending wave after wave of intense satisfaction crashing through me.

"Is this what you wanted?" DJ asks between thrusts, his tone teasing yet heavy with lust as he spanks me again, once, twice.

"Yes," I manage to gasp out, the words barely audible above the sound of our slick bodies moving together. "Yes, DJ, yes, don't stop."

DJ chuckles softly and his pace increases, his movements becoming more forceful as he pounds into me.

Another spank lands on my throbbing, stinging ass, the pain sharpening the pleasure twisting through me until I'm moaning incoherently beneath him, the sensation unlike anything I've ever felt before.

DJ's control is impeccable, his strokes calculated to drive me wild. The mix of sharp, sweet pain and deep, fulfilling thrusts pushes me toward the edge again.

"Look up, Syd. Look at us," he commands harshly, and I obey, realizing the mirror over his dresser reflects us perfectly.

For a breathless moment, our eyes lock. Watching his cock pump in and out of my ass, his hands alternating caresses with hard smacks on my abused skin, sends a new wave of unbridled arousal through me. The visual is raw, primal, impossible to look away from.

DJ's eyes, focused and intense, hold mine in the reflection, a silent challenge that provokes an unbearable response in my core.

His strokes pick up pace, relentless now, and another climax builds, fierce and unstoppable. "Tell me you're mine," he growls roughly, reaching one hand around to rub hard on my aching clit.

"I'm yours," I breathe out, the words a white-hot truth in the tumult of sensations overwhelming me. As the words leave my lips, DJ's hand connects with my rear again, sharper and more possessive than before, cementing his claim.

One deep thrust and a smack that resonates through my entire body and I shatter once more.

My vision blurs with tears of intense release as DJ continues to thrust relentlessly, his movements becoming more erratic and desperate until, with a guttural roar, he finally spills himself deep inside my ass, his body shuddering against mine.

We collapse together, a tangle of limbs and sweat-slick skin, breathing heavily. DJ rolls off me and lies back on the bed, pulling me close. His heartbeat is fast but steadily slowing, a comforting rhythm that echoes my own.

After a stretch of silence filled only with our synchronized breathing, DJ kisses the top of my head again.

"That was..." he starts, but seems at a loss for words.

"Incredible," I finish for him, smiling into his skin. He nods, his fingers lazily tracing patterns on my back.

"Yeah. Incredible," he agrees, his voice tinged with awe.

"Better than two puck bunnies at once?" I half-tease, worrying the jealousy shows in my voice even as the words come out of my mouth.

But DJ just laughs, the sound rich and reassuring. He tightens his hold around me, pulling me closer against his chest.

"Nothing compares to you, Syd," he replies, pressing a kiss to my forehead, and I relax into him.

His fingers continue their idle dance along the curve of my spine, sending shivers across my skin. The room is quiet now, the earlier storm of passion giving way to a peaceful intimacy that I hadn't realized I'd been craving. It feels safe here in DJ's arms, a feeling so unfamiliar that I almost can't name it at first.

And as I tumble into sleep, I can't help but think I'm getting far too used to this.

CHAPTER 19
SYDNEY

THE TANTALIZING AROMA OF FRESHLY BREWED COFFEE HITS MY nose, urging me awake. I blink open my eyes to see DJ's chiseled face gazing down at me, a steaming mug in his tattooed hands.

"Rise and shine, gorgeous," he says with a crooked smile that makes my heart stutter.

I sit up and gratefully take the mug, the heat seeping into my hands.

"You're a lifesaver," I say. "What time is it, anyway?"

"Early. I wanted to catch you before I had to head out. Game day." He leans in and presses a soft kiss to my forehead. "Sleep okay?"

"Mmm, very okay, thanks to a certain someone wearing me out last night," I tease, sipping the deliciously strong brew.

I don't know what I did to deserve to wake up to this perfect man bringing me coffee in bed, but I'm not questioning it.

"That's what I like to hear." DJ flashes a smug grin before flopping down next to me, careful to avoid jostling my mug.

Leaning back against the headboard he casually drapes an arm around my shoulders and I nestle instinctively into his side. His large, solid presence makes me feel warm and protected.

Cherished.

God, am I in trouble.

"Any big plans for today?" he asks, idly running his fingertips up and down my arm and raising goosebumps in their wake.

"Oh you know, the usual—catching up on paperwork, making sure the team has what they need to succeed, that sexy counselor life. If I've got the time, maybe a quick yoga class online before work." I snuggle against him, reveling in his earthy, masculine scent.

DJ chuckles. "Yoga, huh? Don't go getting too flexible without me."

"No promises. A girl's gotta stay limber." I wink at him over the rim of my mug.

"Is that so?" DJ plucks the coffee from my hands and sets it on the nightstand. Then he's rolling me beneath him, his athlete's body flexing as he cages me in. "Let's test that limberness some more, shall we?"

I loop my arms around his neck, drinking in his playful brown eyes and roguish smile. "I thought you had to get to game prep, hotshot?"

"I've got a few minutes." He ducks his head and brushes his

lips over the sensitive spot beneath my ear, making me shiver. "Besides, I'm the two-time MVP. They'll wait for me."

I'm about to give in, leaning in for a kiss when DJ says thoughtfully, "I hope everything's okay with Tyler."

"With—what?" The change in subject leaves me reeling.

"Oh yeah, I didn't tell you. He and I were going to tackle all that sushi last night, that's why I ordered so much. But he had some kind of family emergency." DJ's voice is tender, his eyes concerned. "I hope everything worked out okay."

Wait—Tyler was coming here? To DJ's apartment? Those were the plans that fell through last night?

My heart plummets into my stomach as the realization dawns: there's more between DJ and Tyler than I realized. Flirting and attraction, that's one thing, but it sounds like they're actually exploring a relationship—that Tyler's *letting* himself explore his attraction, which is a huge step.

Guilt crashes over me in unrelenting waves.

Oh god, what have I done?

Tyler trusted me, opened up to me about his feelings for DJ. The thought of him finding out about me and DJ, seeing it as the ultimate betrayal...it makes me physically ill.

"I...I have to go," I stammer, scrambling to my feet and fumbling for my clothes from last night. "I just remembered...an appointment. I totally forgot."

DJ frowns, rising to follow me to the door as I pull my cotton dress over my head with an unsteady jerk.

"Now? Are you sure?" He reaches for my hand but I yank it away.

"No, I really need to go. I'm sorry. This was...I shouldn't have..." The words stick in my throat. I flee for the door.

"Sydney, wait!" DJ calls after me, his voice laced with confusion. "Did I say something wrong? What's going on?"

But I'm already out the door, blinking back the hot tears pricking at my eyes. As I race down the hall, a silent vow echoes in my mind: *Never again.*

I'll never let myself be so weak, so selfish again. DJ and Tyler both deserve better than this.

Better than me.

I try to sneak into the apartment quietly, hoping Selena is either still asleep or already on her way to work, but of course her voice rings out from the living room as soon as the door clicks shut.

"Well, well, well, look what the cat dragged in!" She's sprawled on the couch in her favorite pink pajamas, a huge bowl of Lucky Charms balanced on her lap. The TV is paused on the opening credits of a housewives reality show. "And where have you been?"

I wince, guilt chewing at my insides. I was really hoping to avoid this conversation.

What kind of sister does that make me, that I don't want to tell Selena the details of my life? But I barely want to admit to myself what I've done...

Sighing, I trudge over and collapse on the other end of the

couch. "Morning. Thought you had work today?"

I reach over and steal a marshmallow from her cereal.

"Nope, day off! And just in time to catch you doing the walk of shame, it seems." She lifts her brows questioningly, her eyes dancing with delight. "Soooo, who's the lucky guy? Spill!"

"No one. I was just...out." I avoid her probing gaze, focusing intently on picking at a loose thread on the couch cushion.

"Uh huh, sure. And I'm the Queen of England." Selena rolls her eyes. "Come on Syd, we used to tell each other everything! What happened to twin telepathy?"

"Pretty sure that's not a real thing."

I force a chuckle, but it comes out strained. And just like that, awkwardness hangs thick in the air between us.

Things still aren't back to normal after everything with Paul, the way I basically ghosted her for years, barely returning her texts. Paul always told me Selena was controlling and overbearing, that I needed to get out from under the burden of my twin-sister identity and fend for myself.

Took me far too long to realize Selena wasn't the controlling one.

I clear my throat, hating the distance between us but unsure how to fix it.

"Anyway, it's nothing serious," I tell her. "Just blowing off some steam."

"If you say so..." She looks unconvinced but lets it drop with a shrug, unpausing her show. "Guess I'll have to live vicariously through Teresa's screaming matches instead."

I let out the breath I was holding, waiting for relief that I successfully avoided the conversation.

But as the moment to confide in Selena slips away, regret instantly washes over me. *Can I do anything right?*

"Well, I better get ready for work," I say, forcing a smile. "Duty calls."

"Okay, have a good day, sis," Selena replies, studying me with a hint of concern in her eyes. She can probably sense something is off, but thankfully doesn't press the issue.

I head to the bathroom and crank the shower as hot as it will go, desperate to scald away the guilt clinging to every inch of skin DJ's hands caressed last night. As the steaming spray hits my face, I squeeze my eyes shut.

What the hell am I doing?

Hooking up with one of the players—*twice*—is beyond unprofessional. Plus I totally betrayed Tyler's trust. I was the one encouraging him to explore his attraction to DJ. And now I'm sleeping with DJ behind his back?!

Enough, Sydney. Focus on work. This team is counting on you. No more slip-ups.

Easier said than done when my treacherous body still tingles with the memory of DJ's touch. I vigorously shampoo my hair, trying to wash him from my thoughts.

Needless to say, it doesn't work.

CHAPTER 20
DJ

I SIT ON THE BENCH IN THE LOCKER ROOM, METHODICALLY wrapping ice packs around my aching knee.

The sharp pain that flared up a few days ago has stayed at a manageable level thanks to my diligent recovery routine—rest and ice at every opportunity. Hell, I've even been avoiding any unnecessary strain during sex, though that thought makes me smirk to myself.

My mind drifts to flashes of last night with Sydney—the sultry look in her eyes as she undressed me, the silky touch of her hands on my body, the breathy moans escaping her lips...

"Yo DJ, what's good bro?"

Jason's voice snaps me out of the erotic reverie as he strolls into the locker room with a few other teammates.

I quickly rearrange my expression into an easy grin. "Oh you know, just the usual. Getting ready to dominate out there."

"Hell yeah, that's what I like to hear!" Gabe chimes in, clapping me on the shoulder. "But hey, you sure you're good, man? Saw you limping a bit at practice yesterday..."

The others exchange worried looks.

"Nah, I'm all good, just tweaked it a little. Nothing that'll slow me down," I assure them, flexing my leg for emphasis and taking care not to wince at the dull ache.

The last thing I need is the team knowing I'm hurting and making a big deal out of it.

"Alright, if you say so," Jason says, looking me over skeptically. "Just don't push it too hard out there."

I keep my voice light as I steer the conversation to safer territory. "No worries, I got this. Now let's focus on what really matters - we're gonna wipe the ice with the Kings today, yeah?"

The guys whoop and holler their agreement, and soon the locker room is a flurry of activity as everyone gets into game mode. I keep icing my knee while the usual pre-game rituals and pep talks swirl around me.

After 10 minutes, I unwrap my knee and slowly flex my leg, relieved to find that the movement produces nothing more than a dull throb. It'll have to do. With the crucial game against our biggest rivals coming up, I can't afford to let this injury hold me back.

Failure is not an option, especially not with so much on the line.

❄

From the moment the puck drops, energy buzzes through the arena, charged with bitter history: The Vortex aren't ranked well and yet beat us horrifically last time we matched up. The whole team is hungry to regain our pride by delivering a victory today.

I snag the puck and weave between two defenders, my skates carving the ice in decisive slashes. With a flick of my wrists, I send a crisp pass to Lukas streaking up the left side. He catches my feed in stride and snaps a wrist shot that beats their goalie over the blocker.

The red goal light ignites, and the crowd erupts as we take an early lead. *Damn, that felt good.*

I pump my fist and holler at Lukas, "Beauty, bro! Right where I wanted it!"

He grins back at me through his cage. "Put it on a platter, DJ! Keep 'em coming!"

The Vortex try to answer back immediately, coming in hot off the next faceoff. They gain the zone and their top winger rips a heavy one-timer, but Tyler slides post-to-post like a big cat, snagging the puck out of thin air.

A moment later, he kicks out the rebound of a point shot, staying big and square to the shooter. The puck deflects into the corner and we clear it out to relieve the pressure.

I feel a surge of pride watching my boy in his element, anticipating each play before it develops. *Dude's in straight beast mode.*

Not gonna lie, it puts some decidedly un-teammate-like thoughts in my head about what else those lightning reflexes might be good for...but I shut that down real quick.

Eyes on the prize, DJ. Plenty of time for scoring off the ice after we put this game away.

The clock ticks down, each second an eternity. Sweat drips into my eyes as I dart across the ice, my knee screaming in protest. But I can't stop now. Not when we're this close.

"Come on DJ, you got this!" Tyler yells from the goal, his voice cutting through the din of the arena.

I catch his eye and nod, a silent promise. Then I'm off, intercepting a sloppy pass from the Vortex's defenseman. The puck settles onto my stick like it was drawn by a magnet.

The eyes of the crowd are on me as I weave through the opposing players, their shouts fading into white noise.

One defenseman left to beat.

My knee twinges again, sharp and insistent.

Gritting my teeth, I push through the pain, juking left before cutting hard to the right. The defenseman bites on the fake, his momentum carrying him out of the play.

It's just me and the goalie now. I can see the whites of his eyes, wide with anticipation.

Time seems to slow as I wind up for the shot, the puck rocketing off my stick. It sails through the air, a black blur against the stark white of the ice.

The red goal light flashes. The horn sounds. Pandemonium erupts.

"FUCK YEAH!" Jason bellows, throwing his arms around

me as the rest of the team piles on. We're a tangle of limbs and laughter, adrenaline and elation coursing through our veins.

In that moment, nothing else matters. Not my aching knee, not the grueling schedule ahead. All that exists is the pure, unbridled joy of victory.

Amid the team huddle Tyler finds me, his hand lingering on my back a beat too long, and a different kind of heat blooms in my chest. Our eyes meet in the chaos, a charged look passing between us.

I lick my lips, tasting salt and anticipation.

Yeah, I know just how I want to celebrate this win.

After changing out of my skates, I realize that Tyler's nowhere to be seen in the raucous locker room. A man on a mission, I slip out discreetly and begin methodically checking all the spots he likes to frequent. And in the equipment room, there he is.

Alone, stripping off his pads. Our eyes lock and the air sizzles between us.

I don't hesitate. In two strides I'm on him, my hands grasping his face, my lips crashing into his. He groans into my mouth, kissing me back fiercely.

God, the taste of him. The heat. It makes my head swim.

We stumble backwards, a tangle of desperate limbs and roaming hands. I nip at his lower lip and he shudders. His fingers dig into my hips, pulling me closer. He's rock hard through his compression shorts.

Ty suddenly flips us around and shoves me against the wall. His eyes are molten with lust as he yanks my pants down.

Holy shit. Is he really going to...?

"I've never done this before," he rasps out. "But I want to. I want you on my tongue, DJ."

Then he's on his knees, mouthing me through my briefs. I let out a shaky exhale, my head thudding back against the wall.

Tyler Simmonds is about to suck my cock. The hottest goddamn goalie I've ever seen is on his knees for me.

He tugs my briefs down and I spring free. Ty looks up at me from under his lashes as he takes me in hand. The visual alone nearly does me in.

Then his perfect lips are wrapping around my tip and I swear I see stars. He starts bobbing his head, taking me deeper into his mouth each time.

"Shit, Ty," I groan, barely able to form the words. "So good, baby."

My hands slide into his hair, tugging lightly. He moans around my shaft, the sound vibrating straight to my core. For a first-timer, he's a fuckin' natural. Eagerly licking and sucking like he's starving for it.

For me.

Ty reaches up to roll my balls in his palm as he picks up speed. Hollowing his cheeks and swirling his tongue. It's sloppy and messy and incredible.

My orgasm builds, my abs clenching. I'm not going to last. Not with Tyler Simmonds worshiping my cock like it's his new religion.

Breathless, I gasp, "Ty, I—I'm close, man."

His eyes flick up to meet mine, lit with a wicked glint that says he knows exactly the power he holds right now. He doubles his efforts, drawing me even deeper.

Everything narrows down to just this: the pressure building, Ty's relentless mouth, and the ferocious need clawing at my insides.

It's almost too much—too intense—and yet, not nearly enough.

"Fuck, Tyler—" The words are a strangled moan as I hit my peak, my vision blurring. His grip on my hips is sure and strong, grounding me as I shudder through the climax.

There's a pause where the world stops spinning and all I can hear is my own ragged breathing. Slowly, Tyler eases back, letting me slip from his lips with almost reverent care. Eyes still locked on mine, he wipes his mouth with the back of his hand, a pleased look in his eye.

"It was alright?" he asks, a little self-conscious.

I draw him up to me for a rough, breath-stealing kiss, tasting myself on his lips.

"You're a goddamn prodigy," I mumble between kisses, my hands roaming over his broad shoulders and down the sinewy muscles of his back.

He responds with a low chuckle, pressing me back against the stacked crates of hockey equipment.

A sharp edge digs into my back, but the discomfort fades fast as Tyler's hands slip under my shirt, tracing the ridges of my sore muscles. The heat from his fingers burns my skin, igniting a fire that runs rampant through my veins.

"DJ," he murmurs against my neck, his breath hot and heavy. He bites down gently, and I can't help the moan that escapes me. My hands find their way to the top of his shorts as he continues to mark my skin with his lips and teeth.

"Your turn," I whisper against his ear, my voice hoarse with desire. Tyler grins, his eyes lighting up in anticipation.

He pulls back just enough to look at me, his hands still caressing my body as if they can't get enough. "Anything you want," he says, and there's a challenge in his tone that sends another jolt of arousal straight to my cock.

I spin us around, swapping our positions without breaking contact. He watches intently as I kneel in front of him, mimicking his earlier actions with deliberate slowness, yanking down his shorts and freeing him.

His breath catches in his throat, and the sound alone is nearly enough to drive me wild.

Looking up at him, I give him a sly smile before I take him into my mouth. Tyler lets out a low groan, his hands finding their way into my hair, guiding me deeper. I set a rhythm that has him gasping, teasing and taking in equal measure.

It doesn't take long for Tyler to be whispering my name, his hips bucking slightly as he struggles to keep control. I hum in satisfaction. *I've got him exactly where I want him.*

My tongue swirls around him, drawing out all the sounds I love to hear from those lips.

He tenses, his grip on my hair tighten. "DJ," he breathes out, a warning or an invitation—I take it as both.

"Come on, Ty," I coax, stroking him with my hand. "Let go for me."

And as soon as my mouth envelops him again he does. With a broken groan, Tyler's control snaps, and he surrenders to the sensation, his climax overtaking him in a delicious rush. Gradually, I ease him through his release before rising back to my full height and pulling him into another searing kiss.

His arms wrap around me tightly, nearly lifting me off the ground, before he pulls back to meet my eyes.

"That was unbelievable," he says softly, his gaze open and sincere. "You're unbelievable."

The words warm me more than any post-game shower could. We stand there for a moment longer, holding each other in the afterglow.

What a damn perfect day.

CHAPTER 21
DJ

I SINK ONTO MY COUCH, LETTING OUT A HEAVY SIGH. THE HIGH from last night's win has faded, replaced by a gnawing sense of unease in my gut that won't let up.

Tyler. Sydney. God, what am I doing?

I run my hands through my hair, unsettled by my intense turmoil.

My phone sits accusingly on the coffee table, the black screen reflecting my troubled expression. *I should call them. Explain.* But the words stick in my throat.

I'm DJ fuckin' Johnston, sex god. I should be the biggest poly advocate of them all. I'm the one who always preaches about honest communication.

And here I am, too chickenshit to pick up the phone.

I groan, flinging my head back against the cushions. *When did it get this deep?* It was supposed to be casual—some hot sex, a few laughs.

Not this ache in my chest whenever I think about hurting either of them.

I've royally fucked this one up. Ty and Syd are friends. If they compare notes, realize I've been less than upfront...I could lose them both. The thought makes my stomach drop.

"Fuck." The curse echoes in my empty apartment. I need to fix this. Time to practice what I preach.

I snatch up my phone, my thumb hovering over their contacts. *Who first?* My chest tightens. I care about them both so damn much.

In the end it's Slade's name I tap.

My leg jiggles restlessly as I listen to it ring. Once. Twice. It's enough to make me lose my nerve and I almost hang up, but then—

"DJ? What's up, man?"

I swallow hard. "Hey, Slade. You got a minute? There's something I want to talk to you about..."

I slump into the sticky booth, the smell of spilled beer and stale pretzels filling my nostrils. Slade peers at me from across the table, his brow furrowed with concern.

"Alright man, out with it. What's got you looking like someone pissed in your protein shake?"

I let out a long sigh. *Where to even begin?* "Ah, man, I got in way over my head..."

As I explain the situation with Syd and Ty, I'm relieved to

see that Slade doesn't seem too scandalized about the whole teammate/counselor element—or at least he's got a good poker face. But I can't read his expression as I conclude my dilemma.

"So anyway, I'm crazy into both of them but I haven't exactly been honest about the fact that I'm hooking up with both of them."

"Mmm." Slade takes a long swig of his IPA.

I grip my beer, the condensation slick against my palms. "Dude? Some advice?"

"Fuck, DJ." Slade shakes his head. "You know that keeping secrets never ends well. Trust me, I've been there before Emma and the guys."

"I know, I know." I huff irritably. "I just got so caught up in the excitement, and then I didn't want to scare them off, you know?"

"I get it, bro. But you gotta rip the bandaid off sooner rather than later."

I nod miserably. "So what do I do now? I'm terrified I've fucked up something amazing with both of them."

Slade rolls his eyes affectionately. "First off, breathe. It's not like you've had any define-the-relationship talks with either of them so far, right?"

I shake my head, a hopeful spark in my chest.

"Good. So there's still time to come clean. Just be honest—- tell them you're crazy about both of them but you don't do monogamy. See how they respond."

"But what if it's too much? What if I lose them both?" I can hear wavering desperation creeping into my voice.

Slade reaches over to grip my forearm bracingly. "You gotta have more faith in what you've built with them, man. If they really care for you, they'll at least hear you out. You're a catch. They'd be idiots to shut this down without a conversation."

I let out a long breath. Slade's right. I need to man up and lay it all out there, terrifying as it is.

"When did you get so wise about this shit?" I quirk an eyebrow at him.

Slade chuckles. "Lots of trial and error. This thing with Emma, Alex, Ryan and Lukas didn't fall into my lap. It took vulnerability, tough-ass conversations...and," he glowers meaningfully at me, "a fuckton of honest communication."

"Ugh, I get it, I get it," I groan dramatically.

Slade holds up his hands with a conciliatory look and then reaches for his beer. "To having the balls to put your heart on the line."

I clink my pint against his. "And to praying to god I don't get kicked in them."

Slade punches my shoulder and I let out a relieved laugh as we settle back and focus on draining our beers.

The night flies by, the air thick with the mixed aromas of greasy food and optimism—or maybe that's just my newly buoyed spirits. Slade's advice rings in my ears like a halftime pep talk and suddenly everything seems so simple.

I just need to be honest. Totally, utterly honest.

And what better way to do that than invite Sydney and Tyler over for a face-to-face showdown? Okay, not a showdown, but a reveal—all cards on the table.

I leave the bar feeling less like I'm walking to my car and more like I'm lacing up my skates for the most important game of the season. By the time I'm home, it's nearing midnight, but sleep is the last thing on my mind.

I pace back and forth across my living room, rehearsing lines that sound more like cheesy movie scripts than genuine conversation starters.

"Hey guys, so...I love fucking you both and—nope." I cringe at myself in the mirror hanging near my front door.

Too direct? Definitely. Fuck, how am I going to do this? Before I can spiral further into doubt, my phone buzzes in my hand—a text from Slade.

"Remember, just be YOU. That's who they fell for."

Fueled by Slade's midnight encouragement, I finally muster up the courage to send the texts. My thumbs hover over the screen, heart thumping against my ribs.

"Hey Syd, how about dinner at my place tomorrow? There's something important I'd like to talk about with you."

I send the same to Tyler.

There. Sent. The messages are out there, and now all I can do is wait for their replies.

My phone vibrates almost immediately. Sydney. Her response is simple yet nerve-wracking. "Sounds good, DJ. See you then."

And after an agonizing eternity, Tyler: "Sure thing, man."

Casual as ever, but my stomach twists knowing what's on the line.

There are so many ways this could go totally wrong.

CHAPTER 22
SYDNEY

I STAND OUTSIDE DJ'S APARTMENT, MY HEART HAMMERING against my ribcage like it's trying to make a jailbreak. I raise my fist to knock on the door but hesitate, my hand hovering in midair.

I've been dreading this ever since I got DJ's text inviting me over, impending doom sitting heavy in my gut.

Because I know what's coming. The big reveal about him and Tyler being together.

And where exactly that leaves me—alone on the sidelines, watching the two of them ride off into the sunset together.

I take a deep breath, steeling myself. *I can do this. I* have *to do this.*

DJ and Tyler deserve to have a chance at happiness together, no matter how much it hurts to step aside. Those stolen moments between DJ and I, those scorching hot hookups...they can't hold a candle to the years of history DJ has with his goalie.

I knew what I was getting into from the start.

Another deep breath. *In and out. You've got this, Syd*. With a burst of determination, I rap my knuckles against the door.

A few endless seconds later, it swings open to reveal DJ. His dark hair is perfectly tousled, his chiseled jaw dotted with just the right amount of scruff. He's shirtless, miles of tattooed muscles and smooth skin on display.

Hockey has been very, very good to him. I have to stop myself from openly ogling his godlike physique.

"Hey Syd," he greets me, a small smile tugging at his full lips. But I can see the unease in his brown eyes. "Come on in."

I step inside, my stomach churning with nerves. *This is it. The moment of truth.*

I open my mouth, the words I've rehearsed a hundred times poised on the tip of my tongue. But what comes out instead is:

"I know about you and Tyler. And it's okay. Really. I'm happy for you both."

DJ blinks at me, clearly taken aback. He runs a hand through his hair, mussing it further.

Damn him for looking so fucking good without even trying.

He looks down at the floor, a flush rising on his cheeks. "Syd, I...I don't know what to say. This thing with Ty, it's new. We're still figuring it out ourselves."

I nod, a lump forming in my throat.

"I get it, DJ. And I meant what I said - I'm happy for you. You guys clearly have something special." I square my shoulders. *This is what's best.* "I don't want to get in the way of that. So I'm going to step back, give you two some space to explore this."

DJ takes a step closer, his eyes stormy with regret. "Syd, no, that's not what I want. You're important to me too."

"I should go," I say firmly, turning to leave before I lose my nerve.

"Syd, wait—" DJ calls, just as the door opens again and Tyler walks through.

My eyes widen as Tyler steps inside, looking as surprised to see me as I am to see him. He's dressed casually in a faded Blizzards t-shirt and jeans, his dark blond hair still damp from a shower. Those piercing blue eyes of his flick between me and DJ, assessing the situation.

"Sydney. Hey." Tyler's voice is cautious, hesitant. He shuts the door behind him with a soft click.

DJ clears his throat. "I, uh, asked you both to come over. I think the three of us need to talk. But first… is anyone hungry?" He smiles weakly.

I take a sip of my wine, laughing at Tyler's story about the puppy he had growing up that ate his science fair project.

"The teacher didn't believe me even after my parents vouched for me!" Tyler chuckles.

"My childhood dog once got into my secret stash of Halloween candy," DJ says with a grin. Noticing our alarmed expressions, he hastily adds, "he was fine, puked everywhere before the chocolate made him too sick. But cleaning that up was not fun, and I got in trouble for hoarding."

"I always wanted a pet, but we moved around too much," I share wistfully, feeling a twinge of old longing.

DJ reaches over and squeezes my hand. "Well, maybe someday we can get a dog."

My heart skips at the casual domesticity of his comment. *Together?*

I'm saved from responding when DJ pops up to clear our dinner plates and grab the dessert he has prepped.

Tyler and I dig into the sinfully delicious flourless chocolate cake before us, and DJ clears his throat.

"So, uh, I have something to say to you both. And I'm not sure how it's going to go..."

Tyler and I exchange cautious glances.

"I'm poly," DJ continues. "Ethically non-monogamous."

"Okay..." I say slowly, absorbing the information. I knew that DJ was never tied down to any one person for long, but I didn't realize there was more to it than that.

Tyler's face is unreadable.

DJ clears his throat nervously. "That means I'm capable of having romantic feelings for multiple people at once. And right now, those people are you. Both of you."

DJ's brown eyes are earnest as they flick between me and Tyler.

"You...want to date both of us? At the same time?" Tyler clarifies, clearly thrown.

DJ nods. "I like you both. I'd like to keep exploring what we have, see where it goes. Together. But I'll understand if you're not up for that."

My mind is spinning. I suddenly feel like I'm teetering on the precipice of something big, something that could change my whole life.

Share DJ...with Tyler?

The idea is strange but oddly thrilling. A fresh start, totally different from what I had with Paul. Freedom to explore, to be myself, to be part of something new.

"I'm in," I hear myself say. DJ's face lights up. He turns to Tyler expectantly.

"Um. Wow." Tyler rubs the back of his neck. "I like you, man. And Syd, I mean, you're amazing, I respect you so much, I think you know that. But this is a lot. I think I need some time to wrap my head around it, y'know?"

"Of course, take all the time you need," DJ says reassuringly.

Under the table, his hand finds mine again and gives it a hopeful squeeze. I squeeze back, my pulse thrumming with nerves and excitement.

This is so not how I thought this conversation was going to go...not that I'm complaining.

Tyler rises from the table, those bulging biceps flexing as he stretches. "I should probably head out," he says, glancing towards the door.

DJ shoots Tyler a probing look. "I'll walk you out, man."

Tyler nods and meets DJ's intense gaze. Something heated sparks between them. I gulp, suddenly flushed. Avoiding their gaze as they walk towards the entryway, I give them a moment of privacy by bringing my wine glass into the living room and finding a comfortable seat on the couch.

Low murmurs drift in from the hallway, voices too quiet to make out. Then the talking stops, replaced by a loaded silence.

My imagination runs wild picturing what they might be doing out there. Tyler pressing DJ against the wall, their hard bodies aligned. DJ's hands fisting in Tyler's sandy hair as they kiss heatedly...

Oh god.

Arousal pools hot and heavy in my core and suddenly I can't resist. This whole night has been like a surreal dream and in one impulsive move, I wriggle out of my pants and kick them aside, pushing aside the thin lace of my panties with my fingers.

The first touch of my fingers against my aching clit has me biting back a moan. I stroke myself slowly, picturing these two gorgeous men—men that I've been attracted to both individually and together for a long while now, if I'm honest—making out right outside the door.

Just then DJ opens the door and steps inside, freezing when he sees me sprawled on the couch in just my top, my hands in my panties. His eyes widen for a second before a smirk spreads across his handsome face.

"And here I thought we already had dessert," he drawls. His gaze rakes over my curves appreciatively.

A flush spread across my skin under his heated stare. A thrill zings through me. I've never been this bold before, stripping right in someone's living room.

"I was waiting for you," I say, trying to sound seductive.

DJ stalks towards me, peeling off his shirt to reveal chiseled abs. "Is that so?" He kneels on the couch, hovering over me. "Lucky me."

I reach up and trail my fingers over the hard ridges of his stomach. *God, he's ripped.*

"I think we could both get lucky," I murmur brazenly.

He chuckles, a deep, masculine sound. "Oh, I like the way you think, gorgeous."

Then his mouth is on mine in a searing kiss. I moan against his lips as his tongue sweeps inside to tangle with mine. Large hands skim down my sides to grip my hips. I arch into his touch, my body already aching for more.

DJ kisses a path down my neck, teeth grazing my collarbone. I gasp as he nips at the top of my breast. Nimble fingers unclasp my bra and toss it aside.

"Beautiful," he rumbles, before lavishing attention on my newly bared skin.

I'm lost in a haze of sensation as his wicked mouth explores my body. My hands fist in his hair.

"Please," I whimper as he kisses lower, teasing the edge of my panties. I need him so badly it hurts.

He hooks his fingers in the lace and drags them down my legs. I kick them off impatiently. Then he's spreading my thighs, his hot breath fanning over my most sensitive parts. The first swipe of his tongue has me crying out.

DJ licks and sucks until I'm writhing beneath him. When he slides two fingers inside me, I nearly come undone. He pumps them in and out, curling them to hit that perfect spot as his lips close around my clit. The dual sensations send me flying over the edge.

I shatter with a hoarse cry.

He gentles me through the aftershocks before surging up to kiss me fiercely. I can taste myself on his tongue. I shove at his jeans and boxer briefs frantically, needing to feel all of him. He helps me strip off the rest of his clothes.

Then he's lifting me into his arms and lowering us to the plush rug in front of the couch. He settles over me, his hard length nestling between my thighs. I wrap my legs around his waist.

"Beg for me," DJ says roughly. His eyes burn into mine.

I whimper. "Please, DJ. I need your cock inside me. Please, I'll do anything."

With a groan, he thrusts forward, filling me in one smooth stroke. I gasp at the exquisite stretch. He pauses, letting me adjust. When I roll my hips, he starts to move.

He sets a deep, steady rhythm that has my eyes rolling back. I meet him thrust for thrust, our bodies moving in perfect sync. Pleasure builds and builds as he takes me higher.

I'm so close, teetering on the brink. "Don't stop," I pant.

He drives into me harder. "Never, baby. I'll give you everything you need."

A few more powerful thrusts and I'm flying apart, his name a euphoric scream on my lips. DJ follows me over with a guttural moan, his hot length pulsing deep inside me.

❄

Later that night, tangled in DJ's silk sheets, I lie there breathless and flushed. DJ dozes peacefully beside me, his chest rising and falling in a slow rhythm, but sleep eludes me.

My mind keeps drifting to Tyler, imagining his strong hands caressing my skin as DJ's talented lips trail fire down my neck.

A delicious shiver runs through me at the taboo thought, igniting a fresh tingle of arousal despite my satisfied exhaustion. I picture Tyler's intense eyes piercing into mine as DJ works his magic, the three of us joined in passion.

It's a desire that defies convention, but who says that means it can't work?

I know it's the unspoken connection between DJ, Tyler and I that makes what DJ and I share so electric. It's like a live wire, a current of mutual attraction binding the three of us together. Part of me longs to reach out and grab that connection with both hands, to fully embrace the freedom and exhilaration it promises.

But another part wonders if I'm really ready, this soon after Paul, to dive headfirst into something so deliciously complicated.

Sighing, I nestle closer to DJ, resting my head on his chiseled chest. The steady thump of his heartbeat soothes my racing thoughts. I gaze up at his handsome face, his full lips curved in a slight smile as he sleeps.

Maybe I'm overthinking it.

Maybe I should just enjoy this wild ride, no matter where it leads. For the first time in forever, I'm following my heart instead of my head. And right now, my heart wants DJ and Tyler.

Both of them.

CHAPTER 23
TYLER

I take a deep breath as I lace up my skates, trying to focus on the familiar ritual and push away the thoughts swirling in my head. Dinner with DJ and Sydney last night was...a lot. The idea DJ proposed—exploring something more, together, the three of us—it's intriguing but scary as hell.

I'm still wrapping my mind around being bi, and now this? *Fuck.*

I step out onto the ice, surprised to see Ryan already out there waiting for me. He gives me a knowing look, like he can see right through me. *Great.*

"Hey man, ready to get those legs pumping?" Ryan calls out, skating over.

"Always," I reply, falling into rhythm beside him as we start warm-up laps. "What's with the look?"

"What look?" He feigns innocence that I'm not buying but I'm all too happy to keep the conversation to a minimum.

We pick up speed, making tight turns around the goal posts. My mind keeps flashing to DJ's lips on mine, imagining Sydney joining us, her soft body pressed between our hard...

"Tyler!" Ryan's voice jolts me back to the present. "Get your head in the game, bro. Those posts aren't going to dodge themselves."

"Sorry, just...distracted," I mutter, focusing on my stride.

"This about DJ?" Ryan asks casually as we switch to suicides, sprinting back and forth.

My feet nearly tangle and I have to windmill my arms not to face-plant on the ice.

"What?" I sputter. "Why would you think that?"

"Dude, you've been drooling over him all season. Anyone with eyes can see it. And lately...seems like you guys are getting closer, that's all."

Thankfully the arrival of the rest of the team and Coach's whistle saves me from responding. We spend the next hour running drills—passing, shooting, checking.

But when we break for lunch, I know I'm not getting away that easy. Ryan suggests burritos and I agree, if only to get out of the locker room and away from DJ's curious, charged glances.

"So?" Ryan demands around a mouthful of carnitas as we sit tucked in a back booth. "What's going on with you and DJ?"

I push rice around my plate, hesitating. It's probably not the best idea to talk about this with another teammate, right? Sydney technically being the team counselor and all...

But I know Ryan won't judge me, and I do have a lot I need to sort out...

"He umm...he sort of asked me... totryadatingthingwithhimandSydney," I mumble.

Ryan's eyebrows shoot up in surprise. "Like a throuple? Damn." Then he grins. "Something in the water on this team."

I pause. I vaguely knew that Ryan was involved with a few other players and Emma, our newest coach, but I've never brought it up, unsure if it's cool to ask for details.

"Yeah..." I drop my fork, raking a hand through my hair. "It's a lot. I mean, I like them both so much but...I don't know, man. This polyamory thing is way outside my wheelhouse."

"I get it," Ryan says candidly. "When I first considered the poly thing, I felt so lost. It took me a while to really understand and accept that it could work for me."

"Really? I had no idea." Suddenly I don't feel so alone.

"Not exactly something I shouted about in the locker room," he shrugs. "But yeah, it's a journey. There's no roadmap."

His words strike a chord in me. My truth...maybe it's not the conventional white picket fence fantasy. Maybe it's messy and complicated and beautiful in its own way.

"I really care about DJ," I confess. "And Sydney, actually. Both of them. And I don't want to screw it up, hurt either of them."

"Then don't," Ryan says simply. "Talk to them. Be honest. It won't be easy, but the best things in life rarely are. You just have to decide if it's worth it to you."

Deep down, I already know my answer. DJ and Sydney bring me alive in ways I never imagined. *If there's even a chance...*

"Thanks man," I bump Ryan's fist. "I think I know what I need to do."

The next night, the cheers booming through the home arena thrum in my bones as we skate out onto the ice. This a crucial game, a game we have to win to keep our playoff hopes alive. The pressure would be crushing if I weren't getting used to it by this point.

DJ skates over and taps his stick against my pads with a friendly, uncomplicated smile. "You got this, Ty. Let's shut these fuckers down tonight."

I nod, his simple words filling me with confidence. "Damn right. They won't know what hit 'em."

The puck drops and the game is on, a frenzied back-and-forth right from the start. I'm lasered in, tracking every play, challenging shooters, kicking out pads to deny their scoring chances. We trade goals, neither team able to pull away.

By the second period, my legs are jelly but I dig deep, determined not to let the team down. Gabe slides to block a shot and when the rebound squirts free, I dive for the save.

But the puck sails just past my glove, hitting the back of the net with a devastating swish.

Dammit! I should have had that one.

Pissed at myself, my eyes dart across the ice to DJ, unconsciously seeking his reaction. But my mistake flies to the back of my mind when I see that DJ's unfocused, skating gingerly, his movements slightly awkward.

You wouldn't know it unless you knew the way he moved like I do—he's hiding it well—but I instantly realize something's wrong.

What's going on with him?

I try to ignore it, to get my head back into the game.

But as the clock ticks down in the second period, I can't stop glancing over at DJ, wondering if he's okay, if he'll be able to finish out this critical match. My mind isn't fully on the ice and it shows.

Another shot squeaks by me.

The opposing team whoops and high-fives and the crowd groans.

I slam my stick against the goalpost in frustration.

"Fuck!"

The self-doubt creeps in, an all-too-familiar voice. *You're just Adam's backup, in over your head. You'll never be as good as a real starting goalie. Never be the star your brother Steven is.*

The buzzer pierces through my spiraling thoughts, ending the disastrous second period. I skate to the bench, shoulders slumped, avoiding eye contact with my teammates.

In the locker room, I rip off my mask and collapse onto the bench, head in my hands.

"Simmonds!" Coach Daniels' gruff voice booms out. I look up to see him standing over me, arms crossed.

Here it comes, the tongue-lashing I deserve.

But his expression softens. He claps a meaty hand on my shoulder pad.

"Tyler, you're doing great out there. A few unlucky bounces, that's all. I've got full faith in you, kid. This team needs you. Now get your head on straight and finish strong, you hear?"

I nod, a lump in my throat. "Yes, Coach. I won't let you down."

"I know you won't." He gives my shoulder a final squeeze and strides off.

I take a deep breath, rolling my neck, shaking out my arms, and closing my eyes to get myself in the right headspace.

Coach is right. I've trained my whole life for this. I can do this. I *will* do this.

By the time I skate back out for the third period, a sense of calm determination has washed over me. I deflect shot after shot, my movements fluid and precise. The minutes tick down and we hang onto our narrow lead.

The final buzzer sounds and my teammates mob me, a mass of sweaty limbs and joyous shouts.

Over their heads, I see DJ beaming at me with pride, and something warm unfurls in my chest.

Like everything is finally clicking into place.

The locker room erupts in cheers and high fives as we clatter in, still high on adrenaline from our big win. The sweat soaking my jersey has begun to chill against my skin but I don't even care.

Playoffs are in reach.

"Yo, day off tomorrow! Where are we hitting up tonight to celebrate our win—and the fact that we don't have to wake up early?" Mikey hollers, toweling off his shaggy hair.

I lock eyes with DJ across the room.

The last time we all went out drinking as a team...well, things didn't go so well. DJ raises an eyebrow at me and it's clear we're both thinking the same thing: *we can't let that shitshow happen again.*

Someone needs to step in and derail this plan, and soon, because the team's enthusiasm is gaining momentum.

"Actually, I got an idea," DJ pipes up, his voice carrying over the rowdy chatter. "Let's do something where everyone can join, and we don't have to feel awkward about doing two separate things. Like dinner at a nice restaurant, call ahead, no booze at our tables. Keep it chill, you know?"

"Hell yeah, I'm down," I chime in. "Mad respect for our boys staying sober. We're a team, we stick together."

To my relief nods and words of agreement ripple through the group. Slade claps Tomas on the shoulder, and I see Jason aiming a grateful look at DJ.

"Means a lot, guys. Seriously," Tomas says gruffly.

"Then it's settled!" DJ grins at me, a spark in his eye. "Ty, wanna help me set it up?"

"For sure, bro." I match his grin, my stomach fluttering.

I might even find the stones to talk about his crazy proposal that's been playing on an endless loop in my mind—sharing him with Sydney. I bite my lip.

And maybe...we'll do more than just talk.

CHAPTER 24
SYDNEY

THE RESTAURANT PULSES WITH ENERGY, THE TEAM'S RAUCOUS laughter and animated conversation filling the air. Several large tables are pushed together to accommodate the boisterous crew, soda glasses clinking and fists bumping in celebration of their hard-fought victory.

I don't usually join team dinners, but Coach Daniels asked me to tag along tonight to keep an eye on everyone in a social setting since he wasn't going to be there. I feel a bit like a narc, but I can't lie that I'm thrilled to spend any extra time with DJ... and Tyler...

I weave my way between the tables, soaking in the atmosphere, and am pleased and gratified to see that nobody is drinking tonight.

What a meaningful show of support for my three patients.

"Syd!" Tomas waves me over, his grin wide and eyes bright.

"Did you see that goal I made? Thought the net was gonna rip off!"

I've been trying to attend as many of the home games as possible so the team sees that I'm supportive. I high-five him with a laugh.

"Legendary shot! They'll be showing that highlight for years."

"All thanks to my man Jase's sick pass," Tomas claps Jason on the back. "This guy's a magician on the ice."

Jason smirks, taking a swig of his soda. "Just doing my job, bro. But we all played our top games tonight. Helluva team effort."

I'm struck by the genuine camaraderie flowing between them, the way they prop each other up and share the glory, no hint of jealousy or one-upmanship. It's a far cry from the toxicity and distrust the team displayed when I first started this job.

Tomas leans in conspiratorially as I perch on the arm of his chair. "I gotta say, Syd, having you around has been huge for me and Jase. Knowing we've got someone in our corner, keeping us on track..." He glances at Jason, who nods emphatically. "Means more than you know."

A swell of warmth blooms in my chest. "I'm so proud of you both. Your strength, your commitment to your sobriety and each other—it's been inspiring to witness."

Scanning the rowdy tables, I can't help but notice one glaring absence: Mikey is nowhere to be seen. His sulky presence is impossible to miss, and a twinge of disappointment needles me. But I shake it off.

I'm here to celebrate with the team, and I won't let one patient's progress—or lack thereof—ruin the pride I have for the two who are doing so well.

The dimly lit restaurant pulses with laughter and chatter as I squeeze past the crowd of hulking hockey players to reach the booth where Slade and several other senior members of the team are holding court.

"Hey, look who decided to join the party!" Vincent calls out. He grins and pats the seat beside him. "Have a seat, Doc. We've got a smorgasbord of deep-fried delights here for your scientific analysis."

I laugh and slide into the booth, finding myself sandwiched between a group of imposing athletes.

The table before us is piled high with baskets of every type of fried appetizer imaginable—glistening mozzarella sticks, golden onion rings, crispy chips drizzled with cheese and bacon. The mingled scents of grease and spice and salt make my mouth water.

"As a member of this team's medical team, I have to advise against consuming this much saturated fat in one sitting," I deadpan.

Slade chuckles, a deep, rumbling sound. "Don't worry, we'll work it off at practice tomorrow. Besides, everyone knows post-game food has no calories. It's science." He winks at me conspiratorially.

"Is that so?" I arch an eyebrow. "Fascinating theory. I must have missed that class in med school."

Vincent nudges a basket of jalapeño poppers toward me.

"C'mon Doc, live a little! Let's see that discerning palate of yours in action. Rate these babies on a scale of one to orgasmic."

I snort inelegantly and pop a fried pepper in my mouth, the cream cheese and spice bursting on my tongue. "Mmm, not bad. I'll give it a seven—tasty, but not exactly mind-blowing."

"Tough critic!" Jason whistles. "What about these bad boys?" He waves a fried pickle spear enticingly.

I take a tentative bite and immediately wrinkle my nose. "Ugh, sorry, that's like, a two for me. I think pickles should remain in their natural, un-battered state."

The guys hoot with laughter at my reaction.

"See, this is why we need you around!" Slade grins, slinging a companionable arm around my shoulders. "To keep us in line and make those adorable disgusted faces."

I roll my eyes but can't fight back a smile. It's strange—with Paul, I always felt like I had to filter myself, to flatten my personality to avoid setting him off. But here, among this rowdy group of overgrown frat boys, I'm free to let my freak flag fly.

To banter and joke and just be authentically myself.

As if sensing the direction of my thoughts, Slade leans in closer, his voice lowering so only I can hear his next words.

"Seriously though, how are you doing with everything? We're all here for you, you know. If you ever need to talk..."

I stiffen slightly, suddenly exposed. *Does he know about the fragile, undefined thing developing between DJ, Tyler and me?*

I search Slade's face, but his expression remains casually friendly, inscrutable.

"I appreciate that," I say carefully. "You're all very sweet. I'm...figuring things out."

Our gazes remain locked for another moment as I try to discern what Slade knows. Then Jason cuts in, brandishing a tray of fried mac and cheese bites, and the spell is broken.

As the night winds down, the restaurant staff starts sweeping the floors and wiping the surrounding tables. The Blizzards linger over the remains of their fried feast, but gradually the group dwindles as players head home for the night.

I steal a glance across the room and catch Tyler's eye, his gaze smoldering with an intensity that sends shivers down my spine. All evening, there's been a magnetic orbit between Tyler, DJ and me—a pull drawing us together, even as we try to play it cool in front of the team.

Tyler makes his way over, shoulders set with determination. My pulse quickens.

After our dinner last week, I have no idea where his head is at. DJ's unusual proposal took me by surprise so I can only imagine how Tyler, who's also working to embrace a whole new element of his sexual identity right now, feels.

I swallow as Tyler slides in beside me. "How's it going, Doc?"

"Just enjoying the celebrations," I reply, trying for nonchalance even as Tyler's proximity sends my heart rate skyrocketing; his solid, muscular presence affects me just as much as ever, even with all the complications of our...situation. "How about you?"

A ghost of a smile tugs at his lips. "Same. Though I have to say, the view's gotten significantly better in the last few minutes." His eyes rake over me appreciatively.

My cheeks flush hot. *Damn, when did the shy goalie turn into such a smooth talker?*

"Is that so?" I tease, emboldened by the heated look in his eyes. "And here I thought you only had eyes for someone a little...taller than me."

Tyler throws his head back and laughs, his hand coming to rest lightly on my knee. "Only? Or also?"

A warm tingle spreads through me at his touch and I grin at his response. Hyper-aware of the weight and heat of his hand, I'm reminded of how connected I am to Tyler, how much I've come to care about him already in the brief time we've known one another.

"So how's your sister Leah doing? Last we talked, things were a bit rocky with her husband."

"Actually, they started couples therapy recently. Seems to be helping. Leah sounded more upbeat when we chatted the other day." Tyler's fingers trace idle patterns on my skin as he speaks.

"That's great, I'm glad they're working things out." I smile up at him, genuinely pleased to hear his family is doing well. I shift slightly so my bare leg presses against his under the table.

Tyler's eyes dart to my thigh and darken. He bites his lip. "Me too. Everyone deserves a chance at happiness, you know?"

All of the sudden it seems like he isn't talking about Leah anymore.

"Couldn't agree more," I murmur, pulse quickening.

In my peripheral vision, I catch sight of DJ across the room, his penetrating gaze locked on us. A delicious shiver runs through me, imagining him watching, wanting...

Unable to stop myself, I lean in closer to Tyler, letting my hand rest on his muscular forearm as I grin mischievously. "So, any other family updates? How are your parents enjoying retirement in Florida?"

We chat and laugh, the conversation light but our body language speaking volumes. I angle myself towards Tyler, running my fingers through my hair, savoring the sensation of DJ watching us.

To an outside observer, we're just two people engaged in friendly discussion.

But sexual energy is simmering between all three of us, building with every teasing touch and meaningful look.

God, it's such an illicit thrill, performing for DJ's viewing pleasure, wondering what filthy thoughts are running through his head...

Unable to keep his distance any longer, DJ strides over, his tall form towering over our booth. He braces a hand on the table, looming over us with a smirk.

"You two seem to be having all kinds of fun without me. What do you say we take this party back to my place?"

His gravelly voice drips with insinuation, full of dark promise. Tyler and I exchange a glance and I blush, wondering if Tyler realizes the show I've been putting on—or if he was putting on one of his own?

Because his eyes are bright and he replies instantly.

"I'm in."

CHAPTER 25
SYDNEY

THE RIDESHARE TO DJ'S PLACE IS FILLED WITH A LOADED SILENCE. DJ and Tyler sit on either side of me, our thighs brushing against one another's with each turn. My skin prickles with anticipation and pent-up desire.

I can't believe this is really happening.

It's surreal, like a heady dream—and I never want to wake up.

The moment we step through the door into DJ's sleek modern apartment, the tension that has been building all evening explodes. DJ pins me against the wall, his chiseled body pressed to mine as his lips claim my mouth in a searing kiss.

"I've been dying to do this all night," he murmurs huskily. His tattooed arms cage me in as his tongue delves deep, tasting me.

My mind goes deliciously blank, only aware of DJ's hard

muscles and Tyler's heated gaze on us. I moan into DJ's mouth, my body melting against his.

Tyler steps closer, his broad shoulders filling my vision. "Fuck, that's hot," he says, voice rough with want. "I want a turn."

DJ releases me with a cocky grin. "She's all yours, bro."

Then Tyler is on me, kissing me with a desperate hunger, large hands gripping my hips. I lean into him, fingers tangling in his sandy hair. He groans as I nip at his full bottom lip. His mouth is so right on mine. I can't believe it took us this long to kiss.

DJ steps up behind me, leaning in to nibble at my neck, and I moan into Tyler's mouth as he presses in for another kiss.

My mind a haze of desire, I dimly marvel at how perfectly the three of us fit together, like puzzle pieces finally snapping into place. DJ's deft fingers find the zipper of my skirt and tug it down slowly, his knuckles grazing my ass and legs and leaving trails of heat in their wake.

"God, you're stunning," he breathes reverently as the garment pools at my feet, leaving me in just my black silk top and panties. His brown eyes rake over me hungrily.

Tyler pulls back to drink in the sight as well, his Adam's apple bobbing as he swallows hard.

"So fucking gorgeous," he agrees, rough hands skimming my sides before moving up to cup my breasts.

I gasp as Tyler rubs the pads of his thumbs over my nipples through the delicate lace of my bra. They pebble instantly under his touch.

Not to be outdone, DJ drops to his knees behind me, kissing a path along the lacy edge of my panties.

"Bedroom. Now," DJ commands after a dizzying series of teasing, light touches. They maneuver me down the hall, stripping their clothes and the last of mine as we go until I'm laid out on DJ's king bed wearing nothing at all.

DJ slides a tattooed hand up my thigh, pushing apart my legs. "Damn, Syd. You're a fuckin' vision," he says reverently.

I flush at the raw need in his dark eyes. Tyler stretches out beside me, kisses along my throat, making me shiver.

"I can't believe this is happening," I gasp out.

DJ watches us both, eyes flaring with heat, as Tyler caresses my breasts again. Then DJ slides one hand to my already wet pussy, fingers delicately exploring—and when Tyler moans beside me, I realize DJ's other hand is wrapped around Tyler's cock.

My mind spins at the erotic sight of DJ stroking Tyler's impressive length. Tyler's eyes flutter shut in bliss as he thrusts into DJ's grip. I'm transfixed, heat pooling low in my belly. DJ's fingers continue to tease my slick folds, circling closer and closer to where I'm throbbing for his touch.

"Please," I whimper, arching my hips towards him.

DJ grins wickedly. "Please what, baby? Tell me what you want."

"Touch me," I beg. "I need you."

"Mmm, I love hearing you beg for it," DJ growls approvingly. He slides one long finger inside me, curling it to hit that perfect spot, making me cry out. "Fuck, you're so tight and wet."

His thick finger slides in and out, tweaking against my clit and then thrusting into me again and again as I moan incoherently.

Tyler leans down to capture my nipple in his hot mouth, swirling his tongue and sucking hard. The combined sensations make me writhe and gasp. DJ adds a second finger, pumping them in and out, his thumb rubbing tight circles on my clit.

The exquisite pleasure builds and builds until I'm right on the edge, my thighs trembling, DJ's skilled fingers driving into me relentlessly as Tyler nibbles and sucks at my breasts. It's almost too much stimulation to handle.

"That's it, baby, come for us," DJ urges huskily, brown eyes blazing into mine.

His words send me flying apart, my back arching off the bed as ecstasy crashes through me in wave after wave of pure bliss. I cry out their names, seeing stars behind my eyelids.

DJ works me through it, drawing out my climax until I collapse back against the sheets. He slides his fingers out of my fluttering pussy and brings them to his lips, licking them clean with a low groan of satisfaction.

"Goddamn, you taste incredible," he rasps. "I could get addicted to this sweet pussy."

Tyler lifts his head from my chest, lips swollen and hair mussed. "My turn," he says roughly.

He kisses his way down my body, settling between my splayed thighs. The first swipe of Tyler's tongue through my sensitive folds has me gasping and fisting my hands in his hair.

He licks a long, slow stripe up to my clit before swirling his tongue around the aching bud.

"Oh God, Ty," I moan brokenly, my hips rocking up to meet his hungry mouth. He consumes me like a starving man, lips and tongue and even a hint of teeth driving me wild.

DJ kneels on the bed, one hand lazily stroking his thick cock as he watches Tyler devour me.

"Fuck, that's the hottest thing I've ever seen," DJ says, voice gravelly with lust. "Look at him eating your pretty pussy, Syd. He can't get enough."

Tyler groans against my core, the vibrations making me gasp. He seals his lips around my clit and sucks hard, making my thighs quake. Fuck, Tyler's mouth is pure magic, shooting sparks of pleasure through my veins.

I'm already so worked up from before that it doesn't take long until I'm hurtling towards another peak.

My moans echo around DJ's bedroom as Tyler's tongue drives me closer and closer to the brink. He alternates between swirling around my swollen clit and thrusting deep into my core, fucking me with his tongue. My fingers twist in his hair, holding him right where I need him most.

"That's it, Ty, make our girl come again," DJ urges, his deep voice sending shivers down my spine. He's still kneeling beside us, slowly pumping his fist over his shaft as he watches. The erotic sight combined with Tyler's relentless licking and sucking pushes me over the edge.

I shatter with a hoarse cry, my second orgasm ripping through me even more intensely than the first. Tyler doesn't let up, prolonging my pleasure as I shake and tremble beneath his wickedly talented mouth. He laps up my release like he can't get enough, groaning appreciatively.

"Fuck, Sydney, you're so goddamn sexy when you come," DJ says roughly. "I need to be inside you, now."

Tyler releases me with one final lick, his blue eyes hazy with desire as he turns to look at DJ.

DJ moves to take Tyler's place between my trembling thighs, one hand guiding his thick cock to my entrance. He teases the head through my slick folds, making me whimper with need.

"Please, DJ, I need you," I pant, reaching for him.

With a low growl, he sinks into me, stretching and filling me so perfectly that my toes curl. "Fuck, baby, you feel incredible," DJ groans, bottoming out. "So fucking tight and wet, just for us."

He sets a deep, driving rhythm, hips snapping against mine. I cling to his tattooed shoulders, nails digging into his skin as he pounds into me. The drag of his hard cock against my sensitive walls is divine.

Tyler stretches out beside me again, capturing my lips in a blazing kiss. I moan into his mouth as he twines our tongues together, swallowing down the little cries DJ is fucking out of me with each relentless thrust.

DJ changes the angle slightly and I see stars, a high-pitched keen escaping my throat.

"Oh fuck, right there," I gasp out, my back arching as DJ hits that perfect spot inside me over and over. The coil of tension in my core winds tighter and tighter, my body straining towards release.

"You gonna come on my cock, Syd?" DJ grunts, thrusting his hips faster. "Want this sweet pussy to squeeze me tight as you let go."

His filthy words combined with Tyler's wet lips and tongue trailing along my neck send me flying. I come apart with a wordless cry, my inner walls clamping down on DJ's thick length as ecstasy crashes over me. He groans deeply, continuing to pump into my pulsating heat, drawing out my climax.

Tyler reaches down to circle my clit gently with his fingers and I nearly scream, the added stimulation almost painful in its intensity. But he keeps the pressure light, helping me ride out the waves of pleasure until I collapse back against the sheets, thoroughly satisfied.

DJ's rhythm starts to falter as I flutter around him, his face tight with concentration. "Fuck, I'm gonna come," he warns breathlessly.

"Yes, do it, fill me up," I urge, clenching my inner muscles around him. "Come inside me, DJ."

With a guttural groan, DJ slams into me one last time, burying himself to the hilt. His cock twitches and pulses as he spills himself deep within my core, his release triggering after-shocks of pleasure that make me tremble and gasp.

"Fuck, Syd," he pants, resting his forehead against mine. "That was unreal."

He kisses me deeply before carefully pulling out and flopping onto his back beside me. I feel the loss of him immediately, my body already missing being so thoroughly filled.

And moments later Tyler takes DJ's place, his blue eyes blazing with lust and need as he hovers over me. "I have to have you, Syd. I can't wait another second. Can I?"

"Yes, please, Ty," I breathe, spreading my legs in wanton invitation. The idea of Tyler fucking DJ's release deeper into me is so wickedly erotic.

He notches himself at my entrance and surges forward, sliding in easily through the combination of my arousal and DJ's cum. We both groan at the sensation, Tyler's thick length stretching me in the most delicious way. He's huge inside of me, aided by how sensitive I am from DJ's thorough fucking.

"God, Syd, you take my cock so well," Tyler grunts as he bottoms out inside me. "Love how slick and messy you are, all full of DJ's cum. Fuck, that's so hot."

"Yes, fuck me, Ty," I moan shamelessly, hooking my legs around his trim waist.

Tyler sets a relentless pace, driving into me hard and deep. The wet squelch of him moving through DJ's release is downright filthy and I can't get enough. Knowing they've both claimed me, marked me, is the most arousing thing I've ever experienced.

"That's it, squeeze my dick just like that," Tyler growls, hammering into me faster.

DJ props himself up on one elbow beside us on the bed, watching intently as Tyler fucks me. He reaches out to thumb at my clit and my back arches off the bed, the extra stimulation sending lightning bolts of pleasure zinging through my body.

I'm reduced to pure sensation as the two men I've been dreaming about for months break me down. Tyler's thick length dragging over my sensitive walls, DJ's fingers dancing on my clit—it's the most exquisite sensory overload.

Tyler leans down to capture my lips in a bruising kiss, his tongue delving deep to tangle with mine. I cling to his strong shoulders, fingernails digging into taut muscle as his hips piston faster.

"I'm gonna come, Syd," he pants against my mouth.

My pussy clenches tight around his cock at his words. "Yes, Ty, come in me too," I urge breathlessly, inner muscles squeezing him. "Fill me up."

"Fuck, Syd!" Tyler cries out, slamming into me one final time before his release overtakes him. His thick length pulses and twitches deep inside me as he spills himself with a low groan.

The sensation triggers my own climax and I shatter beneath him yet again, my vision whiting out as ecstasy washes through me in dizzying waves.

DJ's fingers stroke me through it, dragging out my pleasure until I'm boneless, trembling with aftershocks. Tyler collapses on top of me, his weight a delicious blanket I never want to take off. We lay there tangled together, hearts pounding, slick skin cooling, just basking in the afterglow.

Eventually, Tyler rolls off and I whimper at the loss, empty without him in me, on top of me. But then DJ is there, gathering me into his inked arms and pulling me to lay across his chest.

Tyler curls up around us, wrapping a strong arm around my waist and nuzzling into my neck. I snuggle between their warm, solid bodies. DJ's heartbeat is steady beneath my cheek, his fingertips tracing idle patterns on my shoulder.

I turn my head to meet Tyler's lips in a sweet, lingering kiss, almost unable to believe how right this all feels. How comfortable, how natural.

This is something I never could have imagined exploring with Paul, a level of intimacy and trust that I never thought possible.

In the arms of these two incredible men, I'm seen and cherished in a way I never have been before, the entirety of myself laid bare.

Can it really be this easy?

CHAPTER 26
DJ

MY EYES BLINK OPEN AND I LAY STILL FOR A MOMENT, SAVORING the sweet ache of satisfied muscles and the comforting weight of Tyler and Sydney on either side of me. Memories of last night, of tangled limbs and breathy moans and ecstatic pleasure, bring a grin to my face.

I turn my head to admire the sight.

Tyler's sandy hair is adorably mussed, his chiseled chest rising and falling evenly in deep slumber. Sydney's raven locks are splayed across the pillow, her lush curves pressed against me deliciously.

God, they're beautiful. How did I get so lucky?

My life has always been hockey and hookups. No strings, no complications. Catch feelings? No thanks. But this, right here...it's different somehow. Like pieces clicking into place. Like I've stumbled into something real without even meaning to.

Careful not to wake them, I prop myself up on one elbow to get a better view.

The sheet has slipped down to Sydney's waist and my fingers itch to trace the dip of her spine, to skim over the smooth swell of her hip. Tyler makes a soft sound and nuzzles into the pillow, biceps flexing. I swallow hard.

Waking up to the two of them...a guy could get used to it. But what does it mean?

We haven't put any labels on this thing between us. Haven't made any promises. The last thing I want to do is screw it up by overthinking or pushing for more than they're ready for.

I'm not even sure what *I'm* ready for.

Still, I can't ignore the contentment humming through my veins, the sensation of rightness, of home. For the first time, the idea of belonging to someone—or someone*s*—doesn't make me want to bolt. It's exhilarating and terrifying all at once.

Sydney stirs, interrupting my musings. Her eyelids flutter and she looks up to face me with a sleepy smile that makes my heart thud against my ribs.

"Mmmm...morning," she purrs.

"Morning, gorgeous." I tenderly brush a lock of hair from her cheek, marveling at how precious such a simple gesture feels with her. "Sleep well?"

"Very." Her hand skims across my abs and her smile turns wicked. "Though not much actual sleeping happened, as I recall."

I catch her hand and bring it to my lips, grazing her knuckles with a kiss. "Any regrets?"

"None," she says firmly, her eyes soft and sincere. "You?"

I shake my head, throat suddenly tight with emotion. "Definitely not."

On my other side, Tyler rolls over and flings an arm across my waist. "Why're you two awake?" he grumbles without opening his eyes. "It's too early for talking."

"Sorry, sleepyhead," I murmur, running a hand over his shoulder. "How can I make it up to you? Hmmm….how about a lazy morning in bed, then decadent breakfast at this killer diner I know? They serve it all day, so no rush..."

Before I can even finish the thought, Tyler is rolling me onto my back and capturing my lips in a fierce kiss. His hands roam possessively over me as Sydney watches us.

"Fuck, that's hot," she murmurs.

Not wanting her to be left out, I scoot in closer to her, trailing open-mouthed kisses along the elegant line of Sydney's neck as Tyler's hands move to her breasts.

She arches into our touch with a breathy moan.

"Ah! You boys are insatiable," she gasps, eyes sparkling with arousal.

"Can you blame me?" I ask huskily. "Just looking at you two gives me all sorts of naughty ideas….in fact, Sydney, you like me telling you what to do, right?" She blushes and nods. A rakish grin spreads across my face. "Good. I'll be in charge again—of both of you."

Tyler's eyes go wide and he swallows hard. "Shit, DJ, that's...I wouldn't guess I would find that so fucking hot but...yeah. Tell me what to do."

I smirk, loving this new side of Tyler. *Cocky, dominating DJ: activated.*

"You got it, babe." Then I drop my voice, letting it grow rough. "Both of you, lie down."

They scramble to obey, spreading their bodies out before me like an offering; Tyler's all golden skin and taut muscle, Syd's a masterpiece of soft, generous curves. My eyes rake over them hungrily.

I take a moment to appreciate the sight, letting my gaze linger on every delicious inch of exposed skin.

"Fuck, you two are a work of art," I growl.

I turn to Sydney first, capturing her lips in a demanding kiss that leaves her breathless.

"Syd, I want you to put on a little show for us. Touch yourself, nice and slow. Let us see how much you're aching for it."

Her eyes darken with lust and she obediently trails a hand down her body, teasing over her breasts before dipping between her thighs. She parts her legs, giving us a tantalizing view as her fingers start to circle her clit.

"Like this?" she pants.

"Just like that, gorgeous. Tyler, doesn't she look delicious? I bet you want a taste, don't you?"

Tyler nods eagerly, his cock already standing at full attention. "Fuck yes. Please, DJ..."

"Go on then, put that tongue to work. Make her come for us."

He doesn't need to be told twice. Tyler settles between Sydney's thighs, replacing her fingers with his talented mouth.

She lets out a keening moan, hands clenched in his hair as he laps at her eagerly.

"That's it, Ty. Just like that," I encourage huskily, palming my own aching erection as I watch them. The sight of his tousled blond head moving between her thighs, her back arching off the bed in ecstasy...it's the hottest thing I've ever seen. "Fuck, you two are so fucking sexy together."

Sydney is panting now, her cries filling the room as Tyler works her over with lips and tongue and deft fingers. He knows just how to drive her wild, alternating between teasing licks and firmer strokes. Her thighs start to tremble, a telltale sign that she's getting close.

"Don't let her come yet," I command, voice harsh. "Make her wait for it."

Tyler obeys instantly, easing off and lifting his head. His chin is slick with her arousal and it takes every ounce of my willpower not to tackle him to the bed and have my wicked way with him. But I'm not done playing with them both.

"Please DJ, I need to come so badly," Sydney whimpers, desperation coloring her voice. Her hands clutch at the sheets, hips circling restlessly as she chases the release Tyler denied her.

I tsk at her gently, even as my own cock throbs in sympathy.

"Patience, babe. I promise it'll be worth the wait." Turning to Tyler, I crook a finger at him. "Come here, you. Let me have a taste."

He crawls up the bed eagerly and I yank him into a filthy kiss, plundering his mouth and groaning at the taste of Sydney on his tongue. "Mmm, delicious. Though I think I need to sample it from the source, don't you?"

Tyler's eyes are glazed with lust as he nods. I maneuver us so that he's propped up against the headboard with Sydney draped over his lap, her back to his chest. She gasps as the movement causes his erection to slide between her cheeks.

"Ty, be a good boy and keep her nice and spread open for me," I instruct. He reaches around to hook his hands behind her knees, pulling them back and exposing her glistening pussy to me.

She looks like a goddess splayed out for me like this, all soft skin and tempting curves. I can't resist leaning in to run my tongue along her slit, savoring her sweet musk.

"Oh god, DJ!" Sydney cries out, head falling back against Tyler's shoulder as I lave her sensitive flesh.

I take my time exploring her, alternating between broad strokes and teasing flicks, dipping inside to taste her essence before returning to circle her clit. She writhes between us, caught between the dual pleasures of my mouth and Tyler's hard length pressing insistently against her backside.

"Look at you, so desperate for it," I murmur against her heated skin. "You love having both of us worship this sweet pussy, don't you Syd?"

"Yes!" she sobs as I suckle her clit. "Please, I need...ah!"

"I know what you need, gorgeous." Sliding two fingers into her hot channel, I pump them slowly, curling to brush that sensitive spot inside. She keens, moving her hips in an attempt to force herself deeper onto my fingers. "Ty, pin her down."

Tyler's hands clamp down on Sydney's thighs, holding her open and immobile as I work her over mercilessly with lips and tongue and fingers. She thrashes between us, completely at our mercy, a litany of broken pleas falling from her lips.

"Please, please...I'm so close...need to come so badly..."

I redouble my efforts, tongue flicking rapidly over her clit as I thrust my fingers deep. Her body goes taut as a bowstring, inner muscles clenching down on me in fluttering pulses. *She's right on the edge, just needs one little push...*

With a final hard suck to her clit, I send her over the threshold. Sydney comes with a hoarse cry, back bowing, juices flooding my mouth as bliss jolts through her. I lap it all up greedily, prolonging her peak until she's limp and panting.

"Fuck, that was so hot," Tyler groans, his rigid cock still nestled between her ass cheeks. "Watching you make her fall apart like that...god damn."

I crawl up their bodies to capture his mouth, letting him taste Sydney's pleasure on my tongue this time. "You were so good for me, both of you. Now I was thinking..."

I pause and relish the way they both look at me, expectant.

"Maybe we should get cleaned up?"

I walk over to the door to my en suite, where the massive modern shower awaits.

I glance back over my shoulder with a roguish grin. "Well? You two coming or what?"

Sydney and Tyler scramble off the bed eagerly, following me into the luxurious bathroom. I turn on the multiple shower-heads, steam quickly filling the glass enclosure.

"After you," I say, ushering them in with a playful smack to each of their delectable asses. They yelp and laugh, retaliating by pulling me under the warm spray with them.

Water sluices over our bodies as we take turns soaping each other up, hands roaming and teasing. Tyler captures Sydney's lips in a deep kiss and I press against her back, my reawakened erection sliding between her slick cheeks.

She moans into Tyler's mouth, one hand reaching back to grip my hip.

"Insatiable, remember?" I growl in her ear before nipping at the sensitive lobe. She shudders between us, already needy again despite the intense orgasm I just gave her.

"We've created a monster," Tyler jokes breathlessly as he kneads her breasts, rolling the pebbled nipples between his fingers.

"Time for me to take care of you two," Sydney coos, playfully pulling away from us and taking each of our cocks in hand.

Sydney strokes us slowly, her grip slick and firm under the cascading water. Tyler and I both groan, pressing into her touch. My head falls back against the cool tile as she works us over with knowing hands, the dual sensations of the warm spray and her skillful caresses driving me crazy.

"Fuck, Syd, yes," I pant, hips rocking into her fist. Beside me, Tyler is in a similar state, eyes heavy-lidded with pleasure as she pumps his thick length.

"Mmm, you two are so hard for me already," Sydney purrs

sultrily. "I wonder what I should do with these big, aching cocks..."

She sinks gracefully to her knees, the steamy water plastering her dark hair to her neck and breasts. Keeping her grip on our shafts, she leans forward to lick a bead of precum from my tip. I shudder, barely suppressing the urge to thrust into her hot little mouth.

Sydney smirks up at me before turning to lap at Tyler's crown, tonguing his slit. He curses under his breath, fingers tangling in her wet hair. She takes him into her mouth, sucking and slurping noisily, making a show of it.

The sight of her plump lips stretched around him, cheeks hollowed as she bobs up and down his length, is almost too much for me to take.

"Syd, baby..." Tyler groans brokenly. His head thunks back against the tile wall, abs tensing as she takes him deep.

She releases, only to swivel and engulf me instead. I hiss out a breath as her warm mouth surrounds me. Her tongue swirls around my tip before she sinks down, relaxing her throat to take more of me in.

It's exquisite torture, the suction and pressure and heat taking me right to the brink of my control.

"Fuck, just like that, gorgeous," I growl, fighting the desire to buck into her face. She hums around me and the vibrations nearly send me over the edge.

Sydney pulls off and sits back on her heels, water sluicing over her devastating curves. Her lips are swollen and shiny with spit, eyes dark with lust.

"So responsive," she murmurs approvingly.

Stroking us both, Sydney smirks mischievously.

"Now I have an idea. Why don't you boys put on a little show for me together?"

Tyler and I exchange heated glances, instantly on board with her naughty suggestion. I reach out and yank him to me, capturing his mouth in a hard, domineering kiss. He groans into it, hands roaming greedily over my slick skin.

Without breaking the kiss, I walk us backwards until Tyler's shoulders hit the tile wall. Aligning our hips, I take both our straining erections in hand, gripping them together. We both gasp at the electric slide of hard, hot flesh.

"Fuck, DJ," Tyler pants against my lips. "Feels so good."

I start to thrust, our cocks gliding together deliciously as the warm water pours over us. Tyler matches my rhythm, strong hands gripping my ass to pull me closer.

"God, that's hot," Sydney moans from where she's still kneeling and watching avidly. Her own hand has slipped between her thighs to circle her clit. "You two are so fucking sexy together."

I groan into Tyler's mouth at Sydney's words, our kiss turning even more heated and desperate. The knowledge that she's touching herself while watching us rutting together is almost too much to handle. Tension coils tighter and tighter in my groin, balls drawing up close to my body.

"Fuck, Ty, I'm close," I grit out, my hips snapping faster. The wet glide of our cocks is exquisite, the pressure and friction making control impossible.

"Me too," he gasps. "God DJ, want to come all over you…"

"Do it," Sydney urges breathlessly. I glance over to see her fingers moving frantically between her legs, her arousal ratcheting even higher at the sight of us so close to the edge. "Come for me, both of you. I want to see you lose it."

That's all it takes. With a guttural moan, I pulse hot and hard over our fists and Tyler's abs. A second later he's joining me, his release mixing with mine as we stroke each other through the intense climax.

"So fucking hot," Sydney pants. Her thighs clench around her hand as she reaches her own peak, crying out as pleasure sparks through her. The sight and sound of her coming undone prolongs my own orgasm, tremors wracking my body well after the initial peak.

Tyler and I slump against each other, panting, the water washing away the evidence of our passion. He drops his forehead to my shoulder, hands gentling their grip on my hips.

"Christ, that was intense," he murmurs, nuzzling my neck. "Watching Sydney get herself off to us…"

"I know," I rasp. "So fucking sexy. This woman will be the death of us, just watch."

Sydney rises gracefully to her feet, a satisfied smirk playing about her lips as she takes in the sight of Tyler and I still tangled together, pleasantly dazed in the aftermath of our mind-blowing releases. She steps closer and trails a teasing hand down each of our chests.

"Well, that was quite the show, boys," she says with approval. "I think I could get used to waking up like this."

Tyler huffs a laugh and reaches out to pull her into our embrace, sandwiching her between our slick, heated bodies.

"Mmm, you and me both, beautiful. DJ definitely knows how to start the day off right."

I just smile to myself as I finish rinsing off, feeling smug and sated and so damn lucky to have these two incredible people in my arms, in my bed, in my life.

CHAPTER 27
SYDNEY

I WAKE UP SQUIRMING AND BREATHLESS, MY HEART POUNDING AS the steamy details of my latest dream linger in my mind. *DJ's smoldering gaze as he slid his hands up my thighs, Tyler's lips trailing hot kisses down my neck...*

God, it felt so real.

It's not a total surprise. My dreams the past few days have been...very realistic. Ever since that night with Tyler and DJ, it's like my subconscious can't stop rehashing every moment of our time together.

I roll over and check my phone, seeing a string of flirty texts from the boys that immediately bring a grin to my face.

DJ: "Morning gorgeous. Can't stop thinking about the way you taste..."

Tyler: "The other night was unreal, though, seriously. Round 2 tonight?"

DJ: "Calm down stud, let's win this game tomorrow and get

into the playoffs first....can't be staying up all night right before a big game."

Tyler: "Fine, but don't be surprised if I find you in the locker room later."

I can't help but giggle at their boldness. It's like they've awoken this wild, insatiable side of me that I never even knew existed.

Part of me still can't believe this is really happening—that I'm really hooking up with not one, but two incredible, sexy hockey players.

I fire off some playful responses before reluctantly dragging myself out of bed to get ready for another day of trying to keep the Blizzards in line. My cheeks flush—that makes me think of the naughty things DJ whispered in my ear about "punishing" any bad behavior...

Focus, Syd.

After throwing on a pencil skirt and silky blouse, I grab my bag and float down the hall on a cloud of bliss, stopping to grab a yogurt from the kitchen.

When I close the fridge door I nearly shriek at the sight of Selena sitting at the table behind it, nursing a mug of coffee. Her amused smirk deepens at my surprise.

"Looks like someone's a little distracted this morning," she teases, eyeing my disheveled hair and probably the dopey grin I can't seem to wipe off my face. "C'mon, you're practically glowing. Who's the lucky guy?"

I grab a mug and pour myself some coffee, taking a moment to savor the rich aroma before joining her. My cheeks heat as flashes of the past few days replay in my mind—*hands caressing bare skin, breathless moans, the exquisite push and pull of three bodies moving as one...*

I shake my head to clear the erotic montage.

"It's, um, a bit complicated actually," I hedge, sipping my coffee to hide my flustered expression. But Selena knows me too well.

"Ooh, I sense juicy details! Come on, you can't hold out on me now. I want the whole steamy story." She waggles her eyebrows suggestively. "You're my twin, you owe me this!"

I sigh, knowing resistance is futile when Selena has that gleam in her eye.

"Okay, fine. But you have to promise not to judge me."

"Cross my heart. Now give me the goods, woman!"

I take a fortifying breath. "I'm kind of...seeing two guys on the team. Together. And they're also seeing each other." I peek over at her, bracing for her reaction.

Selena blinks for a moment, processing. Then she throws her head back and laughs, loud and uninhibited.

"You're in a throuple? Oh my god, Syd, that's the last thing I ever thought you'd say! What is it about that team and polyamory!?"

Selena's laughter slowly subsides as she fixes me with a genuine smile.

"Seriously though, I'm so happy for you," she says. "It's about damn time you let yourself have some fun after everything you've been through. If getting sandwiched between two hunky hockey players is what puts that spring in your step, then you do you, boo!"

I flush crimson, nearly choking on my coffee.

"Selena!" I sputter. "It's not just about the sex. I mean, don't get me wrong, that part is…unreal. But DJ and Tyler…they're amazing guys, inside and out."

I fiddle with my mug, a soft smile playing on my lips as I think about how attentive and caring they've been, both as friends and now as lovers.

"They make me feel special. Safe. Like I can finally be myself again after walking on eggshells for so long with Paul."

Selena reaches across the table to squeeze my hand, her expression sobering. "Oh honey, I'm so glad to hear that. You deserve to be treated like a queen after putting up with that asshole's crap." Her gaze grows pointed and protective.

"I know I do." I squeeze her hand back, feeling a surge of gratitude for my ride-or-die sister. "And you know what? I think I'm finally starting to believe that myself."

Selena grins, her eyes twinkling with mischief once more. "Atta girl! Embrace your inner goddess."

She's still chuckling as I head out the door for work. I shake my head, her unwavering support only widening the smile on my face.

For the first time in a long time…I'm happy.

❄

My day starts off like any other—I have a great session with Jason, who is all smiles lately. Then one of the team members shows up unplanned to talk through his stress and learn some new coping strategies.

After lunch, though, I drum my fingers on my desk, glancing at the clock for the hundredth time in five minutes.

Mikey is late for our session, a disturbing reminder of our early days. I've been sitting here for 20 minutes already and—I check again—there's no email from him, nothing to say that he's on his way or even that he won't be able to make the appointment.

Just as I'm about to send him a text, he barrels through the door, disheveled and scowling.

"Nice of you to join me, finally," I say evenly, taking in his bloodshot eyes and rumpled clothes. *It can't be...is he using right now?*

He slumps into the chair across from me, mouth twisting into a sneer. "Don't give me that condescending therapy bull-shit, Sydney. I know what you really are."

My stomach clenches. I force myself to meet his glare head-on. "And what is that, exactly?"

"A slut who spreads her legs for any pro athlete who looks her way. God, I can't believe I ever took you seriously as a counselor. What a joke."

His words slice through me like razors.

I grip the edge of my desk, knuckles turning white, willing myself not to flinch. *How dare he speak to me this way, belittle my credentials, my profession, everything I've worked for?*

Tears prick the back of my eyes but I blink them back furiously.

"Mikey, you're out of line." My voice wavers and I curse myself for it. "If you're not here for a productive session, then—"

"Oh, I bet you want to be real productive, huh? Get on your knees and suck my—"

"Get out!" The words burst out of me, my whole body shaking with rage and humiliation. "Get the hell out of my office, now!"

Mikey shoots to his feet, kicking over the chair as he does. "With fucking pleasure. Have fun whoring yourself out, bitch."

The door slams behind him like a gunshot. I sink back in my chair, burying my face in trembling hands.

Oh god. Oh god oh god oh god.

Sobs burn my throat as hot tears finally spill over, smearing my mascara.

How could he treat me like that? Call me those vile things? I search my spinning thoughts, trying to pinpoint where I went wrong, how I failed him as a therapist.

The glazed look in his eyes, the slurring...he had to be high or drunk or both. And I couldn't get through to him, couldn't do my damn job.

Failure.

The word pulses in my head like a migraine.

Whore. Failure. Slut. Worthless.

It's too much. I need to get out of here, away from this place that suddenly feels tainted.

Grabbing my purse with numb fingers, I stumble out to my car, not even bothering to lock up behind me. Sobs wrack my body the whole drive home until I'm hiccupping and snotty.

Pathetic.

The first thing I do when I get to my apartment is peel off my clothes and jump in a scalding shower, trying to wash the shame from my skin. It doesn't work. Afterwards, I pull on my fuzziest plaid pajamas and crawl onto the couch, queuing up some brainless reality show on my laptop.

I need to disappear for a while, to forget the sting of Mikey's accusations and the ruins of my self-worth scattered at my feet.

Hours later I'm crumpled on the couch, the screen of my laptop frozen where I've paused the episode of a vapid luxury real estate show, unable to focus on the drama. My eyes are puffy and sore from crying, my throat raw.

Mikey's cruel words keep echoing in my head, an endless, taunting loop.

The sound of the door opening and footsteps walking inside makes me jump, my heart leaping into my throat. Oh god, is Selena back with her latest date? I can't handle making small talk tonight.

I sink farther into the couch and tug the blanket up over my head, hoping they'll just pass me by in the dark.

"Syd? Why are you hiding here in the dark?"

Embarrassed, I lower the blanket to see Selena and Emma

settling down onto the couch on either side of me, their faces etched with concern.

"I'm fine," I choke out, pushing the hair out of my face and sitting up straighter. "Just a rough day at work, that's all."

Emma raises an eyebrow. "Bullshit. What's going on?"

I shake my head, clamping my mouth shut as more tears threaten to fall. *I can't burden them with this.*

But Selena reaches out and squeezes my hand. "Syd, come on. It's us. We're here for you, no matter what."

Her gentle touch breaks my resolve. The words start pouring out of me like a waterfall.

"It's Mikey. That asshole rookie I told you about. He...he called me a slut today. And a whore. Somehow he knows about me and DJ and Tyler, I guess."

Emma sucks in a sharp breath, her eyes narrowing. "He did not."

I nod miserably. "It was so humiliating. And it brought up all this shit from—from what happened with Paul."

Selena's jaw tightens at the mention of my douchebag ex. "That fucker. I swear, if I ever see him again—"

"It's not even about him," I interject. "Not really. It's just...god, maybe Mikey's right. Maybe I am a slut for being with the guys. Maybe I'm not cut out for this job if I can't even keep my hands off the hockey players. And not even just one of them!"

"Listen to me," Emma says fiercely, leaning in. "There is nothing wrong with loving multiple people. I would know." She smirks, lightening the mood. "Dating pro athletes isn't easy, trust me. Everyone thinks they get to have an opinion on your sex life. But screw them."

"Damn straight," Selena chimes in. "You're amazing at what you do, Syd. What happened with Paul...that kind of shit messes you up. It takes time to heal. Be patient with yourself. Don't let some little drunk prick make you doubt yourself."

I let their words wash over me like a soothing balm. Emma and Selena always know exactly what to say.

I may be a mess, but at least I have my sister and my best friend to pick me back up.

"You're right," I say finally, squaring my shoulders and taking a deep breath. "I'm done letting Mikey walk all over me. First thing Monday, I'm going to Coach Daniels and making a plan for an official intervention. We need to set some firm guidelines and warn Mikey about consequences. This kind of behavior is unacceptable."

"That's our girl," Emma grins, and walks to the fridge to grab a bottle of white from the door. "And speaking of interventions...I think this calls for a glass of wine."

I hiss at her bad joke and move to jokingly swat her but she dances out of my reach.

Thank god for the girls. As Emma pours wine and Selena launches into a hilarious story about her latest Tinder disaster, the knot in my chest starts to loosen.

CHAPTER 28
TYLER

THE ARENA LIGHTS GLARE DOWN ON THE ICE AS I TAKE MY position between the pipes, my skates digging in and head bowed for a moment of focus before the puck drops. The din of the opposing team's crowd washes over me in waves, adding to the weight of expectation hanging heavy in the air.

This is it—the final key game before playoffs.

The Blizzards need this win to progress or our whole season goes down the drain.

I block out the noise and zero in on the ice as the ref blows the starting whistle. The puck skitters back and forth, blades flashing. Axel snags it, weaving between defenders with that unreal agility of his. He passes to Griff, who winds up for a slapshot. I hold my breath but the goalie snags it from the air.

Close one.

The puck bounces back into play and the battle continues.

Minutes tick by and the score stays stubbornly tied. My

nerves crank tighter with each rush at the goal. I lunge left and right, batting away shots, but one almost sneaks by, pinging off the goalpost.

Too close. Can't let them score.

The pressure mounts and doubt creeps in, the tension coiling in my gut. I can practically hear my brother Steven's voice in my head, mocking me, telling me I'm going to choke like always.

DJ shouts encouragement from down the ice as if he can hear my thoughts. "Keep it up, Ty! We've got this!"

I meet his eyes briefly, drawing strength from his unflinching confidence in me and the team. I shake off the negative thoughts, my grip tightening on my stick. We've worked too damn hard to let it all slip away now.

But I can feel the doubts edging their way back in as the puck comes down the ice towards me.

I grit my teeth and brace myself as the puck hurtles towards me, my glove hand shooting out to snatch it from the air. *Not this time.*

The rubber disc slams into my palm with a satisfying thwack.

"Nice save, Ty!" DJ shouts, flashing me a grin. I nod back, trying to stay focused. Can't let my mind wander, not even for a second.

The first intermission can't come soon enough.

The locker room is all nervous energy, guys pacing and muttering as Coach lays into us about playing tighter defense. I sit in my stall, head hanging, replaying that close call over and over.

DJ plops down next to me, our shoulders brushing. His warmth seeps through my pads.

"You're killing it out there, Ty," he murmurs, bumping his knee against mine. "Don't let the pressure mess with your head. Trust your instincts."

I blow out a breath, trying to absorb his easy confidence. "Easier said than done. If I mess this up..."

He grabs my shoulder, forcing me to meet his gaze, his brown eyes unusually warm. "You won't."

His faith wraps around me like armor and I sit up straighter, some of the tension draining away. "Thanks, man. I needed that."

"Anytime." His hand lingers a beat longer than necessary before he stands. "Now let's get back out there and kick some ass."

The second period is a blur of close calls and near misses. We're scrambling, the other team smelling blood in the water. They pepper me with shots but I hold the line, DJ's words ringing in my ears.

Trust my instincts. Be the rock.

The clock winds down toward the second intermission and we're locked in a 1-1 stalemate. Exhaustion weighs on me like a lead blanket. My reactions slow a fraction.

And that's all it takes.

The forward winds up and fires a rocket from the point. I lunge...but I'm a heartbeat too late.

PING! The puck ricochets off the post and in, the goal light flashing red. *Failure.*

Devastated, I crumple to my knees as the crowd erupts in cheers, their triumphant roars salt in the wound.

Skating to the bench for the second intermission, I can't meet my teammates' eyes. The air crackles with barely contained anger and disappointment. *They trusted me...and I blew it.*

Slumping onto the bench, I stare at the floor, shame burning my face. Someone taps my pads.

"Hey. Chin up, kid," DJ says softly. "It's just one goal. We'll get it back."

I swallow hard and nod, but the lump in my throat remains. All I want to do is hide from the crushing weight of my failure. But I can't. I'm the goalie—there's nowhere to run. I have to suck it up, stuff down the hot sting of tears, and find a way to finish this game.

The final buzzer sounds and the Blizzards squeak out a 5-4 victory, no thanks to my lackluster performance in goal tonight. I skate off the ice with my head hung low, feeling the disappointment like a lead weight in my stomach.

As I make my way to the locker room, I spot a familiar face in the hallway.

Steven.

What the hell is he doing here? He never comes to my games. I plaster on a fake smile as we hug.

"Hey bro, surprised to see you here," I say, trying to sound upbeat.

"Had to see my little brother starting in goal for myself," he says, giving me an assessing look. I've been starting for most of the season but of course Steven chose *tonight* to swing by and judge me, a game where everything was on the line. "Let's grab some food and catch up."

We end up at a nearby sports bar, burgers and beers in front of us. I can already tell this isn't going to be a pleasant brotherly chat by the critical look in Steven's eyes.

"So how's it going, moving into the big leagues?" he asks, taking a swig of his IPA.

I shrug. "It's a big adjustment, a lot of pressure. But I'm working my ass off."

Steven snorts in amusement. "You might want to step it up. You looked like a fucking rookie flailing around out there. At this rate, you'll be warming the bench again in no time."

His words hit me like a punch to the gut. I stare down at my plate, appetite gone. "I let in a couple bad goals, I know. I'm still adapting to—"

"Save the excuses," Steven cuts me off. "Words aren't worth shit in hockey. You either perform or you're out. And tonight, you sure as hell didn't perform."

I feel my face flushing with embarrassment and frustration. Getting reamed out by Coach is one thing, but by my own brother? The brother I've always looked up to, wanted to emulate?

"If you're gonna make it in the pros, you need to be lights out, every single night," Steven continues. "No room for fuck-ups or off games. Goalies are the backbone of any team. You lose your edge, you're disposable."

I sit in miserable silence, each word from him chipping away at my already shaky confidence. He's only saying what I've been thinking myself.

That I don't have what it takes.

That I'll never live up to his legacy.

Steven was a first round recruit straight out of college and did five years in Denver before an injury cut his career short. He's ten years older than me, which made him old enough to idolize, and also far enough in age that we were never close.

He used to come criticize my high school hockey games when he was a pro. I've spent every year since then chasing his approval, eager to show him that I can be just as good of a player as he was.

"Guess I should be grateful I even made it this far," I mutter, more to myself than him.

"Damn right you should. It takes a hell of a lot more than just talent."

I know he's right, but I resent the way he says it—like I'm the runt of the litter, perpetually destined to fall short. The sting of inadequacy settles in my chest as I force down the rest of my burger.

This night can't end soon enough. I stare down into my beer, looking for answers I know I won't find.

All I want to do is go home, crawl into bed, and forget this whole humiliating day.

I trudge down the dimly lit hallway of my apartment building, my muscles aching, shoulders slumped under the weight of defeat. The only sound is the soft scuff of my shoes against the worn carpet. As I round the corner, I stop short.

DJ and Sydney stand outside my door like two gorgeous sentinels, mirrored concern on their faces.

"Hey, Ty," Sydney says softly, reaching out to touch my arm. "Are you okay?"

I force a smile. "Yeah, I'm fine. Just tired."

DJ frowns, unconvinced. "Bro, I saw your face after those goals went in. You're beating yourself up, aren't you?"

"Nah, it's all good," I lie, avoiding his probing gaze.

Sydney pulls me into a hug, enveloping me in her jasmine scent.

"It's not your fault, Tyler," she says. "The whole team was off tonight."

"She's right," DJ agrees, wrapping his tattooed arms around us both. "You're an amazing goalie. A few bad goals doesn't change that."

I want to believe them, but the tight knot in my chest won't unclench. The phantom red goal lights flash behind my eyes.

"I don't know," I mutter. "Maybe I'm just not cut out for this."

"Hey!" DJ grips my shoulders, forcing me to meet his eyes. "That's bullshit and you know it. You're Tyler fucking Simmonds. You're the wall, remember?"

I manage a weak chuckle at our old inside joke. "Some wall I am, letting pucks through like a sieve."

"Stop that," Sydney chides gently. "You're human, Ty. You're allowed to have off nights." She cups my cheek, her brown eyes luminous with affection.

I sigh, leaning into her touch despite myself. My body craves their comfort, even as my mind rebels against it.

"I just feel like I let everyone down, you know? The team, the coaches, the fans..." I swallow hard. "You guys."

"You could never let us down," DJ says fiercely. He presses a kiss to my temple, his lips lingering.

Sydney nods, rising on tiptoe to brush her mouth against mine. "We're here for you, always. You're stuck with us, hotshot. Now...are you going to let us into your place or what?"

"Much as this hallway has its charms," DJ quips, "it could sure use a bunch more soft furniture for what I have in mind..."

A real smile tugs at my lips, even as exhaustion pulls at my eyelids. "Thanks, guys. I totally would invite you in...next time. I think I just need to crash, try to sleep this off."

They exchange a worried glance but don't push any further, each giving me one last squeeze before stepping back.

"Call us if you need anything, okay?" Sydney says. "Even if it's just to talk."

"Or not talk, if you know what I mean," DJ adds with a wink.

I snort. "I'll keep that in mind. Night, guys."

I close the door behind me with a heavy click. The apartment seems cavernous, empty. I strip off my suit, not bothering with the lights, and fall into bed.

But sleep eludes me. I stare at the dark ceiling, the game playing over and over in my mind's eye like a grotesque highlight reel. Every goal, every missed save, every disappointed face in the crowd.

My chest constricts, breath coming short and sharp. *How can I face them again? My team, my coaches, my fans?*

I close my eyes, trying to summon the feeling of DJ and Syd's embrace. But all I can see is the puck sliding past me, the red light glaring.

Failure.

With a groan, I roll over and bury my face in the pillow.

CHAPTER 29
DJ

I'M PRACTICALLY WEARING A PATH INTO THE POLISHED HARDWOOD floor of Slade's sprawling living room, my sneakers squeaking in protest with every agitated stride. This house reeks of good taste and even better paychecks—high ceilings with crown molding, state-of-the-art technology, endless plush couches that are begging for lazy days, and art on the walls that I'm damn sure didn't come from a thrift store.

"DJ, if you keep pacing like that, you're gonna drill a hole straight to China," Emma teases from her cozy nest of throw pillows, not bothering to look up from her tablet.

"Sorry, Em," I mutter, pausing to flash her a grin. She's the kind of girl who can pull off bedhead and PJs like it's high fashion, and right now, she's all Sunday morning ease with her hair in a messy bun and a steaming mug of something caffeinated on the table beside her.

"Got your jockstrap in a twist over Ty?" Ryan asks, poking

his head out from the kitchen, where he's probably pilfering someone else's snacks. Guy's got an appetite that could rival a bear pre-hibernation.

"Something like that," I admit, scrubbing a hand through my hair.

Slade lounges in a leather armchair like it's his throne, his grey-blue eyes sharp and assessing.

"Just spit it out," Slade commands, but there's a warmth there that says he's already halfway to my corner.

"Tyler's a mess, man," I start, throwing my hands out, tattoos stretching with the motion. "The guy won't stop beating himself up over the last game. I mean, we clinched our spot, and he's acting like he single-handedly tanked our chances."

Slade nods, the corners of his mouth pulling down. "He puts too much pressure on himself."

"Exactly." I flop down onto the opposite chair, my body language broadcasting frustration. "You know how he gets—like he's trying to shoulder a mountain or something."

"Okay, so what do we do about it?" Slade leans forward, elbows on his knees, looking every inch the captain ready to lead us out of rough waters.

"Distraction. He needs something to take his mind off the ice," I suggest, hoping the vague idea blossoms from there.

"Like a group outing? Just the guys, no hockey talk allowed?" he offers, tapping a rhythm on his thigh that suggests he's already plotting the guest list.

"Perfect. And maybe...throw in some friendly competition? Something stupid and fun without any stakes, like laser tag."

My lips quirk up at the thought of Tyler decked out in neon gear having a blast, momentarily free from his self-inflicted goalie's guilt.

"Or paintball," Slade fires back, a mischievous glint lighting up his eyes. "Nothing bonds a team like colorful bruises."

"Genius." I can't help but laugh. "It's settled then. Operation Distract Tyler is a go."

"Operation Keep Our Goalie Sane," Slade corrects with a smirk, and I have to agree—it does have a better ring to it.

"Alright, let's get this planned, captain," I say, feeling the band of tension in my chest begin to loosen. With Slade on board, Tyler doesn't stand a chance against this impending morale rescue mission.

"Time to blow off some steam, boys!" Slade announces the next day as we pile out of our cars in front of a local paintball arena.

The place looks like a freaking war zone—inflatable bunkers, stacks of tires, wire spools, and camo netting everywhere. I grin. A little friendly competition and adrenaline is just what the doctor ordered.

We suit up in camo jumpsuits and protective masks. Tyler and I exchange a knowing glance as we strap on our gear, hands brushing.

My pulse races and it's not just from the impending paintball battle.

"I call DJ!" Jason yells. "No way I'm letting that bastard snipe me again."

"In your dreams, Jace. I'm sticking with my boy Ty, you'll never see us coming." I slap Tyler on the back, letting my hand drift lower than strictly necessary. He flashes me a crooked grin.

We break into two teams and disperse to opposite ends of the arena. As smaller groups splinter off to strategize, Tyler discreetly pulls me behind a stack of crates.

"So what's the play?" he asks teasingly, those baby blues boring into me.

I swallow hard. "Uh, Jason and Slade are the biggest threats. Let's try to take them out first. You hang back, pick 'em off from a distance. I'll draw their fire."

"Draw their fire, huh?" He steps closer, crowding into my space and lowering his voice. "You sure that's a good idea with your bum knee?" He studies my face, something like worry in his eyes.

Concern spikes through me. *He doesn't know it's hurting again, does he?*

"Wow, you really know how to sweet talk a guy," I deadpan, keeping my voice intentionally light. "My knee is fine. It's sweet of you to worry though, babe."

Tyler rolls his eyes but I catch his smile at the endearment. "If you say so. Don't come crying to me when you're limping later."

"Oh, I can think of a few other reasons I might be limping..." I joke, moving to slide my fingers up his chest.

He shoves me, blushing. "Dude! The guys are right there."

I drop my arm, chuckling. "Relax, they can't see us. But you're right, we should focus. Let's light these mofos up." I clack my paintball gun for emphasis and Ty's face splits into a wide grin.

The whistle blows and chaos erupts. Paint splatters the bunkers in streaks of neon, shouts echo across the arena. I duck and weave, trying to draw the opposing team's attention. A paintball whizzes past my ear. *Too close.*

I spot Jason crouched behind a stack of tires. *Gotcha.* I line up my shot, exhale, and—

Whap! A paintball explodes across Jason's chest.

Behind me, Tyler whoops. "Sit down, son!"

We fall into an easy rhythm, moving in sync. He lays down cover fire while I advance. Slowly, we pick off the others until it's just Slade left standing.

"Where is he?" Tyler hisses.

"No clue. Tricky bastard." A paintball pings off the bunker by my head and I flinch. "Shit!"

"You okay?"

"Yeah, just startled me." I risk a peek around the edge of the bunker, scanning for any sign of Slade. Nothing. *Dammit.*

"I'm gonna make a run for that SUV. Cover me."

Tyler frowns. "DJ, wait—"

But I'm already off, zig-zagging toward a rusted-out SUV in the middle of the arena. Paintballs splatter the ground at my feet. *Almost there.* I dive for cover...

And collide with a warm, solid mass. Slade grins down at me, paintball gun leveled at my chest. "Gotcha."

We stare at each other for a breathless moment...then crack up laughing.

"Man, I really thought I had you!" I wheeze.

"That's why I'm the captain," he says smugly. "Better luck next time, rook."

The whistle blows, signaling the end of the match. I'm still grinning as we exit the arena, riding high on endorphins and camaraderie. The guys are ragging on each other good-naturedly, all jokes and easy rapport.

Even Tyler looks relaxed, a genuine smile stretching across his face. *Damn, he's beautiful.*

I take a little longer than necessary stripping out of my jumpsuit in the locker room. Tyler notices, his eyes tracking my movements as I peel the sweat-soaked fabric off my skin. When I head for the bathroom, he follows.

As soon as the door swings shut behind us, he crowds me against it, claiming my mouth in a passionate kiss. I moan into it, my hands roving the hard planes of his back.

He tastes like adrenaline and desire, a heady cocktail.

"Been wanting to do that all day," he murmurs against my lips.

"Kiss me? You didn't want to shoot me?" I joke breathlessly.

"Bit of both, honestly," he quips with a wry grin. "You're a pain in the ass, but God, you're hot as fuck. Especially in camo."

I drag him back in for another kiss, licking into his mouth.

He groans, hands sliding down to palm my ass. Things are just starting to get interesting when—

"Yo, you guys fall in or what?" Jason's voice rings out.

We spring apart.

"Uh, just finishing up!" Tyler calls, his voice strangled.

"I wish!" I hiss to him in frustration, and he shushes me.

I press my forehead to his, both of us shaking with barely suppressed laughter.

"To be continued," I promise in a whisper.

He nips at my bottom lip. "Count on it."

With one last stolen kiss, we disentangle and exit the bathroom. The thrill of almost getting caught simmers under my skin. I know it's a risk but damn if it doesn't make it even hotter. As we rejoin the group, I catch Tyler's eye, a secret little smile playing about his lips.

Oh yeah. I'm in trouble.

The next day, I frown as I look out onto the ice, the cold air chilling my lungs as I take a deep breath. But the energy in the rink is anything but refreshing today. Tension crackles in the air like static electricity as the team runs through drills.

Mikey slams into Jonesy, our big defenseman, with way more force than necessary. "Watch where you're going, asshole!" Mikey barks.

Jonesy whirls around, eyes flashing. "Me? You're the one who came in late on that play, dickwad."

They square off, facemasks nearly touching as they jaw at each other. I skate over quickly, Slade right beside me. We muscle our way between them, pushing them apart.

"Enough!" Slade roars, using his Captain Voice. "We're a team, for fuck's sake. Act like it!"

Mikey and Jonesy keep glaring but stand down.

I shake my head in disgust. *So much for us coming together after that shitshow in Canada. Fragile egos and testosterone, man.*

We resume drills but it's a disaster. Passes going wild, guys not communicating. I keep my eye on Tyler in the net and what I see only makes my heart sink.

He looks shaky, fighting the puck, body language defeated. *Damn, I hate seeing him like this.* I really thought he was in a better headspace after yesterday's excursion.

After practice ends, I hustle to catch up to Ty as he stalks off the ice.

"Hey man, wait up! You wanna grab a protein shake, talk it out?" I reach for his shoulder.

Tyler flinches away from my touch, and I'm surprised by how much the rejection stings. "Nah, I gotta jet. Got stuff to do," he mumbles, not meeting my eyes.

"Ty, c'mon..." Desperate to get through to him, I lean closer. "Don't shut me out, babe. Let me be here for you."

For a second he melts into me and I'm relieved, thinking he's let me in. But then he tenses again.

"I can't, DJ. I just...I can't right now." He ducks under my arm and practically sprints away.

"Fuck!" I spin and smash my fist into a locker, putting a sizeable dent in the metal. Pain explodes in my knuckles but I barely even notice. *What the hell was that?*

I flex my bloodied hand, examining it idly as my mind works in overdrive. This thing between me and Ty...it's too important to let some macho hockey bullshit torpedo it. But how do I get that through his thick, beautiful skull?

I slump down onto the bench and cradle my head in my hands. One way or another, I need to make Tyler understand what he means to me.

That I'm here for him, for us. Even if it means confronting shit he'd rather avoid.

Because Tyler Simmonds is worth fighting for, and I'm not about to give up now.

CHAPTER 30
SYDNEY

I GLANCE AT THE CLOCK AS ETHAN FINALLY STRIDES OUT OF MY office, his lanky form disappearing down the hallway. 5:47 PM. *Shoot, there goes my plan to hit the gym before heading home.*

I'm only two days into this week and it's already been totally brutal, back-to-back sessions and meetings with barely a second for myself. It also started badly, with me having to tell Coach Daniels about Mikey's progress–or lack thereof–and the way he talked to me at our last session.

Coach was pretty disturbed by the whole thing. We've been in extra meetings all week putting together a performance and behavior plan.

With a sigh, I start shoving files into my bag. These long days are really doing a number on my energy levels.

A knock sounds at the door. I look up to see Jamie poking his head in, his boyish face creased with worry.

"Hey Syd, you got a minute?"

I plaster on an encouraging smile.

"Of course, come on in." I gesture to the chair across from my desk as I sit back down. "What's on your mind?"

He settles into the seat, hands clasped tightly. "I just can't shake the bad vibes of that last game, you know? I mean, we won, but even now...the energy on the ice feels so hostile. And the guys...everyone seems on edge."

I nod, leaning forward. "That's totally understandable. High-pressure situations can really amp up emotions and adrenaline."

"Yeah, I guess. I'm just not used to feeling so anxious about my performance, or everyone else's." He runs a hand through his dark curls, agitated.

"Well, let's talk through some de-stressing techniques. Have you tried any mindfulness or breathing exercises?" I suggest. His skeptical look makes me chuckle. "I know, I know, it can feel a little woo-woo at first. But studies show..."

We spend the next twenty minutes going over various relaxation methods - progressive muscle relaxation, guided imagery, the works. By the end, Jamie looks noticeably more at ease, his shoulders no longer up by his ears.

"Thanks Syd, I think those will really help," he says earnestly as he stands to leave.

"Anytime. My door is always open." I give him an encouraging grin as he departs.

No sooner has Jamie vacated the doorway than Lukas appears, his hulking defenseman frame making the room feel instantly smaller. *Oh boy, here we go again.*

"Hey Sydney, I was hoping I'd catch you," he says, an uncharacteristic vulnerability in his usually confident voice.

I stifle my exhaustion, waving him in. "Well, you're in luck. What's up?"

As he starts unloading about his anxiety over his slipping performance stats, the weight of the job presses down on me. *Player after player, worry after worry...I'm starting to feel like a sponge that's soaked up all it can hold.*

I glance longingly at my phone, wishing I had the energy to text DJ or Tyler to see if they want to grab a much-needed drink....or maybe work out our stress in the bedroom.

But who am I kidding? By the time I'm done listening to Lukas pour his heart out, I'll barely have the mental capacity to drive myself home and face-plant into bed. And it's not like Ty has been around much lately, anyway...

Sighing inwardly, I try to focus on the stressed man in front of me, knowing that I'd give a lot to trade this conversation for one with Tyler, where he really opens up to me about what's going on with him...

The next morning I sit across from Tomas in my cozy office, eyeing him with concern. He hunches forward, elbows on his knees, mouth turned down at the corners.

Something is clearly weighing heavily on him today.

"What's on your mind, Tomas?" I ask gently, giving him an

encouraging smile. "This is a safe space. You can talk to me about anything."

He exhales slowly and runs a hand through his short, dark hair. "It's just...things with my girlfriend. They're not good." His accent thickens, the way it does when he's upset.

I nod, letting him take his time. We've discussed his relationship issues before, but he hasn't been ready to make any big changes yet. *Here's hoping that starts today.*

"She yelled at me on the phone again last night. Called me stupid, worthless." Tomas's jaw clenches. Pain flashes in his eyes. "Said I care more about hockey than her and I'll never amount to anything."

"I'm so sorry she said those things to you. She's abusing you, Tomas." Keeping my voice calm and nonjudgmental, I hold his gaze. *I'll keep telling him this for as long as he needs to hear it.* "You don't deserve to be treated that way by anyone, especially your partner."

"I know." He shakes his head. "And I keep making excuses, but...it keeps getting worse. The insults, the anger, the jealousy. She's so controlling. I feel trapped."

As Tomas shares more examples, each one breaks my heart. Every time we discuss this it hits too close to home, reminding me of how Paul used to berate and belittle me. No wonder Tomas always seems on edge lately. Living under constant criticism would erode anyone's self-worth.

"Can I share something from my own experience?" I venture when he falls silent.

At his nod, I take a deep breath.

"I was in an abusive relationship too," I say, "not that long ago. Similar to what you've described—the cruel put-downs, explosive outbursts, possessiveness. It started small but escalated over time."

Tomas's eyes widen. "Really? But you seem so...strong. Put together."

"It can happen to anyone," I assure him. "Abuse is insidious like that, chipping away at you bit by bit. But Tomas, leaving was the best and bravest thing I ever did. As painful as it was, I'm happier and healthier now. I got myself back."

"I want that too. To feel...free again. Like myself." He straightens up, something shifting in his expression. Determination mixed with grief. "I have to end it with her, don't I? Forever?"

"That's a big decision, and it has to be yours. But I think you're incredibly strong for even considering it. For valuing yourself enough to walk away from a situation that's hurting you." I reach out and squeeze his shoulder. "You have so much to offer, Tomas. You deserve a relationship built on love, trust and respect. Never let anyone make you feel 'less than.'"

Tears glisten in his eyes but don't fall. He swallows hard and nods.

"You're right. I know you're right. I've been thinking it for a while, I just..." His hands clench. "I have to do it. I have to break up with Alicia. No more living like this."

Pride and relief swell in my chest. *This is a huge breakthrough.* "I'm so proud of you for making this choice. I know it isn't easy.

And I'll be here to support you every step of the way, okay? You're not alone in this."

"Thank you, Sydney," he says hoarsely. "For listening, for understanding, for...everything. I couldn't have gotten to this point without you."

"You did the hard work," I tell him firmly. "This is your strength. And things will get better from here, I promise."

We spend a few minutes going over safety strategies and self-care for the difficult days to come. As our session winds down, I'm filled with bittersweet elation.

I'm overjoyed for Tomas and the abuse-free future that awaits him.

But it's also stirring up a lot of feelings about my own healing journey. I know I still have work to do on rebuilding my sense of self, but helping Tomas makes me feel like I've taken a big step forward.

Tomas stands to leave and I walk him to the door with a warm smile. "Brighter days are ahead, Tomas. For you and the team."

Tomas smiles back, then mutters under his breath, "Unless DJ's knee's shot again and we're all screwed."

I grab his shoulder before he can leave. "Wait, what? What's wrong with DJ's knee?"

Tomas waves it aside as if it's none of my concern. "Oh, nothing—I just noticed that DJ was limping off the ice today, made me kind of nervous that his old injury's acting up again." He shakes his head. "Last fucking thing we need right now. Anyway, thanks again, I'll keep you updated."

With that, Tomas exits, leaving me blinking in surprise. *DJ's hurt?*

I finally find DJ limping across the parking lot, favoring his right knee as he hauls his hockey bag toward his Mustang. Worry shoots through me at the sight.

"DJ, wait up!" I call out, jogging over to him. He turns, his dark eyes wary as I approach. Up close, I can see the exhaustion etched on his chiseled face. "Can I talk to you for a sec?"

He sighs, dropping his bag with a thud. "Look, it's not a great time, okay?" His voice is weary, defensive. "It's been a really long day."

I frown, not wanting to let him go in this state. "It's just I...noticed you were skating differently at practice today. Like you were in pain." I search his face, trying to gauge his reaction. "Is your knee bothering you?"

DJ stiffens, his jaw tightening. "You spying on me or something? Did the coaches put you up to this?" His words come out sharp, accusatory.

"What? No, of course not!" I protest, taken aback by his hostile tone. "I'm just worried about you, that's all. If you're injured, you need to get it checked out before it gets worse."

Why is he being so prickly?

"I can handle it," he snaps coldly. "I don't need some shrink babysitting me or telling me what to do. Just stay out of my business, alright?" He savagely throws his bag into his car and moves to get inside.

Tears spring to my eyes at his harsh dismissal. *This was a mistake. He doesn't trust me, doesn't want my help.*

"Fine," I choke out. "Excuse me for giving a damn."

Before he can respond, I spin on my heel and make a beeline for my car. DJ calls after me but I don't look back, blinking furiously to hold back the flood threatening to spill over.

I yank open the door and peel out of the parking space, not daring to glance in the rearview mirror as I speed away. Hot tears stream down my face.

Tyler's avoiding my calls, and now this... Suddenly, the joy of last week feels very out of reach.

CHAPTER 31
TYLER

S WEAT DRIPS DOWN MY FACE AS I LAUNCH MYSELF ACROSS THE ice, my muscles burning with each explosive movement. The sound of my blades carving across the frozen surface echoes through the empty arena.

Just me, the goal, and the puck.

"Looking sharp, Ty!" Marcus calls out as he sends another puck my way. *Okay, and Marcus.*

I snap my glove out to snag it midair. "One more!" I shout, tossing it back.

He shoots again and I slide into a split, deflecting it wide. The searing pain in my groin tells me I'm pushing it too far, but I ignore it.

I have to be better. Faster. Unbeatable.

"Dude, it's getting late," Marcus says, skating over. "We should call it a night."

I shake my head, pulling myself up. "Nah, you go ahead. I'm gonna run a few more drills."

He frowns, his brow creasing with concern. "You sure, man? You've been at it for hours already. Don't want to over-train and injure yourself."

"I'm good," I insist, even as my legs tremble beneath me. "Seriously, I'll catch up with you later."

Marcus hesitates, but finally nods. "Alright, well, get some rest tonight, yeah? See you at morning skate."

He heads off the ice, leaving me alone in the cavernous space. I retrieve more pucks and set them up, running the drills again.

And again.

Each time pushing harder, desperate to prove to myself that I have what it takes. That I won't let the team down when it matters most.

But even as I make save after sprawling save, the doubt lingers like a shadow in the back of my mind. *You're an imposter,* it whispers. *You'll never be as good as Steven. You'll choke when your team needs you and cost them everything.*

My phone buzzes in my bag on the bench—probably Sydney checking in to make sure I'm still alive. Or DJ wanting to grab a beer and unwind. Or my sister, worrying like always. But I can't face any of them right now.

Can't let them see how close I am to cracking under the pressure.

So I keep skating, keep drilling, keep pushing, even as the

minutes turn to hours. My body screams for mercy but I shut it out.

Mind over matter. I'll rest when we've got that Cup in our hands. Until then, this is all that matters. Hockey is all that matters. I'm a Simmonds, this is what we do.

I try to let that confidence fill me, the knowledge that hockey is in my blood. But all I can hear is the doubt.

I lean my head against the cool tile of the shower stall, wincing as the hot water pummels my battered muscles. Today was brutal. And, as the adrenaline fades, exhaustion seeps into my bones.

What the hell am I doing? If I keep this up, I'm going to crash and burn spectacularly.

I need a new game plan, and fast.

After toweling off, I grab my phone from my locker. My thumb hovers over the screen for a moment before I pull up our Adam's number and hit call. He picks up on the second ring.

"Ty? What's up man?"

"Hey, you got a minute to talk? I could really use some advice from the master."

Our injured goalie chuckles. "Sure thing. Why don't you come over? We'll crack a few beers and break down some tape."

"Sounds perfect. I'll grab a pizza on my way. Meat lover's?"

"Is there any other kind? See you in 30."

I hang up, already feeling a little lighter. Adam always has a way of putting things in perspective.

His place is sleek and modern, all glass and chrome. I balance the pizza box as I knock. Adam opens the door, his easy grin setting me at ease instantly.

"Ty! Come on in. I've already got the last game queued up."

We settle on a plush leather couch, demolishing the pizza as we pore over every second of footage. Adam pauses and rewinds, pointing out tiny adjustments to my stance, my timing. His insight is invaluable—this guy has more goalie knowledge in his pinky finger than I have in my entire body. But it's his steady, encouraging presence that really gets me.

He believes in me, even when I'm struggling to believe in myself.

"Look at this part," he says, jabbing a finger at the screen. "Your lateral movement is a little sluggish here. I think if you..."

As Adam drones on, I can feel something flickering to life in my chest. A small, tentative ember of hope. *Maybe I can do this. Maybe I'm not a complete lost cause.*

We work until my eyelids grow heavy. I stretch and stand, joints popping.

"I should get out of your hair. Thanks for this, man. Seriously. I owe you a case of beer. Or ten."

Adam waves a hand. "Don't sweat it, that's what friends are for. You got this, Ty. I know you do."

As I'm stepping out the door, my phone buzzes in my pocket. I pull it out and my heart jolts when I see DJ's name on the screen. My thumb wavers over the answer button. I've avoided him and Sydney for days, telling myself that I'll reach out once I'm not in such a black mood.

Maybe it's finally time.

Swallowing hard, I accept the call and lift the phone to my ear.

The moment I step through DJ's doorway his lips are on mine, hard and demanding, his hands roaming across my back. I lean into the kiss, desire flooding through me.

Fuck, this feels so right.

"Bedroom?" DJ murmurs against my mouth.

I nod eagerly. We stumble down the hall, leaving a trail of discarded shirts and jeans behind us. When we reach the bed, both in just our underwear, a flicker of nerves surges through me.

Just tell him.

I pull back slightly.

"I've been thinking..." I meet DJ's eyes, swallowing hard. "I want you to...you know." Heat rises in my cheeks. "Fuck me."

The words come out quietly but DJ hears them loud and clear.

His eyes sparkle with a dark gleam but his handsome face softens. "We'll take it nice and slow, Ty. I've got you."

DJ kisses me again, this time tender and reassuring.

My heart pounds as he eases me back onto the mattress, his fingertips skimming along my abs. I'm already moaning as DJ hooks his fingers in the waistband of my boxer briefs. "This okay?"

"Yes," I breathe out. "Please."

With a smile, he tugs them down, exposing me completely. I'm already achingly hard, and DJ meets my eyes, a gleam in his eye, before wrapping his mouth around me, so tight I see stars.

His lips glide along my shaft, tongue swirling, as he takes me deep. I gasp and buck my hips involuntarily.

"Fuck, Deej, that feels incredible..."

DJ hums around me, the vibrations sending shockwaves of pleasure radiating through my body. He works me slowly, purposefully, building me higher with every slick slide. My fingers thread through his hair, needing something to anchor me.

He pulls off and before I have time to miss him he's crawling up my body, kissing and nipping at my heated skin.

"I'm gonna make you feel so good, baby," he purrs. "Gonna take such good care of you."

I capture his mouth in a searing kiss, our tongues tangling, the taste myself on his lips dizzying. Breaking away, DJ reaches over to the nightstand, fumbling in the drawer before pulling out lube and a condom. The snick of the cap sends a thrill down my spine.

"Just breathe," DJ soothes as he drizzles the cool liquid over his fingers. "I'll go slow, I promise."

The first press of his finger into my ass makes me tense reflexively. But DJ peppers soft kisses across my face, my jaw, down my neck as he works me open with gentle persistence.

By the time he's three fingers deep, I'm a writhing, desperate mess beneath him.

"Please, Deej," I beg, my voice wrecked. "I need you inside me. Now."

DJ groans, his eyes flashing with desire. He withdraws his fingers and I whine at the emptiness. But then he's positioning the blunt head of his cock at my entrance.

"Ready?" he asks, holding my gaze.

I nod frantically. "Yes, god yes."

Slowly, torturously, DJ pushes forward. The stretch and burn as he breaches me makes me gasp. His fingers were one thing, but Christ, his cock feels so big.

"That's it, Tyler, you're doing so good," he says gently, leaning down to kiss me again. "God, you feel unreal around me."

When he's fully seated, DJ stills, giving me a moment to adjust. It's unlike anything I've ever felt before—so full, split open on his thick length. My cock is so hard it almost hurts.

I experimentally squeeze my muscles around him and we both moan.

"Christ, Ty," DJ grits out. "You keep doing that and this is gonna be over embarrassingly fast."

I grin up at him, feeling a rush of power. "Then you better start moving."

DJ answers with a deep, primal kiss as he starts to roll his hips. His thrusts are measured at first, letting me get used to the sensation. But soon, the intensity builds until he's driving into me relentlessly, hitting a mind-blowing spot deep inside with every snap of his hips.

I'm reduced to a string of broken moans and gasps, my cock smearing pre-cum against my stomach as it bounces with the force of his thrusts.

"Fuck, I love the feel of your tight ass," DJ growls in my ear.

His filthy words spur me higher, pressure coiling tighter in my core. I'm hurtling towards that edge, my whole body drawn taut. DJ must sense how close I am because he wraps a hand around my weeping erection, stroking in time with his thrusts.

"That's it, come for me, Ty."

A few more rough pumps of his fist and I'm gone, my orgasm slamming into me like a freight train. I spill over DJ's fingers with a ragged shout of his name, my release painting my chest and abs. DJ works me through it, milking every last drop as I shudder and clench around him.

My ecstasy proves his undoing. With a guttural moan, DJ buries himself to the hilt, pulsing deep inside me as he finds his own release. For a long moment, we remain locked together, chests heaving, hearts pounding in sync as the aftershocks rock through us.

Finally, with a soft kiss to my forehead, DJ carefully pulls out and disposes of the condom. He grabs a washcloth from the en suite, cleaning us both up with tender efficiency before crawling back into bed and gathering me close.

I tuck my face into the crook of his neck, inhaling the musky scent of his skin.

"How are you?" DJ murmurs, his fingers tenderly stroking up and down my back.

I let out a strangled laugh, unsure how to even put the experience into words. "I'm...I'm perfect."

DJ laughs, intentionally misunderstanding my words. "You *are* perfect, Ty. I hope you know that."

I huff. "Far from it. But that definitely helped take my mind off things for a while."

DJ's arms tighten around me. "Hey, I mean it. You're so strong, pushing through all this pressure and uncertainty. I'm in awe of you, honestly."

I swallow around the lump forming in my throat, staring up at DJ's ceiling. "I don't feel very strong lately. I'm barely keeping my head above water."

I take a deep, shuddering breath, collecting my thoughts as DJ waits patiently beside me. Finally, the words come, a jumbled rush at first but then steadier, more sure.

"Growing up, it was always hockey first, you know? My parents were so busy, working their asses off to support us and pay for equipment and ice time. I know they loved us, but a lot of the time, it felt like they just weren't...there."

I swallow hard, old hurts resurfacing. "So it was me, my brother, and my sister against the world. And Steven, man, he was larger than life to me. This hotshot hockey prodigy that I desperately wanted to be just like."

DJ makes a soft noise of understanding, his thumb rubbing soothing circles on my shoulder. It gives me the courage to keep going, to put words to the things I've never said out loud.

"But Steven...he was brutal, Deej. Constantly telling me I wasn't good enough, fast enough, tough enough. That I'd never make it if I didn't push myself harder. And I took it all to heart, let it fuel me. I thought that's just how it was—that I needed to be hard on myself to succeed."

I let out a humorless laugh, the sound hollow in my chest.

"Turns out, it just made me a fucking mess. I'm only realizing now how much it fucked me up."

DJ shifts to face me, his brown eyes intense and full of empathy.

"Ty, listen to me. You are not a mess. You're human, dealing with a metric fuckton of pressure and childhood baggage. But you know what else you are? Incredible. Resilient. One of the strongest, most wonderful people I've ever met."

His words wash over me, soothing the ragged edges of my psyche. *I want so badly to believe him.* DJ cups my face, his calloused thumb brushing over my cheekbone.

"I know it's not easy to shake that shit off. Trust me, I've got my own steaming pile of mommy and daddy issues. But you're not alone anymore, Ty. You've got me, Syd, the whole team in your corner. We are going to the fucking playoffs, and there's no way that would be happening if you weren't amazing."

Emotion clogs my throat. I turn my head to press a kiss to DJ's palm. "I...thanks, Deej. I'm…" A pressure builds behind my eyes, and finally, finally, I let go and cry.

DJ gathers me close as the tears spill down my cheeks, his strong arms enveloping me in warmth and safety. I bury my face in his chest, my shoulders shaking.

"I've got you, Ty. I'm right here," he murmurs, his lips brushing the top of my head.

For the first time in longer than I can remember, I don't feel the need to be strong, to keep up the unshakable facade. With DJ, I can just...be. Messy, vulnerable, completely raw.

And that inner voice isn't yelling at me, telling me I'm weak, that I need to man up.

For the first time in a long, long time, that voice is quiet.

CHAPTER 32
DJ

A WARM, WET MOUTH ENVELOPS MY NIPPLE AND I MOAN, MY BODY responding instantly. My eyes shoot open to see Tyler's sandy hair, sleep-tousled and sexy as hell, as he licks and sucks his way across my chest to my other nipple.

"Mmm, good morning," I mumble, my voice rough with sleep and arousal.

Tyler glances up at me through his lashes, his blue eyes filled with mischief. "Morning, you. Did you get any sleep?"

"Oh yeah. After our amazing performance last night I could've slept through a hurricane." I stretch languorously, letting the sheet slide down to reveal my rapidly hardening cock.

Tyler's lips curve into a smirk. "Mm, maybe we could have an encore this morning? If you're up for it, that is." He trails his fingers teasingly along my shaft.

I grin cockily. "Oh, I'm definitely up. In more ways than one." I tense my abs, making my hard dick jump.

Tyler snorts a laugh, shaking his head. "Syd was right. You're insatiable, DJ." I feel a tweak of guilt at Sydney's name—I was totally out of line with the way I treated her the other day. I called her that night and begged for her forgiveness, but I still feel like she might be upset with me.

Before I can spiral about my bad behavior, Tyler is already shifting down the bed, his big, calloused hand wrapping around my length.

I groan as his hot mouth slides over the head of my cock, tongue swirling, taking me deep. *Holy shit, Ty's mouth should be illegal.* My hands fist in the sheets as he sucks me hard and fast, building me up in record time.

Just when I'm about to blow, he pulls his mouth away. I growl in frustration, but then Tyler is crawling back up my body, his own rock-hard erection dragging along my thigh.

"Fuck me, DJ," he pants against my lips. "I need you inside me."

I growl, flipping us over in one swift move. I reach for the lube and slick myself up hurriedly, my control rapidly fraying. Tyler watches me with hooded eyes, his chest heaving, legs spread in wanton invitation.

I line up and press forward, sinking balls deep into his tight heat in one smooth thrust. We both moan loudly at the intense sensation. I start to move, pulling out slowly before slamming back in.

"Yes, fuck, just like that," Tyler gasps, hands reaching to grip my ass. I set a punishing pace, the room filling with the sounds of skin slapping against skin and our harsh breaths.

Last night was about Tyler's exploration, about tender emotional connection. But this? This is pure, carnal need. Hard and fast and primal. The rest of the world falls away until there is only Tyler—his body, his moans, his scent surrounding me. His tight ass clenching hard on my cock with every thrust.

I pause to compose myself, my cock buried deep in Tyler's tight ass. *Fuck, he feels amazing.* I suddenly wish Sydney was here to see this and get an idea. One that might make her feel a little warmer toward me.

Leaning down to grab my phone from the nightstand, my fingers are slick with lube and fumbling as I dial Sydney's number.

After a couple rings, she picks up, her voice thick and groggy.

"Mmm, hello?"

I put her on speaker, letting her hear Tyler's needy moans as I slowly rotate my hips, grinding into him. "Hey baby, sorry to wake you. Ty and I were just thinking about you."

"Oh yeah?" Her voice perks up, taking on a flirty tone. "And what exactly are you two doing?"

I smack Tyler's ass, making him yelp. "I've got my cock stuffed in Ty's perfect ass and realized you were missing out. Thought you might want to join the fun?"

"God, you guys are so hot," she breathes out. I hear rustling through the phone, like she's pushing the covers aside. "I wish I was there with you."

"Rub that sweet pussy for us, Syd. Let us hear you." I start thrusting into Tyler with more purpose now, spurred on by Sydney's whimpers echoing through the room.

Tyler grips the sheets, his muscular back flexing as he pushes his hips back to meet my strokes. "Fuck, your cock feels so good," he pants.

I lay my body over his, reaching around to fist his erection as I pound into him. Our sweaty skin slaps together obscenely. "That's it Ty, take my cock."

"Oh fuck, I'm close!" Sydney cries out. Her breathy moans crescendo through the speaker.

That's all it takes to send me over the edge. I slam deep and empty myself inside Tyler with a low groan. He tenses and spills over my fist with a shout, his ass clenching around me.

We collapse onto the messy sheets, chests heaving. Sydney lets out a satisfied sigh. "Mmm, good morning to me."

"Just wait until we have you here in person," I say with a smirk she can probably hear.

"Looking forward to it. But you boys better get moving—big day today. Bring home a win for me tonight!"

"You know it, babe. Talk to you later." I end the call and drop a kiss between Tyler's shoulder blades. He wraps his arms around me, pressing soft kisses to my sweat-dampened temple.

"Thanks for last night," he mumbles into my shoulder. "Sorry to break down on you like that…"

I lift my head to look at him, cupping his jaw tenderly. "Hey, you have nothing to apologize for, okay? I'm glad you felt safe enough to open up to me." I brush my thumb over his stubbled cheek. "I want to be here for you, Ty. In every way."

Tyler's eyes search mine, vulnerability shimmering in their blue depths. "This thing between us...it's real, isn't it? It's not just sex anymore."

My heart stutters in my chest. *He's right.* Somewhere along the way, amid the flirting and fucking, real feelings have taken root. Deep, powerful emotions like nothing I've ever felt before.

"Yeah," I whisper roughly. "It's real. So real it scares the shit out of me sometimes."

A smile blooms across Tyler's face, boyish and beautiful. "Me too. But it's the good kind of scary, you know? Like...like we're on the edge of something amazing here."

I nod, throat too tight for words. Instead, I lower my head and capture his lips in a passionate kiss, trying to pour all my feelings into the press of my mouth on his.

And then I reluctantly pull away and slap Tyler's ass, herding us both up and out of bed. Syd's right, it's time to get our game faces on.

The Cup is waiting.

The roar of the crowd thunders in my ears as I glide onto the ice, the weight of their expectations bearing down on me like a physical force.

Game one of the playoffs... here we go.

Across the rink, Tyler takes his place in the net, lean muscles rippling beneath his jersey. Even with the tension I know he's carrying, his movements are fluid and graceful, like a panther stalking its prey.

The puck drops and the game explodes into a flurry of sticks and skates. These guys came to play today. I dart between defensemen, the cold air burning my lungs as I push for the goal. Ty makes a spectacular diving save and I can't hold back a whoop.

"Yes Ty, that's my boy!"

But the other team is hungry. They slam us against the boards, fighting for every inch. I wince as pain shoots through my bad knee on a pivot. *Can't let it slow me down. Team needs me. Mom needs me.*

Back and forth we battle, the scoreboard slowly climbing. Tyler is a wall in the net, but I see it wearing on him, eyes clouding with doubt when one slips through.

"Shake it off Ty, you got this!" I call, but he doesn't meet my gaze.

I fake out their center and shoot—denied!

Frustration boils in my gut as we head into the third period tied 2-2. We need this win. The team needs it, the fans need it...Tyler needs it. I catch his eye as we line up for the face-off.

There's a wealth of emotion swirling in those baby blues—determination, fear, exhaustion. But beneath it all, trust. Trust in me, in us.

The puck drops and I surge forward, my muscles screaming as I push hard, determined to bring home a victory at any cost. Their defense descends on me but I spin away, peripheral vision locked on Tyler's crease. One of their goons slashes at my sore knee and I stumble, biting back a cry of pain.

Ty shouts my name, his voice cracking with worry. It's like a shot of adrenaline straight to my heart. Gritting my teeth, I straighten up and charge ahead.

I won't let him down. Not now, not ever.

Their goalie squares up as I approach, his stance textbook perfect. But there—a flicker of uncertainty in his eyes, a twitch of his blocker. I see my opening and I take it.

The puck rockets off my stick, sailing over the goalie's left shoulder and hitting the back of the net with a satisfying swish. The red goal light blazes to life and the arena absolutely erupts.

"Fuck yeah!" I scream.

We manage to hold on to the lead until the buzzer sounds. I slam into Tyler, crushing him to me in a fierce hug.

"You were incredible," I murmur into his neck.

But he's stiff in my arms, shrinking from the cheers and stick taps. I can feel the tension still coiled within him, the demons still not conquered. Well, it's not as if one night of opening up is going to undo a lifetime of abuse from Ty's asshole brother.

As we head down the tunnel, I vow to myself: I'll do whatever it takes to prove to Ty how amazing he is, to heal the wounds his dickhead brother left.

To show him he deserves every ounce of love, on and off the ice.

CHAPTER 33
TYLER

TONIGHT, I'M SUPPOSED TO BE AT A TEAM-WIDE DINNER WITH our owners, a celebration of the start of our playoffs run. Compulsory fun that will be fun for no one. But before I can even start getting ready for it, there's a knock on my apartment door.

Huh, I'm not expecting anyone.

I open the door, only to discover Sydney and DJ standing on the other side, both wearing playful grins and outfits that are absolutely too casual for dinner with our billionaire overlords.

"We have something for you," Sydney says coyly, brushing past me and into the apartment.

DJ holds up an envelope between two fingers and saunters past me as well. I grab it from him and rip it open, intrigued.

Holy shit.

I stare at the glossy Bulls/Lakers tickets in my hands, blinking back surprise and sudden emotion as a lump forms in my throat. Sydney and DJ watch me with eager smiles, her eyes sparkling and his lips curving up in that signature cocky grin.

"Happy playoffs, baby," DJ drawls, giving my ass a quick squeeze. "We know you've been dying to see the Lakers."

"And now you finally can, with us," Sydney adds warmly, her delicate hand resting on my arm. "A night away from hockey to just enjoy ourselves."

I swallow hard, overwhelmed by their thoughtfulness. They know how much this means to me. With the demands of my own career, I've never managed to catch the Lakers when they're in town, despite being a diehard fan for years. But it's more than just the tickets.

It's Syd and DJ showing up for me, supporting me, during the nerve-wracking emotional rollercoaster of playoffs. Despite my self-doubts and the team's toxic crap, these two amazing people have my back.

"But the team dinner?" I ask, looking between them.

Sydney shrugs. "I told Coach Daniels you needed a night off of team obligations to de-stress. He took my counsel seriously."

"I—this is incredible. Thank you both so much," I stammer, my tongue tripping over the words. "Really, I'm so grateful—"

"Then show us your gratitude, stud," DJ interrupts with a wicked smirk. He nods toward my bedroom. "Go get that sexy ass changed so we can grab drinks and dinner before tip-off."

Sydney laughs and gives me a gentle shove. "You heard the man. Hurry up, hot stuff!"

As I head to my room to change, tickets clutched to my

chest, a huge grin spreads across my face. *Damn, how did I get so lucky?*

I find myself sandwiched between Sydney and DJ in a dimly lit cocktail lounge, their warm thighs pressed snugly against mine. Syd's hand wanders teasingly up my leg, her fingertips grazing over the growing bulge in my pants before disappearing just as quickly. DJ's fingers trail along my other thigh, tracing circles that inch higher and higher.

They're making it hard to focus on the light, flirty conversation bouncing between us.

"So, Tyler, how's it feel juggling a polyamorous relationship?" Sydney asks, her voice a seductive purr in my ear. "Must be a lot of...pressure."

"Oh, he can handle the pressure," DJ chimes in with a smirk. "Our boy's got talented hands. Among other things."

I nearly choke on my whiskey. "You guys are relentless."

"Aw, like you don't love every minute of it." Sydney winks, her hand finding its way back to my crotch.

"Yeah, Ty, we know you're enjoying this," DJ whispers, his warm breath tickling my neck. "No need to play coy."

"Who's playing?" I grin, feeling bold. "Maybe I'm just getting started."

"Oh really?" Syd arches an eyebrow, her expression a challenge. "Wanna show us what you got?"

DJ flags down the waiter for the check. "I think that's our cue to take this party somewhere more...private."

"Lead the way." I down the rest of my drink, pulse already racing in anticipation.

The moment the bill is settled, we're stumbling towards the bathroom, giddy, barely able to keep our hands off each other.

As soon as the door locks behind us, DJ pushes me up against the wall, his mouth hot and urgent on mine. I lose myself in the taste of him, in the feel of his hard body pressed against mine. Sydney works at my belt, her nimble fingers making quick work of it.

When she takes me into her warm, soft hand, I groan into DJ's mouth.

I catch sight of us in the mirrors lining the walls - a tangle of groping hands and writhing bodies. It's the hottest thing I've ever seen. DJ notices me looking and flashes a wolfish grin.

"Like what you see, Ty?" He nips at my throat. "'Cause I sure do."

He turns his attention to Sydney, scooping her up and setting her on the black marble counter. She gasps as he tugs her panties down her long legs and pushes her skirt up around her waist. Watching him dip his head between her thighs, seeing her fingers tangle in his dark hair as he devours her—fuck, it's almost too much.

"Don't just stand there," DJ barks, coming up for air. "Get over here and fuck our girl. Now."

His tone brooks no argument. I can only obey, moving to

slide my hard length into Sydney's slick heat as DJ watches intently, his own hand working at his cock.

Sydney moans, throwing her head back as I fill her. "God, Tyler, yes..."

I set a hard, fast rhythm, driven by the intensity of DJ's stare and the intoxicating sounds spilling from Syd's lips. She feels incredible, her tight walls clenching around me with each deep thrust. I grip her hips, pulling her to meet my increasingly erratic strokes.

"Fuck, you two are so hot like this," DJ growls approvingly. He steps closer, fisting a hand in Sydney's hair. "Ty, think you can hold our girl up while you fuck her? I need that mouth on me."

Sydney stands, groaning as I slip out of her, and I spin her around and hitch her hips up until I can fill her again.

DJ grins. "Good boy. Now don't let her go," he instructs, and then grabs a fistful of Syd's hair, dragging her mouth down to his straining erection until she's braced between us. "Open up, baby girl. I know how much you love choking on my cock."

She parts her lips eagerly and I watch, mesmerized, as she swallows him down. The sight sends a jolt of lust straight to my own throbbing dick. My hips stutter, my climax building embarrassingly fast.

"That's it, Ty, fuck her harder," DJ commands breathlessly. "Make our girl come all over that big cock. Fuck her into me until my cock fills her throat."

Jesus, the things he says.

I piston into Sydney, my grip tight on her hips, slamming

her back into me with everything I've got. She whimpers around DJ as his cock moves deeper into her mouth, the vibrations making him curse and tighten his grip on her hair.

"Shit, just like that...I'm gonna come down your throat, Syd."

My hips snap forward, driving into Sydney's slick heat as DJ's words push me over the edge. "Fuck, Syd, I'm gonna come," I grunt, my fingers digging into the flesh of her hips.

She cries out around DJ's cock as her own orgasm crashes through her, the sensation of her clenching around me making my eyes roll back. I empty myself inside her with a hoarse shout, pumping into her throbbing heat until I'm completely spent.

DJ throws his head back with a growl, his entire body going taut as he reaches his peak.

"Take it, baby. Swallow every drop," he growls, holding Sydney's head still as he spills himself down her eager throat.

She does as she's told, gulping and gasping as she works to accommodate his release. When he finally pulls out, Syd falls back against my chest, still trembling. I wrap my arms around her, holding her up, as DJ tucks himself back into his pants with a self-satisfied smirk.

"Damn, you two are a sight," he rumbles appreciatively, his eyes roaming over our slick, entwined bodies. "I could watch you fuck our girl all day, Ty."

"Ditto," I manage, still trying to catch my breath. "That was...intense."

"The best kind of intense," Sydney purrs, twisting in my

arms to plant a messy kiss on my mouth before tugging her dress down. "But I think we have a game to get to, hey?"

The game blurs past in a rush of adrenaline and arousal, my body still buzzing from that hot-as-hell hookup in the bathroom. I can barely focus on the action on the court, my mind replaying flashes of DJ's cock in Syd's mouth, the way her tits bounced every time I thrust. Beside me, Syd and DJ are cozy, sharing nachos and nudging me with sly grins.

"Best game night ever, am I right?" DJ murmurs, his breath hot on my ear. "Beats the hell out of some boring team dinner."

I smirk back at him, enjoying his closeness. "Definitely more fun than listening to Luca drone on about defensive strategies over bland chicken."

Syd laughs, her eyes sparkling. "You guys are terrible. But I have to agree, this is way better."

She leans into me, her curves soft and tempting, and I drape an arm around her, savoring the rightness of being here with them, laughing and flirting without a care. For a blissful stretch of time, I forget about the pressure, my asshole brother, all of it.

I'm just a guy, living the dream with his two gorgeous lovers.

Then the final buzzer sounds and the crowd explodes into cheers, but Syd pays no attention, going rigid against me. I glance down to see her staring at her phone, her face ghostly pale.

"Syd? What's wrong?" Icy dread runs through me at her expression.

"It's Mikey," she says tightly. "He just showed up wasted to the team dinner with the owners. He's totally out of control. I have to go do damage control before this turns into a complete disaster."

My chest clenches as she grabs her purse and bolts up from her seat, already halfway up the aisle before DJ and I can react. We exchange a loaded, worried look.

"Shit," DJ mutters. "Poor Syd. And fucking Mikey, that idiot."

I'm already moving, pushing past the oblivious celebrating crowd. "Come on, we have to go help her salvage this. Before it ruins everything she's working for. That we've all worked for."

This is the type of thing the media would absolutely eat up. We've just finally salvaged our reputations, turned the conversation back to our skills on the ice.

Something like this could really fuck up our team's synergy and lose us the playoffs.

DJ is right on my heels as we rush after Sydney's retreating form, my buzz completely killed.

CHAPTER 34
SYDNEY

I BURST THROUGH A SET OF ORNATE DOUBLE DOORS INTO UTTER pandemonium. The swanky restaurant looks like it's been hit by a tornado of panicked hockey players and staff. Vincent, our GM, is pacing the room like a caged tiger, barking orders left and right.

"I don't care what it takes, just find him, and now! And where the hell is Sydney?" he shouts into his phone.

"Right here," I call out, raising my hand meekly. Vincent whips around, his eyes flashing. I gulp.

Scanning the room, I spot the team owners huddled in the corner. The Prescott family, billionaires who made their fortune in corn futures before buying the struggling hockey franchise as a vanity project.

Mr. and Mrs. Prescott are frantically tapping on their phones, no doubt doing damage control.

But it's their daughter who catches my eye. Tall and willowy with striking emerald eyes, she stands apart from the chaos, calmly observing the madness. Our gazes meet and there's an odd sense of kinship. Another woman thrown into this testosterone-fueled world, a fellow outsider.

"Some party, huh?" I joke weakly.

She gives me an appraising look. "You must be Sydney, the team's addiction counselor. I've heard about you. I'm Amelia Prescott."

"Nice to meet you, Amelia. Sorry it's under such crazy circumstances." My heart sinks even lower as my gaze moves back to Vincent, still furiously stalking around the restaurant shouting into his phone. *This is on me.*

Amelia touches my arm gently. "Hey, don't be hard on yourself. This isn't your fault. Addiction is a beast. All we can do is be there to support Mikey when he's ready."

Her compassion—both for me and for Mikey—takes me by surprise. Before I can respond, Vincent strides over, clapping a meaty hand on my shoulder.

"Syd! Stop disappearing. Oh—" his voice softens. "I see you've met our future team owner," he booms with false joviality. "Amelia here is shadowing her parents to learn the ropes."

I plaster on a bright smile, suppressing my rising shame. *Just smile and spin, that's my job now. Never mind that I'm failing miserably at actually helping these players...*

Vincent steers me away, updating me on what's happened. Mikey showed up high as a kite and made a massive scene, screaming at the serving staff and getting belligerent with the restaurant's manager when he tried to intervene.

It was ugly…and extremely public. Mikey's already left the premises, so there's not much I can do until he's located.

"No luck yet," Vincent grunts. "We've tried his home, his girlfriend's place, his favorite restaurants. Any ideas?"

I chew my lip, racking my brain. *Where would a troubled young athlete go to escape? To get away from the pressure, the scrutiny, the constant fear of screwing up?*

Suddenly it hits me. "The rink," I blurt out. "He'd go to the one place that feels like home. Where he feels safe and in control."

Vincent's eyes widen. He whips out his phone and starts barking orders. Within minutes, we're racing across town in his sleek Audi, tires squealing as we take corners at breakneck speed.

As we pull up to the darkened practice arena, my heart is pounding.

Please let him be here. Please let him be okay.

Vincent uses his master key to let us in the back entrance. The cavernous space is eerie, all shadows and silence. Our footsteps echo as we make our way down to the ice.

And there, sitting hunched in the center of the ice, is Mikey. My heart clenches at the sight of him. Slowly, I make my way across the ice to join him, my shoes slipping on the slick surface.

Mikey's bloodshot eyes peer out at me. "Whadda you want?" he slurs.

"We're here to help, Mikey." I keep my voice gentle but firm.

"You need to get treatment. We'll be with you every step of the way."

He stands, then nearly slips.

Vincent has walked up behind me and steps forward to catch his elbow. "C'mon, son. Let us help you."

Mikey looks between us, his face sad and exhausted, and suddenly his shoulders sag, the fight gone out of him. He lets himself be led off the ice.

An hour later, Mikey's quietly checked into rehab and I'm in a conference room, staring down a social media nightmare. Coach Daniels paces while Chloe scrolls through her phone with a deepening frown.

"TMZ's already picked it up," she reports. "Photos of Mikey leaving the restaurant drunk off his ass with a black eye and a bloody nose. Speculation about him groping the team owner's daughter."

Coach slams a fist on the table. "Goddamnit!"

I massage my temples, a headache building. It was my job to prevent this exact scenario. Some addiction specialist I'm turning out to be.

Paul's mocking voice slithers through my mind. *"You're out of your depth, Syd. You can't handle this. You're going to fail, just like always."*

I shake my head, trying to dislodge his poisonous words. But they cling like cobwebs, sticky and cloying.

Vincent catches my eye from across the table, his gaze concerned.

I look away, shame burning my cheeks. *I've let him down. Let them all down.*

"We need to release a statement," Chloe is saying. "Something to explain Mikey's absence, spin this in a sympathetic light..."

Their voices fade to a distant buzz as Paul's taunts grow louder, drowning out all else. *"You're weak, Syd. You'll never be enough... Where were you when this was going down? Fucking some hockey players like a slut?"*

I squeeze my eyes shut, pressing the heels of my hands against them, willing Paul's voice to disappear.

A gentle touch on my shoulder startles me and my eyes fly open. Coach Daniels is crouched beside my chair, his eyes soft with concern.

"Hey," he says quietly. "You okay?"

I swallow hard, trying to find my voice. "I'm fine," I rasp unconvincingly.

Coach studies me for a long moment, his gaze knowing. "You're not fine, Syd. And that's okay. This was an intense night."

He pats me on the shoulder and stands back up. "How about you take yourself home, get some rest?"

I nod numbly, grateful for the out. I need to escape this room, these accusing stares, my own self-loathing thoughts. Gathering my things with shaking hands, I slip out, avoiding eye contact with anyone.

The cold night air slaps me in the face as I exit the arena, bracing and sobering. I gulp it in, trying to clear my head.

Fishing out my phone, I debate calling DJ or Tyler, updating them on where I am, everything that's happened.

But I keep hearing the echo of that word in my head, in Paul's voice. Mikey's.

Slut.

My fingers open up the rideshare app and call a car almost before I know what I'm doing.

I just need to go home.

I stumble into my dark apartment, kicking off my heels and shucking my purse onto the entry table. Exhaustion weighs on me like a fifty-pound barbell as I drag myself to the couch and collapse onto the soft cushions.

What a clusterfuck of a day.

My stomach churns with anxiety and bitter regret. I know what I need to do, but god, it's gonna hurt like a bitch. With shaking hands, I pull out my phone. DJ and Tyler's faces smile up at me from the lock screen—a silly selfie we took not long ago, laughing and carefree.

Shit, I can't back out now.

Taking a deep breath, I tap on DJ's contact and hold the phone to my ear. Voicemail.

I swallow hard.

"Hey DJ...I'm sorry to leave this as a message but...I think I need to take a break from you and Ty. With everything going on with the team, I just...I need to focus 100% on work right now."

Tears prick at my eyes but I blink them back.

"You and Ty both mean so much to me, you know that. But I can't give my all if I'm...distracted. You deserve better. I'm so sorry."

The goodbye tastes bitter on my tongue as I end the call. *One down, one to go.* This time, the tears fall freely as I listen to Tyler's outgoing message.

"Ty...god, I don't even know what to say." A humorless laugh escapes me. "You and DJ...you're everything I never knew I needed. But the team has to come first right now. I fucked up by not being there today."

I angrily swipe at my damp cheeks.

"Just...take care of each other, okay? I'll miss you both so damn much."

I end the call and hurl my phone across the room. It bounces harmlessly on the rug. Pulling my knees to my chest, I bury my face and let the sobs come, my shoulders shaking with the intensity of my grief.

It's the right thing to do. It has to be.

Then why does it feel like my heart is being ripped out of my chest? I cry until my throat is raw and my eyes burn. Emotionally spent, I uncurl my aching body and stumble to the bedroom, not even bothering to undress before collapsing onto the bed.

Tomorrow I'll focus on fixing this mess with the team.

Tonight...tonight I'll let myself mourn the loss of the two best things that ever happened to me.

CHAPTER 35
DJ

I GRIT MY TEETH AS I TAKE ANOTHER LAP AROUND THE ICE AT practice, trying to ignore the twinges of pain shooting through my knee with every stride.

I should probably be resting, letting my body heal, but with the playoffs in full swing and the team's morale at rock bottom after Mikey's drug-induced blow-up with the owners went viral, I can't afford to show any weakness.

Gotta keep up the facade of DJ the indestructible stallion, even if my body's screaming otherwise underneath the pads.

And even if all I can think about is the voicemail from Sydney last night, shattering the fragile thing that she and I and Tyler had been building...

I shut down that line of thought. I can't think about Sydney if I want to be at all functional during practice.

The news about Mikey fell like a bomb in the locker room. I

skate past huddles of the guys muttering grimly about the social media shitstorm.

"—PR nightmare. Trending on Twitter all night—"

"—suspension for sure. At the worst possible time—"

The toll it's taking is plain to see. Nerves are frayed raw. During drills, guys snap at each other over botched passes.

"Watch the fucking puck, Rook!" Lukas snarls at the new guy after a sloppy turnover. The poor kid blanches like he took a sucker punch to the gut.

On breaks, the team's usual banter dies on their lips. Everyone just slumps against the boards, eyes vacant, lost in their own heads. Slade gives me a hopeless look. I can tell he's been trying all morning to get the guys to shape up, but no dice so far.

Pulling myself together, I try to inject some pep, get everyone focused on the task at hand. "Let's clean it up out there, boys! Playoffs on the line. No passengers—we need all hands on deck!"

My voice strains with projected positivity, but inside, I'm fraying at the seams. *How am I supposed to hold this ship together when my own foundation is crumbling?* This shit with Syd is throwing me way off my game.

She's shutting me and Ty out, slipping through our fingers, and I have no idea how to put everything right.

We're halfway through the latest drill when things start to really fall apart. At first all I notice is that some of the team isn't where they're supposed to be on the ice. Gaps yawn where usually there'd be bodies filling the lanes.

Then I realize why—Nikolai's off his angle, lagging behind the play. And so is Marcus...*shit.*

I charge across the ice, my skates sparking shavings as I throw myself between the two of them. They're grappling like a pair of angry bears, gloves and sticks scattered around them.

"Break it up, you meatheads!" I yell, trying to pry them apart.

Their sweaty jerseys slip through my fingers. My own frustration is bubbling up inside me, ready to blow. It's been building all damn practice.

Nikolai spits out his mouth guard. "Stay out of this, DJ! This prick needs to learn how to pass."

"Screw you," Marcus snarls back. "Maybe if you could skate half as fast as you run your mouth—"

I shove my way between them again as they lunge for each other. "I said knock it off!"

Marcus sneers at me, his lip curling. "Oh, look who's talking. Big man DJ, always sticking his nose where it doesn't belong. I see you trotting after Sydney like a little puppy dog. You sniffing around the new shrink or something? Bet it'd be easy enough to dazzle her, use her and lose her like everyone else who's unfortunate enough to land in your bed. How about you focus on that?"

My vision flashes red. I feel the anger rising up my throat like bile.

How dare he bring Sydney into this, implying I'm taking advantage of her?

He has no idea about the connection we have, the way she makes me feel seen and understood for once in my life...

"You don't know what the hell you're talking about," I growl.

"Hit a nerve, huh? You're just pissed Sydney won't let you hit something else..." Marcus makes a crude gesture and the other guys snicker.

Something snaps inside me.

Without even thinking, I rear back and my fist collides with his jaw with a sickening crack.

Marcus staggers back, eyes wild with shock and fury. Before I can even process what I've done, he launches himself at me in a flurry of fists.

We tumble to the ice in a tangle of limbs, gouging and pummeling each other like rabid dogs. The coppery taste of blood fills my mouth as his knuckles smash against my teeth. Searing pain lances through my already battered knee when it twists beneath his weight.

Dimly, I'm aware of the chaos erupting around us—skates scraping, voices shouting, hands grabbing at our jerseys trying to haul us apart. But I'm too far gone, operating on pure primal instinct as I snarl and thrash against Marcus's grip.

It takes three guys to pry us apart, our chests heaving, glaring daggers at each other across the ice.

Coach's livid voice cuts through the haze of rage and adrenaline.

"Johnston! LeBlanc! What in the ever-loving *fuck* was that? You wanna beat the shit out of each other, you do it on your own time, not on my goddamn ice!"

His face a mask of disappointment, he gestures furiously at the mess we've made in the brawl—blood spatters on the ice, equipment scattered everywhere. "Hit the showers, both of you. And don't even think about suiting up next game until you get your heads out of your asses."

Shame sits like a lead weight in my gut as I limp toward the locker room, the adrenaline leaching out of my system and leaving behind only throbbing pain and bitter regret.

What the fuck was I thinking, throwing hands with Marcus like that? Letting him get under my skin, giving in to my anger? Some role model I am, completely losing my shit in front of the whole damn team.

I can feel their eyes boring into my back, a mix of shock and judgement and pity that makes my skin crawl. *The great DJ Johnston, unraveling at the seams for all to see. Pathetic.*

Stripping off my sweat-soaked gear with jerky, agitated movements, I don't meet anyone's gaze. The only one I want to look at right now is the one person who seems to be avoiding me like the plague.

Where the hell is Tyler?

I scan the room, but his stall is empty, his pads and skates nowhere to be seen. Did he book it out of here the second practice ended, not even bothering to wait for me? The thought sits like a stone in my chest.

I know I shouldn't push, but more than anything I want to talk to Sydney right now. Somehow I know that she'll be the only one who gets it.

But that's not an option right now. After I shower and get

dressed, I decide to head upstairs for some fresh air, maybe that will help me clear my head.

As I'm leaving the locker room, Grady says, "Yo, DJ! Coach is looking for you man—"

"Can't talk now bro, gotta hustle!" I shout over my shoulder, slipping past him. The fluorescent lights of the narrow hallway blur as I pick up speed. More shouts and the scuff of cleats on the rubber mat flooring chase after me. These fools aren't gonna let me off easy.

I'm closing in on the metal double doors at the end of the hall when—*shit*. Coach's unmistakable broad silhouette steps out from the equipment room. I hit the brakes so hard I nearly wipe out.

Nope, not happening, I am *not* ready for the verbal thrashing he's gonna unleash on my ass.

Whirling around, I dash back the other way, shouldering my way through the gaggle of dudes gathering to gawk at my walk of shame.

"Move, I'm coming through!" Keeping my eyes downcast, I brush past them and beeline for the stairwell.

Taking the steps two at a time, I emerge onto the roof, the chilly air whipping across my overheated skin.

Chest heaving, I stalk to the edge and grip the metal railing, the city skyline wavering in my vision.

"Shit," I groan, tilting my head back. I royally screwed the pooch back there. The media shitstorm, Mikey acting the fool, Syd caught in the crosshairs trying to clean up the mess...

It's all turned to chaos.

And then there's the dull ache pulsing in my knee.

I pace back and forth, thoughts racing.

This thing with Syd and Ty... We fit, I can feel it deep in my bones. But both of them are wrestling demons that make my issues look like a paper cut.

I want to be there for them, take on their battles.

Syd's got such a bleeding heart, wanting to save the world. And Ty, king of the mind-fuck, convinced he has to be something he's not...

Before I even realize what I'm doing, my feet carry me back down the stairs and through the now empty halls. Like a goddamn magnet, I'm drawn to her, ending up in front of Syd's office door, fist poised to knock. I hesitate.

Maybe this is a bad idea. We both need space, time to process this fuckery.

I should respect her request from the voicemail last night, not push her right now. But I ache with missing her, missing *them*, so viscerally my vision nearly blurs.

I can't leave it like this.

Rapping my knuckles against the wood, I suck in a sharp breath. "Syd? You in there? It's me. Can we talk?"

CHAPTER 36
SYDNEY

A KNOCK AT MY OFFICE DOOR JOLTS ME OUT OF THE PAPERWORK trance I've thrown myself into for the past hour. I look up to see DJ standing in the doorway.

At first I think he's here to give me some impassioned speech about our three-way relationship in response to my voicemail, and I don't think I can take it. I stand to ask him to leave, but then look at him properly.

His broad shoulders are slumped in defeat and his dark eyes are bloodshot, purple half-moons sagging beneath them. My heart clenches at the sight of him looking so broken.

I swallow the urge to take him into my arms to comfort him and force a tight smile.

"DJ, come on in," I say, gesturing to the seat across from my desk. "It looks like you're here in a professional capacity...right? Not to talk more about...well, us?"

He sighs heavily and drags himself over, sinking down into

the cushions. "To be honest, I was hoping we could do both." He catches my wary expression and sighs again. "But I know it's not right to push you right now. I can respect that boundary. I just don't know who else to go to…is it okay if we just talk?"

I nod, grabbing my notepad and pen. "So," I begin gently. "Tell me what's going on."

DJ rakes a hand through his perfectly tousled hair. "I really fucked up, Syd. At practice today…there was a fight. Marcus and Nikolai were going at it, I tried to break it up but…"

He shakes his head.

"I don't know what happened. One minute I was pulling them apart, the next I was swinging at Marcus myself. Took three guys to pull me off him." His voice cracks. "I've never lost control like that before."

My hand itches to reach out and soothe him, to smooth the anguish from his chiseled features. I grip my pen tighter instead. "These things happen sometimes in high-stress situations. Hockey is an intense, physical sport. Emotions can boil over."

"But I'm supposed to be a leader," DJ says bitterly. "Not flying off the handle and brawling with my own teammate. And I'm always going off about the toxic masculinity in hockey and how dumb it is. God, I'm so ashamed of myself right now. I'm such a fucking hypocrite."

"Let's unpack that," I suggest. "What emotions were you feeling leading up to the fight? Before you intervened?"

He thinks for a moment. "Anger. Frustration. My damn kn —well, I—I haven't been playing my best." He trails off, looking chagrined. "Sorry, you know what? You don't need to hear about my problems. I should go."

"That's what I'm here for," I assure him before he starts to rise. "And it sounds like you've got a lot on your plate. You're human, DJ. Cut yourself some slack." I soften my voice. "Beating yourself up won't change what happened. The important thing is that you learn from this and do better next time."

I could learn from my own advice here. The irony nearly kills me. Every piece of me is aching to take DJ into my arms, to burst right through those professional boundaries I insisted on building back up. But somehow, I hold back.

"You're right, Doc," he says heavily. "I will. I gotta make this right with the team somehow..."

I watch the play of emotions across his ridiculously handsome face, the yearning to lean across the table and kiss him rising up strong and intense.

"One step at a time," I advise, focusing very hard on his eyes and shutting down my thoughts. "For now, let's explore some strategies for managing your stress in healthy ways."

"There's something else," he interrupts, his eyes not meeting mine.

DJ shifts uncomfortably on the couch, his dark eyes darting away from mine. "I...uh, my knee has been killing me lately. I think you know that." His words come out rush, like he's embarrassed to admit any weakness.

My heart squeezes at his vulnerability. *DJ never talks about his injuries. This is huge.*

"Your knee?" I try to keep my tone gentle and non-judgmental.

He nods tightly. "Yeah. I had a major injury in college, it wiped me out a whole semester. I thought it was totally healed but... It's been aching more and more the last few weeks. Especially after games and hard practices."

I want so badly to reach out and squeeze his hand in reassurance. To pull him into a comforting hug and let him know it's okay, that I'm here for him no matter what. But I restrain myself, clasping my hands tightly in my lap instead.

"I'm glad you told me, DJ. That must have been really hard for you to admit out loud." I give him an encouraging smile. "Have you thought about getting it checked out by the team doctor?"

DJ's jaw clenches and he looks away again. "Nah, it's not that bad. I can handle it."

Classic stubborn athlete. I sigh inwardly.

"DJ, your health needs to be your top priority. If your knee is hurting, you owe it to yourself to get it looked at. At the very least, the doc might be able to give you some stretches or PT exercises to help manage the pain."

He's quiet for a long moment, his fingers drumming restlessly on his muscular thigh. Finally, he blows out a breath.

"Yeah, okay. You're right. I'll make an appointment to see the doc this week."

Relief rushes through me and I beam at him. "I think that's a great decision. I'm really proud of you for taking this step."

DJ meets my gaze, his dark eyes stormy with emotion.

"Thanks, Syd. For listening and not making me feel like a total wuss about this." He reaches out like he wants to take my hand, then thinks better of it and stops himself.

Oh god, I want to touch him so badly. To feel his warm skin against mine, to interlace our fingers...

But no. I can't. Slowly, regretfully, I inch my hand back and clasp them together again.

"Of course, DJ." I keep my voice steady and expression neutral, even as my heart cracks.

This is ridiculous—I can't be a good counselor to this man, not with the way I care about him.

"Although...I do think it'd be better for you to see someone else for a while, you know, for counseling. To maintain proper boundaries, you know? I can...I can make a referral."

His face shutters closed, going carefully blank. "Right. Boundaries. Got it."

It physically hurts to see him withdraw so completely. But I know deep down this is the right call, painful as it is.

We both need some space. I can't do my job without it.

I walk him to the door, longing to reach out and smooth the tension from his shoulders. "Take care of yourself, okay? Keep me posted on what the doc says."

"Will do. Thanks again, Sydney." DJ hesitates, then gives me one last piercing look before striding away down the hall.

I close the door and sag back against it, letting out a shaky breath. It's only after I can no longer hear DJ's footsteps that I let the tears come.

I bury myself in my work for the next few days, determined to be the best addiction counselor I can be. There's no time to dwell on the smoldering, longing looks from DJ and Tyler that set my body on fire.

My patients need me focused and clear-headed. That's the most important thing now.

I'm practically glued to Tomas's side as we head to practice. "Remember, progress isn't linear. Setbacks are a normal part of recovery."

Tomas nods, jaw clenched. "I know. It's just hard, seeing Mikey struggle like this."

"You're a good friend to him. He's lucky to have your support." I squeeze Tomas's shoulder reassuringly before he takes the ice.

In the stands, I spot DJ stretching, his chiseled muscles rippling beneath his tight gear. Our eyes lock and electricity crackles between us. I flush and quickly glance away.

Not going there, I remind myself sternly.

The next few days pass in a stressful blur of therapy sessions and team meetings. I'm constantly on the move, coffee in hand, typing notes on my laptop.

"The urge to use can be so intense, like a tidal wave threatening to pull you under," Jason confesses at a check-in, bouncing his leg anxiously. "I'm trying to ride it out, but man, it's brutal."

"You're doing great, Jase. Those urges will pass. Let's talk through some triggers..."

By the time I collapse into bed each night, I'm thoroughly drained. But sleep proves elusive as forbidden fantasies of DJ and Tyler continue to invade my mind—the brush of their fingers on my skin, their lips on my neck, hands roaming my curves...

I toss and turn, aching for their touch.

Get a grip, I scold myself. *You were the one who chose to end things. This is the right decision.*

But keeping my distance is pure torture, especially with the tension of playoffs ratcheting higher with each passing day. I just pray I can hold it together without completely losing my mind.

After a particularly long day I collapse onto the couch, feeling like I just played a triple-header of championship games without any breaks. Every muscle aches but it's my mind that feels most battered, thoughts swirling nonstop.

The front door swings open and Selena struts in, her electric blue bodycon dress as bold as her personality. "Syd! Get your cute butt up, we're going out!"

I groan, burying my face in a throw pillow. "I can't, Sel. I'm exhausted."

She perches on the armrest, narrowing her smoky eyes at

me. "You've been hiding in this apartment all week. You need a night out with your sis! Flirty bartenders, spicy margaritas..."

"I'm too stressed and tired for all that." I pull the pillow tighter.

"Babe, I'm worried about you." Her voice softens. "You can't just work and wallow. If you aren't going to let yourself be happy with your guys, then—"

"Don't." I sit up abruptly. "I'm fine, okay? I just...need rest."

Selena sighs, her brash exterior dropping away to reveal the concern underneath. "Alright, alright. Get some sleep then. Love you."

She drops a kiss on my head before slipping out.

Alone again, I trudge to my bedroom and flop onto the rumpled sheets. I toss and turn for hours, my mind a battleground.

Did I make a huge mistake ending things with DJ and Tyler? Am I an idiot for choosing work over a shot at real happiness?

Paul's mocking voice slithers through my brain. *"You'll never be good enough, Syd. Not for them, not for your patients. You're going to screw it all up like always."*

I squeeze my eyes shut, trying to block him out. I picture Jason, Tomas. I'm helping them heal. That has to mean something, right?

But Paul's sinister whisper persists. *"Who are you fooling? You can barely handle your own issues. How long until you crash and burn?"*

The tears finally break free, soaking my pillow as I curl into myself. The harder I try to be strong, to do the right thing, the more I feel like I'm losing everything.

I'm terrified that Paul was right. That no matter what I do, I'm going to end up broken and alone, a failure at my job and at love.

God, I wish I could silence the doubts and fears. I wish I knew what the hell I'm doing.

I wish...I wish I was back in DJ and Tyler's arms, even just for a moment of peace.

But I made my choice. No matter how much it hurts, I have to see it through. For my patients. For myself.

Even if it means facing the demons in my head alone.

CHAPTER 37
TYLER

THE BREAK-UP VOICEMAIL FROM SYDNEY HAS BEEN ON A LOOP IN my head for the past two days, like a terrible jingle that just keeps repeating itself. I've tried calling her, texting. But no response.

DJ and I caught up on the phone last night about it and he told me he went to see her in her office and she gave him the full-on professional treatment.

So brutal. She must be hurting so much—but just not letting us in.

My mind snaps back to what I'm doing as Carlos, one of our trainers, steps back over to my mat. Damn, I've been doing that a lot—zoning out, losing track of what I'm doing. *Bad sign for tonight's game.*

"Come on Tyler, keep that core engaged," Carlos urges as I stretch my hamstrings.

The spacious gym is empty except for us, the clanking of

weights and whir of treadmills conspicuously absent. It's just me, Carlos, and the endless loop of thoughts dancing around in my head.

I force a grin that feels more like a grimace. "You got it, boss."

My quads are on fire as I pulse deeper into the stretch, trying to focus on the burn instead of the ache in my chest. Nothing like a little physical pain to distract from the emotional shitstorm raging inside me.

Carlos eyes me skeptically, clearly not buying what I'm selling. "What's going on with you, man? You're wound tighter than a drum." He tosses me a foam roller. "Work out those knots before they turn into a pull."

I catch the roller and flop onto my back with a grunt, viciously attacking my IT band. "Just pre-game jitters. I'm good."

The pressure borders on excruciating as I dig in, teeth clenched.

"Bullshit." Carlos kneels down, pinning me with his stare. "This isn't like you. If your head's not in it, you've got no business on the ice tonight."

Anger flares in my chest and I sit up abruptly, hurling the roller against the wall.

"I said I'm fine," I snap. "I don't need a fucking babysitter."

Carlos raises his hands in surrender, jaw tight.

"Look, I'm not trying to bench you. But you've been pushing too hard. Rest up before the game, get your head straight. Team needs you at a hundred percent." His voice softens. "And I'm here if you need to talk."

I deflate, scrubbing a hand over my face. *He's right and I fucking hate it.*

"Yeah, okay." I stand, shoulders slumped in defeat. "I'll see you tonight."

Carlos claps me on the shoulder as I head for the door, his eyes worried. If only he knew the half of it—that my heart's as bruised as my body, that losing Syd has me twisted up in knots.

That I'm not sure I can be the man, the goalie, that everyone needs me to be.

I paste on a hollow smile and shoot Carlos a half-assed salute. But as I exit into the harsh afternoon sun, all I can think about is squeezing in a few more drills before grabbing a pre-game meal.

Rest is for the weak, and I can't afford to be weak. Not now, not ever.

❄

I'm taping up my stick, going through my usual pre-game routine, when a sudden commotion outside the locker room breaks through the whir of my tumultuous thoughts. Confusion knits my brow as I set down the tape and pad over to the door, poking my head out.

"Ty!"

My sister Leah stands there in all her glory, her face split in a proud smile, hands clutching a big homemade sign with my name covered in glitter and hokey motivational phrases.

My heart seizes in my chest at the sight of her, emotions welling up and catching me completely off guard. Seeing her care so much, show up when I need her most even though I didn't realize how badly I needed her until right this second...it bowls me over.

Before I know it, she's got me wrapped up in a bear hug, the posterboard crinkling between us. I breathe in the familiar scent of her flowery perfume, letting it center and ground me.

"Come here," I tug her elbow, leading her to a quiet alcove away from the pre-game hustle and bustle. We huddle close together, making the most of these stolen seconds.

"I've missed you," she murmurs, looking me over with obvious concern in her eyes. "How are you holding up, really? With the playoffs and everything with Mikey going down in the press..."

A sigh escapes me. After how chill Leah was when I came out, I knew I was safe telling her about my relationship with Sydney and DJ. She's been a nonjudgmental safe harbor for me recently.

"I just—I don't know what to do," I tell her. "Syd's completely shut me and DJ out ever since Mikey relapsed. Won't talk to us, won't let us be there for her. I get it, but..."

"But it still hurts like hell," Leah finishes gently when I trail off.

I nod, throat tight. "Yeah. And the pressure of stepping up, being the guy the team is counting on in goal...it's a lot. I don't want to let anyone down."

Leah rubs my arm, her touch soothing and reassuring in a way only a big sister's can be. "You could never let anyone down, Ty. You're so strong. You've got this. I believe in you, and I know Syd and DJ and the boys do too, even if things are hard right now."

That well of emotion rises again in my chest, a swelling of gratitude and affection and the sting of tears. I blink them back, not wanting to get too sappy before a big game. "Thanks, Lee. I really needed to hear that."

The concern doesn't leave her eyes, but she nods, giving me one last quick squeeze. "Anytime. Now go get 'em. I'll be cheering my head off from the stands!"

"Wouldn't expect anything less." I flash her a smile, genuine if a bit tremulous, then duck back into the locker room to finish getting in the zone.

Her words turn over and over in my mind as I strap on my pads—*strong, believe, got this*. I cling to them like a lifeline, hoping against hope that she's right.

The puck whizzes past my head, deflecting off the post behind me with a loud clang. *That was a close one.* I quickly recover, holding my stick out to deflect the rebound attempt.

Not on my watch, buddy.

I settle back into position, sweat dripping down my face.

These guys are relentless tonight, peppering me with shots. But I'm in the zone, laser-focused.

At least I'm trying to be. But as the forwards line up for the faceoff, my mind can't help but drift to Sydney. The way her voice sounded on that voicemail when she broke things off. The fear and hurt on her face when she found out that Mikey had relapsed, when we were at the basketball game. The desperation with which she took off, ready to make things right with the team.

Snap out of it, Tyler. Head in the game.

The ref drops the puck, and the action starts up again, fast and furious. Their top line comes charging into the zone on an odd-man rush. I track the puck carrier, square to the shot. He dishes a quick pass and I push off hard, extending my pad just in time to deny the one-timer.

They're knocking on the door but I'm turning them away. *C'mon boys, help a goalie out. Let's get some offensive zone time.* As my d-men finally clear the puck out of danger, I can't resist hazarding a glance up into the stands.

I scan the crowd...nope, no sign of Sydney with the rest of the staff, but the arena is packed tonight, so it's impossible to know for sure.

I wonder if she's still coming to games, or if she's staying away.

A clear thought comes to me that feels so obvious and right that I can't believe I didn't reach this sooner: DJ and I need to go get our girl.

As soon as this game is over, I'm going to talk to him about it.

With that in my mind, I'm able to focus back entirely at the game playing out in front of me. The hours pass in a blur.

And at the end, DJ hits an incredible slapshot. The puck rockets off his stick and flies past the other team's goalie's outstretched glove to bury itself in the back of the net. The arena erupts in screams and cheers as the final buzzer sounds.

Blizzards win!

After the game, I'm getting worked over by a massage therapist when DJ tracks me down.

"Yo, what's up?" I ask him quietly once we're huddled in the corner. "Any word on Syd?"

He shakes his head, frustration written all over his face. "Nah man, nothing. She's not answering texts or calls. I don't know what to do."

I chew my lip and then say, "I've been thinking about this, man. What we need is a grand gesture, like in the movies. Y'know, run through an airport, stand outside her window with a boombox, some epic romantic shit."

A chuckle bursts out of DJ, the first real I've heard from him in days.

I know it's over-the-top, but I think I'm on to something.

"You're right, we need to do something big to win her back,"

DJ muses. "I'm thinking... skywriting? Flash mob? Ooh, what about a puppy dressed as Cupid?"

I snort. "With our luck, it'd probably piss on her shoes."

We're both cracking up now, the tension from the game and this whole effed-up situation finally easing a bit. This is what I need right now—DJ, a dash of self-deprecating humor, and the spark of a plan.

"C'mon," I say, holding my fist out. "Let's get out of here and figure out our grand gesture. Operation Woo Sydney starts now."

DJ bumps my fist with his, grinning. "Let's do this."

As we head out, tossing increasingly wild ideas back and forth, hope flickers in me for the first time in a while. DJ, Syd and I—we've got something special, something worth fighting for. And if a ridiculous, sappy, made-for-the-movies grand gesture is what it takes?

Then that's exactly what we'll do.

CHAPTER 38
SYDNEY

My car creeps along the dark Chicago streets, my mind too numb to pay attention to anything but the exhaustion seeping into my bones.

What was I thinking, going to that game? Stupid, Syd.

So stupid to put myself through that, sitting in the shadows, heart racing every time DJ or Tyler skated by, terrified they might somehow sense my presence. But how can I do my job if I stay away?

Tomas and Jason and Mikey deserve better, someone who can really be there for them, not drowning in heartache…

I stumble through the door, kicking off my sneakers with a groan. The little voicemail icon blinks on my phone screen accusingly. *Damn it, I must have forgotten to turn the ringer back on after the game.*

I flop onto the couch and reluctantly press play, closing my eyes.

"Hey Syd, it's me. Listen, I know things have been...complicated between us. But Tyler and I really need to talk to you. Can you make some time tomorrow? We miss you." DJ's velvety voice wraps around me, tugging at something deep in my chest.

I toss the phone onto the cushion with a sigh. *Will they ever stop wanting me? More importantly, will I ever stop wanting them?*

I can still picture it so vividly—DJ's sparkling eyes and Tyler's crooked grin, their hands reaching for me. The memories twist like a knife.

The idea of seeing them again is so tempting. But nothing has changed, and facing their disappointment in person...I'm not sure my fragile heart can take it. DJ and Tyler are too good, too bright and beautiful.

I'll only drag them down.

No, better to hide away, nurse my wounds in private. Even if it's torture. Even if it means never experiencing the electric feel of their touch on my skin again.

I grit my teeth and tell myself that somehow I'll be able to keep doing everything I need to do—stay away from DJ and Tyler, be there for Tomas and Jason and Mikey, the rest of the team.

Piece of cake.

But the bone-deep exhaustion I'm feeling makes it hard to believe my own little pep talk.

❄

I stare up at the shadows dancing on my bedroom ceiling, my mind spiraling in endless circles. I've been tossing and turning all night, the sheets tangled around my sweaty limbs. Finally, as the first pale streaks of dawn creep through the window, I sit up with a heavy sigh, resigned to being awake.

My heart feels like a stone in my chest as the realization settles over me.

I can't do this anymore.

DJ and Tyler are under my skin, haunting my every waking thought. The magnetic pull to fall back into their arms is a constant, irresistible force, but I know it would be a disaster for the team, for my ability to do my job.

What if I'm so distracted mooning over those two that I miss something critical with Tomas' recovery? Or screw up Jason's treatment plan because my mind is in the gutter instead of focused on being the kick-ass trainer I know I can be?

I'd never forgive myself.

Rubbing my hands over my face, I let out a shaky breath. There's only one solution, as much as it guts me to even think it.

I have to resign from the Blizzards.

Walk away from the team that's become my family. Find a colleague who can step in and give the guys the undivided support they deserve, without the...complications of wanting to bang two of the star players.

"Shit," I mutter, the word bitter on my tongue.

Swinging my legs over the side of the bed, I stumble to my closet to start getting ready, my actions stiff and mechanical. I swipe on some concealer to hide the dark circles under my eyes and pull my hair into a sleek bun.

Padding into the kitchen, I start the coffee maker and lean against the counter, staring unseeingly at the backsplash tiles. In my head, I rehearse what I'm going to say to Vincent.

"You know I love this team. Working with the Blizzards has been a dream come true and I can't express how much I appreciate the opportunity. But I'm just not in a headspace to give the guys my full focus right now, and they deserve better. I think it's best if I step back..."

I suck in a sharp breath, the thought of leaving DJ and Tyler behind almost incomprehensible. But even as tears prick behind my eyes, a strange sense of calm settles over me.

I know, deep down, that this is the right decision.

The only way to untangle the mess I've made and do right by the team. *I just hope the guys can forgive me, someday.*

With a fortifying sip of coffee, I square my shoulders and head for the door, my future unwritten and my heart already aching with loss.

I swipe at my eyes with the back of my hand, trying to clear the blurry film of tears as I pack up the last of my things in the tiny office that had become my refuge. The resignation had been even harder to deliver than I'd imagined, and I can't quite believe this is goodbye.

A knock at the door makes me jump. I look up to see Coach

Daniels filling the doorway, his broad shoulders nearly brushing the frame.

"Hey Syd, you got a sec?" His deep voice is gentle, concerned.

I nod, quickly wiping my eyes again. "Yeah, of course. Come on in."

He steps inside but doesn't sit, shoving his hands in his pockets as he studies me. "I just wanted to say, well, that you've been incredible for the team. The progress you made with Tomas and Jason... I've never seen anything like it. They're like new men out there."

I try to smile but it comes out more like a grimace. "Thanks Coach. That means a lot coming from you."

"I mean it, Syd. You have a true gift. It kills me that we're losing you." He shakes his head. "And I hope you know that what happened with Mikey, that's not on you. The kid's got his own demons to battle."

I nod automatically, but inside a voice whispers that he's wrong, that I failed Mikey when he needed me most.

If I had just paid more attention, been there for him more...

"Well, I appreciate you saying that," I say, carefully placing a framed photo of me and Selena as children in the box of my belongings. "But I should probably get going..."

Coach holds up his hand. "I get it. But promise me you won't be a stranger, okay? My door is always open if you need anything. I mean that."

Tears sting my eyes again at his kindness. I manage a real smile this time. "Thanks Coach. For everything."

We shake hands and then he's gone, leaving me alone once more. I look around the barren office a final time, a heaviness settling in my chest. Then I grab my box and walk out, the click of the lock sounding with depressing finality.

Outside, I stop and take one last look up at the arena, weighed down with regret and sorrow. *I failed here, failed the team and Mikey and myself.* As I turn and trudge off into the weak winter sun, I feel utterly lost.

What do I do now?

When I arrive home all I want to do is collapse into bed and pull the covers over my head, but as soon as I open the door Selena's voice cuts through the silence.

"Oh no you don't, missy. We're going for a walk."

She's lounging on the couch in yoga pants and a T-shirt but jumps up as soon as she sees me, grabbing my arm.

I groan. "Selena, please, I just want to go lay down—"

"Nope. Emma called me, told me what happened. We're getting out of this house." Selena grabs her purse and two iced coffees from the kitchen counter, shoving one into my hand. "Let's go."

I sigh but reluctantly follow her out the door, sipping my coffee. As we meander down the street, couples stroll hand-in-hand, groups of friends laugh together on patios. Everyone seems so carefree and happy.

Must be nice.

"I know you're upset about resigning, but Syd, you are smart and amazing and talented," Selena says gently, looping her arm through mine. "One bad season, one jerk of an ex, doesn't change that. You'll get through this."

"Will I though?" I mutter glumly. "Feels like everything is falling apart."

"Hey." Selena stops walking and turns to face me. "You are Sydney freaking Nelson. My brilliant sister, the talented addiction specialist, the strongest person I know. You've overcome so much already. This is just a bump in the road."

I manage a small smile at her words. Selena always knows what to say to make me feel better, even just a little. I may have resigned in disgrace, torpedoed my own career...but at least I still have my sister by my side. Her unfailing support means everything.

We continue walking as the cool breeze ruffles our hair. I'm still reeling, my professional future as shaky as my legs in these worn-out sneakers. But Selena's right about one thing, at least —I can't let myself spiral.

I have to pick myself back up somehow.

I loop my arm tighter through hers as we turn the corner. The future terrifies me...but for now, I'll face it one step at a time, with my sister at my side and an iced coffee in my hand.

It's a start.

CHAPTER 39
TYLER

I SLIDE IN ACROSS FROM DJ AT THE TINY TABLE, OUR KNEES knocking beneath. The cafe near the arena bustles with the usual lunchtime rush but it all fades away as I meet his troubled gaze. He looks as exhausted and heartsick as I am.

"Any luck?" I ask, already dreading the answer.

DJ shakes his head grimly. "Nada. Straight to voicemail again. Texts still on 'unread.' It's like she's vanished off the face of the earth, bro."

I scrub a hand over my face. "Fuck. What are we gonna do, man? We can't lose her. Not like this."

"I know." DJ toys with the wrapper from his sandwich, jaw clenched. "It's killing me, Ty. I can't stop thinking about her, worrying if she's okay. If she hates us now."

"She doesn't hate us," I insist, though uncertainty gnaws at my gut. "Sydney's just...processing. So much has happened. She needs time."

"And space, apparently." DJ's voice cracks and he looks away, blinking hard. "Away from us."

My chest constricts. It physically pains me to see him hurting like this. Impulsively, I reach across the table and grip his hand.

"Hey. Look at me." I wait until DJ's glistening eyes meet mine. "We're gonna fix this, alright? Failure is not an option. Not when it comes to Sydney."

He swallows thickly. "I want to believe that, but...what if we *can't* fix it? What if we pushed her away for good? I mean...she resigned. It can't get more final than that, right?"

I refuse to even entertain that possibility. "Nope. I won't accept that. We fight for what we want, remember? And there is nothing I want more than the three of us, together. We'll make her see how much she means to us. Whatever it takes. We've just gotta make it through the playoffs and then we can focus on getting our girl back."

DJ searches my face for a long moment before managing a small nod. "Okay. You're right. We can't give up." He squeezes my hand. "Thanks, Ty."

I squeeze back, mustering up a smile I don't quite feel. The thought of flying off tomorrow and facing our biggest rivals without Sydney by our side just doesn't feel right.

This can't be how our story ends. Not when it feels like we're just getting started.

❄

The next day I'm staring out the airplane window watching the clouds below, lost in thought.

"You okay, man?" DJ asks from the seat next to me, nudging my arm.

"Yeah, just...thinking about Sydney."

DJ sighs. "I know. Me too. But she'll come around. It's like you said, we'll figure out how to get through to her." He rests a reassuring hand on my shoulder, his touch lingering.

I glance over at him and manage a half-smile. "I don't know what I'd do without you."

"Probably be even more of a moody goalie," he teases with a wink.

I roll my eyes but can't help chuckling. "Whatever, dude. You love that I'm dark and broody."

"Among other things..." DJ murmurs, his gaze heated as it roves over me. I inhale sharply, my body reacting to the fire in his eyes despite the swirl of nerves in my stomach. *Damn, if only we were alone...*

My filthy mind would love to drag him into the bathroom and join the mile high club, but these toddler-sized airplane toilets barely fit one fully grown professional athlete, let alone two. That would be quite the show for everyone.

The plane hits some turbulence as we start descending and I tense up, my flying anxiety flaring. DJ notices and slides his hand over to rest on my thigh, squeezing gently.

"Almost there, Ty. Just focus on me, okay?" His deep brown eyes lock onto mine, grounding me. I nod, trying to match my breathing to his.

Noticing that I need a distraction, DJ slips me some noise-canceling headphones, and I put them on gratefully, staring blankly at the screen in front of me. Some colorful Bollywood movie plays out, the dramatic scenes and dance numbers oddly mesmerizing.

Before I know it, we're touching down, the plane rattling as the wheels hit the runway. I let out the breath I was holding.

As we deplane, I can practically feel the nervous energy vibrating through the team. The gravity of this playoff game settles over us all. It's time to box up all the feelings once again and get in the zone.

Focus on nothing but hockey and getting the W.

Celebratory shouts and laughter of my teammates echo off the locker room walls. Sweaty bodies jostle around me, hands slapping my back, ruffling my hair. I force a grin, accepting the barrage of congratulations, but inside I feel numb. Hollow.

"Tyler, my man!" DJ slings an arm around my shoulders, his lean muscles glistening. "You were on fire out there! Those saves were straight out of a highlight reel."

"Thanks, bro." I manage a weak smile. "Couldn't have done it without the rest of you beasts."

"Nonsense. This win is all you. When Adam went down, we thought we were screwed. But you? You stepped the fuck up." He leans in closer, his breath hot against my ear. "I knew you had it in you."

My throat tightens. DJ's proximity, the warmth radiating off his inked skin, sends a shiver down my spine. I swallow hard, stepping back. "Just doing my job."

"Well, you were perfection. This calls for a proper celebration! Steakhouse on me, boys!" DJ announces to the room. Whoops and cheers erupt in response.

I plaster on a smile, but my heart's not in it. As the guys file out, eagerly discussing dinner plans, I hang back. Slowly, methodically, I peel off my gear. The pads that felt like armor on the ice now suffocate me.

"You coming, Ty?" DJ pauses at the door, his brow furrowed.

"You know, I think I'm gonna sit this one out. Feeling pretty beat."

It's not entirely a lie. Exhaustion weighs on me, but it's not just physical.

DJ studies me for a moment, his gaze probing. "You sure? We can always grab a quiet bite, just the two of us."

The offer is tempting. Too tempting. *DJ deserves better than my mopey ass right now.*

"Nah, man. You have fun. I'm just gonna crash."

He nods, but the concern doesn't leave his eyes. "Alright. Get some rest, superstar. You've earned it."

With a final clap on my shoulder, he's gone. And I'm alone. In the suffocating silence of the empty locker room.

I make my way back to the hotel, each step heavier than the last. The door to my room clicks shut behind me, sealing me in. I survey the generic decor—the bland walls, the impersonal furniture. It's a perfect reflection of the void inside me.

This is it. The moment I've dreamed of since I first laced up skates. A crucial playoff win. A chance to prove myself. To step out of my brother's shadow.

But as I sink onto the bed, staring blankly at the ceiling, I realize the bitter truth. None of it matters. Not without her. Not without the woman who completes us.

I close my eyes, picturing her face. The way she looks at me, like she sees past the mask I wear. The way she fits so perfectly in my arms, in DJ's arms. The three of us, an unbreakable unit.

But she's not here. And the victory turns to ashes in my mouth.

CHAPTER 40
SYDNEY

I STARE AT MY HANDS FOLDED IN MY LAP AS THE LATE afternoon sun slants through the blinds of Dr. Carter's cozy office.

"I just feel so...stuck," I admit, my voice quavering. "Like I'm paralyzed by everything that happened with Paul. I don't trust my own judgment anymore."

Dr. Carter leans forward, her kind eyes focused intently on me. "Sydney, it's completely normal to have doubts after an abusive relationship. But don't let Paul's actions color your view of yourself and what you're capable of."

A lump forms in my throat.

She's right, I realize with startling clarity. *I've been letting Paul win, even now that he's out of my life. By not believing in myself, not chasing my dreams, I'm still giving him power over me.*

"You were following your passion when you went to medical school," Dr. Carter continues gently. "Don't let anyone, especially not Paul, take that away from you. It's not too late to go back and finish a residency."

Tears blur my vision as the truth of her words sinks in. "I want that," I whisper hoarsely. "I want to help people, to do something meaningful. I just...I'm scared. What if I fail?"

Dr. Carter smiles and reaches for the box of tissues on the side table.

"Failure is a part of growth," she says, handing me a tissue. "But I have a feeling you're stronger than you realize, Sydney. Look how far you've already come."

I dab at my eyes and manage a watery grin. "You know, I never thought I'd be the one on this side of the conversation," I joke weakly.

She chuckles. "Oh, believe me, therapists need therapy more than anyone. We deal with a lot of heavy stuff in our line of work!"

I nod, breathing deeply as I regain my composure. She's right—I've made so much progress already. Confronting my past, working through my trauma, rebuilding my sense of self.

I can do this. I will *do this.*

Pride blooms in my chest as I thank Dr. Carter and head out to my car. I'm taking care of myself, finally putting my needs first. It's a good feeling.

But as soon as I slide into the driver's seat, the tears flow freely again, years of pent-up pain and self-doubt pouring out of me. I rest my forehead against the steering wheel and just let myself cry.

Thank God I have another appointment in two days, I think

wryly as I turn the key in the ignition. *This healing thing is hard work.*

The cafe bustles with the chatter of lively conversations and the clink of silverware against plates. The scent of freshly brewed espresso mingles with the warm aroma of buttery croissants. Golden sunlight streams through the windows, bathing our little corner table in a cozy glow.

Selena takes a sip of her oat milk latte, her bold red lipstick leaving a perfect imprint on the mug. "So Syd, how did your session go?"

She fixes me with her caring but intense gaze, false eyelashes fluttering.

I fiddle with my napkin, suddenly feeling exposed even in the anonymity of the crowded cafe. "It was good. Really good, actually. Dr. Carter helped me realize some things..."

Emma leans in, her blue eyes wide with interest. "Like what? Do tell!" She grins encouragingly.

I take a deep breath. "Like...maybe it's time I stop letting other people dictate my life. Maybe it's time to dig deep and remember what I want for myself and my career."

"Hell yes!" Selena exclaims, earning a few startled glances from nearby tables. She lowers her voice. "It's about time. Paul totally railroaded you."

I wince at the mention of my ex's name but nod. "Totally. And I've been thinking...what if I picked back up with my residency, completed my medical training? Finished what I started before everything with Paul."

Emma clasps her hands together, practically bouncing in her seat. "Sydney, that's amazing! You'd make an incredible practicing psychiatrist. Just think of all the people you could help, especially with your experience with addiction."

Selena reaches over to squeeze my hand. "We'll support you every step of the way, sis. Whatever you need."

Tears prickle at the corners of my eyes. After feeling so lost, so disconnected from myself for so long, their unwavering faith in me is almost too much to handle.

Emma slides a napkin across the table with a wink. "No need to cry into your salad, though."

After we finish eating the three of us pull out our laptops, planning on getting a few hours of work in. I don't have any clear plans—being currently unemployed and all—but when I check my email, I can hardly believe my eyes.

My fingers hover frozen over the keyboard.

Could this actually be real? A second chance?

"Syd, what is it?" Selena asks, her voice tinged with curiosity. She and Emma both look up at me from across the cafe table.

I glance up, unable to believe my old mentor at Harvard Med got back to me so quickly. "It's an email from Dr. Janssen. He thinks he might be able to pull some strings and get me interviews for residency programs."

"Oh my god, Syd, that's amazing!" Emma exclaims. She reaches over to squeeze my hand. "See, I told you things would start looking up for you!"

"It's not a done deal yet," I say, trying to tamp down the balloon of optimism inflating in my chest. "Interviews are just the first step. Those happen in the fall and winter, and then I'd still have to actually get accepted somewhere. It would be another year until I started a program. If I get into one."

Selena waves a dismissive hand, her bright red nails flashing. "Please, once they meet you, any hospital would be crazy not to take you."

I give her a wobbly smile, remembering all the late nights we spent as kids playing doctor. Selena always enjoyed creating dramatic backstories for her 'injuries' and I was always the brilliant physician who cured her.

Somewhere along the way, I lost sight of that dream.

"I'm really proud of you, sis," Selena says softly. "I know this last year has been rough, but look at you—taking charge and going after what you want. Paul can suck it."

I chuckle at that, even as a shiver goes through me at her repeated use of my ex's name. Emma notices and shoots Selena a look.

"The point is, we're here for you, Syd," Emma says, turning back to me. "Whatever you need, we've got your back."

I nod, blinking back fresh tears.

"Thanks guys," I say, my voice thick with emotion. "I don't know what I'd do without you."

"Um, crash and burn, obvs," Selena teases with a wink.

I laugh and swat at her arm. "Watch it or I won't give you any free medical advice when I'm licensed."

※

I take a deep breath and smooth my pencil skirt as I walk into the sleek glass lobby of the Midwest Addiction Treatment Center. *Relax Sydney, you've got this. You already aced the phone interview, so meeting a few people in person will be no sweat.*

The receptionist smiles warmly as I approach the front desk. "Addiction specialist interviews?" she asks. "They're expecting you in Conference Room B."

I follow her directions down a brightly lit hallway, swallowing my nerves. This is a perfect opportunity for me—a short-term gig that would pay the bills while I try to get back on the residency track.

My first interviewer is an austere woman with steel-gray hair pinned in a tight bun. She squints at my resume over her bifocals. "I see you took some time off from your psychiatry residency, Ms. Nelson. Can you explain that gap?"

My throat tightens. I can't exactly say, *"My abusive ex-boyfriend made me question my self-worth and abandon my career goals."*

I paste on a polite smile. "I wanted to explore addiction counseling before committing to a medical specialty. But I'm eager to complete my training now."

She makes a noncommittal, "Hmm," and scribbles a note. *Great start, Syd.*

The next two interviews go more smoothly. I bond with a jovial social worker over our shared passion for holistic treatment approaches and the medical director seems impressed by my knowledge of the latest harm reduction strategies.

By the time the final interviewer walks me out, my nerves have settled. She gives my hand a warm shake. "I shouldn't say anything yet, but between us, I think you've got this position in the bag."

I beam at her, giddy relief flooding through me. A fresh start, doing meaningful work, Selena and Emma nearby for support—it's all coming together.

So why does it seem like something crucial is still missing?

CHAPTER 41
DJ

THE GOAL HORN BLARES AND MY TEAMMATES MOB ME IN celebration, but despite scoring a crucial goal in a crucial game my head isn't in the moment.

Agony radiates from my knee and it takes everything in me to keep the pain from showing on my face.

We glide back to the bench for a line change and I catch a flash of dark hair in the stands. Just for a second, my heart leaps, thinking it's Sydney.

But of course it's not.

She's back in Chicago, hundreds of miles away, probably not even watching the game now that she's not on staff. The familiar weight of her absence settles like a stone in my gut.

Coach gives me a nod as I ease myself onto the bench, grimacing. "You good, DJ?"

"Always, Coach. Just need a breather." I flash him a cocky grin that I hope masks the truth.

My knee is getting worse every day. The pain meds and cortisone shots aren't cutting it anymore. But like hell am I gonna sit out when we're this close to the Cup.

I lean my head back and close my eyes, trying to center myself. I picture Sydney's face, her beautiful brown eyes, that crooked smile that makes my heart race.

God, I miss her. I miss the sound of her laugh, the feel of her body pressed against mine. I even miss the way she calls me on my bullshit. Keeps me honest.

The whistle blows and I push myself to my feet, ignoring the bolt of pain that shoots up my leg.

Can't think about that now.

Can't think about anything except the next shift, the next play, the next goal. We're so close to everything we've ever wanted.

I just wish she was here to share it with us.

I collapse onto the locker room bench days later, my knee throbbing with a familiar searing pain. Another grueling practice in the books, but at what cost? Gritting my teeth, I bury my face in my hands. This injury is going to be the death of me.

Or at least the death of my career.

"Yo DJ, you alright?" Tyler's concerned voice cuts through my spiraling thoughts. He plops down beside me, his solid warmth both comforting and unnerving.

I debate lying, plastering on a smile and cracking a dirty

joke like always. But I'm so damn tired. Tired of pretending everything is fine when my body is betraying me and my future is balanced on a knife's edge.

"No, Ty, I'm really not," I admit, the words bitter on my tongue. "It's my knee. I...I don't know how much longer I can keep playing through the old injury."

Tyler's brow furrows as he listens intently. I lay it all out— the pain, the fear, the pressure.

If I can't play, can't earn that fat NHL paycheck, my mom is royally screwed. Her underwater mortgage, my little sister's college fund...it all hinges on me. Some cocky, queer jock with a bum knee.

"Dude, you need to see the team doc ASAP," Tyler insists, his large hand coming to rest on my shoulder. Sparks zing through me at the contact despite everything. "I get it, you don't want to let anyone down. But running yourself into the ground helps no one. You're always calling out the toxic masculinity bullshit around here...don't fall into that same trap, DJ."

I blow out a breath, hating that he's right.

"I hear you, man. I'll make an appointment." The thought terrifies me, but the alternative is watching my body give out and my life fall to pieces. "Just...don't say anything to the other guys yet, okay? Last thing I need is a bunch of pity looks in the locker room."

"Your secret's safe with me." His hand lingers another moment before he stands. "But you better actually go. I'll sic Leah on your stubborn ass if I have to."

I snort out a laugh in spite of myself. Tyler's sister is a force to be reckoned with.

Must run in the family.

"Message received, you menace." I flash him a weak grin, pushing to my feet with a wince I can't quite hide. "Thanks, Ty. For listening and knocking some sense into me."

"It's what I'm here for, idiot," Ty says affectionately. "We still on for later?"

"Count on it," I say, holding his eyes with mine.

Tyler's bed squeaks as we tumble onto it, a tangle of limbs and searing kisses. My hands race over his chiseled chest, pushing his shirt up and off, admiring him for the hundredth time.

Hockey bods, man. Nothing better.

"Need you," Ty breathes between kisses, tugging at my belt. I help him out, shucking my jeans and boxers in record time. His eyes go wide as I spring free. *That's right, drink it in.*

"Like what you see?" I smirk, stroking myself.

"Fuck yes," he groans, gripping his own hard length through his shorts. I bat his hand away and palm him myself, relishing his gasp. He lifts his hips to help me slide his shorts and tight blue briefs down his muscular thighs.

We crash back together, naked and aching. The press of his body against mine lights me up like the goal siren. Our hips grind in a filthy rhythm as we devour each other, tongues sliding slick and hot. His hands map my ink, tracing the swirls and edges.

I kiss a path down his chest, flicking my tongue over his nipples just to hear him curse. He fists a hand in my hair as I mouth at his abs, his v-lines, the jut of his hipbones.

"DJ, please..."

Music to my ears. I lick up the velvety underside of his thick cock and swallow him down. He cries out, arching off the bed as I work him with lips and tongue.

Soon we're both slick with sweat and need. I rummage in my discarded jeans for lube and a condom. Ty eagerly rolls to his hands and knees, presenting that perfect ass. I get him ready with slick fingers, tease and stretch until he's rocking back and begging for it.

Then finally, I line up and slide home. The tight hot squeeze almost undoes me before we even start and I have to pause, panting into his shoulder blade. He clenches around me and I nearly lose it all over again.

Judging from the muffled groan he makes, he feels the same.

"Move, dammit," he grits out.

And finally, I do. I pull back and slam in again, setting a deep, driving rhythm. He pushes back to meet every thrust, sweat-slick skin slapping loudly. It's frantic and messy and so goddamn good.

As I push into Tyler again and again, surrounded by his heat, something clicks into place deep inside me.

This is right. This is real.

Him and me, connecting on a level I never knew I was missing. It feels so good to have finally shared everything with him, to not be holding back.

Tyler cries out as he comes untouched, spasming around my cock and pulling my own climax from me. I muffle my shout against his neck as I shoot into the condom, dizzy with pleasure and emotion.

After, we collapse in a sweaty heap. I gather him close and he nestles into my chest, humming contentedly.

Shit, that was amazing. It's always amazing.

I pull back to cradle Ty's face in my hands, leaning in for a kiss and then resting my forehead against his.

Tyler's blue eyes bore into mine, filled with emotion in the dim light of the bedroom. "I'm in love with you, DJ. Completely, totally in love with you."

I reach out to caress his chiseled jaw, tracing the stubble with my fingertips, his words sending a careening feeling through my insides.

I've never exchanged "I love you" with a partner before. I've never let myself get this close to someone. I thought I was happier without it, the pressures and expectations of that oh-so-heavy word.

Love.

And I thought that wanting a non-monogamous lifestyle meant that I *couldn't* have it. How could you love someone but also want more? Who would want to be with someone so greedy? Even though I've been happily poly for years, that part never clicked into place for me.

I didn't allow myself to even hope for love, because I never expected to receive it in return.

But now... My throat tightens, and I swallow hard. This thing with Tyler—and with Sydney, for as long as it lasted—has fundamentally changed me. Allowed me to see that love doesn't have to be defined in a traditional way. That it can grow, and adapt, and fit into whatever space you give it.

Love wants to be found. It wants to be embraced. And it's for everyone.

"I'm in love with you too, Ty," I tell him softly. "So damn much."

He leans in and kisses me, tenderly. I know this is as big of a moment for him as it is for me, to tell another man that he's in love with him.

I press my forehead against head and breathe him in for a moment, proud of us both.

As we pull apart, his brow furrows with concern. "Your knee...you've been limping all night. I'm worried about you, babe."

I sigh heavily. He's not wrong. The pain has been getting worse, harder to ignore.

"I don't want you to stress about hockey or what comes next," Tyler continues, voice gentle but firm. "You are so much more than what you do on the ice. And no matter what, I'll be right here by your side."

Emotion clogs my throat. *This amazing, wonderful man...I'm so damn lucky to have him.*

"I made an appointment with the team doc for tomorrow

morning," I admit quietly. "I'm done pretending this injury isn't a big deal. Time to face reality."

Pride shines in Tyler's eyes. "I'm so glad, DJ."

"I never would've gotten here without you," I tell him solemnly. "Your support means everything. And Syd's too, honestly. She really made me see I need to deal with this."

We both go quiet for a moment, feeling Sydney's absence like a physical ache.

The post-coital bliss fades as reality seeps in, cold and harsh. Tyler's strong arms wrap around me but the empty space behind speaks volumes. It's a Sydney-shaped void, a gaping absence where her body should be tangled with ours, our missing puzzle piece.

I sigh heavily. Tyler stays silent, lost in his own head. I know we're thinking the same damn thing: *how the hell did we let our girl slip away?*

"This isn't over," I finally say, my voice low but determined. "We can still fix this. Syd belongs with us. We belong together, all of us."

Tyler lifts his head, a flicker of hope passing across his blue eyes. "Damn straight. I'm not giving up on her, on us. We'll do whatever it takes to prove how much she means to us."

My mind races, flipping through ideas like a Rolodex. Grand gestures, heartfelt pleas, skywriting her name...and then it hits me. The big play to end all big plays.

I sit up slowly, my abused knee twinging. "I think I've got it, Ty. The move that'll win our girl back. But I'm gonna need reinforcements to pull this off."

Tyler props himself up on an elbow, his chest a work of art in the dim light. "Movie gesture moment, for real this time?"

I grin. "You know it."

As I start revealing the master plan, Tyler's eyes light up, his grin stretching wide. This crazy scheme might be our Hail Mary pass, but I'll be damned if we don't score the ultimate goal.

Sydney back where she belongs, in our arms and in our bed.

Game on.

CHAPTER 42
SYDNEY

I stare at my reflection in the full-length mirror critically. It's my first day at the new addiction counseling center and I want to make a good impression, so I've dressed up more than I usually do, and my reflection in the mirror looks more like Selena than myself.

I tuck a stray lock of chestnut hair behind my ear and sigh.

"You're going to crush this, Syd," Selena says from her perch on my bed. She's still in her pajamas, sipping coffee and scrolling through her phone. "You look hot *and* professional. They're going to love you."

I shoot her a grateful smile. "Love you," I say, grateful that at least all the drama lately has had the side effect of bringing us closer together.

"Love you more. Now go kick some addiction ass!" She smacks my butt playfully as I roll my eyes, grab my purse and head out.

The L ride to the center is a blur. I'm too keyed up to read the novel I optimistically stuffed in my bag. I put in my earbuds instead, cranking up my "Badass Bitch" playlist and trying to psych myself up.

You're overqualified for this, I remind myself. *You'll be great, you were a get for this role.*

I'm feeling cautiously optimistic as I walk up to the converted warehouse that houses the center. But as soon as I step inside, my stomach plummets.

Every TV in the sunny, open concept space is tuned to sports news. And there, larger than life on the biggest screen, is a freeze frame of DJ's grinning face as he shoots the game-winning goal...

I gulp, feeling dizzy.

Of course. The Blizzards' unexpected road to the championship is the biggest story in Chicago right now.

There's no escaping it, or them.

Get it together, Nelson, I order myself sternly. *DJ and Tyler are just guys. Impossibly hot, charming, amazing guys who you maybe could have loved...*

"No," I say out loud, earning a puzzled look from the receptionist. I kick myself, pasting on a bright smile. "Hi there! I'm Dr. Sydney Nelson, the new addiction counselor? I'm here for orientation."

The rest of the day passes in a haze of HR paperwork, facility tours, and meeting new colleagues. Everyone is warm and welcoming, passionate about the work in a way that energizes me. I can see myself really thriving here.

But every time I pass a TV or overhear a conversation in the break room, there's an unwanted jolt of recognition.

"Did you see that pass from Johnston to Armstrong in the second period? Brilliant!"

"Simmonds absolutely stood on his head in the net last night, eh? I think the kid's finally hitting his stride..."

Each casual comment knocks the breath from my lungs. It's impossible to escape the reminders of DJ's wicked eyes and Tyler's bashful smile. The phantom feeling of their lips on my skin, their hands in my hair...

Will I ever be able to escape them?!

I roll over in bed, blinking against the sunlight streaming through the blinds. *Ugh.*

Today is the day. The championship game.

Despite my best efforts to avoid anything hockey related, the fact that it's happening tonight is inescapable, seeping into my consciousness like spilled coffee on a white shirt.

My fingers itch to grab my phone, to call DJ and Tyler and check in on them. See how they're holding up under the immense pressure. Make sure their heads are in a good place before the big game. But I resist the urge, shoving my hands under my pillow instead.

It's my day off and I fully intend to spend it in blissful, hockey-free isolation. A pint of indulgent ice cream, a dumb reality show marathon, and my cozy couch are calling my name. The perfect distraction from Stanley Cup madness.

A loud rap on my bedroom door jolts me out of my reverie. Selena pokes her head in, a wide grin splitting her face.

"Rise and shine, sis! We've got plans today." She has a sneaky look in her eye that makes me throw a pillow at her.

I groan and burrow deeper under the covers. "Selena, no. I'm not leaving this apartment. It's trash TV and ice cream day, remember?"

"Nuh-uh, no way." She marches over and rips the blanket off me. "It's a beautiful day and we are not wasting it! Shopping and sisterly bonding await!"

I scowl at her, mourning the loss of my cozy cocoon. "Can't we bond with some housewives? And mint chocolate chip?" I give her my best puppy dog eyes.

"Not a chance." She grabs my arm and hauls me upright with surprising strength. "You've been moping around for long enough. Time for some retail therapy and vitamin D! Doctor's orders."

I grumble but let her pull me to my feet, anyway. Resistance is futile and all that.

My mind flits unwittingly to DJ and Tyler again as I stumble towards the shower. *God, I hope they're ready for tonight. I hope their teammates have their backs and their heads on straight.*

I shake my head, dispelling the thoughts.

No. Not going there.

Today is about me.

And apparently, being dragged out into the world against my will by my annoyingly perky twin.

But as I step under the warm spray, I can't help but smile a little. Selena's right—moping around isn't doing me any good. It'll be nice to get outside, be distracted.

Hours later, I shift irritably in my new dress, turning to complain to Selena about going out after a long day of shopping, but my jaw drops when I realize where our rideshare has taken us.

"You—you tricked me!" I gasp, staring at the arena. "Selena, I can't be here right now, you know that!

The Stanley Cup finals—how could she spring this on me?

I'm definitely not mentally prepared to face DJ and Tyler so soon.

"I can't do this," I protest. "Not after my resignation, the way I left things with the guys..."

"Yes you can," Selena insists, bodily pushing me out of the car. "It'll be good for you! Look, Emma and everyone is here for you!"

My mind still reeling, I glance over to see Emma waving excitedly, flanked by my former coworkers decked out in team jerseys. Their joyful smiles make my heart swell.

Maybe I can do this. For them.

"We're going," Selena states, tugging me toward the entrance. "Those boys need to see the confident, sexy Sydney I know is in there." She winks. *Well, that explains the shopping spree...*

I take a deep breath, squaring my shoulders. I guess I can't avoid DJ and Tyler forever. And seeing my friends' support…

I feel a flicker of my old fearless self coming back.

"Fine, let's go," I declare, allowing Selena to lead me inside.

The Blizzards hit the ice with explosive energy, skating and passing with lightning speed. I rise to my feet along with the rest of the roaring crowd as the puck drops. Slade snags it and takes off down the rink like a shot, weaving between defenders with fluid grace.

My eyes dart to the bench, searching for DJ's familiar smirk and swagger, but his spot is glaringly empty.

An uneasy feeling twists in my stomach.

For DJ to miss a critical playoff game, something must be seriously wrong. *Is his knee acting up again? Did he injure himself worse?*

I chew my lip anxiously as my gaze returns to the frenetic action on the ice. The Blizzards are playing like men possessed, forechecking aggressively and peppering the opposing team's goalie with blistering slapshots.

The arena buzzes with energy—the fans can sense that this team is on a mission tonight.

Slade fires a shot that pings off the crossbar. The crowd

groans in unison. I'm only half-watching the game, my mind churning with concern for DJ.

I sigh and turn my attention back to the ice, trying to lose myself in the drama of the game, rejoicing every time Tyler gets another amazing block in.

As the second period winds down, the Blizzards are clinging to a precarious 2-1 lead. The intermission buzzer sounds and I slump back in my seat, exhaling deeply.

"You okay, Syd?" Selena asks, her brow furrowed with concern. "You seem distracted."

I force a smile. "Yeah, I'm fine. Just...wondering where DJ is, I guess."

Selena nods knowingly. "I'm sure your boy will make a dramatic entrance any minute now. He always did have a flair for theatrics."

I roll my eyes but can't help the small grin tugging at my lips. She has DJ read. Suddenly, the arena lights dim and a hush falls over the crowd. I sit up straighter, craning my neck to see what's happening.

The Blizzards are skating back out onto the ice, but instead of taking their positions, they start gliding into some kind of...formation? Murmurs of confusion ripple through the stands.

I squint, trying to make out what they're doing.

Then the jumbotron flickers to life and a collective gasp echoes around me. The camera pans out to an aerial view and my jaw drops. The players have arranged their bodies to spell out three letters:

SYD

My name, splashed across the ice in human form. Heat rushes to my cheeks and I bury my flaming face in my hands, unable to process what I'm seeing.

This can't be real.

"Sydney, look!" Selena grabs my arm, yanking my hands away. She points to the jumbotron, where a new message is flashing:

"WE LOVE YOU SYDNEY!"

Tears prick the corners of my eyes. I blink rapidly, hoping the moisture doesn't spill over.

And then I see them. DJ is standing at center ice, a bulky knee brace strapped to his leg, but his megawatt grin firmly in place. He looks directly at me and waves, his eyes crinkling with warmth. Tyler is beside him, waving too, his boyish face split in a huge smile.

I stare at them, my heart swelling with an emotion I can't name. After everything we've been through...

As quickly as it began, the moment ends. The players disperse, skating to their positions for the third period. I remain frozen, my mind reeling, barely registering Selena's excited chatter beside me.

"Holy shit," Selena keeps repeating beside me. "Holy shit!"

I nod dumbly, stunned into silence. I have no idea what just happened. But I know one thing for sure—I'll never forget this game. Not for the rest of my life.

The rest of the game passes in a blur. I barely register it, too caught up in the way that little display made me feel.

Seen. Special. Appreciated.

And DJ and Tyler were behind the whole thing.

The final buzzer blares and the arena explodes in a cacophony of cheers, whoops and joyful screams.

Glittering confetti rains down from the rafters as the Blizzards pile onto the ice, a mass of sweaty, exuberant bodies. Fans in black and white jerseys pour over the boards, flooding the rink to embrace their triumphant heroes.

It's utter pandemonium on the rink, but I'm focused, on a mission. My eyes dart through the boisterous crowd, seeking out two familiar faces.

I spot DJ's dark hair first. Tyler is right behind him, his goalie mask pushed up on his head, sandy hair tousled. They're fighting their way through the jubilant throng, eyes locked on mine.

My heart pounds against my ribs as I start pushing through the crowd, dodging leaping fans and dejected opponents. We're inexorably drawn towards each other, the pull growing stronger with each step. The din of the arena fades away until there is only the thrum of my pulse in my ears.

As we close the distance, I see the intensity burning in their eyes, the set of their jaws.

And then, in a moment I know will be forever etched in my memory, Tyler drops to his knees before me, right there on the ice. DJ comes up behind him, resting his hands on Tyler's shoulders, his full lips quirked in that signature cocky smirk. Tyler's cheeks are flushed, his blue eyes full of nervous hope and yearning.

"I'd get on my knees too," DJ says, "but..." He glances down wryly at the brace around his leg.

The roar of the arena fades into a dull hum as I stand on the ice, the world shrinking until it's just me, Tyler, and DJ, our faces flushed and breaths coming fast in the chilly air.

DJ catches my gaze, his dark eyes soft and vulnerable in a way I've never seen before.

"I wasn't at the game tonight because Tyler helped me realize I needed to put my own health first for once. Rest up my bum knee before I wreck it for good." He shakes his head ruefully. "Apparently I can't be there for you guys if I'm not there for myself first. Who knew?"

My chest tightens. I want to reach out, to pull him close, but I hold back, still frozen in place.

"I want to be the kind of man who can be real with you, Syd. The kind who's not too proud to lean on you when I need to."

Tyler shuffles closer on the ice. "We want to be there for you too, Sydney. With your job, figuring out what comes next..." I swallow hard at the raw emotion in his voice. "That's what love is. And we...we love you."

The words hang in the air, far more exhilarating and terrifying than anything else that happened on this ice tonight.

"If you'll have us, we want to be with you," DJ adds softly. "However you want this to go."

I look back and forth between DJ and Tyler, my eyes stinging with unshed tears.

Then I launch myself forward, throwing an arm around DJ and hauling Tyler up into our fierce embrace. I end up with my face smashed into DJ's shoulder, Tyler's hair tickling my cheek. I'm shaking.

Shaking, and laughing, and crying all at once.

"You're crazy," I say, my voice muffled. "You planned all of this for me? And I'm guessing Selena was in on it?"

The sheepish looks on their faces is enough to tip me off without them saying a word. And suddenly I realize something with stunning clarity.

"I love you too," I say, the words sounding right for the first time in years. "Both of you. So much."

I didn't know if I would love again after Paul. Certainly not this soon, or in a relationship this unexpected. But the two of them—their devotion, their unwavering support, our *chemistry* —has a beautiful hold on me.

Their arms tighten around me but it's complete and utter relief that knocks the air from my lungs.

Distantly, I register the crowd screaming their heads off, the team whooping and whistling. But I don't care.

Let them stare. The whole damn world can know.

I'm in love. We're in love. And I'm ready to take a chance on this.

Ready to open myself up again.

CHAPTER 43
SYDNEY

As soon as the three of us stumble through DJ's front door, all eager hands and hungry kisses, DJ growls into my ear. "I've been dying to get you two alone all night."

We had to go to a celebration party before this, and while it was nice to see the other players, it was pure torture not getting to be alone with my guys.

"Me too," I admit breathlessly, my skin already tingling with anticipation. I can't believe this is finally happening.

Me, DJ and Tyler, together again at last.

Part of me still can't quite believe I'm bold enough to do this, to dive headfirst into a polyamorous relationship with two insanely hot hockey players. *Old Sydney would never.*

But I'm not that broken, beaten down girl anymore. With DJ and Tyler, I'm powerful, desired, alive.

DJ's kisses trail fire down my neck as he walks me backwards toward the bedroom, his big hands spanning my waist.

Behind him, Tyler is already stripping off his shirt, revealing that muscular goalie body I've been pretending not to fantasize about for weeks.

We barely make it to the massive bed before the rest of our clothes go flying. I pause to drink in the sight of them—two flawless male specimens, bodies honed to perfection, cocks already hard and heavy. For me.

"God, you're breathtaking," Tyler murmurs, blue eyes roving over my naked curves with open appreciation—and then flicking to DJ, his eyes hot with arousal as he soaks in the sight of our other partner.

DJ slides up behind me, strong arms encircling my waist as he nuzzles into my neck.

"And you're all ours, baby," he says, his voice thick with satisfaction. "We're going to take such good care of you."

I flush with pleasure, still not used to feeling so precious, so adored.

My breath whooshes out as DJ spins me around and throws me onto the soft bed. I squeal and turn and then moan at the sight of Tyler's hands holding both his and DJ's cocks, stroking.

"We've been dreaming of having you back in this bed," Tyler whispers hoarsely, and then the men exchange a look so full of dark promise that I nearly lose it right then.

"Get her ready," DJ growls, and Tyler eagerly moves to the bed. "We're going to both take you—at once."

His voice is firm as he gives the order but his eyes dart to me, a silent question for permission. I nod frantically, already dripping in anticipation. I've never done anything like this.

I can't wait.

Tyler moves down the bed until he's between my legs, and DJ steps to the side until he has a perfect view. "Start with two fingers," he orders, "and just tease her with your tongue."

Tyler settles between my spread thighs, those blue eyes flashing with heat as he gazes up the length of my body.

"You're so fucking beautiful, Syd," he breathes reverently. "I can't believe we get to share you."

Then his fingers are on me, teasing through my slick folds with a feather-light touch that has me arching off the bed, desperate for more. True to DJ's command, he slides two long fingers inside me, crooking them just right to hit that perfect spot. I cry out, hands fisting in the sheets.

"That's it, Ty," DJ praises huskily from beside the bed, slowly stroking his own gorgeous cock as he watches us. "Get her nice and ready for us."

Tyler leans in, dragging the flat of his tongue along my slit in a long, slow lick that ends with a teasing flick to my clit. Pleasure sparks through me and I moan, hips rolling to chase his touch. He laps at me in light, playful licks, his fingers still moving in a steady rhythm that has me climbing higher and higher.

"Please," I whimper, head thrashing on the pillow. I'm so close already, wound tight just from the electrifying knowledge that I have both of them, that this is really happening. "I need..."

"I know what you need, baby," DJ says, voice rough with arousal.

DJ crawls onto the bed, kneeling up near my head. His hand

tangles in my hair, tugging just enough to send shivers racing down my spine. "Open up for me, gorgeous."

I part my lips obediently and he feeds his cock into my eager mouth. I moan around him as I start to suck, the taste and weight of him on my tongue pushing me even closer to the edge.

Tyler chooses that moment to wrap his lips around my clit, sucking hard as he pushes a third finger into my dripping core. The dual stimulation is too much. I shatter with a garbled cry, my body shaking and clenching around Tyler's fingers as DJ fucks my mouth.

"That's it," DJ groans above me. "Fuck, I love the feel of your mouth around my cock."

I whimper, still shuddering as I come down. Tyler gentles me through it, licking and stroking until my tremors subside.

But they're far from done with me.

DJ pulls out of my mouth, then grips the base of his cock, rubbing the spit-slick head against my lips. "You ready for us both, sweetheart?"

"God, yes," I breathe, dizzy with how badly I want them. "Please, I need you."

I feel the blunt head of Tyler's cock nudging at my entrance as DJ moves down my body to position himself alongside Tyler between my quivering thighs. My nerves thrum with anticipation.

Tyler pushes forward slowly. The thick length of his cock makes me moan, my back lifting off the bed at the exquisite intrusion. DJ's hand caresses my inner thigh, his feather-light touch sending ripples of pleasure radiating across my fevered skin.

"That's it, Ty," DJ encourages, his voice a low rumble. "Fuck, you both look so hot like this. I can't wait to be inside her with you, feeling you together."

Tyler bottoms out with a groan, his hips flush against my ass. He stills for a moment, letting me savor the feeling of him so deep inside. Then with a sudden move he flips me around until I'm straddling him, the change in position pushing him even deeper into me.

I cry out and grind down, wanting even more.

"Hold her still for me," DJ orders, his eyes meeting Tyler's. "Don't let her move."

Tyler's hands grab my hips, pulling me down hard, and sparks flash behind my eyes, so that I also miss that DJ's grabbed the lube from his bedside table and slicked his fingers up. But it's impossible to miss when he sinks a finger deep into my ass.

I moan, wriggling with pleasure, but Tyler's hands hold me firm.

DJ works me open slowly, thoroughly, his slick fingers stretching and probing until I'm a writhing, desperate mess. The feeling of DJ's finger and Tyler's throbbing cock inside of me at the same time is almost too much to handle.

I can't imagine what it will be like when DJ's inside of me too, and just thinking about that pushes me closer to the edge.

"Please," I whine, my voice high and needy. "I'm ready, I need you, please just fuck me..."

"Shh, we've got you, baby," DJ soothes, pressing a kiss to my shoulder blade. "We'll give you what you need."

He slips his fingers free and I shiver in anticipation. But then the hot, blunt pressure of his cockhead nudges against my rear entrance. Tyler shifts his hips slightly, and the movement sends sparks skittering through my core.

I'm so full of him already, I don't know how I can take any more.

But oh, how I want to.

DJ pushes forward, breaching me with excruciating slowness. The stretch is almost too much, skirting the knife's edge of pleasure and pain. I sob out a broken moan, my body trembling between the two men as he pushes in deeper.

"Fuck, Syd, your ass is so goddamn tight," DJ grits out. I can hear the strain in his voice, feel the tension in his body as he fights to control himself.

Tyler moans as the pressure of DJ's cock stimulates his own hard cock, already deep inside of me.

I feel impossibly full, stretched to my absolute limit with both their cocks buried deep inside me. The sensation builds until I'm dizzy with it. Tears leak from the corners of my eyes as I try to breathe through the overwhelming intensity.

"Shh, you're doing so well, baby," Tyler soothes, his hands petting over my sides. "Just relax, let us make you feel good."

DJ bottoms out with a low groan, his hips nestled snug against my ass. He drapes himself along my back, his chest heaving against my shoulder blades as he adjusts to the vice grip of my body around him.

"Fuck, the way you're squeezing us both," he pants. "You love our cocks, don't you sweetheart?"

"Yes," I whimper mindlessly, too lost in sensation to form coherent thoughts. "Yes, oh god, I need..."

And then they start to move, slowly at first, rocking in tandem in a way that has fireworks erupting behind my eyelids. The sliding of their cocks inside me is unimaginably erotic, stroking and stimulating secret places, and I can't stop the moans that fall from my lips.

"That's it, take it," DJ growls, snapping his hips harder, driving deeper. "Fuck, you feel incredible."

Tyler is more gentle but no less intense, rolling his hips in slow, deep thrusts. Their differing rhythms, DJ's rough and demanding, Tyler's smooth and worshipful, blend together into a symphony of bliss that carries me higher and higher.

"I can feel you, Ty," DJ groans, his voice tight with strain. "Feel your cock rubbing against mine inside her. Fuck, it's so good."

Tyler lets out a broken moan, his hands flexing on my hips. "It's better than I ever imagined."

Their dirty words only ratchet my arousal higher, the perverse thrill of being so thoroughly claimed by them both reducing me to wordless cries and desperate whimpers. My body is no longer my own. I've become pleasure itself.

It builds and builds, cresting like a tidal wave, until release crashes over me with shattering force. I scream my ecstasy, walls clamping down on their cocks. They fuck me through it relentlessly, wringing out every last shudder and spasm.

"Holy shit," DJ pants harshly. His hips bounce erratically against my ass as he chases his own end. "I'm gonna come, Syd..."

"Do it," Tyler urges breathlessly. "Come in her with me, DJ."

With a primal roar, DJ slams into me one last time and stills, his cock pulsing as he spills himself deep inside me. The hot flood of his release triggers Tyler's own climax, and he thrusts up hard, groaning deeply.

I shudder in bliss, thoroughly sated and filled their combined essence. It's filthy and depraved and I've never felt more deliriously satisfied in my life. They both remain buried inside me as we catch our breath, all slick skin and heaving chests.

DJ presses open-mouthed kisses along my spine, murmuring praise into my sweat-dampened skin. "You were incredible, baby."

Tyler's hands stroke soothingly along my trembling thighs, his softening cock still twitching inside me. "You're amazing, Syd. I can't believe how lucky we are to have you."

I hum contentedly, too blissed out to form words. I've never felt so...worshiped. The fears that plagued me before, the scars from my past, all melt away in the face of their devoted affection.

Carefully, DJ pulls out of me with a hiss and I whimper as Tyler slips out next, feeling momentarily empty and open. But they maneuver me gently onto my side, DJ spooning up behind me as Tyler curls around my front, cocooning me in their strong arms.

And then I am perfectly, utterly content. My body aches in the best way, every nerve ending still tingling from the mind-blowing pleasure they wrung from me.

"That was…" I trail off, at a loss for words to describe the magnitude of what we just shared.

"Earth-shattering? Life-altering? The best sex of your entire existence?" DJ supplies with a grin, nuzzling into my neck.

I giggle and reach back to swat at his firm ass. "Someone's confident."

"He's not wrong though," Tyler murmurs, brushing a tender kiss to my forehead. "I've never felt anything like that. Being inside you, with DJ, it's…it's..indescribable, I guess."

"Mmm, eloquent as always, Ty," DJ teases, but there's a note of pure affection beneath the playful jab.

I smile softly, my heart so full it could burst. "I love you both so much. I didn't know it was possible to feel this way about two people at once, but god, I do. I really do."

"We love you too, baby," DJ says without hesitation, his arms tightening around me in unison with Tyler's. "More than anything."

It suddenly strikes me that what I feel for DJ and Tyler is so different from what I felt for Paul, from what I thought was love.

"I need to tell you more about…about my romantic past," I whisper, and squeeze my eyes as tears start to form. "I'm bringing a lot of baggage with me. Maybe more than it's fair for me to ask you both to handle."

Tyler cups my face gently, tilting my chin up to meet his

earnest blue gaze. "Hey, no, don't talk like that. We're in this together, Syd. Your past, your baggage—it's part of you, and we love every part of you."

"He's right," DJ affirms, his voice low and sincere against my ear. "We're not going anywhere, sweetheart."

A tear slips down my cheek at their heartfelt words and Tyler brushes it away with the pad of his thumb, his touch infinitely tender. I take a shuddering breath, trying to center myself, to believe that I deserve this, that I'm worthy of their devotion.

"I want to tell you everything," I continue. "I don't want there to be any secrets between us. But it's...it's hard. Remembering how I let my ex break me down, chip away at me until I hardly recognized myself..."

DJ's arms tighten around my waist, anchoring me. "What that bastard did to you wasn't your fault, Syd. He took advantage of your big, beautiful heart. But he didn't break you. Look at you now. You're so strong, so brave to open yourself up to us after everything you've been through."

"We've got you," Tyler promises fiercely. "No matter what you tell us, no matter what happened in your past. We're not going anywhere."

I sigh, and tension I didn't even know I was holding finally releases. "I will. I'll tell you. I feel so safe with you both. But tonight, maybe you can both just..."

"Hold you?" Tyler asks, reaching one hand up to cup my face. "Anything you need."

"Mmm," I hum contentedly, wiggling a little and then realizing that DJ's cock is already half hard again behind me. "Oh, hello there," I coo, and giggle into Tyler's neck, almost delirious from the emotion and the pleasure I've felt tonight.

Tyler's hand lazily reaches around me, finding DJ's cock and slowly stroking. "Mmm, ready for round two already?" DJ murmurs, his voice husky with sleep and renewed arousal.

I shiver with anticipation as they both turn their attention to me. "With you two in bed with me, how could I not be?"

This time, there's no frantic urgency, no desperation. We take our time savoring each other, worshiping every inch of skin with lips and fingertips. As one by one we succumb to bliss, there's a profound sense of connection, of rightness. We finally collapse into a sweaty, satisfied tangle of limbs, trading gentle caresses as we drift off to sleep.

Some time later, I wake slowly, awareness returning in stages. The first thing I feel is contentment, a deep-seated calm that seems to originate from my very bones. Sandwiched between Tyler and DJ, their warm bodies pressed close, I'm whole, peaceful in a way I never knew with Paul.

The realization washes over me like a revelation: everything about this is different. Not just the mind-blowing sex, but the closeness, the care, the complete acceptance of who I am, flaws and all. There's no judgment here, no impossible standards to meet.

Just a beautiful, complex, wholly unique bond of love and desire.

I snuggle deeper into their embrace, a smile curving my lips.

For the first time in so long, I can breathe again.

CHAPTER 44
SYDNEY

Three Months Later

The colorful balloons sway in the breeze as we approach Emma's imposing greystone, a "Welcome Baby" banner fluttering above the door. My heart races, palms sweaty as I squeeze DJ and Tyler's hands.

Our first official team event as a throuple.

No pressure, Syd.

Slade opens the door, and a smile spreads across his chiseled features at the sight of us.

"Hey, you three! Welcome, come on in." He pulls me into a warm hug, his citrus cologne enveloping me. "I'm really happy for you guys," he murmurs discreetly in my ear before releasing me to embrace DJ and Tyler.

Slade's genuine acceptance and support means the world, dissolving the anxious knot in my stomach. I blink back tears, determined not to become a blubbering mess thirty seconds into this baby shower.

We enter the living room, and the guys grab drinks and start making the rounds, leaving me to take in the festive scene. Pastel streamers twist across the ceiling and a towering diaper cake serves as the room's centerpiece. It's like Pinterest threw up in here, but in the best way possible.

My gaze lands on Jasons's wife Melissa, positively glowing in a flowing floral maternity dress that drapes over her seven months pregnant belly. Her chestnut hair tumbles over her shoulders in glossy waves and her skin has that luminous mama-to-be sheen. She's a vision of fertile goddess beauty.

Definitely puts my simple sundress and sneakers to shame.

"Melissa, you look absolutely radiant!" I exclaim as I approach, marveling at her serene smile. "Pregnancy suits you."

She laughs and waves off the compliment. "You're too kind, Sydney. It's really sweet of everyone to make such a big fuss over this baby shower considering it's our second kid."

"Are you kidding? The team wouldn't miss a chance to celebrate you and Jason, especially with everything you've been through lately. This little one is a symbol of Jason's incredible recovery journey too."

Melissa's eyes mist over as she rubs her belly. "That's true. We're so grateful for the support. I don't know how we would've made it through otherwise."

As she mentions recovery, my mind wanders to Tomas and his continued sobriety alongside Jason. They've been pillars of strength for each other. If only Mikey had been so lucky...

He relapsed again recently and the sting of it still feels raw. Maybe if I had noticed the signs earlier or reached out more...

Rationally I know addiction doesn't work that way, but the guilt still gnaws at me. The Blizzards had to cut ties with him last month, which was brutal but necessary. I have to believe we did everything we could for him.

You can't help someone who doesn't want to be helped. As someone who spent years filled with denial in an abusive relationship, I know that firsthand.

I blink, pushing the somber thoughts aside, and refocus on Melissa's angelic face. Today is about celebrating new life and fresh starts.

For all of us, in our own way.

Nearby, I spot Tyler engulfed by a gaggle of teammates, their boisterous laughter carrying across the room. Curious, I meander closer, snagging bits of the animated conversation.

"Congrats man, officially our starting goalie!" Ryan says. "It's about damn time."

"Seriously, you're gonna crush it out there," Alex agrees. "Adam left big skates to fill, but if anyone can do it, it's you."

Over the summer, Adam decided to retire instead of coming back. His injury was still not totally healed, and he didn't want to risk making anything worse. It was a tough decision for him, but one that lead to Tyler getting permanently promoted, so I can't feel too bad about it.

Tyler ducks his head, a shy smile tugging at his lips. "Thanks guys, that means a lot. I've got a solid team backing me up, so I know we'll kill it this season."

Pride surges through me, warming me from the inside out. That's my man, humble as ever. He's worked his ass off for this and he deserves every bit of recognition.

Watching him navigate the spotlight, I can't help but reflect on the rocky road that led here. Tyler's come so far, not just in his career but in his personal life too.

You'd think that his asshole brother would've been thrilled by Tyler's promotion. Instead, Steven was snide about it, making cutting comments about how Tyler was always picking up everyone else's sloppy seconds.

The awful subtext about our relationship went unnoticed by no one.

In the end, Tyler chose himself. Chose us. He told Steven where he could stick it and hasn't talked to him in months.

I couldn't be prouder. Screw anyone who can't see how amazing he is, brother or not.

As if to punctuate that thought, I notice the casual way our teammates include DJ in the conversation, clapping him on the back and drawing him into their circle. It's a small gesture, but it speaks volumes.

This team, this beautifully unorthodox family, has embraced every facet of who we are, no questions asked. The gratitude that washes over me is staggering.

Lost in my musings, I startle when a fruity concoction appears under my nose.

"Penny for your thoughts?" Emma grins, pressing the chilled glass into my hand.

I take a sip, the fizzy mocktail dancing across my tongue. Mm, passion fruit and...is that a hint of ginger?

"Just soaking it all in," I reply, linking my arm through hers as we amble toward a quiet corner. "It's surreal, you know? Being here, like this, with the guys..."

Emma nods sagely. "The Blizzards have a way of sneaking into your heart like that. They're good people."

We settle onto a loveseat, the buttery leather sighing beneath us. From our cozy nook, the party ebbs and flows in a vibrant swirl of laughter and chatter, a live jazz quartet laying down a smooth soundtrack.

"So," Emma leans in conspiratorially, "a little birdie told me residency interviews are coming up. How're you feeling about that?"

And just like that, the contented bubble bursts, anxiety zinging through my veins.

Ah yes, the looming specter of my future, come to rain on this beautiful parade.

I gnaw my lip, the question I've been avoiding for weeks pushing to the forefront. What if I match somewhere far away? Will a long-distance relationship even work?

DJ and Tyler's careers are here and I can't—*I won't*—ask them to uproot their lives.

"I'm excited about restarting my career," I tell her honestly. "But I'm trying not to think about the possibility that I don't end up in Chicago. Like...what if I match in *Texas*?"

DJ approaches, the warmth of his presence enveloping me

like a protective shield. His arm slides around my waist, pulling me flush against his lean, muscular frame.

The contact ignites a flurry of butterflies in my stomach, and I instinctively melt into his embrace.

"Don't worry about that," he says, clearly having overheard our conversation. "We'll figure it out when the time comes. And besides...even Texas has hockey teams."

I laugh, leaning further into his solid chest. The steady thrum of his heartbeat beneath my cheek is a soothing metronome, grounding me in the here and now.

Tyler materializes on my other side, his broad shoulders and chiseled jaw a striking contrast to DJ's dark, tattooed beauty.

"We'll be fine, Syd," he says softly, his calloused hand finding mine and twining our fingers together. "No matter what."

I glance between them, my heart so full it feels fit to burst. DJ, with his razor-sharp wit and fiercely protective nature. Tyler, steady and strong, an unwavering pillar of support. Two sides of the same coin, each completing me in ways I never knew I needed.

In this room full of people, I've never felt more seen, more cherished, more wholly and completely myself.

The fears that plagued me earlier—the residency, the future, all the unknowns on the horizon—suddenly seem small and inconsequential in the face of this love.

As DJ leans in to brush a feather-light kiss across my temple and Tyler rests his forehead against mine, I close my eyes, silently pledging to nurture and protect this precious, unconventional love we've fought so hard to build.

Come what may, we'll face it as one. Always.

THANK YOU

First off, a HUGE thank you to my newsletter subscribers for taking a sneak peek look at the ARCs for this book. I can't tell you how much I appreciate you. Your support means the world to me!

And a massive thanks to you, my dear reader, for giving this author a shot. I hope you loved Sydney, DJ and Tyler's story as much I as loved writing it for you!

Want to share your thoughts? If you liked this book, please consider leaving a review on Amazon or sharing your thoughts on TikTok or Instagram. Your opinions mean the world to me and I cannot tell you how much I appreciate you spreading the word about my little book.

If you'd like to receive an exclusive deleted scene between Sydney and DJ, sign up for my newsletter! (https://subscribepage.io/jUDsP2)

ALSO BY ALEXIS BARLOWE

Don't miss the story of how Coach Emma fell for her own four hockey hunks in the first book in the Team Players series!

Read Pucking Amazing now!

ABOUT THE AUTHOR

Alexis Barlowe is a Midwesterner at heart and hockey fan who loves to write swoon-worthy romance set in the thrilling world of sports. When she's not dreaming up new HEAs, you can find her in her kitchen baking (especially anything chocolate), or curled up with a good book and cup of tea.

You can follow Alexis on Instagram @alexisbarloweauthor.

Printed in Great Britain
by Amazon

46448602R00228